Praise for Jacquelin

"Like Perkins-Valdez's *Take My Hand*, Friedland's novel exposes a shocking betrayal of women by government institutions . . . incredibly resonant in these uncertain times."

—Fiona Davis, *New York Times* bestselling author of *The Spectacular*

"Friedland fearlessly explores issues of incarceration and eugenics . . . a riveting, compelling story—but it's also an important one, reminding us that history's darkest aspects can echo forward into our present day."

—Kelly Rimmer, *New York Times* bestselling author of *The German Wife*

"*Counting Backwards* is more than a powerful read. Ultimately it teaches us *all* how to move forward."

—Lisa Barr, *New York Times* bestselling author of *The Goddess of Warsaw*

"A tightly woven dual-timeline novel that explores the sins of a family member . . . Jacqueline Friedland's ripped-from-the-headlines story is an *Erin Brockovich* for our times."

—Jill Santopolo, *New York Times* bestselling author of *The Light We Lost*

"*Counting Backwards* examines the ways women's bodies have been used against them in American society both past and present . . . Friedland explores both responsibility and redemption with heft and grace."

—Jo Piazza, national and international bestselling author of *The Sicilian Inheritance*

"Jacqueline Friedland uncovers a shameful moment in our country's history and in so doing, brings into the light people whom time has largely forgotten."

—Daisy Alpert Florin, author of *My Last Innocent Year*

"*Counting Backwards* is truly a book for this moment . . . a tour de force about family, female independence, and embracing what really matters."

—Lynda Cohen Loigman, author of *The Love Elixir of Augusta Stern*

"Bold, timely, and inspired by shocking real-life events, *Counting Backwards* had me gripped from its opening chapter . . . Friedland doesn't shy away from tackling hard questions about social responsibility, ancestral loyalty, and—perhaps most crucially—what we owe ourselves."

—Carola Lovering, bestselling author of *Tell Me Lies* and *Bye, Baby*

"A gripping, timely, and important read. In *Counting Backwards*, Jacqueline Friedland has crafted a nuanced, powerful, and eye-opening novel, driving home the urgency and fragility of women's reproductive rights. This is a thought-provoking story, perfect for lively book club discussion."

—Yvette Manessis Corporon, internationally bestselling author of *Daughter of Ruins*

"*Counting Backwards* sheds light on historical and modern injustices against women through two resilient female leads, court cases that will leave you stunned, and twists you won't see coming."

—Gabriella Saab, author of *The Last Checkmate*

COUNTING BACKWARDS

COUNTING BACKWARDS

a novel

JACQUELINE FRIEDLAND

Counting Backwards

Published by Harper Muse, an imprint of HarperCollins Focus LLC.

This book is a work of fiction. All incidents, dialogue, and journal entries, and all characters with the exception of some well-known historical figures, are products of the author's imagination. Where real-life historical persons appear, the situations, incidents, and dialogues concerning those personas are entirely fictional and are not intended to depict actual events or to change the entirely fictional nature of the work. In all other respects, any resemblance to persons living or dead is entirely coincidental.

Any internet addresses (websites, blogs, etc.) in this book are offered as a resource. They are not intended in any way to be or imply an endorsement by HarperCollins Focus LLC, nor does HarperCollins Focus LLC vouch for the content of these sites for the life of this book.

Library of Congress Cataloging-in-Publication Data

Names: Friedland, Jacqueline, author.
Title: Counting backwards: a novel / Jacqueline Friedland.
Description: Nashville: Harper Muse, 2024. | Summary: "Inspired by true events revealing America's troubling past involving Pre-War eugenics practices, this emotionally riveting dual timeline novel brings together the lives of two inspiring women while exploring the timely and important themes of immigration, fertility, and motherhood"—Provided by publisher.
Identifiers: LCCN 2024042002 (print) | LCCN 2024042003 (ebook) | ISBN 9781400347308 (paperback) | ISBN 9781400347346 (library binding) | ISBN 9781400347315 (epub) | ISBN 9781400347322
Subjects: LCGFT: Legal fiction (Literature) | Novels.
Classification: LCC PS3606.R555224 C68 2024 (print) | LCC PS3606.R555224 (ebook) | DDC 813/.6—dc23/eng/20240906
LC record available at https://lccn.loc.gov/2024042002
LC ebook record available at https://lccn.loc.gov/2024042003

Printed in the United States of America

25 26 27 28 29 LBC 5 4 3 2 1

Dedicated to all the women who are fighters

Jessa

January 2022

If he caught me in the act, he'd be furious. I grabbed the white cardboard box off the bathroom counter and started tearing it into penny-sized pieces. I made sure to render each piece small enough that the picture of the baby on the packaging would be impossible to make out. After I'd created a small pile of fragments on the marble countertop, I wiped the whole mess into the shopping bag from the pharmacy, tied the handles into a tight knot, and tossed the bag into the trash. The test stick was resting between the double sinks. Behind it, a glass bottle holding a bouquet of skinny reeds emitted a pungent citrus scent. The air freshener had been a holiday gift from my friend Tate, but now the cloying notes of grapefruit were nearly turning my stomach. Maybe it was a sign.

Less than two minutes had elapsed so far. I stared at the strip of paper inside the little testing window, bending closer as it gradually became saturated. The control line had already begun to appear, faintly at first, but then stronger, a pink promise that this test was functional.

I stared so intently at the test that my vision began to blur, the one pink line morphing into a wavy haze of nothingness. If

I focused hard enough, could I see just what I wanted to see? At the sounds of movement on the other side of the closed door, I flinched—Vance was waking up and beginning his day.

The timer on my phone showed another two minutes and fifteen seconds before the test would be finished.

"Jess?" Vance called from outside the door, his deep voice still thick with sleep. His footsteps came closer, and he jiggled the locked doorknob. "Can I come in?"

My eyes shot back to the test.

"Um . . . yeah! One sec!" I grabbed the stick and stashed it in the cabinet below my sink. Tossing a few tissues into the trash to bury the pharmacy bag, I gave the toilet a quick flush for good measure and then opened the door.

Vance waited at the threshold with bleary eyes and a dark shadow of stubble blanketing his wide jaw. The old Tufts University t-shirt he'd slept in stretched against the muscles of his chest, and his olive-toned legs, thick like logs, were on display beneath his black boxer briefs. The chain necklace he wore was askew, with its silver Star of David pendant dangling off to the side near his left shoulder. The necklace had belonged to his grandfather, and Vance almost never removed it.

"Babe," he said as he pressed his warm lips to my forehead and then made his way past me toward the toilet. "Why'd you get up so early?" He didn't wait for me to answer before adding, "I think I drank three liters of seltzer before I fell asleep. All that ponzu sauce at dinner. Salty."

Vance and his business partner, Arjun, had taken a client out the night before. They'd gone to some fancy new Japanese restaurant on the Upper West Side that everyone was raving about. It was hard to keep track of the many trendy eateries that Vance and his partners visited in their ongoing efforts to impress their high-maintenance clients.

Turning his back, he began to relieve himself. I wanted to keep guarding the hidden test, to make sure he didn't go digging for shaving cream or extra deodorant in that undersink cabinet. But he would know something was off if I just stood there watching him urinate, wouldn't he?

"I'd better get dressed," I said. Even so, I made no move to leave. Instead, I studied myself in the wide mirror that was mounted on the wall behind the sinks, buying time by taking in my appearance. Unlike many of my friends, I thought I looked my best first thing in the morning. Right after waking up, there was a slight puffiness to my face that rendered my sharp cheekbones a little less severe and made the angles beneath my hazel eyes more mellow. I smoothed my brown curls half-heartedly, not minding that they were wild as usual. My mother, whose own bouncy curls had once rivaled my own, used to describe their constant tangles as "chaos incarnate." All these years later, I could still hear the jingle of her laughter as she joked that trying to brush my hair in the bath was like participating in a sporting event. But I loved my hair. Not just because of the way the long flouncy curls seemed to be bursting with life, but also because of how each coiled tress allowed me to see a piece of my mother every time I glanced at my own reflection.

I leaned closer to the mirror, noticing a hint of purple beneath each eye. At thirty-one, I was often mistaken for a younger woman, which was fine, except at work. My physical appearance was just one more obstacle standing between me and the respect I wanted at my firm. The respect I deserved. I should have earned it by now. Instead, I was still scrambling to prove myself.

Vance looked over his shoulder at me as he continued to empty his bladder.

"You're going in today?" he asked.

"Just for a couple of hours. LDP depositions start on Tuesday, remember?" I heard the snippiness in my tone. It was harsher than

I'd intended, but I didn't have it in me to apologize. Instead, I left him there and made my way to the closet in hopes that my exit from the bathroom would hasten his own.

When we'd found our apartment last summer, it had been a definite upgrade from the prewar walk-up we'd shared since our wedding five years earlier. The amenity that finally convinced me I could handle leaving the West Village to relocate to the stodgier, uninspired streets of the Upper East Side like Vance wanted was not one but two walk-in closets in the bedroom. The eat-in kitchen and spare bedroom weren't so bad either. During our first visit to the apartment, we'd smiled tentatively at each other and talked about one day turning that second room into a nursery. My chest constricted as I recalled how hopeful we'd been then, even when we were still raw from our recent loss.

Choosing a semi-sheer floral blouse and a pair of navy slacks, I could already hear Tate in my mind, ribbing me for refusing to wear jeans to the office, even on a Saturday.

Vance was still clanging around in the bathroom, and it was all I could do not to shout at him to hurry it up. How much longer until I could get back to those results?

He called out to me then. "You remember I made us lunch plans with Mandy and Lou, right?"

Yeah. I remembered. But it wasn't just Mandy and Lou. It was Mandy, Lou, and AnneElise, their adorable, pink-cheeked, eight-month-old baby girl.

"Yup." My voice was still more brittle than I intended, my frustration about the interrupted pregnancy test getting the better of me.

He came out of the bathroom then, wiping a smudge of toothpaste from the corner of his mouth. I was buttoning my slacks and didn't turn away from the mirror, but he must have noticed something in the twist of my lips.

"You're seriously mad about the depositions?" he asked. "I didn't forget. I never forget."

It was true. Vance always listened attentively when I talked about work, especially cases that were giving me trouble. He'd advise me about the right course of action, steering me through complicated corporate situations or tricky client relationships, his focus always on making sure I'd come out smelling like a rose. Vance was a finance guy, so the substance of his work differed from mine, but the attendant aspects of his banking job sounded very similar to my experiences in the corporate litigation world. We were both subjected regularly to dauntingly high expectations, rigid procedural rules, complex office politics, and clients whose demands were often well beyond the realm of possibility. On more nights than I could count, unloading work-related predicaments onto Vance had been the only way I managed to unwind. When he threaded his fingers through mine, telling me just what I should do about whatever I'd described, it was a balm to the frustrations I'd brought home from the office.

It had been almost seven years since I graduated from law school. Seven years. I'd given myself exactly that long to make partner at a law firm. Several of my peers had already reached that milestone at other firms, and even at my own office, a few had jumped the line ahead of me. I'd been working my tail off since the day I took the job at Dillney, Forsythe & Lowe, LLP, putting in brutally long hours and so many late nights. After one Big Mistake in my fourth year, I'd doubled down, out-billing every associate in the firm ever since. And now, finally, I was the lead attorney on one of the firm's big cases. Other attorneys in the office had begun seeking me out for advice on their own matters, and things were looking up. Now that New Year's had passed, new partners would be announced in a matter of days.

In a perfect world, I would have been four months pregnant by now. I could see it all in my mind's eye: I'd be wearing loose, flowy tops, hiding a belly that was just beginning to bulge. Then, after being named partner, I'd start wearing all the cute, fitted maternity clothing that showed off my adorable bump. The other lawyers might be disappointed to discover that one of their new partners was pregnant. They'd worry, perhaps, about my continued dedication to the job, but by then it'd be too late for anyone to take back my promotion. Then I'd continue to wow them with my stellar work anyway, and soon they'd wonder why they'd ever been concerned in the first place.

But this was not a perfect world. In this world I'd gotten pregnant accidentally the year before. It had been too soon, before I was ready to focus on anything other than meeting my career goals. When I miscarried at nine weeks, my primary emotion had been relief. But now, after the fourth month in a row of actively trying to make a baby, I still wasn't pregnant. Four months wasn't so long. I knew that, but I couldn't shake the feeling that it was karma, payback from the universe for my dark thoughts the last time.

With each passing month that we tried and failed to conceive, my anxiety escalated. For so long, I had told myself that once I had a baby, once there was another person in the world who shared a portion of my parents' combined DNA, the massive hole inside my heart would begin to repair itself. But when I peed on test stick after test stick, each stupid strip of paper producing only a control line, it occurred to me that I might never have the baby I so desperately wanted. I knew how badly Vance wanted the baby too, a child we would raise in the Jewish faith. He didn't mind that I chose not to convert, so long as we converted the baby and carried on his family's religious traditions. My own parents were basically lapsed Catholics. The only holiday we even recognized was Christmas, and I knew by the time I was eight or nine that they just did it for me. Every year, I was given the choice of blowing off the holiday in favor of a trip to Orlando, but I always picked painting new ornaments with

Mom and trying to wait up for Santa with Dad. If raising our future children Jewish meant more opportunities to celebrate holidays with family, I was all in.

Vance made his way across the room to the wide dresser beneath the wall of windows. Against the backdrop of the morning light, he stood suddenly motionless, regarding me. Maybe something about the pointed way I was still staring into the mirror gave me away, or maybe the despair was coming off me in waves so thick it was just impossible to overlook.

"This isn't about the depositions," he said. It wasn't a question.

"What do you mean?" I reached for a tortoiseshell hair barrette on the vanity table and placed it between my teeth, using both hands to twist pieces of my hair into place. I risked a glance at him. The sun shining through the window behind him was already so bright it felt glaring. I blinked and turned back to my own reflection. I didn't want to engage in another shouting battle. Vance was so convinced that the only thing holding us back from conceiving was my own neurosis—my anxiety and my hyperfocus on the situation. After our last argument, he'd made me promise to stop taking pregnancy tests all the time, to at least wait until my period was late before peeing on another stick. He said the constant checking was too much pressure, that it felt excessive. I had acquiesced, even though the checking didn't feel over-the-top to me. It felt comforting, like at least I knew where things stood inside my body. The wondering just made everything feel worse, as far as I was concerned. But I didn't want to fight, so I'd agreed. Then yesterday, he'd walked in on me, stick in hand. My period wasn't due for two more days, and we both knew it.

"You just don't seem like yourself," he said as he opened a drawer and pulled out a pair of running shorts.

I clipped my hair into place and didn't respond.

"I'm trying to help you relax here," he continued, "not stress you out even more. I can see the way everything is getting to you, even if you can't. It's like you've got blinders on. That's why I've been saying you should cut back at work."

As he uttered those words, I bit my lip so hard that my mouth filled with the taste of metal. If I were a man, no one would suggest taking it easy at work as a solution to fertility issues. Maybe it was Vance's body that was failing us, not mine. And anyway, whether my ovaries were underachievers had nothing to do with how many hours I was billing at work, and I knew it. Why didn't Vance know it too?

I whipped away from the mirror to face him, my anger getting the better of me.

"We're doing this again?" My voice rose. "At the same time that you're taking on more responsibility, raising your hand for every new client the firm brings in? And don't get me started on the podcast, which was supposed to be a little hobby, a little something you were doing on the side, right? You're treating it like a second full-time job. Meanwhile, I should just curl up in a ball and give up everything I've worked for? All these years you've been supporting my career only to take it all back as soon as my baby-making skills aren't up to snuff?"

"Now it's my fault that the podcast took off? That people are interested in hearing what I have to say? You know full well that getting my name out there is going to open doors for me in the future. We've talked about this."

Tapping into his due diligence skills, Vance had started a podcast to help descendants of Holocaust victims track down lost or stolen heirlooms. As the show began to get more traction, he started getting invitations from financial institutions seeking advice about authenticating various financial assets. The networking opportunities had been piling up. Not to mention the synagogues and Jewish organizations that had taken an interest in him for leadership roles.

"Apparently, hundreds of listeners think I know my shit," he continued. "It'd be nice if you could show a little support here instead of thinking all the time about what a victim you are, poor little Jessa. When I say that you should take a step back, it's not because we, as a couple, have too much to do. It's because you cannot handle the stress you're putting yourself under."

"Support?" I growled back at him. "I'm not the one failing to show support!"

"Jessa." His tone was maddeningly calm, a tactic he liked to use to highlight my own volatility. I was hot-blooded, sure, but I didn't feel like apologizing for my big emotions.

I stared back at him, hands perched on my hips as I waited for him to say something else, hopefully to offer an apology of his own.

"I'm just pointing out what you're refusing to see. You can't do everything, and nobody's asking you to," he said as he stepped into his shorts.

If this were any other morning, one where we weren't so thoroughly attacking each other, this would be the moment when I'd point out that it was too cold to go running in shorts. He was going to freeze, running like that in the middle of January, but I was too irritated to start our usual back-and-forth about his exercise gear, where I'd suggest sweatpants and he'd insist he was impervious to the cold. I would chuckle at his pigheadedness, and he'd smile back indulgently. For once, the predictability of it all didn't feel enchanting.

He moved toward the unmade bed and began pulling up the comforter, putting everything back into its proper place.

Instead of helping, I stayed where I was, sizzling with indignation. This was the third time now that he'd declared I was working too hard, that my job was impacting whatever was or wasn't happening inside my uterus. Each time he said it, I felt like he was thinking mostly about the baby we'd lost, implying that if I'd taken it easier the year before, maybe we'd already have the child for which I was now so desperate.

"Look, I know how important this is to you, but you need to calm down about it all," he said as he tossed a pillow into place. "We don't want to become that couple friends with kids feel they have to tiptoe around. People will think we've become fragile, sad little flowers because you're not yet 'with child.'"

As he raised his hands to make air quotes, I curled my own fist at my side, pushing my fingernails into my palm. I stayed silent and he added, "We're tougher than that. I know we'll get there eventually. But you need to exhale a little in the meantime."

Vance was lucky. His parents were alive, and he had three vibrant brothers and an entire army of first and second cousins. His family celebrated not only the Jewish holidays they'd observed since he was a child, but thanks to multiple interfaith marriages, they'd also happily adopted the Christian and Hindu holidays of my sisters-in-law Laura and Jiyana. Vance's oldest brother, Darren, was the only one who'd married a Jew, my sister-in-law Vicky. But as long as all the children were raised Jewish, including an Orthodox conversion after being born to a non-Jewish mother, everyone was happy. His parents continued in their volunteer positions at the family's Reform synagogue, happily bringing the rest of us into the fold. I'd joined his family at one joyful occasion after another—festive bris ceremonies for our nephews Jonah and Kian, bar and bat mitzvahs for our teenage nephews and nieces as well as several of their cousins, and a never-ending cycle of other holidays and family celebrations. As much as he tried, Vance could never really understand what it was like for me to be an only child with deceased parents, to have spent eleven consecutive Thanksgivings at a quiet table for two with Gram. It colored everything.

I didn't want to yell at him though. Continuing to argue wasn't going to achieve anything.

"I just need to finish out this last week knowing I've done everything in my power," I said. Whether I received that coveted brass ring or not, in eight days I'd be able to shift more energy to figuring out how to get pregnant. It seemed that having sex most nights of the week, like we'd been doing intentionally since October, simply wasn't enough. There were tips to learn about what to eat, how to time intercourse, what kind of underwear men were supposed to wear. But with the demands at the office, I hadn't found a second to spare for that kind of reading. Frankly, we were lucky there'd even been time for the sex.

He opened his mouth to respond, and I felt myself bristle in anticipation. But then I reminded myself of how much I loved him and of the certainty he brought to my life. I would be wise to take greater care with our relationship.

"You know what?" I interrupted before he could say something that would only stoke the flames of my temper. "It's a beautiful Saturday morning. Go enjoy your freezing run along the river. I don't want to argue with your cute face." I moved to where he was standing and placed a gentle kiss on his lips. I pasted on a smile so he'd accept my olive branch and continue on his way toward the kitchen, or even out of the apartment. Then I'd be able to get back to that pregnancy test, which was still waiting in the bathroom cabinet. I could feel it calling to me, the invisible pull getting stronger by the second.

If Vance was surprised by my sudden shift in demeanor, he didn't show it. Instead, he sighed as he looked down at me. I knew it would take time before things felt easy between us again. As much as I hated going behind his back with the pregnancy tests, I was sure that if I didn't keep checking myself over and over, I'd be too distracted to function. And this was not the week to be off my game at work. If only I were more confident that Vance would be able to understand that kind of uneasiness. We had argued more in the past few months than in all five prior years of our marriage.

"Tell you what," Vance said. "Give me two seconds, and I'll walk out with you."

"Now?" I balked. "You go on ahead. I'm not ready."

"Yes, you are," he said, his eyes roving over me. "You look great. *And* I'm skipping coffee this morning. Something new I'm trying."

Was this something about caffeine and fertility?

He tossed the final velvet throw pillow onto the bed. "Let's go," he said, taking the Velcro band for his phone from the top of his nightstand and wrapping it around his arm, just above his bicep.

I glanced back toward the bathroom. These days, I felt like he was suspicious of me every time I went into a bathroom. Even if I'd been imagining the way his eyes bored into my back, I didn't have the bandwidth to deal with another argument about it at that moment. How could I possibly get back in there without tipping him off? The test's instructions had been very clear that after a certain length of time, the results could no longer be considered accurate. And first thing in the morning was the best time to test. If I didn't look before we left the apartment, it'd be a full day before I could try again.

"I just have to . . . I have to . . ." I started toward the bathroom, feeling so frantic in my need to retrieve the little stick that I completely blanked. I looked back at Vance, whose head was cocked to the side as he waited for me to finish. The harder I tried to think of a word, one single reasonable word to end my sentence in a logical way, the more I struggled. I winced, and the silence started to get weird. All those years of therapy as a child, and apparently panicking and freezing were still a part of who I was. Now that I'd faltered so conspicuously, anything I did behind a closed door in the bathroom would seem suspect.

"Never mind," I finally said, forcing myself to think about the big picture. If it meant protecting something between Vance and me, I could wait. There was nothing I could do except give in to him. I beelined for the bedroom door, grabbing my work tote from the floor along the way. "I'm good."

Carrie

1912

It was one of them blindingly bright Virginia summer days. That's what I remember most about the morning the ladies came to take me away. I was home watching after the babies like usual because Mama was downtown again, looking to find herself a day's work. Doris was crawling across the dusty floor, stopping now and again to stare at her toes, and I felt a little sorry at the way the milk-white skin of her knees had gone gray from the dirt of the planks. Baby Roy was asleep in the old bassinet we'd got from Miss Jenny, who lived with her brother's family on the second floor of the house. Our family had two rooms on the first floor, right below them. I was just six years old at the time, you understand, but I loved to look after my own brother and sister, to be the one taking charge. Even if they was only half-related to me, that one-half was enough.

When Doris tired herself out and set to acting fussy, I took her up on my lap and read to her from the newspaper Mama had brought home the week before. Mama told me she'd found the paper lying flat down on the ground on Main Street, where it didn't matter to nobody, and she knew I'd want to see it. Most of the words were too big for me to make out on my own, but the more times I went over it, running my finger nice and slow under each letter, the clearer it would come to me. There were some pictures that helped me make sense of the writing too, like the advertisement for Old Henry Whiskey. I recognized that picture of the bottle easy.

Doris was too young to care anyhow whether she understood what I was saying. Even if I'd read it all perfect, she'd still be paying more mind to my hair, pulling the dark strands to her mouth. Mama was always after me to tie up my locks with twine, but I preferred to keep them loose. I already knew I wasn't a pretty girl, not like Lorna Mayfair, a girl my age from up the hill who looked just like one of those dolls behind the glass at the store. My hair was the one thing about me that made me proud, standing out sharp as it did against my white skin. So that's how we were that afternoon, Doris in my lap, sucking on my hair, Roy still sleeping peaceful, and me studying the photographs in the paper, when there came a pounding on the front door.

I hoisted Doris onto my hip and went looking, figuring it was someone searching for Mr. Gibson upstairs. Folks was always after him about monies he owed. When I opened the door, I found that lady, Miss Drummond, waiting on the splintered porch. She wore a slim skirt and buttoned-up blouse, her pale yellow hair pulled back so tight it gave me a headache just to look at it. There was another lady with her who I'd never seen before.

Miss Drummond looked over my shoulder to see behind me before she even spoke, like she wanted to know what-all was going on inside our little house.

"Hello, Carrie," she said, her words as crisp and tight as her hairdo. "Is your mother at home?"

I shook my head at her as I squinted out into the sunlight. I didn't think to ask how she knew my name. "She's gone out for a workaday," I said.

The two ladies shared a look at that. I figured they thought I was telling fibs and that my mama was with a man, but she only took up with men on days when she couldn't find other work. Ever since my da left four years before, Ma did what she needed to take care of us. I'd heard her talking with her friend Sally from up the road. One night, the two of them sat on the steps of our porch, chewing tobacco and taking turns spitting into a can. Ma told Sally that the Olsens, who she cleaned house for, had moved to Tulsa. She shook her head when she said that, then complained that she'd needed to spend the afternoon with a fellow who gave her money for laying down with him.

I didn't understand back then, but I heard enough folks say that what Mama did with the men caused us to end up with Doris and baby Roy. They said it like them babies were a punishment. Ma didn't see it that way though. She always talked about my brother and sister being gifts from the Lord during hard times. She needn't have told me that bit, about them being little treasures, because I knew it on my own. Especially Doris. When she held on to my pinkie finger with her whole fist or looked up at me with her dark round eyes, I knew I couldn't love anybody more than I loved her.

"We'd like to bring you down to the CHS today for a stay. Do you have any belongings you'd like to pack up before we go?" Miss Drummond said.

Everyone around our parts knew about Miss Drummond and the CHS. She ran the Children's Home Society, where they took kids whose folks didn't want them no more. There weren't no reason why I should be going to a place like that.

"I can't go nowhere with you," I told her. "I'm looking after the babies now."

The woman beside Miss Drummond sucked in a breath so loud it was almost a hiss.

"But you're only five years old," the lady said, as if I couldn't care for my own kin.

"Six," I said, sticking my chin in the air. "Since last month."

"Well, why don't you go gather the other little one, and he can come along too."

"Ma won't want us leaving without her knowing about it first," I told them. "She'll have my hide about it." And that much was the truth.

"Oh," Miss Drummond said, looking real sad. Her eyes went down to the newspaper pages still hanging from my hand. "You like to read?" she asked.

I shrugged, wanting her to leave. "I guess."

"Hmm." She seemed like she was thinking on something as she looked again at the lady she'd brought with her. "It's too bad you can't come back with us. There's story time happening in an hour, and Miss Willis always likes to have children read along."

I did think a story time seemed like a nice thing to do, nice enough that it might even be worth a walk with Miss Drummond and her friend. Still, I didn't want to disobey Ma.

"I could leave a note for your mother, if you'd like. As long as she knows where you've gone, she'll think you've been responsible. I believe they're reading *Old Mother West Wind* today. Isn't that right, Mrs. Vestry?"

Now, I didn't know much about different children's books, but it just so happened that Miss Drummond had mentioned the very same book that Wendy Dinkins was showing off about just the week before. Her rich uncle from Norfolk had sent it, and she wouldn't let none of the neighborhood kids even touch the drawing on the cover.

Thinking about Wendy's neat yellow braids, and all them peppermint candies her uncle sent too, I was suddenly gathering up baby Roy out of the cradle. I told Miss Drummond that we didn't have a pram for ferrying either of the little ones, so she would have to carry Doris.

It wasn't but two hours later when Ma showed up at CHS.

I was sitting beside Miss Willis, the reading lady, looking at a picture book while two older boys hunched over a small table across the room, working on a drawing together. Miss Willis was asking me questions about the pictures we was looking at, like why was the bunny smiling, and what did I think that bunny was going to do with her bowl of porridge. That was when I heard shouting from down the hall. It only took a few seconds for me to recognize the rumble of Ma's husky voice, coming loud as if she was using a blow horn.

"You can't just come to my home and take them all!" she hollered. "Who do you people think you are, stealing my babies?"

I stood up from the small mat where we were sitting and peeked out the open doorway of the little library room. There was Ma in her work smock. Even from the other end of the hallway, I could see smudges on her arms, and I knew those spots of grime meant she'd got herself some cleaning work for the day. It looked like she'd been sweeping out somebody's hearth and chimney. She might have gotten paid in kind, like happened sometimes, when she traded her services with folks and came home with a sack of food. I was hungry just thinking on the grits and butter cake she'd got the week before.

My ma was a thick woman, tall too, with dark brown hair she kept short and blunt like the edge of a box, never letting it grow past her ears. Her sleeves were rolled higher than her elbows, probably for the hot day, and her thick muscles were plain to see even from looking at just the bottom half of her arms. I wondered if that skinny Miss Drummond was afraid, standing across from Ma's big body and all that shouting. But then Miss Drummond took up like she was the one in charge, and I suppose she always was.

"Now, now, Miss Buck," she said in a calm voice.

"It's *Mrs.*," Ma snapped back. "Mrs. Buck."

Miss Drummond started over. "*Mrs.* Buck, we were just minding the children for a time so Carrie could come get a sense of the place. You needn't get out of control. You can go on and take them home as soon as you like. But we hoped Carrie might like to stay on with us here."

To stay at the CHS? I ought to have known. That Miss Drummond had tricked me. I should have remembered seeing Mallory Johnson's aunt after seven-year-old Mallory had gone to the CHS. It was only a few days later that the girl was living with a whole new family. Her aunt Tilly had celebrated with a fresh bottle of whiskey in the street, hooting that she no longer had to look after her sister's brat.

But I didn't remember. Not then. What I was focused on in that moment was the small wooden shelf that must have held at least eight more books for children. I wanted to know what was inside each one. When Miss Drummond came to ask me what I wanted to do, whether I wanted to stay a little longer, it didn't take much for her to convince me.

Once I agreed, Miss Drummond went and had a quiet conversation with my mama down the hall. I never did learn what she said to Ma in those hushed whispers, or why Ma agreed. She let Ma take Doris and baby Roy back home, keeping only me. Later, after everything that happened, I told myself that Miss Drummond must have made some awful threats to make Ma leave me the way she did. And Ma must never have realized what-all would happen next or how it would change everything.

Jessa

February 2022

I stared blankly at the list of interrogatories I was supposed to be editing. It wasn't even lunchtime yet, but the sky outside my office window was dark gray, filled with ominous rain clouds that added to the malaise I was already feeling. It had been four weeks since the managing attorneys announced new partners. Although the list included thirteen new partners worldwide, the New York office of Dillney, Forsythe & Lowe had chosen just two. Maybe the fact that only two new partners were from New York should have lessened the sting of not making the cut.

It didn't.

The verdict was in, and I guess I just wasn't partner material. No matter how hard I tried to be taken seriously, it seemed I'd never be invited into that inner circle, never follow in my father's footsteps or live up to the memory of my great-grandfather in the ways I'd envisioned. Had my parents still been around, I'm sure they would have said I should be proud of my effort even though things hadn't panned out as I'd hoped. My dad would have looked me in the eye and tried to comfort me with one of the many quotations he liked to toss around. I could picture him with that crooked half smile, a hand resting on my shoulder. He'd have said something like, "Remember: 'Big shots are just little shots who keep on chasing the stars.'" Even so, I couldn't help feeling like a disappointment.

A knock sounded against the open office door, and I looked up to see Dustin Ortiz's perfectly coiffed head poking into the room. Even before noticing the smug tilt to his lips, I knew my morning frustration levels were about to get worse.

"Stan just added me to Hannity Blue," he said, referencing one of the firm's biggest cases. It was a securities litigation that I'd been working on with Stanley Rubin, a senior partner, for close to a year.

I considered why Stan would have added Dustin to the team. It was true that I'd been spending less time at the office during the last few weeks, still licking my wounds from being passed over. I'd been arriving slightly later in the mornings and sometimes using lunchtime to catch up on things I'd neglected for too long amid my quest for partnership, like dental checkups and eyebrow waxing. I'd even scheduled a lunch with my college friends, Sophie and Jane, whom I'd nearly fallen out of touch with during my prolonged efforts to rise to the top. Even with that little bit of self-care, I was still billing more than forty hours per week. And billable hours didn't account for all the time I spent at work that couldn't be charged to a specific client. Just because I wasn't using face time or all-nighters to prove my dedication anymore didn't mean I was slacking. Yet apparently, my marginally breezier lifestyle came with this unfortunate new consequence.

I couldn't stand Dustin. He was a few years older than me, but he'd only recently graduated from law school and had been working at the firm for less than a year. Supposedly, he'd spent several years traveling the world and working odd jobs along the way so he could earn just enough to continue his blithe, nomadic manner of living. I didn't know what had inspired him to finally set down roots in New York and pursue a more traditional career path, but I also didn't care.

Wanderers and free spirits like that were antithetical to me. My negative feelings toward people who didn't push themselves toward success were perhaps irrational and unfair, but I knew too well that life was a finite gift. I didn't have patience for people who didn't try to make the very most of the time they'd been given, whether by working toward personal accomplishments or endeavoring to improve the world around them. Somehow, slacking off on beaches the world over didn't seem like the most productive way to use years of your life, no matter how a person spun it.

I might have tried to overlook my distaste for Dustin's personal history, but then I got to know him. The more time I spent in his presence, the more infuriating I found him. He seemed to think his age offered him seniority he hadn't yet earned, and he somehow found every opportunity to question my actions. From "Why are you using this conference room?" to "Don't you think there's a more efficient strategy for reviewing those documents?" Dustin always seemed to think he knew better.

Yet if I complained about him being staffed on the Hannity case, it would only look like sour grapes after my lack of promotion.

I shoved my chair out from the oversized desk and moved toward the box of binders that had been delivered to my office that morning. I'd been planning to spend the next day and a half organizing them, but fine. I'd let Dustin do it.

"I assume Stan sent you the complaint and the other digital files. Why don't you read over those to start, and then you can take these flagged docs"—I lifted the heavy box and pushed it toward him—"and arrange them by topic."

"Yup, should have expected that," he said, taking the box and holding it with considerably more ease than I had managed a moment before. "Give the new guy the grunt work."

I rolled my eyes before I could stop myself.

"Who do you think was going to do that before you decided to pop by?" I moved back toward my desk and dropped into the chair. "These are the documents that were flagged for privilege. Stan wanted to review them over the weekend, but before we have them couriered to his country house tomorrow, they need to be checked again. And organized." I turned back to my computer pointedly, dismissing him.

He made a noise in the back of his throat, indicating his annoyance at the task, my sharp tone, or both, but then he turned and disappeared back into the hallway.

With that interruption complete, I reopened the document I'd been working on but couldn't focus. After reading the same line of text three times, I clicked on my internet browser instead. One upside of my stagnant career trajectory was that I had more time available for other research. In the past few weeks, I'd scoured articles, books, websites, and social media, seeking tips and tricks for trying to conceive—or TTC, as the great wide internet called it. I'd found suggestions that ranged from eating celery to taking vitamins to wearing wool socks during intercourse to even dancing under a full moon. No joke.

Earlier that morning, I'd used another ovulation test strip, one of the many commercial items for TTC support about which I'd recently learned. It functioned similarly to a pregnancy test, but the results would tell the user when she was most fertile. That morning, two lines had appeared on my test. After so many pregnancy tests showing only one stripe, it was a relief to see a second bar showing up on *any* type of test I took. According to the package insert, the second line meant I was having a surge of luteinizing hormone, a chemical released by the pituitary gland that would trigger ovulation.

Focusing so intently on the science of it all was perhaps not the most exciting way to look at baby-making, but I didn't mind; I was tired of waiting. Vance, on the other hand, didn't want to hear anything about timing or motility or hospitable testicular environments. He was already starting to complain about our sex feeling clinical. He grumbled about on-demand performances and got annoyed when I positioned my pelvis over a pillow, creating an angle to give the sperm their best chance of reaching their intended destination.

I wondered if I should prepare a romantic dinner at home to ease the tension we'd both been feeling. If we shared a bottle of wine, Vance would start to get handsy before long. Cabernet and candlelight always led us to the same place. I wouldn't have to ask him for anything, and we could just allow the night to take its natural course.

In the meantime, law firm partner or not, I still had work sitting on my desk that required my attention. I let out a long breath and pressed a couple fingers to my forehead, trying to force myself to focus. Thanks to Dustin, I no longer had to sift through those painfully tedious binders. Still, I found myself procrastinating every way I could. I clicked over to my email, which I'd checked only minutes before. There was just one new message, an office-wide note from Don Halperin, the head of the pro bono committee. He was looking for attorneys to collaborate with Legal Aid in defending people being held at an ICE detention facility.

Long ago, I had expected I would do oodles of pro bono work during my legal career, using my success to help the less fortunate the way my great-grandfather had done with healthcare back in the day. But then I got so busy hustling to prove myself, to show the older partners at the firm that my dad wasn't the only great attorney to come from the Gidney family, that I'd let other priorities fall by the wayside. With my intense caseload, I'd only taken on one non-billable case a year, and never anything time-consuming. But as I reread Don's email, I realized that being promoted wasn't the only way I could have made my parents proud. I turned back to my screen and tapped out a message offering my help, immediately feeling better about myself than I had in weeks.

~

Twelve days later, I walked into the US Immigration and Customs Enforcement Detention Center in Hydeford, New Jersey. The squat concrete building sat in the middle of a large open field, where it was surrounded by nothing but barbed wire and dry, yellowing grass. The stark flatness of the land and lack of trees and shrubbery gave the impression that I was somewhere more like Kansas than New Jersey. How amazing that a place this desolate could be located only ninety minutes from Manhattan. I didn't know the exact size of the property, but from the looks of it, I'd have guessed the building sat on something like thirty acres. As I headed toward the main entrance, past a parking spot designated for the employee of the month, I noticed a smattering of outbuildings in the distance as well.

Having never previously visited an immigration detention center, I'd expected something akin to a state prison. There were certainly many similarities, like the bleak architectural style of the cream-colored building, the cameras mounted in every possible corner, the preponderance of armed guards, and the metal detector I had to pass through before entering the facility. I hoped that on the other side of that locked door, I might find some differences too.

I made my way past rows of nailed-down plastic chairs in the lobby area to a desk where two guards, a man and a woman, sat sorting through papers. After I presented my identification and explained that I'd come for a legal visit with Isobel Pérez, the guards showed me how to use quarters to store my belongings in a small locker. If not for the bulletin board announcing a set of visitation rules and an ad for Global Tel Link—a phone service to "connect you with your incarcerated loved one"—the little lockers would have brought to mind an ice-skating rink. After stowing everything other than my memo pad and two pens, I approached the male guard, whose plastic name tag read "Doherty."

"Legal visitation is permitted until 4:00 p.m.," he said as he punched a code into a rectangular device beside a heavily reinforced door. I already knew that visiting hours ended at four, even with the more generous visitation time frame provided for lawyers over family and friends. I'd be able to stay with my new client for as long as three hours that afternoon, if need be.

"You got lucky today," he continued as a buzzing noise sounded and the door unlocked. He led me into a hallway of fluorescent lighting and gray concrete walls. The flooring was a dusty, epoxy-type material that might once have been white but now nearly matched the gray of the walls. Small piles of trash lined the edges of the floor, empty paper cups and gobs of tangled hair, the sight of which made me want to gag.

"The private meeting rooms are usually full long before lunchtime, but today's been quiet. Can't say why," he added, glancing back at me over his shoulder.

I was surprised by the officer's friendliness. The Legal Aid materials I'd been given in preparation for this case provided lengthy information about how difficult ICE facilities could make it for inmates to communicate with their lawyers. Unlike criminal defendants who were entitled to free legal counsel in the US, ICE detainees had no such right. They either had to pay for representation themselves or find lawyers willing to represent them pro bono, like I was doing. During the hour and a half I'd spent traveling from Manhattan to get here, I'd wondered if ICE had chosen the remote location strategically to make it harder for lawyers from the city to visit their clients in person. I hoped not, since detained people with counsel were ten times more likely to win their immigration cases than those without a lawyer, at least according to what I'd read.

"Where would we have been able to talk had the private rooms been full?" I asked, picturing myself sitting inside a jail cell with a woman I hadn't even met yet.

"Multipurpose room," the guard answered without looking back.

At the end of the hallway, we came to another locked door with another little keypad where the guard entered a code. Once we passed through, entering what seemed to be the main part of the facility, I was hit immediately by the strange smell of the place. The closest comparison I could draw in my mind was a school locker room, but not exactly. A moldy aroma mixed with scents of sweat, citrusy cleaning supplies, and something reminiscent of oatmeal. The air was thick and stale, and I felt a flutter of dread, wondering if I had the guts to stay in such a place even for the duration of a short visit.

Doherty led me past a room that looked like a cafeteria filled with plastic picnic-style tables but entirely enclosed with metal bars like one giant prison cell. At the only occupied table inside, a heavyset middle-aged woman in a pale blue jumpsuit sat opposite three people in street clothes, an older man and two teenagers.

"That's multipurpose," the guard said, pointing toward the room. "Bunks are down that way." He gestured vaguely toward the right before adding, "Meeting rooms are down here." As he talked, a thunderous whirring began in the ceiling above us. The guard paid it no heed, so I just followed behind him, turning left down another hallway. As we began passing the meeting rooms, each with one large window in the center of a closed door, I could see one-on-one meetings taking place between inmates and people dressed in business clothes.

"Why are the women in different-colored jumpsuits?" I asked, raising my voice to be heard above the loud machinery.

"Threat level," the guard called back.

As we moved farther down the hall, the noise finally began to fade. He set to unlocking the door of the empty meeting room and explained over his shoulder, "Blue is for petty offenses or no criminal history, pink is for repeat offenders, and red is for serious threats. The color codes keep us safe in here when we need to make snap decisions."

My heart jumped at the realization that I'd just walked myself into a place full of criminals. He must have noticed something change on my face.

"Most of them aren't violent here. You'll be fine." He opened the door. "Go on in." He glanced at the electronic tablet he was holding. "They're bringing up 246 now."

I knew 246 represented the last three digits of the A-Number, or alien registration number, for my client, Isobel Pérez, but I hadn't known that was how people were referred to in here.

Before I had time to say anything else, a female guard appeared leading a petite young woman with a long dark braid. The prisoner was pretty, with a youthful smattering of freckles across her nose. I was glad to see that my new client was wearing powder-blue coveralls.

"Just hit the call button when you're finished," the male guard said, pointing to a small box mounted on the wall near the door. He then glanced at the inmate and told her sternly, "Make sure you're back for count."

She gave him the kind of small nod that is only marginally more polite than an eye roll. Then she moved to one of the seats at the rectangular metal table.

After the door clicked closed behind the guard, Isobel spoke first.

"Welcome to my humble abode," she said in perfect English as she lowered herself into her seat. "You're from Legal Aid?"

I should have known the woman wouldn't have a Spanish accent. I was embarrassed to have expected otherwise, as the case file had been clear about Isobel's history. She'd been only three years old when she arrived in the US from Mexico and had lived nearly her whole conscious life here. Even so, the simple fact that the case involved a client in an immigration detention center somehow led me to expect a foreigner, not someone who sounded like she'd been raised in the Bronx. Looking across the table at Isobel now—at a woman so close to my own age who'd grown up in New York, attending American schools, watching American TV, hearing American music—I felt my nerves suddenly stand at attention. I'd never represented an immigrant before. Sure, I could call myself a talented attorney when it came to corporate litigation and negotiations. But, I realized with a start, there was no guarantee I'd be able to help this woman. Maybe this was just one more task I wasn't fit to undertake.

The edges of my vision began to blur as a familiar sense of panic set in. How could I have thought I was capable of helping an immigration client when I knew nothing at all about US immigration law? What if this woman got deported simply because of my own incompetence? As my vision grew fuzzier, I fought the urge to vomit. I was well accustomed to these sensations, the beginning of the "freeze" response, which my therapist had explained was a reaction to acute stress. I'd learned as a child that freezing was not an unusual phenomenon for young people who'd suffered severe trauma. But I couldn't freeze here, not now, when someone else's future was at stake. I pinched the inside of my wrist, grounding myself in the moment, just as I'd learned to do years earlier. Taking a deep breath in through my nose and sending a quick prayer up to my parents, I tried to force myself to a calmer state. An image of my dad flashed in my mind. I couldn't say whether it was a dream or a memory. He was waving me on, telling me to get started, and thankfully, it was just what I needed. My vision began to normalize, and I was able to look my client in the face again, forcing a smile onto my own.

"No," I finally answered. "Not Legal Aid exactly. I work at a firm called Dillney, Forsythe & Lowe." My words were emerging stilted and stiff, like a script I'd rehearsed. "We partner with Legal Aid periodically. I'm here to help you with your application for a stay of deportation." I opened my memo pad to take notes, then accidentally knocked both pens to the floor. Sweat was forming on my brow, and I wiped at it as I leaned down for my pens.

"Girl," Isobel said, "how come you're the one who's nervous? It's my ass on the line."

I opened my mouth to respond, but I couldn't think of how to answer.

"I'm your first immigration client; am I right?" Isobel asked. Her tone was kind, almost sympathetic.

"How did you know?" I asked, finally finding my words.

"Well, first off, you got that baby face, but something tells me you're older than you look. Still, someone around here gets a lawyer for free, either they got hooked up with a charity organization and lawyers who do cases like this all the time, or else it's some fancy lawyer who wants to do some community service or whatever." She looked down at my right hand, where two delicate gold bracelets dangled off my wrist.

"I'm guessing," she continued, "that most lawyers who work for charity groups don't have silver pens with their initials engraved on them. You got another eight just like those two at home, I'm betting. Right next to the jewelry box with more of those fancy bracelets."

"Oh, I . . ." I did own a whole set of the pens. She was so astute that I almost started explaining how I'd splurged on them after orchestrating a lucrative settlement for a client the year before. But then I realized how tone-deaf that would sound and how naïve I'd been to bring them. I'd put on my mom's gold charm bracelets for luck that morning, then tossed a couple of my favorite pens into my bag. But it was dawning on me that my choices had been callous and obtuse—simply more evidence that portended poorly for my instincts with this case.

Before I could come up with a proper response, maybe an apology, Isobel continued.

"I'm not trying to give you a hard time. Sometimes I just say too much too fast. Calling it like I see it and all that." She shrugged lightly and pulled her long braid around from her back to let it hang over her shoulder. As she fiddled with it, I saw that her fingernails were bitten down to the quick. "Don't think I'm not grateful you're here," she continued. "Everyone calls that same hotline, and usually nobody comes for them. Anyhow, you're smart, right? Went to some fancy schools, I bet. You'll figure it out. Then you'll just tell me what I need to do. And trust me, I will do it because I have got to get out of this place."

Her words helped, yanking me back from the abyss of self-doubt that had been pulling at me. Yes, exactly. I would figure this out, just like I'd mastered so many other areas of the law. And then we would work together to get Isobel back to her old life. There was no time to waste.

I launched into the interview questions I'd prepared and started to find my groove. Isobel answered one question after another, explaining that when she'd been sent to the United States from Mexico as a toddler, it was because her mother couldn't afford to care for her back home. Isobel was raised by her grandparents in East Tremont, New York, where she'd made friends, gone to school, and met her long-term boyfriend, Iggy. She and Iggy had always planned to get married but never quite got around to it, and then Iggy drowned in a fishing accident shortly before Isobel was arrested by ICE for marijuana possession. Even though New York had since legalized marijuana, Isobel's status as undocumented became known to the authorities from the arrest, and her immigration situation was a separate matter for which she could still be held.

"Our daughter, Sia, she's about to turn eleven," Isobel said, all her features softening as she mentioned the girl. "She's living with my grandparents now, and they're raising her up just like they did me."

I thought of mentioning that I, too, had been raised by a grandparent, having moved in with my grandmother immediately after my parents died. But this meeting was not about me.

"Money's always been tight for us," Isobel continued. "My grandparents, their English isn't so great. They work hard, for sure, but things have always been rough. They have enough expenses just looking after themselves and now Sia too. And my *abuelo* with his diabetes and the gout, and on and on it goes. They've got so much debt already."

I wasn't sure whether Isobel was trying to explain why she didn't already have an attorney or why no one had posted a bond for her release. Maybe she was simply elucidating the fact that she hadn't come from the easiest circumstances.

"I mean, what do they think I'm going to do back in Mexico?" she asked. "I don't know anyone there, or where anything is. I've been living in this country almost thirty years. Been here since before I could tie my own shoes."

"Okay, well, the first step," I told her, "is to fight for cancelation of the removal order." I had more to say, but I was distracted from my next thought when Isobel suddenly started fanning herself furiously with her hand, as if we were sitting outside in oppressive summer heat.

"Oof, I'm sorry," she said, shaking her head at me. "I get these hot flashes." She rubbed her sleeve across her forehead, and it darkened with sweat.

"Hot flashes?" I asked, turning back to the manila folder open on the table to look at Isobel's data. "Aren't you just thirty?"

Isobel nodded. "Premature menopause. Since a few months back. They had to remove my uterus."

"Oh. I'm so sorry," I answered, processing how Isobel was already finished bearing children even though she was still a young woman. Nearly the same age as me. I wondered what that was like for Isobel, to know that even once she was outside the facility, she would never, under any circumstance, be pregnant again. "Were you sick? Oh!" My hand shot to my mouth, as if to prevent more words from escaping unbidden. "That's your private medical business. Please. You don't need to answer that."

"No, I don't mind." Isobel shook her head. "Just had some cramping, see, and the doctor said I had a cyst on my ovary, said they could fix it . . ." She trailed off, squinting her eyes like she was searching her mind for more information. "I don't know. Once I woke up and they told me what they'd done, I guess there wasn't anything else to ask, you know?"

I wasn't sure I'd understood properly.

"Are you saying they removed your uterus and didn't tell you until afterward? They didn't explain everything to you in advance?"

Isobel hesitated a moment.

"I don't . . ." Her eyes shuttered for a moment. "I've been trying not to think about it too much, mostly."

My mind jumped without warning to the baby I'd lost so many months before and the doctor's promises that Vance and I would still have plenty of time to create our perfect family. I pushed away the thoughts, scribbling the words "adequate medical care" onto my memo pad and putting three large question marks beside it.

Meanwhile, Isobel cocked her head and looked off to the side, like she was still trying to remember something.

"No one ever said it just like that," she finally answered. "There was a lot they talked about that day in the exam room, risks to my health if we didn't deal with the cyst, issues with insurance. But then that was that." She wiped her hands together like she was ridding them of crumbs. "No use dwelling on it now. The important thing is that I find a way to stay in this country with my daughter."

I wanted to ask why cramping might lead so quickly to a hysterectomy, but I hadn't been called to Hydeford to discuss Isobel's medical history. I quickly crossed out the question in my notebook, drawing several dark lines through it. I had to respect my client's wishes and stay on task, no matter the feeling of unease that was burgeoning in my gut.

"Let's talk about your arrest," I said instead. "Can you tell me about what your job was at the time?"

Isobel let out a long sigh.

"I was working as a manicurist," she said. "I was good at it too. My customers learned they had to call ahead, by at least three days usually, if they wanted to get the seat across from me."

I couldn't imagine what it must have been like for Isobel. Going to her job as a manicurist one day and being incarcerated in an immigration detention center the next.

As we talked more about Isobel's circumstances and her daughter, Sia, I wondered whether I might be able to prove that Isobel's case qualified for the "extremely unusual hardship to a child" exception to removal orders. That avenue could potentially prevent a deportation. But I didn't know what conditions would constitute an extremely unusual hardship. Thus far, I'd read only the file of materials Legal Aid had provided in advance of the meeting, and I was starting to realize that I needed to do much more research on my own.

I berated myself again for thinking I could waltz into an ICE facility and save someone's entire future based on only a couple hours' worth of reading. I'd have to learn so much more about immigration law, everything I could, in order to give this woman the best chance of success. In the meantime, I continued peppering her with questions, copying down notes furiously. It would have been so much easier had I been allowed to bring in my laptop.

I was startled from my focus when Isobel put her hand up to her throat and asked, "You think we could take a break for some water?"

"Oh." I halted midscribble and glanced at the wall clock behind her. "My goodness. I've had you talking for nearly two and a half hours. No wonder you're parched. Yeah, you know what, I have enough. We should wrap up for the day. I'll get to work on all of this, and then I'll make another appointment so we can fill in any gaps if necessary."

I began to push back my chair so I could ring the call button for the guard, but Isobel took hold of my wrist, stopping me.

"Thank you," she said, holding eye contact.

"Oh, you're sweating," I responded without thinking.

"I'm telling you," Isobel said, laughing lightly, "these hot flashes are no joke."

As I drove north on the Turnpike, heading back toward Manhattan, my mind raced. I thought of the many legal sourcebooks and journals I wanted to review that evening, trying to keep a mental tally of what to tackle after I finished dinner with my grandmother.

I'd been meeting my mom's mother for dinner at the Dreamland Diner on the Upper East Side once a month, religiously, ever since I started college. In the past couple of years, I'd begun to feel that the monthly visits weren't enough. Gram was in her eighties, and her mortality suddenly felt glaring to me, even though she was still in relatively robust physical health. Recently, I'd been asking for plans with increasing frequency; museum outings, weekend brunches, walks around the neighborhood. I wanted to soak up all the time I could with her, especially since I'd begun to worry I might never have another blood relative.

As I approached the George Washington Bridge, I thought more about my new client, Isobel, wondering about her childhood and whether she and I might have had similar experiences growing up despite our different backgrounds. It sounded like Isobel's grandparents had sacrificed so much to raise her. Having always been so focused on my own suffering, I hadn't given much thought to what my grandmother might have sacrificed, becoming responsible for a child again in her midsixties. When I moved in, newly orphaned at age twelve, she had showered me with hugs and attention, trying single-handedly to fill the void left by the car crash that killed my parents. They'd been on their way home from parent-teacher conferences when they hit a patch of black ice. For all the years that followed, Gram showed nothing but affection and pride in me, guiding me and loving me. But maybe it hadn't always been so easy to be pseudomother to her grandchild, to have to give up the freedoms of later adulthood. Perhaps it was time I asked her these questions myself.

As I pulled into a spot in the parking garage, I felt a familiar gush between my legs. But I prayed I'd mistaken the sensation. It couldn't be my period, not yet. It was three days early. Maybe it had just been my imagination, or random bladder leakage. Or plain old sweat. But in my heart, I knew. It was the end of another cycle, another month of wasted effort and fruitless hope. As I reset my imagined pregnancy timeline yet again, my thoughts flashed to Isobel and how that high-spirited woman's body had been altered irrevocably, in a manner that would prevent her from ever having another child. Even with the disappointment of passing time, at least I still had a chance.

Carrie

1920

As we walked toward the railroad tracks, Billy was talking a mile a minute. He was my best friend—really my only friend. His family lived on a tidy plot of land just up the road from the folks who'd been fostering me since I was six years old. After Miss Drummond brought me to the CHS facility all those years earlier, it was only a couple of days before she had me placed with Mr. John and Mrs. Alice Dobbs. I still didn't know what Miss Drummond said to my mama that day when I first got took. All I remembered was that while Ma continued carrying on in the hallway of the children's facility, orderlies asking her over and over to lower her voice, Miss Drummond came to talk with me. She said if I went to stay with certain upright folks across town and helped them keep house, I'd get a warm bed all to myself and a chance to go to McGuffey Primary School. She told me I'd be allowed to sit at my very own desk five days every week. When she dangled the possibility of real Crayola crayons, I was ready to do just about anything she asked.

Alice and John Dobbs were all right. They never hugged me up like my mama did, but they didn't beat on me neither. Long as I did my daily chores, the mopping, the laundry, starching, mending, canning, and such, they let me come and go from school, let me have a fair share of their hot food each night. I was one grade behind the other kids my age in school, on account of getting started late, but I didn't mind. Over time, I often forgot I was a year older than the other kids in my schoolroom. Especially Billy, since he always knew so much more than I did anyhow. The placement in a lower grade also kept me farther apart from Loretta Dobbs, which was probably for the best.

Mr. and Mrs. Dobbs, they told me to call them "Mrs. Alice" and "Mr. John" from the start. Loretta was the only child they had of their own. She was two years older than me, and mostly she just ignored me. The only times we had cross words was when she had friends around and wanted to show off by hassling me. Then later, she'd try to make up for it one way or another, pushing her dessert toward me when I cleared the table that night or giving me a piece of her scented soap before I took my bath. I suppose she was glad enough that it was me sweating out the family chores every day and not her.

Miss Drummond never told me how long I'd be staying there with the Dobbs family, but before I knew it, seven some-odd years had passed since I'd started sleeping in the alcove off their kitchen. Other foster kids had come and gone while I was there, especially in the summers when there was more work to be done, but I'd been there the longest. Billy thought the reason the Dobbs family took in fosters was because they needed the money they got from the state each time they did so. I couldn't really say.

As we walked along Second Street, enjoying the first truly warm day that spring, we kicked at pebbles along our way. I watched the dust getting thicker on the laces of Billy's Buster Browns and wondered if his mother would be sore at him for not being careful. The afternoon felt like any of so many others until Billy surprised me.

"How come you're all quiet-like today?" he asked.

I looked at him sideways, noticing his freckled cheeks were pinker than usual. He was one of the shorter boys in the class, and it seemed I was gaining inches on him near every day, tall as I was.

I squinted my eyes back at him, like he was being a numskull. I was quiet most of the time. It's just who I was, so it wasn't worth remarking on it like he'd just gone and done. Once, I heard Mr. Dobbs tell his brother that I was a good foster because I kept mostly to myself, didn't bother nobody—so I didn't know why Billy was always saying I should speak up more anyhow. I never did understand how a body could think of so many things to say aloud all the livelong day.

"Is it because of your mama?" he asked.

"My ma?" We were nearing the corner of Main Street then, and I stopped right there beside the letter box outside Gilmore's Furniture. We never talked about my ma. Ever since I came to live with the Dobbs family, I hadn't been allowed to see her. Not once. Mrs. Alice told me when I arrived that if I wanted to stay on with her family, I had to make sure to be a nice girl and stay away from trouble. She told me Ma was trouble, and that I couldn't be going to the other side of town, not even for a quick visit with her. Mrs. Alice said she and Mr. John weren't rich folks, but they had their reputations at least. I hadn't argued then because I thought for sure Ma would come to see me where I was, so it didn't matter where I was or wasn't allowed to go. But in all those years, she never did come see me even once.

Billy looked then like he was choking on a sucker, his eyes getting wide and cheeks reddening.

"What?" I demanded. "What did you hear? You know something, you got to tell me." Billy had three older brothers, all of them skinny and dark-haired like him, but they was all the most likeable kind of boys, always smiling and goofing off with friends. Their pa worked at the Pepsi-Cola bottling plant in town, and they always had extra bottles of soda pop to share with friends. It seemed anytime something was going on around town, Billy heard about it from one or another of his brothers before any of the rest of us kids got wind.

That's why I believed him even when he said something I never would have expected.

"They took her to the Colony for Epileptics. I heard from Roger."

I wrinkled up my nose. "The Colony?" I said, wondering if he meant the place over in Lynchburg. Kids round our parts liked to tell tales about crazy folk from the Colony coming to Charlottesville and causing all sorts of mischief. We all knew it was pretend when they talked about escaped patients twisting the heads off chickens or snatching children from their beds, but we were afraid of inmates from the Colony just the same. Ma was nothing like any of the monsters from those stories.

"She ain't epileptic," I said.

Three ladies toting packages were walking toward us. One of them carried a basket full-up with items from the apothecary. I recognized among her purchases the Slo Poke caramels Mrs. Alice always kept on hand for Mr. John. Loretta had once passed me one of those candies in secret, and I hadn't forgotten yet the feel of that creaminess against the roof of my mouth. The lady nodded at me as I stepped out of her path.

Billy didn't answer until they'd moved on.

"No, I figured," he said, keeping his eyes to the pavement like he didn't want to say any more. I pushed his arm then, mad, like I was getting ready to fight.

"Say the rest," I told him.

"Roger said the Colony is where they take ladies who've been up to no good."

I knew what he meant by that. I'd heard enough folks whispering with Mrs. Alice over the years about how Ma had been working on the streets, that she was making a living through immoral behavior with men.

"But why now?" I asked. Even though Ma hadn't ever come to see me, I'd hoped she'd been doing all right, that maybe she'd found a better way to look after Doris and Roy, maybe a steady job that was keeping her too busy to check in on me. I liked to think she was just saving up her money until the time was right to come and get me.

Billy shrugged, but I kept waiting on him to give me an answer.

"Don't know," he said. "Maybe she gave a cop some trouble or something." He gestured with a tip of his head that we should take up walking again. I twisted my lips but followed along just the same.

Despite the years that had passed, I hadn't forgot the way Ma could explode when she got angry, her temper turning her into a tornado time and again. If Ma got into a little trouble, she always seemed to make it worse by yelling back too hard. She didn't let nobody tell her what was what—that was for sure.

As we reached closer to the train tracks and the row of houses behind them, I wondered if there wasn't something I could do to help her. I never asked Mrs. Alice nor Mr. John for hardly anything, but I thought that time had come.

When I came upon the house, I found Mrs. Alice already waiting for me. I was old enough to know by then that bad days always had a habit of getting worse, and this day was no exception.

Mrs. Alice was standing on the short wooden steps leading up to the back door, the buttons of her navy housedress pulling against her large bosom, her white hair pinned up in a large, loose bun like always. Some strands had come free now that it was getting late in the day.

"You took your time getting back," she said.

"Ma'am?" I asked, not sure why she was waiting on me anyway. I wondered if I'd left the cheese sitting out on the icebox again, and maybe she was about to have my hide. But what she said instead was the worst kind of surprise.

"Tomorrow's going to be your last day at school."

We still had three weeks left before the end of the term.

"Are we breaking for summer early?" I asked.

Mrs. Alice shook her head, like she was frustrated that I wasn't doing a better job of keeping up. She didn't like to repeat herself.

"You're not taking a break, girl," she said. "You're finished with your schooling for good. You'll be focusing your time on helping around the house now. No need to wait for the end of the school year. You've completed enough of the sixth grade to get credit for it."

"But why? Have I done something wrong?" I was already thinking of all I would miss if Mrs. Alice made good on her threat. Our teacher had been reading to us from *The Story of Doctor Dolittle*, and we weren't nearly finished. Each student had also been working on a special presentation for the last day of school, and I'd been excited about mine, preparing to show how I could fly clothespin airplanes.

"No, nothing wrong. But Mr. John and I, we need your help with the farm now that it's coming on late spring and we've got the new crops this year. You've done all the learning you require. A girl like you has no need for junior high."

Now, I knew I wasn't the smartest girl. Mrs. Alice certainly told me so often enough. But I kept up fine with the lessons in class.

When I didn't just answer "yes, ma'am" to her like usual, Mrs. Alice added, "You'll be fine. Getting through most of the sixth grade is plenty enough of an accomplishment, especially for a foster. It's far more than you'd have done without us, so chin up."

She said that last bit like I ought to have been grateful. I suppose I was glad that I'd been able to spend the last several years living there, having school, staying out of trouble, away from the drunks and the crime on the other side of town. But I didn't think the Dobbses had done anything so special. I earned my keep with them, worked hard seven days a week. It wasn't like they was just giving me everything for free. If there weren't to be no more school, there was hardly reason at all for me to stay with the Dobbses anymore. What good would it be, picking up after them and Loretta all the time, keeping everything just so?

I looked out to the lawn beside the house, or the "farm," as the family called it. It was pretty much just a regular yard, except it was filled with an oversized vegetable garden and a couple of outbuildings for livestock. It wasn't anything like the pictures I'd seen of real farms, tobacco plantations out in the Virginia country, with them sprawling fields of sand lugs all lined up in perfect, neat rows. Even the local peach and apple orchards were more sizable than the dusty plot of land on which the Dobbs family relied. Even so, since he was often busy at his day job doing maintenance for the town's railcars, Mr. John hired a boy or two from time to time to help out with the chickens and goats. The boys would come each day, sweating and grunting out there in the coop, or huffing to themselves in the dry grass while they mended fences.

"But that's the whole reason I even came to stay here in the first," I argued, "so as I could go to the school over here."

"And you did," Mrs. Alice said. "It's been years you've been going. You can still see your friend Billy, if that's what you're worried about. After you finish chores and he's done with his school day."

She was always making comments about me being sweet on Billy, even though I wasn't. I suppose she couldn't imagine that it might be the other way around, that maybe a boy, even a freckled, gangly one like Billy, could take a cotton to a girl with shoulders so broad or a face as plain as mine. I didn't know for sure if Billy liked me that way or not. We didn't talk about those things, and it didn't matter to me anyhow.

"When can I go back to my own mama?" I asked. I'd never said something like that to her before. I didn't know if she knew about Ma being at the Colony, but I figured if Billy knew, maybe someone had told Mrs. Alice too.

She let out a long sigh at my question, like she was trying to blow away all the Virginia dust with that one breath.

"I didn't want to mention it," she said. Then she glanced over her shoulder toward the street, as if to make sure there weren't no one else within earshot before she looked back at me. "Your mother has been committed to a facility. You understand what that means? It was high time somebody intervened. At least she'll have guidance and care in the institution."

"She don't need that kind of help." I couldn't hold my thoughts inside. Without school, there wasn't nothing at the Dobbs house I was scared to lose. "Who's looking after Doris and Roy?" I asked.

I hadn't thought about them at first, when Billy told me the news earlier, but once they came to my mind, it was like they started pounding against my insides with metal spoons.

Mrs. Alice pushed her lips together like she didn't want to talk about Doris or Roy at all.

"I want to go back to my ma's house," I said. "You can tell that lady, Miss Drummond, to come and get me."

I had pushed too far, and now Mrs. Alice turned redder than the Tommy Toes growing in that garden behind me.

"You listen good and close, Carrie." She leaned in and pointed a finger at me. "There is nowhere else for you to go. You leave this farm, and you'll be on the streets, keeping time with men just like your mother did. If you must know about Doris and Roy, I'm told they've been placed in private homes too. At least now you three will stand a chance."

Her words about my brother and sister stopped me short. I wondered if I'd be able to find them, if maybe they'd been put somewhere nearby and might be getting set to attend the same school I was just leaving. They'd be so grown already, I realized, and I worried I mightn't even recognize them. But then I figured a body always has to know her own family. Nothing was more important than blood kin. My mind set to racing, and when Mrs. Alice walked away from me, I was already working on a plan to get my little family back together.

Jessa

February 2022

As I stepped into the Dreamland Diner, I was greeted by the familiar scent of sizzling bacon. I scanned the restaurant until my eyes landed on my grandmother, who was already nestled into a booth beside a large picture window that looked out onto Lexington Avenue. People outside hurried along the street, but Gram had her eyes trained on the Kindle in her lap. Having spent forty years working as a librarian, she could rarely be found without her e-reader, and its extra-large font, somewhere close by.

"Anything good?" I asked as I reached the table.

"Meh." Gram waved a hand in the air. "A thriller, but I knew where it was going by the end of the second chapter." Her blue eyes were bright with triumph beneath her penciled-in eyebrows. People often remarked that my grandmother resembled the dowager countess from *Downton Abbey*, and I agreed. With her wry sense of humor and a watchful gaze that never seemed to miss a trick, ole Betty Gregory could have given Maggie Smith a run for her money.

Gram barely waited for me to slide into my seat on the worn leather banquette before launching into a barrage of questions.

"So tell me about the immigration case," she said as she pushed a large laminated menu across the table. I had to resist the urge to roll my eyes at her question.

Gram had been flush with delight when she heard I would be doing more pro bono work. "Focusing on more altruistic work" was how she'd put it a few days earlier, right before she told me it was nice to see me "finally following a more righteous path, like you were meant for."

I knew she was thinking of her father when she said things like that. Though I'd never known my great-grandfather, I was well aware that he'd devoted much of his life to helping others, starting with the subsidized medical clinic he'd opened in a rural Massachusetts town near where Gram grew up. I'd always enjoyed listening to stories about the welcoming place her father created and the crucial medical care they provided for people who couldn't afford services elsewhere. Grandpa Harry had worked himself to the bone so he and the other doctors at the clinic could improve countless lives. In recent years, it had become increasingly clear that Gram didn't think I was living up to the same standards. The times she'd suggested I consider a lateral move to a firm more focused on public interest were too numerous to count. Or she'd bring up Jiyana's job as a social worker and say, "Maybe something more like that." It didn't seem to matter to her that I'd wanted to be a corporate attorney, like my dad, ever since I was a little kid.

Yet now, with partnership off the table, my plans to follow in my dad's footsteps had been undeniably disrupted. Taking on additional pro bono work wouldn't change that. And in fact, my father had often talked about wanting to build a pro bono program at his firm, well before boasting about charitable work was used as a recruiting tool. Even so, it irritated me that Gram was gloating from across the table.

"It was just a client meeting," I said on a shrug. "The woman was around my age, and nice," I added, even though that wasn't really the point. "I feel sorry that she doesn't have someone more experienced in immigration law to help her." I glanced down at the menu without reading it. We'd eaten at Dreamland so many times that I could practically recite the options from memory.

"Nonsense," Gram said. "You'll do whatever needs to be done." She motioned to a waiter so we could place our order.

We rattled off our usual requests: eggs over easy with sausage and toast for Gram, a Cobb salad for me. After the waiter left, Gram continued with her questions. The level of curiosity she displayed went well beyond the mild, polite interest she usually showed in my commercial cases. She wanted to know everything—from the layout of the detention center to the number of guards to my every last interaction on the property.

I replayed the long day in my mind's eye. Everything I'd encountered at the client meeting had been new to me. "I didn't get to see that much of the place. From what I could tell, it looked mostly how you'd picture a prison, like what they show in the movies. Lots of barbed wire and restricted areas, guards pacing the halls. Some loud machine blowing air. Maybe the biggest surprise was how dirty it was." I thought of the trash that had lined the walls, and that was just in the places where visitors were permitted. I could only imagine that the interior portions of the facility were in worse condition. "I didn't see sleeping quarters, but the parts I walked through were pretty dismal."

"So you didn't see any cages, like they talk about in the news? Children behind chain-link fences like a dog kennel?" The packet of saltines Gram had taken from the breadbasket earlier lay forgotten on the table as she waited for an answer.

I shook my head, remembering the horrible headlines we'd all seen about the centers closer to the Mexican border.

"No, not today, but this isn't a facility in Texas. I can't really speak to what's going on down there."

I reached for my glass and took a long sip of ice water, remembering the relief I'd felt when I stepped back into the parking lot after the visit. The biting February wind came as a welcome cleanse after the few hours I'd spent breathing the stagnant air inside the detention center. As I recalled the dispiriting atmosphere, an image of Isobel fanning herself came back to my mind.

"Actually," I started casually, as if I hadn't been perseverating during the entire drive home, "my client was hot even with how cold they keep the place. She's going through premature menopause because of some procedure they did during her detention."

"A young woman in menopause? What kind of procedure?" Gram asked, her gaze becoming more intense.

"I know," I said, noticing the way her expression had darkened. "It looks like you're having the same thought, maybe about some negligence or substandard care. But the client didn't want to get into it, so I had to let it go."

"No," Gram said.

"No, what?"

"Just wait!" she snapped. "Why can't you wait! Give me a moment."

I was startled by her outburst, but I closed my mouth and went quiet. It wasn't the first time my grandmother had displayed excitable behavior recently. I figured this was a "senior moment" taking hold of her, and given her age, I shouldn't have been surprised to see them happening more frequently these days. Gram turned her eyes up toward the ceiling, as if searching for a thought or maybe just the right words for what she wanted to say, so I waited.

As the silence stretched, my eyes drifted around the room, taking in the other groups of patrons at the kitschy restaurant. I saw a teenaged couple sitting side by side, an elderly man alone, and a table full of middle-aged women in business suits before my gaze settled on a young family at a table across the way. Five of them were crammed into a booth: a mom squirting ketchup onto the plate of a toddler, two slightly older boys playing with action figures, and a ruddy-faced man in a cowl-neck sweater. It looked like the dad was telling them all a story. He was smiling and gesticulating, miming shooting a basketball. None of the others were paying much attention to him, or to each other for that matter.

Watching them, I thought about how I had once taken it all for granted too, the simple weekday dinners, my mom's constant hovering, my dad's chattering about the different people in his office or someone he'd bumped into at court. If Vance and I ever managed to have the babies we were aiming for, I would make sure to do better, to relish every moment and appreciate how lucky we were. I tried to mentally superimpose my own face onto the mom across the room, Vance's onto the dad, imagining what it would be like to trade places. All these years after losing my parents, the desire for a picture-perfect family still followed me wherever I went. Except now, in addition to the constant desperation, I also felt a new sensation of panic—the fear that I wouldn't be able to have a baby, that the family I'd always dreamed of was simply never going to happen.

"Well, don't you?" Gram asked, and I realized I'd missed the first part of whatever she'd been saying.

"Sorry, what?" I asked, my eyes coming back to hers. "Gram, are you okay?" Her face seemed to have turned even paler than usual.

"You can't just let it go," she answered. "You have to protect this woman, make sure she hasn't been harmed." Gram had always been a woman of deep passions, but this reaction seemed aggressive, even for her.

"That's not what I was hired for. It's not my business."

She held my gaze silently for a moment, as if trying to make a point. When I didn't respond, she asked, "Doesn't it concern you?"

Even though she was putting voice to thoughts I'd been considering myself, I kept reaching the same conclusion: Unless Isobel asked for help or divulged more details, there was nothing I could do about her medical procedure. I shook my head. "She didn't really want to get into it with me. She's the client, so she's in charge."

Gram slammed her hand against the tabletop, her voice rising as she leaned toward me. "Well, maybe for once in your life, you should take some charge! Stop letting other people make so many decisions for you. Constantly letting other people steer the ship isn't going to protect you from anything." She pointed a finger and leaned even closer. "Enough with sheltering your tender heart. Enough coddling yourself!" Spittle flew from her mouth as she finished.

"Whoa!" I reared back. Gram was typically the picture of composure, even in anger. This behavior was so out of character, so much more than the little blips of senility she sometimes displayed, that I was instantly concerned. My thoughts jumped directly to worst-case scenarios, as usual. She might be reaching the beginning of the end, I worried, and faster than I'd realized. I didn't know if I could confront a life without Gram in it. I wasn't ready to be the last one from my biological family left on the entire earth.

I knew what I was doing. *Catastrophizing*. Another term my therapist taught me back in my teens. Unfortunately, no therapist had yet trained me to prevent myself from racing immediately, and unjustifiably, toward imagining the worst possible outcomes.

Gram inhaled deeply and then began again.

"I'm sorry," she said, visibly working to calm herself. "It just . . ." She hesitated. "I hate to think of a young woman deprived of choices like that. Should you not, at least, just ask her about it one more time?"

I was so relieved to see her composure return that I felt willing to agree to anything she suggested. The server reappeared beside our table then, placing a steaming dish in front of Gram and my salad before me.

"She didn't exactly say the doctor did it without her consent," I said as the waiter walked away. "Maybe it was just a complicated medical issue that was difficult for a layperson to understand." I felt myself losing confidence in my words even as I spoke them. I actually couldn't recall exactly how Isobel had phrased it. Had she mentioned agreeing to undergo the procedure? "Or maybe she just didn't want to get into her personal medical details with me. A stranger. I was only there to help with her immigration status, not her hot flashes."

Gram pursed her lips, and I got the distinct impression that she was trying to prevent herself from saying something else.

"What?" I asked. "What is it?"

She inhaled deeply, like she was gearing up to reveal something. But then she hesitated again, and her shoulders slumped. "Let's just talk a little more about what you think you should do," she said.

"I should keep trying to get the woman's removal order canceled because that's what she has retained me to do. She doesn't want to get deported to a country that's really never been her home. Maybe we're creating another issue where none exists."

Gram cocked her head to the side, her eyebrows shooting up. "If you really think that, then why did you even mention it to me?" she asked.

When I didn't answer, she reached across the table and took my hand. "Do something for me," she said. "There's a Supreme Court case from the 1920s." She reached into her purse for a pen, tore off a corner of her paper place mat, and scribbled down the name. "Take a look at it."

"Oh, come on," I started, my tone laced with frustration as I took the paper and glanced down at it. It wasn't unusual for my grandmother to refer me to an article or book when trying to make a point. All that time spent working in libraries had left its mark. I hated going on research jaunts whenever Gram wanted to teach me one lesson or another, but I'd learned long ago that protesting was futile.

"It's one that your great-grandfather would have wanted you to read," she added as she held my gaze. It was no surprise she was bringing him up. I could hear about my dapper, intrepid, generous grandpa Harry only so many times without developing a bit of hero worship, and she knew it. "It's easy enough to find," Gram told me. "Just read it. Then we'll talk."

A waiter reappeared to fill our water glasses again, and when he finished, Gram changed the subject.

~

Three days later, I was still anxious about Hydeford. I shouldn't have been surprised that the 1920s case Gram mentioned had struck at the very heart of what bothered me about Isobel's situation. The short case opinion from the Supreme Court had hit me like blunt force to the chest. The horrifying opinion had been written by Justice Oliver Wendell Holmes Jr., who'd always been described in my law classes as a hero of jurisprudence, a humanitarian, and a visionary. Adding to my shock was the fact that long-venerated justices William Howard Taft and Louis Brandeis also signed the opinion of the Court. After I finished reading the case a third time, when I still simply couldn't digest what I'd seen, I'd Googled the plaintiff, Carrie Buck.

As I reached for my cell phone to try calling Gram again, Tate came barging into my office.

"Why haven't you left yet?" she asked.

Tabitha Clifford, who preferred to be called Tate, was a paralegal at Dillney, Forsythe & Lowe. Seven years earlier, Tate happened to be the only witness when I wiped out in the hallway on my very first day at the firm. I could still remember the mortification that coursed through me when my patent leather heel snagged on a piece of carpet and I went tumbling, spilling my iced latte all over myself in the process. Tate was just passing by with a cart full of Redweld folders. After helping me back to my feet, she pulled off her own cardigan to cover the stain spreading across my white blouse. As I joked about literally taking the shirt off her back, I knew I'd found a friend.

"I'm just finishing up," I said, looking up from my computer to see that Tate had pulled her pin-straight blond hair into a complicated twist and was wearing fresh, glossy red lipstick. The sky outside had begun to darken, and my empty stomach was getting impatient for dinner.

"Big plans?" I asked as three emails appeared in my inbox in quick succession, all of them from Dustin Ortiz. Rather than deal with whatever aggravating material was within those messages, I twisted my body so the computer was no longer in my line of sight and returned my full attention to Tate.

"Just that guy from my bridge class." She shrugged, and then her eyes fell to the open folder on my desk. "The deportation case?" she asked. "I thought that one was supposed to be pretty open and shut."

"Yeah." I also glanced down at the folder before looking back at Tate. "It was supposed to be. The woman was arrested for marijuana possession a month before it was legalized in New York. It was her first offense, and only a small amount with no intent to distribute."

"If it's legal now, why's she still in custody?"

"It's still a federal crime. And anyway, once she was arrested, she became known to ICE. Since she was present in the country without authorization, they kept her. The good news is she's got no prior record. She has family here, a daughter who's a citizen. I think I should be able to get the removal canceled."

"Then why are your shoulders all droopy like you've already lost the case?" Tate asked.

Before I could respond, my cell phone started buzzing on my desk. I saw Vance's name flashing on the screen, but I didn't reach for the phone.

"Don't you want to get that?" Tate asked, her eyes darting down to the caller ID.

"We're not . . . No." I shook my head.

She lowered her pale eyebrows with a look of sympathy. "Take the call, Jess," she said, turning to leave. "I'll see you in the morning." Tate knew all about the explosive argument I'd had with Vance two nights before, right after my period had arrived.

Again, he'd acted like I was blowing everything out of proportion. He reminded me that we hadn't been trying all that long, which technically may have been true—but longing so intensely for something that wasn't materializing made each month feel like an eternity. There were so many fertility treatments we had yet to try, he'd said, and then he'd reminded me that if fertility care didn't work out, we could adopt. At the mention of adoption, I'd gone ballistic. I wasn't proud of how I'd behaved, but the cavalier way in which he'd thrown around that word, *adoption*, made me feel like he didn't know me at all. I knew it was all the same to him as long as our kids were raised Jewish, filling new seats in the family's pew at High Holiday services and belting out songs at the annual Passover Seder. But passing down his great-grandmother's hallowed recipe for noodle kugel simply didn't feel like enough. To me, the whole point of having children was to bring pieces of our history back to life, to have more biological relatives keeping us company.

I wasn't willing to consider adoption until we had tried absolutely everything else. Was it so wrong to be honest about it?

On the fourth ring, I reached for the phone and slid my finger across the screen to answer.

"Hi," I said, trying to keep my voice neutral. "I'm just about to leave."

"I made us a reservation at Sushi Seventy," he said, referencing our favorite neighborhood restaurant. His tone was gentle, laced with something hopeful. I pictured him sitting in his office two blocks south of the Plaza Hotel across from Central Park, his collar likely loosened by this time of day, showing off his wide neck. He was probably fidgeting with something as usual, a pen or a coffee mug. "I did some research today," he said, lowering his voice so the colleagues in his open-plan office wouldn't overhear, "about fertility options and medical interventions. And I got the name of the doctor Doug and Maria used. The guy doesn't usually see people until they've been trying for closer to a year, but I sweet-talked the receptionist."

With those words, my lingering anger began to melt away. Vance had gone charging ahead, intent as usual on fixing any situation that caused me distress. That kind of care from him was a hallmark of our relationship. Really, it was part of what had made me fall in love with him in the first place. Even the night we met, when Vance had shown up to a New Year's party full of NYU law students, he'd made it a priority to look out for me. It had been a crazy night, and somewhere amid all the lemon drop shots and Lady Gaga anthems blaring through my friend Carly's apartment, I'd managed to lose a shoe. There was no way I'd have been able to get a cab home on New Year's, and I couldn't walk all the way from Gramercy Park to my building downtown with only one shoe. After making a few jokes about Cinderella, Vance had turned that apartment upside down, insisting that I continue enjoying the party while he searched. He hadn't given up until forty-five minutes later when he pulled the shoe out of the freezer, of all places. I'd already been admiring his soulful eyes and athletic build, but when he closed that freezer door and emitted a triumphant battle cry, I was done for.

Two months later, when things began to feel serious between us, he confessed that he'd had tickets to a late-night Maroon 5 concert on New Year's but had sent his friends along without him. He'd smiled sheepishly, telling me the concert hadn't been nearly as important as helping me find my shoe, or getting my phone number. I'd been so lost back then, still trying to find where I belonged in a world without my parents. When Vance appeared with his vitality and confidence, and his constant ability to take charge, I felt like I was being wrapped in a warm blanket, provided a force field of protection that I'd been searching for all along.

And now, all these years later, he was still going out of his way to take care of me. As I absorbed his words about the new doctor, my imagination took me on a journey of what would follow this conversation. We would find an expert, the very best one, and we'd figure it all out. It would all be fine. Science was amazing, and surely a slew of cutting-edge options were waiting for us out there. It might be a difficult road, but we would have our own child by the end of it.

"Whoever gets to the restaurant first should order the sashimi combo, right?" I asked.

"That's what I was thinking," he said, and I could hear the smile in his voice. We were going to be fine. Everything would be fine. Totally fine. I just knew it.

Carrie

June 1923

Everything started to change a few weeks shy of my seventeenth birthday. Three years had passed since I'd learned about Ma being sent to that Colony for Epileptics and Feebleminded in Lynchburg, and I'd still not managed to do a thing about it. Nor had I found out what had happened to Doris and Roy. Instead, I'd spent endless days hauling feed, cleaning troughs, and collecting eggs from angry hens. That all was on top of the laundering, sweeping, and pressing that had been my job since the day I'd first arrived at the Dobbs home. It didn't leave much time spare for plotting how to reunite my family. And I got distracted from thinking about my family sometimes, so fixed was I instead on my longing to return to school.

Some days I worked extra hard, thinking that if I pleased Mrs. Alice, she'd relent and send me back to the classroom. Other days I'd foul up on purpose, hoping to show I weren't so useful to have around all the time anyhow. But my mistakes never led Mrs. Alice to suggest more school. Instead, she'd just set me to doing over whatever I'd ruined, and I'd be cross with myself for making the extra work. Mrs. Alice said that sometimes it seemed like I was of two fully separate minds, doing my very best or doing my awful worst depending on the day. I reckon she was right. But that was how the time kept unfolding for me, one day after the other, so much the same as each of the days before it.

Loretta Dobbs had married a young man the year before, a homely, churchgoing fellow who came from a family just two roads over. He and Loretta moved farther down south, where the husband was taking a job at his cousin's construction company. I liked to think on her new life and imagine something similar for myself, a love story and an escape. With only one more year remaining until I turned eighteen, I'd talk out my dreams with Billy, guessing on where I'd go after I was legally an adult. Maybe I'd work as a telephone operator and get my own little apartment to rent. Or I might be able to find a position at the glove factory down on Hendricks Street, on account of my experience with so much mending at the Dobbses'. I didn't know what other employ there could be for someone like me, a quiet, hefty girl who'd never gone past the sixth grade. If I managed to get the right job and save some earnings, maybe I could use the money to get my ma free. That was what I hoped. I'd tell them I could look after her just fine all by my lonesome.

That's what I was thinking about that June day as I walked into the dusty shed out behind the house and hoisted a bag of feed onto my shoulder. When I came back outside to bring the feed to the coop, I noticed Mr. John walking up the road with another fellow. Mr. John had lots of friends around town, and it wasn't unusual for him to bring someone by the house, so I didn't pay them much mind.

I was hurrying through my tasks so I could have time left over to walk up the road to the Wilkenses' farm, where they had a litter of kittens. The white-haired wife, Claudia, said I could come feed the little tabbies using milk from a dropper. In the years I'd been living over on Grove Street, that Claudia Wilkens had always been extra kind toward me. Each time she visited with Mrs. Alice, she'd slip me one of her fresh-baked biscuits or offer to comb my hair. Maybe because her own children were grown, she was lonely. Or maybe she just liked having another somebody to watch over. I could understand something like that because that's how I felt about them kittens. It filled me up, looking after little ones like that, much the same as when I'd looked after Doris and Roy.

I was making my next trip out of the shed, the slop bucket full and heavy in my hand, when Mr. John was upon me.

"Carrie," he said. His tone was always the same, deep and strong. Looking back now, I think Mr. John had the kind of voice that belonged on a radio program. His hardy timbre made it so a person would barely notice how his hair had thinned or how liver spots now dotted his face. "This here's Clarence Garland, my nephew, here to work with you." He pointed with a thumb to the young man beside him. When I turned my eyes to greet the newcomer, I near up and lost the use of my tongue. I'd never seen such a looker as him in real life. He was more like the fellows on the giant placards outside the playhouse in town, like that Rudolph Valentino. He was tall, like me, and I was near eye to eye with him. I guessed he was about five years older than me, his dark hair slicked back with some kind of pomade, and his eyes so light they looked almost unnatural.

We already had two farm boys hired up for the year, so I couldn't figure why we'd need yet another, even with all the produce and eggs selling faster than they used to.

"Mrs. Alice and I are heading down to visit Loretta in Durham for a time," Mr. John said, "and Clarence here is going to be looking after the farm while we're gone. He'll stay in the apartment with the other boys," he explained, talking about the spare room over the barn. "You just follow what he says." Mr. John turned back to

Clarence then. "She's a sturdy thing. Good worker. Won't give you no trouble."

I felt my face redden from Mr. John's words. He'd said such things about me plenty in the past, but this was the first time I ever minded it, standing as I was in front of that young man. It was like I suddenly noticed then how my gray dress hung loose and shapeless on me, like a burlap sack, and how my boots were caked in manure and mud. And yet, when Mr. John stood there describing me no different than he would a tractor, Clarence seemed somehow not to notice the unfavorableness of it all.

He smiled back at me, showing me straight white teeth. "Good to meet you, Miss Carrie," he said, like he really meant it.

I wondered where he came from, how long he'd stay, how long Mr. and Mrs. Dobbs would be down there visiting with Loretta, but I couldn't hardly find my words to ask about any of it just then. The pail full of old scraps was still hanging from my hand, weighing me down. I just nodded and went back to work.

Two days later, Mr. and Mrs. Dobbs finally left to stay with Loretta. I kept about my chores anyhow, having long since settled into my routine, taking care of the house in the morning and then heading out to clean the coop and collect fertilizer in the afternoons. I saw Clarence coming and going throughout the day, stopping to check in with Ralph and Tony, the other farmhands. It wasn't until the sun began sinking lower in the sky that first day we were on our own that he approached me.

"Carrie," he said, smiling like he was real glad to see me. "You planning to take supper all alone tonight?"

I didn't tell him I always took my supper alone.

"Why?" I asked.

"I thought maybe you and I could take ourselves on a walk into town. You could show me around. Maybe we stop at a soda fountain?" He smiled at me, and something in his expression made me think he was feeling shy to even ask. But then I thought he probably just felt sorry for me, a girl with nobody to look after her and such. I didn't have any money to spend on a soda pop anyhow, and I didn't want to say so.

"The day's been long and hot," I said. "I'm fixing to stay in." I didn't need someone's pity, not even if that someone was so fine to look at.

Clarence's shoulders dropped a little at my words, and his lips tightened in on themselves like he was truly disappointed. Before I even thought about it, I surprised myself by saying more. "There's extra hash and boiled peas." I pointed back toward the house.

"That sounds like just about the best offer I've had in a real long time." He smiled at me so wide that I couldn't help but smile back.

"Come on then," I said. I was suddenly brimming with a brand-new kind of giddiness.

I set us a place on the back porch where the air was cooler, on account of the sugar maples flanking the house on both sides. I turned two chairs, facing them out to the yard so we could gaze out into the evening. The train tracks were just beyond the yard, and I knew a train would be passing by soon, something for us to watch while we waited for the lightning bugs to arrive. Once we were settled, both of us with full bowls balanced in our laps, the smell of warm dirt still lingering in the air, Clarence set to asking me questions. He inquired about one thing after another, like he needed to know everything there was to know about Carrie Buck. Somehow, we talked for three hours, until the moon was sharp and bright.

After that day, I knew for certain that my feelings for Clarence were more than just friendly in spirit. I couldn't say what he thought in return, except that everywhere I went on the farm, Clarence seemed to show up beside me.

On the fourth day after the Dobbses left, I was hauling a basket of turnips toward the root cellar, and then there was Clarence.

"Let me get that for you," he said, lifting the heaping basket from my hands before I could answer. "Carrying for Carrie," he said, laughing a little at his own joke. I grinned back at him and his foolishness. I stood at the top of the steps, trying to decide whether to follow him down to the cellar, but he made quick work of it. Wasn't even a minute before he was on his way back up, his strong hands free again.

"See ya," he said, winking at me before walking off toward the barn.

He showed up at lunchtime that day too, holding a big yellow flower. I couldn't tell you what type of blossom it was, but I knew it was the kind that grew down by the little crick.

"I saw this and thought of you," he said, pushing the flower gently into place behind my ear. It felt silly to me, wearing my dusty work dress, heading back to the coop to shovel dung while having a flower wedged into my hair. But I left it there just the same.

All the rest of that day, I found my eyes roaming across the property. I looked up toward the barn roof, where Clarence was working and hammering while Ralph stood on a ladder beside him. He didn't look back my way, but I reckoned it was best he kept focused on his balance up there anyhow. As each hour passed, I wondered harder if maybe I'd imagined his interest in me, stocky and plain as I was.

But then he came looking for me again before supper. Not just that night, but every night that week. He'd show up at the back door, offering me that easy smile, his eyes never drifting from my face. As we sat on the back porch night by night, chewing our corn and greens, or anything else I scrounged from the larder, I could feel myself tumbling toward something.

One such night, he told me all about how he came to be here on the farm with us instead of back in Richmond, where his own family lived.

"My father's not like Uncle John," he said before biting into a piece of the sourdough loaf I'd sliced for us. "My old man's always telling me I have to be this way or that. I was getting ready to just take myself on the road when we heard from Uncle John about him wanting my help." He pushed his lips out like he was figuring about something. Then he looked over at me, a flush spreading on his face.

"I don't mean to act sour. Just wondering where life's going to take me next."

"You could stay on here, couldn't you?" I asked, maybe sounding too hopeful. "Mr. John's always hiring one man or another. Why not you?"

Clarence put his dish on the little table between us and looked me square in the face, nodding as he did.

"Why not me." He didn't ask it, but said the words like he was stating his mind. He stared at me longer, and I wondered if I was meant to say something. I didn't know what though, so I just sat quiet while heat rose in my cheeks. I reckon he noted my flush because his lips turned up in a big smile. Then he cleared his throat and turned his eyes back toward the train tracks.

After that night, I started to think that maybe Clarence's arrival at the Grove Street farm was the beginning for me, the first step in my adult life. After he went back to the barn on those nights, I'd lie on my little cot in the alcove and think about what would happen when Mr. John and Mrs. Alice returned, when they saw their nephew's good work on the farm and his growing interest in me.

One afternoon, after the Dobbses had been gone so long it felt like maybe they were never coming back, Clarence came to see me where I was hanging linens on the back line. It was late in the day, but I'd been so busy preparing pepper jams that I was only just finishing the laundry.

Clarence took up the last sheet in my basket and started pinning it to the line.

"How about you come on a walk with me to the creek?" he asked.

"Just let me set this back inside," I said, my blood quickening at the invitation. I lifted the basket with one hand and untied my apron with the other.

Once I'd tidied up, we made our way down the hill, heading west toward the small crick and squinting our eyes against the glare of the sinking sun. Charlottesville was a place that seemed to fill with more buildings and concrete every day, the natural areas getting covered up one after another by the fuss and such of big-city life. Yet this particular area of forest where we were headed, with its trickling stream of water and its tangled thicket of trees, was still holding on.

"I heard from Uncle John today," Clarence told me as we stepped over the fallen branches and the thick cover of leaves. "They'll be back from Durham on Monday."

The news hit me like a weight in my stomach, dropping like a stone.

When we reached the small stream of water, he took my hand in his. I'd never held hands with a boy before, and my palm started to sweat at the touch.

"Will you tell them you want to stay on?" I asked, unable to pretend that wasn't the very question I thought about all the livelong day.

"I sure hope they'll have me," he said, stopping us in our tracks with a light yank and turning so his full body faced mine. He pushed some of my hair away from my eye as he looked at me real intent, like I was all that mattered in the world.

I opened my mouth to answer, but before any words came out, he put his mouth on mine for a kiss. I gasped in surprise, but I kissed him back just the same. When he pushed his tongue between my lips, I think I jumped a little. I didn't know anything about that kind of kissing, and I put my hand against his chest to push him back.

"Shh," he told me. "I've wanted to do this since the first moment I saw you."

I liked hearing that he felt the same about me as I did him, and I put my lips back to his, this time opening my mouth for him to teach me.

Soon he was lowering us to the ground.

"Wait, Clarence," I said, "we can't." I was thinking about the dirt stains that would get on my dress if we did our kissing right there on the muddy forest floor.

"It's okay," Clarence said, continuing to lower me to the sodden ground. "Trust me."

And shame on me, because in that moment, I did.

As soon as we were down against the leaves and muck of the ground, Clarence started pushing up my dress. That was when I realized there was more risk to lying down than just soiling my smock.

"Wait, Clarence, what are you doing?" I pushed at his hands.

He didn't even answer but just kept on shoving up my dress, his breath growing heavy and ragged. He put his lips to my neck and started kissing me there, his mouth making my skin all slick in a way I didn't like.

"Stop it, Clarence," I said, suddenly feeling mad. I pushed against him, but he was lying on top of me, his weight firm. He had me pinned down with one arm, and with the other hand he was fumbling with his own pants, all frantic-like. My dress was up around my waist, and I was pushing, trying to free myself from his grasp. I learned in that moment that I was not as strong as I thought. All that business with Mr. John calling me "a sturdy thing" wasn't but nothing.

"This is what you've wanted," he said, huffing. "You don't have to pretend."

"No, Clarence! Please! No!" I was shouting now, but he clamped his hand over my mouth.

"You stop," he said. "Just keep still so I can . . ."

I cried out against his hand, but the sound didn't carry none, covered as it was. My body went limp against the force of it all. And then my mind did this curious thing, where everything went suddenly and completely blank, all my thoughts shoved into nothingness. Even though I could still feel Clarence up above me, it was somehow like I wasn't there, like I had gone away. I just watched what happened as if I was looking down from up above us. Years later, when I learned the word *obliterated*, I thought back to that moment with Clarence. That was what he had done to me then; I felt obliterated. I wish now that I had fought harder—I wish for that all the time, but I can't go back.

~

He didn't hold my hand as we walked back up the hill, but he talked a bunch just the same as he had on our way down, as if nothing had changed. I might have wondered if I'd imagined everything else, if not for the burning stickiness between my legs and the ache I felt where his thumb had dug into my shoulder.

"Chances are," Clarence said, "Uncle John will send me off after he returns. He doesn't really have enough work for four men, especially with you here doing your share. Don't you think?"

How different a person could feel from one hour to the next. Though I would have been devastated for him to leave just that afternoon, now I couldn't wait for him to go. Whatever I thought I'd felt for him earlier, well, he'd more than extinguished that. If this was how a man loved a woman, I didn't want no part of it.

He glanced over at me when I didn't answer.

"Well?" he asked lightly, like I was the crazy one for keeping quiet. I just wanted to reach the house and get to the washbasin. I was keen to scrub at myself, to wash every part of him off my skin, out of my body. I was crawling with the feel of him.

"Aww." He looked at me with that expression I had mistaken for goodness, the corners of his mouth lifting. "Don't be sore at me for leaving. You know I'll come and see you. You're my girl now."

I didn't want to be his girl. Not anymore, not after the way he'd acted. I didn't know how to tell him that, and I worried he might still do something else to me, so I just kept my lips closed tight.

When we reached the edge of the Dobbs property, he stopped walking and took my chin in his hand, looking me straight in the eye.

"I promise," he said. "I'll be back."

Well, that was just what I was afraid of.

Jessa

February 2022

As I waited for my grandmother to emerge from the apartment building on Eighty-Fifth Street, I pulled my wool hat down around my ears. The old puffer coat I'd grabbed that morning wasn't much of a match for the frigid, damp air outside, and the rawness of it swept right through me, chilling me to the bone.

The day before, Gram had finally answered one of my calls, but only to insist that we needed to speak in person. Had this been a month earlier, I would have pushed back, telling her I could not possibly leave work in the middle of a weekday to meet, and that we should either speak by phone or wait until the weekend. But now, thinking of my dismal prospects of advancement at work, I sighed loudly. There was no use dwelling on the years spent sacrificing for a partnership position that was clearly never going to materialize.

"Hey now."

I turned to see the doorman watching me. He was standing about ten feet away, next to the building's revolving door.

"How about a smile?" he asked. "It can't be that bad."

I considered the older man in his long green overcoat and matching cap, and I wondered if I should tell him that times had changed—that it was no longer polite to tell a woman to smile, that it wasn't my job to decorate the city streets with a smiling face. But then something inside the building caught the man's eye, and he began pushing the revolving door.

A moment later, Gram emerged in a thick cranberry-colored parka that reached nearly to her shins, along with a matching wool hat.

"Good afternoon, Mrs. Gregory." The doorman nodded at her. "You need a cab today?"

"No thank you, Jonathan," she answered as her eyes landed on me. "I'm just going for a walk with my granddaughter."

"Well, you button up now," he told her. "It's a cold one."

She nodded at the man and readjusted the knitted scarf around her neck as she made her way toward me. After a quick kiss on the cheek, she took hold of my elbow and directed us toward Third Avenue.

"You're sure you don't want to find a coffee shop or something?" I asked, just as the wind picked up around us.

She shook her head. "I need the fresh air," she said, "and it's better if no one can listen in on our conversation."

"This sounds serious," I said playfully as we walked in tandem.

She shot me a stern look, effectively wiping the grin from my face.

"Yeesh, sorry," I said, feeling a bit like a reprimanded teenager. "What's this all about?"

We turned north on Third Avenue, heading uptown. "The case I told you to look up . . ." She trailed off, as if she'd forgotten what more she wanted to say.

Another senior moment, I worried. But then I noticed the way she was squaring her shoulders and raising her chin, like she was building up her nerve.

"There's something I need to tell you. You talk about wanting to live up to your family's legacy. Well, now's the time you can. You should know about your great-grandfather's connection to that girl, what he did for her."

~

That night, I sat cross-legged in the middle of the bed surrounded by scattered papers. My computer was open in my lap as I clicked through the pages of yet another website about immigrants' rights. I'd wasted too much time that afternoon thinking about how my great-grandfather wasn't who I'd been led to believe but was, in fact, so much more. I'd always assumed I knew his whole story, all the ways in which he'd sacrificed to help others, but I'd only known one chapter of a much longer story. Now I saw with new eyes why my dad, who'd been so successful in corporate law, always put my mother's family on a pedestal.

At the sound of the apartment door opening, I glanced at the bedside table. My view of the clock was blocked by an empty Chinese take-out container, but I knew it was nearing midnight. Reaching up, I removed the rubber band that had been holding my hair in a haphazard bun. Mascara had surely pooled beneath my eyes in tired smudges, and I had grease stains on my t-shirt from where I'd dropped a forkful of lo mein. I wondered fleetingly if any women had attended the client dinner from which Vance was now returning. All of them would have been more put together than what he was about to find waiting for him.

When he reached the bedroom, his eyes scanned the area. "It looks like a war room in here." In addition to the piles of papers and greasy take-out packages, there was an empty bottle of Diet Coke lying sideways in the middle of the carpet, a bag of Twizzlers open on a pillow, and a few fortune cookie wrappers by my feet.

"Yeah." I stood to start gathering up trash. "I guess I was kind of in the zone." The mess that had accumulated testified to how out of sorts I'd been, thinking about the innumerable ways I could screw up Isobel's case. "No one ever said I did my best work on an empty stomach, right?" I swiped at the duvet with my empty hand, wiping away stray crumbs.

"Yeah, but who are you and what did you do with my neurotic wife?" he joked as he started to unbutton his dress shirt.

"Sorry. It's been so busy at work with Hannity Blue," I said, referencing the corporate (a.k.a. paying) client who had been monopolizing my time for a securities litigation. Even with Dustin Ortiz doing more of the heavy lifting than I frankly would have expected from a reformed deadbeat like him, our whole team had been underwater with it. "And I have Hydeford in the morning. It's like the more I learn about immigration, the more I realize I don't know. The body of law is enormous, and it's all really complex. Making heads or tails of it has been an undertaking for me."

Vance shook his head slightly. "And you have an actual degree in the laws of this country. Imagine how confusing it must be for people who are trying to come here for the first time."

"If you do absolutely everything right when you first arrive in the US, the rules are kind of clear," I said, pausing for a second to wonder if even that much was true. "But once you make one error as a noncitizen, even something small like failing to file a form on time, it triggers all these other laws that seem to have endless possible interpretations."

"It couldn't have been this complicated back in the '40s when my grandparents came over, right?" Vance asked as he sat on the edge of the bed and began removing his shoes.

One of the first things I ever learned about Vance was that his father's parents survived Auschwitz as teenagers. It was because of Vance's grandparents and the horror they'd experienced in Poland that he was so adamant about holding on to his Jewish heritage and raising his own kids Jewish. He'd told me as much long before he proposed. His grandparents were also the inspiration behind his podcast and the hours he spent recording episodes that helped reunite families with their heirlooms.

His entire identity was wrapped up in what his grandparents had suffered, in the stories they'd told him when he was a child. Over time, he'd shared some of the stories with me. I'd heard the bone-chilling account of how his grandmother had watched her own mother and sister get shot by a guard after they were caught reciting a Hebrew blessing over the body of a prisoner who'd died in her sleep. His grandfather, I learned, had been subjected to medical experimentation he refused to discuss, but whatever happened had left him with a significant limp for the rest of his life.

Normally, I was very attentive when Vance spoke about his family and how important they were to him. His attachment to family was one of my favorite things about him. But now I didn't want to focus on his grandma and grandpa Singer, not when I'd learned only hours earlier that my own great-grandparents had lost so much as a result of Grandpa Harry's efforts to help another person. I'd never known. I couldn't say what trait motivated a person to put the needs of others so far before their own, but I hoped I'd inherited it too, that I could live up to that example.

I hadn't decided yet whether I'd share the new pieces of my family story with Vance. My great-grandpa had risked his reputation to help a defenseless girl, and it had ruined him. Vance wouldn't want to hear about anyone in my family being considered a failure, even if it was for all the right reasons. He'd only worry about how it would reflect on us, on him. Whatever fault he might find with what Grandpa Harry did, I didn't want to hear it. So instead, I took my leftovers and the small pile of trash and carried them out to the kitchen.

When I returned to the bedroom, Vance glanced up at me from where he was still sitting on the bed, scrolling though his phone.

"There's more to this pro bono case," I said, lowering myself onto the gray bouclé chair in the corner of the room. "I think some medical abuse might be going on inside the facility. I'm hoping I'm wrong." Then I spoke aloud the decision I had reached hours earlier: "But as Isobel's only advocate right now, I feel like I need to pursue this some more."

Knowing more of my own history had brought the situation at the detention center into clearer focus. The idea that a woman in custody had been subjected to a medical procedure without her full consent, and possibly for nefarious reasons, in the twenty-first century! It was almost too awful to consider. And now, given what Gram had shared, I felt enormous responsibility to help prevent such travesties from ever happening again. So consider it, I must.

"Wow, yeah, for sure." Vance nodded, but his gaze flickered away from me for a moment. I could almost see the gears turning inside his mind, searching for a reason to contradict me. "It sounds like a lot though, doesn't it?" He didn't wait for my response. "You should probably bring in another attorney from your office to deal with this. It shouldn't all be on you. Especially now, when we're trying to keep your stress levels low, right?" He tossed his phone onto the bed and pulled off his socks to begin massaging his left foot.

I watched him push his thumb into his arch, the way he did when his plantar fasciitis acted up. He closed his eyes for a moment to revel in the self-massage, and I took the opportunity to snarl at him. His continued insistence that I couldn't handle the work I was doing was becoming intolerable.

Of course it all had to be on me, I wanted to say. I was Isobel's attorney, and quite possibly her only advocate. If she'd been mistreated in custody, someone needed to stand up for her, just like my great-grandfather had done for the girl in that old case. I didn't want to keep arguing with Vance, begging for his approval.

Mercifully, my phone rang, interrupting us.

"It's Jiyana," I said, raising my eyebrows at the late call. My sister-in-law was one of those people who generally climbed into bed at the same time as her toddlers. "Hey, is everything okay?" I asked as I picked up.

"Wendy just called in sick for tomorrow." Wendy was their über-reliable nanny, the woman who made it possible for Jiyana to work long hours as a social worker, earning overtime to help pay for their son's fancy preschool. This was the first time I'd ever heard of the woman missing a day. "I would never normally ask. I know your job is so crazy, but I have this one meeting I can't cancel, and Will has an on-site in Connecticut. Jonah can stay at daycare till six, but Kian's pickup is at four. If you could just grab him and bring him to the apartment, Will can be back like ten minutes after you get there. Are you too busy?"

I clicked over to my calendar, doing some calculations in my head about driving time to and from Hydeford.

"Yeah, no. I can actually do it. I'll be in Jersey all morning, but I can get back in time."

"Oh my God, Jess. You are the ultimate lifesaver. I cannot tell you . . . I will repay the favor tenfold when you and Vance pop out a few little monsters of your own," she said with a laugh. "Any news on that front, by the way?"

I glanced over at Vance, who was still sitting in the same spot, waiting to finish our conversation. I wasn't sure how he'd feel if he knew I'd told Jiyana we were trying. He loved how close she and I were, but with the whole thing becoming an increasingly sensitive topic, I didn't want to ask now whether he minded.

"Hey, listen," I told her, "Vance is here waiting to talk to me, so I've got to run. But text me the details for tomorrow, and I'm on it."

"You're my hero. Love ya, sis," she said, ending the call.

I turned back toward Vance. "Auntie Jessa to the rescue?" he said.

I smiled. "You know it."

"You see? Working less isn't exactly the end of the world. If you cut back, you could spend your days relaxing, hanging with your nephews, putting your feet up somewhere."

I could feel the disappointment settling over my face at his words, and he clearly saw it too.

"Look, all I was trying to say earlier is that you're not the only person at the firm who could help this client of yours. Can't you just think about it?"

"I'm so tired," I answered, shutting down the conversation before we started another shouting match. "Can we just get in bed?" I twisted my neck to relieve the tension in my shoulders and stood.

Vance opened his eyes and cleared his throat, like there was something else he wanted to say—but I didn't wait before moving to the bathroom and shutting the door between us.

~

The next morning, I passed through the metal detector and then waited for a beefy-armed officer to buzz me into the interior of the detention facility. He ushered me silently through the dusty gray hallways into the same meeting room where I'd sat with Isobel just a couple of weeks earlier. With little more than a grunt, the man promptly left me in the small space, and I presumed he was going to retrieve my client.

I remained near the open doorway, curious about the other parts of the facility. I wondered where Isobel was at that moment. Was she sitting in a cell, bored to distraction? Doing some sort of work program? Writing letters? I felt remorseful that I didn't have a better understanding of what daily life was like for her or for any of the women incarcerated at the facility. While I waited, a sturdy-looking middle-aged woman in green scrubs and a tight blond ponytail came down the hallway, walking briskly past the door. She glanced at me but then looked away just as quickly as she hurried along. After she rounded the corner and disappeared from view, there was little else to look at besides the dingy concrete walls and dusty floor. I moved toward the table, pulling out one of the cold metal chairs. As I opened my notepad and flipped to an empty page, the harried woman in scrubs reappeared, poking her head into the room.

"Hey," she said, her voice quiet enough to suggest she didn't want to be overheard. "You're the lawyer for Isobel Pérez?"

"I am," I said cautiously.

"She's been through a lot. I hope you're able to help her." The woman glanced over her shoulder and then turned back to me.

"Oh." I was glad Isobel had at least one ally in the facility. "Yes, I hope so too."

The nurse opened her mouth to speak again, but then Isobel and the guard rounded the corner. The woman nodded curtly before hurrying away. Given this guard's surly behavior, I could hardly blame her.

I turned my attention to Isobel, offering a subdued smile in greeting as she approached. Her hair was pulled into two braids on either side of her head in a youthful fashion. She nodded back at me as they came closer.

When the officer left, Isobel pulled out the chair opposite me and flinched at the jarring sound of its legs scraping the floor.

"The joys of Hydeford never cease," she said sarcastically, taking her seat.

"I just have a few things I wanted to cover today," I said, regretting the businesslike tone to my voice. I felt a pull to act friendlier toward Isobel, like a girlfriend would. Maybe because we were so close in age, or perhaps because she seemed like someone I might know outside of the detention facility. I wanted to offer her a hug and ask how she was holding up. I wished I could put funds into her commissary account and ask if she needed anything from the outside, but all the paperwork I'd been given by Legal Aid made it very clear that lawyers were supposed to maintain arm's-length relationships with their clients, never becoming overly familiar. My objective was to represent Isobel as effectively as possible, so I forced myself to remain professional.

Before the meeting, I had prepared a list of follow-up questions pertaining to Isobel's initial arrest and her transfer from the New York City Field Office to the current facility. If we could demonstrate any irregularities in the earlier parts of the detainment, that would bolster other arguments as to why Isobel was entitled to a cancellation of the removal order. Even more important, though, was the question of whether Isobel's constitutional right to equal protection had been violated during her time in custody. But first, I needed to know something else entirely.

"Before we get too deep into procedural details," I started slowly, "I wanted to ask you something about a comment you made last time we were together." I noticed myself fidgeting with the pen in my hand, twirling it between my thumb and forefinger. At least I'd remembered not to bring my monogrammed pens this time. I placed the pen down on my notepad. "You're not obligated to talk to me about this, and it won't impact your immigration status in any way, but I'd like to hear a little more about your hysterectomy."

Isobel's head cocked to the side in question.

"My hysterectomy?" she repeated. "Why?"

"Well . . ." I was suddenly reluctant to confess my concerns, wondering if both Gram and I had just been wildly off base in our suspicion. But then I thought of my great-grandfather again. "I just want to make sure you've been receiving appropriate care while in custody."

"Yeah, okay," Isobel said with a shrug.

We were both silent for a beat as I waited for her to say more, but she only raised her eyebrows expectantly.

"Well," I started, reminding myself not to put words into my client's mouth, not to create my own narrative. "Do you remember what the doctor said about why you needed surgery?"

Isobel lifted her hand, tilting it back and forth in the air as if to say her memories were only so-so. "I mean, I'd just had a little cramping and some spotting or whatever. My cousin in Queens, she told me once about her period getting weird as she got older and how her doctor gave her some hormone medicine that fixed her up good. I didn't expect anyone to start talking about surgery to me. I can't really tell you every last detail of what they said, just that they convinced me it was the best thing for my health. I couldn't get, like, a second opinion or anything, so I figured I'd better just do it and take care of myself."

"Is it possible the doctor told you before the surgery that you would be having your uterus removed?"

She shook her head as her lips twisted.

"No, definitely not," she said. "That's something I'd remember. When I woke up, it was all over, and they never said anything about my uterus. The only thing they bothered to tell me before I went under was to count backwards from ten."

Her words hit me with a jolt, triggering a memory I couldn't quite grasp. I shook away the feeling so I could stay focused on Isobel.

"You're absolutely certain?" I asked. "There was nothing else?"

"Look," she said, her voice taking on an edge. "I'm not an idiot. I may not have a college education or whatever, but I know where babies grow. If Choudry or that nurse said anything about taking a piece out of me that I wanted to keep, I would've objected. If I'd understood beforehand that there was even a chance the doctor could decide to remove my whole uterus, I would've waited to see if the cramping and whatnot would get better on its own." Her gaze shifted to the empty wall behind me, her focus intent, as if she were watching a movie of her memories on that wall. Through the silence, I could hear the ticking of the clock mounted in the corner of the room. A door clanged shut somewhere down the hall.

Finally, she shook her head. "Like I told you," she said, "when I woke up from the anesthesia, it was done." She lifted one shoulder in a half-hearted shrug, her eyes finally coming back to mine. "What could I do?"

"Did you talk to anyone about it?" I asked.

"Well, I mean, that nurse you were just talking to. Her name's Fern. She helped take care of me while I was recovering. It was pretty brutal for a few days there. They just sent me back to my cell all bandaged up. Fern brought me Tylenol at least, though it didn't help much. Aside from her, I just talked to Denise, one of the other inmates. She's about my age and can't have kids anymore either."

"But the procedure was necessary for your health?" I said, willing that much to be true because the alternative was still unthinkable.

"I mean, that's what the doctor said. I had cysts or something."

"Did you sign anything before the surgery?"

"Sign anything?" She thought for a minute. "Maybe?" She shrugged again.

When I heard the question in her voice, my heart sank. She should have been informed, clearly and explicitly, about not only the reasons for the procedure, but also the risks of possible side effects and complications. Especially regarding something as permanent as the removal of her reproductive organs. One hardly needed to be a board-certified physician to know that much.

"Would you be willing to give me permission to ask for a copy of your medical records? Just to make sure everything they did was medically necessary. We could have another doctor take a look at the records. A second opinion after the fact."

"I can't pay for that," she said as she shook her head. "And it won't do any good anyhow. It's not like they can put the uterus back in now."

"No, no cost to you. Not a penny." I didn't know how much the firm would allow me to spend on this case, but this was something I needed to pursue, even if I paid out of my own pocket.

"Yeah, whatever," she said again. "I don't mind you trying, but good luck getting anything. Everything takes forever in this place."

She was probably right, but I would at least file the request. Maybe the records would show that the doctor had actually saved Isobel's life but had done a bad job of explaining things afterward. Whatever I found, it wouldn't change Isobel's future or the feats of which her body was no longer capable.

"What about your friend?" I asked. "You said her name is Denise?"

Isobel nodded, her braids moving up and down against her shoulders.

"Has talking to her been helpful?" I asked.

"Well, I mean, yeah." She shrugged again. "She lost part of her fallopian tube, and they didn't know it had to be taken out until the surgery already started, so we had kind of a similar experience. A surgery with a surprise ending. I guess they just do things like that when you're a prisoner."

"Wait." I sat up straighter. "She had the surgery while she was in custody? Did the same doctor do your procedure?"

Isobel nodded. "Dr. Choudry. All of us get taken over to that same clinic to see the gynecologist over there. Pinelands Women's Health, it's called."

Two cases having such similar outcomes was a flag of the brightest red. If nothing else, the incidents clearly indicated that the facility was providing inadequate medical counseling.

"Do you think your friend would be willing to speak to me about her experience?" I asked.

Isobel looked away and began chewing on her thumbnail.

"Just a conversation," I said. "Nothing more than she's comfortable with."

Isobel let out a long, slow breath.

"I mean, I can ask her," she answered on a shrug.

"Great, okay." I figured it was best to close the topic for the day and move on to questions about the specifics of her arrest, as I'd originally planned. Over the next hour, I collected pages of details about her detainment, including facts I thought might truly be helpful in obtaining the cancellation we sought.

After I packed up and headed out to the parking lot, where my car was now covered in a thin layer of snow, I finally let my mind run free. So many questions were nagging at me. Was my own struggle to get pregnant skewing my perception? I hoped so. It would be much better to discover that I was deeply self-involved than to confirm incarcerated women were being subjected to unnecessary, nonconsensual gynecological procedures. And by federal authorities at that. I groaned aloud as I tossed my tote bag to the passenger seat and settled in behind the wheel.

As I turned on the wipers to push the snow off my windshield, I thought again of what Gram had shared with me. Her family had given up so much to protect just one girl—and I resolved in that moment that I would find out what was really happening to the inmates at Hydeford and do whatever it took to help them. I pulled out of the parking spot, heading back toward Manhattan and my nephew's preschool, my thoughts already racing toward my next steps.

Carrie

October 1923

When Mrs. Alice and Mr. John returned from Durham, Clarence spent two long summer days cozying up to them, following Mr. John around the farm, noting all the improvements he'd made while they were gone. There was the roof he'd thatched, he said, pointing, and there was the fencing he'd mended. Clarence took all his meals with his aunt and uncle in the dining room, acting as though he barely knew me. On the third morning though, as I served porridge and griddle cakes to the Dobbses, Clarence's seat at the breakfast table stayed empty.

"Should I keep the oats warm for Mr. Clarence?" I asked as I ladled the food out for Mrs. Alice.

"No need," she answered absently. She mixed blackstrap molasses into her morning tea, making it bitter the way she liked. "He's gone on his way."

The words were such a relief I nearly dropped the pot in my hands. I never did find out where he'd gone. Nobody thought to tell me, and I told myself that I didn't much care, so long as he was far away from me. My only thought then was *good riddance to bad rubbish,* as Mr. John liked to say.

Not until weeks later, after the leaves had started changing color, did I realize my predicament. I was in the back hallway, searching in the closet for the tin of shoe polish we used on Mrs. Alice's boots, when my eye caught the pile of clean sanitary towels folded behind the bath towels. The sight made me realize I'd not had my own monthly in quite some time. Too long. I startled as I suddenly understood why I had been feeling poorly in the mornings, sometimes the afternoon too, and why my appetite had soured. A tiny piece of Clarence had planted itself inside my womb.

I hoped with all my heart that Clarence's seed wouldn't stick. I'd lived on a farm long enough to know that not all pregnancies ended in babies. Sometimes an animal would start bleeding long before it was time, and there'd be nothing to show for the pregnancy except a mess on the barn floor. I knew I'd have to do whatever I could to dislodge that kernel before it grew any bigger inside me, weed the thing out like a dandelion from a vegetable bed. In the meantime, I couldn't tell. Not anyone.

For those next few weeks, Mrs. Alice was happier with me than she'd ever been before, as I worked doubly and triply hard, lifting, carrying, sweating my way through the day, hoping something would shift that baby loose. Then at night, instead of drifting off after a hard day's work, I'd lie awake on my cot wondering what would happen if Clarence found out. Would he want to marry me? I prayed with every ounce of my being that he would not. I didn't realize then that there were worse things to fear than Clarence or how much was going to be ruined for me because of that one afternoon by the crick.

After another month went by, my breasts had grown bigger and my belly was starting to show the slightest bit of roundness. I let out the waists on my dresses, hoping Mrs. Alice wouldn't notice. I knew, eventually, my secret would come out, and I hoped to figure out a plan by then.

It was Billy who said something to me first. Sunday afternoons, he and I liked to go walking across Free Bridge, up above the Rivanna River, one of the tributaries to the James. It was a mild autumn day, the weather less crisp than the few days before, and the sun was beating down on us strong. I was complaining about Mrs. Alice again, going on about how she soiled the good tablecloth with cranberry sauce for a third time. She expected me to rid the material of the deep red stain, yet again, without abrading the fabric none, but Billy interrupted me.

"You ready to talk about what's really on your mind?" he asked, ignoring all I'd said about Mrs. Alice and her cranberry relish.

"Like what?" I asked.

He looked for a moment like he was calling up the nerve to speak, and then he just spit them words at me.

"About how you let Clarence Garland knock you up."

My heart near stopped when he said it. I felt like he'd kicked me square in the chest, knocking the breath from me. "I didn't *let* Clarence do anything!" I said, not yet realizing what I was confessing.

Billy's words had cut me deep, and I was too busy being offended to keep anything inside. His accusation brought to mind all the questions I'd been wondering ever since the crick. *Did* I let it happen? Could I have fought harder or done more to protect myself? Was it my own fault for leading him on right from the get-go? Would I ever feel clean again?

Billy stopped in his tracks, yanking my hand to make me face him.

"Wait. That son of a bitch forced you?" Billy had never cussed around me. His jaw was set tight, looking like he was fixing to hunt down Clarence that very moment, even as we stood there in the middle of the bridge.

"You think I would have done that with him by my own choice?"

"I'm going to murder that bastard," he said, his eyes darting around.

"Billy, stop. I just want to forget the whole thing."

"But you could have him arrested for what he did to you. That's a crime. You can't just let him get away with it." His hands were in fists, and his face was getting redder and redder.

"And who's going to listen to me? I'm just a foster kid who got herself in trouble like that loose mama of hers. And now with another mouth to feed on the way."

Billy stared back at me hard for a long moment. Then finally his face softened, his shoulders coming back down a bit too.

"You know how far along you are?" he asked.

"I reckon the baby'll come around the end of March." I looked off toward the river, unable to meet his eyes. I didn't want to see the judgment there. But then he surprised me.

He grabbed for my hands, both hands now, pulling at me until I brought my gaze back to his own.

"Marry me then," he said, his eyes brightening and his breath starting to come faster.

"What? No." I couldn't do such a thing, not all sudden like this. And not when I'd never felt anything for Billy more than a sisterly love.

"I'll get you a ring. We'll do everything right." Then he started lowering himself onto his knee.

"No, no, Billy." I pulled at his arm so he'd not go down like that. "I can't ask that of you. It just don't feel like the right thing."

"But I'll take care of you," he said, standing back to full height. "We could get our own house. It'd be small until I got more money saved up, but we'd be together." His cheeks were turning pink as he talked. He looked at me so hopefully then that I thought about giving in.

"Look, I know you don't feel that way for me," he said. "I understand that, but there's all different ways to love. The other stuff, maybe that could come in time. And until then, you'd be safe. And maybe happy enough? We could make a life, you and I."

I might not have been a romantic girl anymore, but I couldn't do it, not to Billy. It just felt like taking advantage when he still had his whole life ahead of him. And I didn't want to do that to my one true friend.

"You don't want to be stuck with me," I told him. "Not when you could find a woman who wouldn't be pretending. You deserve a woman who'll love you true."

All the excitement went out of his eyes then, his mouth coming closed and his whole face seeming to sag all at once. He nodded slowly, and I imagined he was replaying my words in his head. I almost wished I could take them back, but I thought I was doing what was best for both of us. I reckoned I'd find a way to solve this problem by myself. I'd been mostly on my own for so many years now.

It was only two days later that I realized how very wrong I had been.

~

Early that Tuesday morning, I heard Mrs. Alice calling for me from the other side of the house. I'd just finished tidying my cot in the alcove, hadn't even started on breakfast yet.

"Carrie!" she hollered again, and I hastened through the house toward the front room. I found her standing beside the large fireplace, like she was waiting for company to arrive. Mr. John was there too, his lunch pail in his hand, fixing to leave for work, it seemed. Before I could wonder why he'd be heading out so early, Mrs. Alice pointed at her favorite rocker and told me to sit down.

I'd never had permission to sit in that chair before, but I did as she said.

"John." Mrs. Alice huffed out the word like a command, telling him it was his turn to talk.

Mr. John cleared his throat and pulled at his starched collar.

"Well, Carrie," he said. He rumbled his throat again but didn't say more, just looked back at his wife.

"For heaven's sake." She sighed, swiping her hands against each other the way she often did before a task. "Carrie," she said, "your condition is becoming obvious."

I was surprised she'd caught on. She paid me so little heed most of the time, only fussing about whether I'd done my chores to her liking. There was no use denying it though. So I just kept quiet.

"It's unfortunate," she said, looking from me over to her husband. "You've been a good worker over the years, especially recently. But we can't have a pregnant girl under our roof, not unwed. You really are no different from your mother. I suppose we should have expected something like this would happen eventually."

Seeing the disappointment in her eyes, I knew what I had to do.

"Mrs. Alice," I said, my voice cracking. "It wasn't my fault. Your nephew, Clarence, he done this to me. Forced himself on me down by the crick while you folks were down there in Durham. I couldn't make him stop. I begged, but he was so strong." I swallowed hard. "You know how strong he is. Billy says he should be arrested for what he done."

I thought maybe Mrs. Alice would take pity on me now that she knew, but instead she kept quiet as Mr. John nearly lunged at me.

"How dare you!" he shouted. "You listen here, missy." He came closer to where I sat and leaned in toward my face. His cheeks were suddenly fiery with rage, and I felt myself afraid of him for the first time since I'd known him. "You'll not be saying such things about my sister's son. Not after we took you in, after all we've done for you, year after year. Clarence is an upstanding boy, a fine young man. You won't be spreading this around town, that he'd hurt a girl, that he'd fornicate in the woods. No, I won't have it."

He studied me a moment, a look of disgust turning his lips down. He was still bent low, his eyes level with mine as they bored into me. I had to lean back in my chair just to put some air between us. But then he straightened to his full height and took in a deep breath. "No one would believe you anyhow, not a girl like you." He ran a hand down his necktie, smoothing the brown fabric back into its place.

I looked over at Mrs. Alice, who was still regarding me as if I was a stray cat in the house. Foolish girl that I was, I'd expected them to be horrified by their nephew's actions, his violent, foul behavior. But Mr. John acted more upset at the idea of me spreading bad news about Clarence than what-all he'd actually done.

Then I thought Mr. John just didn't believe me, which was why he'd got so mad. It wasn't until later that I realized the truth of things didn't matter. Mr. John didn't care what had happened to me. He just didn't want me accusing Clarence of any of it.

"Alice," Mr. John said, looking away from me, "I've got those people to speak to. You keep the girl inside the house until I get back."

When Mr. John returned later that evening, he found me pressing linens in the kitchen.

"Pack your things, girl," he said as he handed me a small travel case. His voice was gruff, like he wouldn't tolerate questions. Much as I wanted to ask where I was going, I stayed silent and did as I was told.

I trudged through the kitchen back toward the cramped, dank alcove where my mattress lay, a place that I had for so long yearned to escape. Yet as I stepped inside and let my eyes rove over the worn bedding on the floor, the lone cubby in the corner with my night-clothes folded inside, I was suddenly reluctant to go. I opened the case Mr. John had given me and began filling it with everything I had to my name. There wasn't much, just a couple of work dresses, my underthings, my old schoolbooks, and some trinkets Billy had given me over the years.

As I loaded the case, it was as if I was seeing each item again for the first time. I realized only then how much of my life at the Dobbses' had been tied up with Billy. Atop my cubby sat the yo-yo he'd loaned me during the third grade and then never wanted back. There was a wooden bell he won for me at a holiday fair the year before, and five genuine Venus pencils that had become a Christmas tradition between us. Billy gave me one every year since the time I'd stopped going to school, on the promise that I'd take pains to remember what I'd learned before my school days came to an end. He was the only decent person I'd known since Ma, and saddling him with Clarence's child to raise . . . I knew for sure that wouldn't have been doing right by him.

I put those pencils he gave me to only one purpose over the years, and that was writing letters to my ma at the Colony. I had to ask permission from Mrs. Alice each time I wanted to send a note because I needed her to give me a postage stamp. I didn't ask more than once or twice a year because I knew what she'd say. Mama never wrote me back anyhow. Sometimes I wondered if the folks in that place she was being kept even let her see the letters at all.

The items in my small case rattled around as I followed Mr. John out of the house. There was a car in the drive waiting for us. I did what he said and got into that back seat, still not knowing what in the world was to become of me.

Jessa

March 2022

As I waited on the small love seat in Dr. LaRusso's Upper East Side office, I checked my phone for a third time. Vance had warned me that he might be late, but I felt uncomfortable sitting there all alone on the floral upholstery, wondering about my fertility, and maybe my entire future, without anyone beside me. I couldn't help imagining myself sitting in the same spot again and again, month after month and year after year. If we kept trying and failing to conceive, eventually Vance would tire of waiting. He'd want to pursue other options, and if I didn't capitulate or surrender to a time frame he deemed reasonable, he would leave. I felt certain of that. And I'd be on my own, abandoned once more.

I was catastrophizing again. I knew that. After all, I was the one intent on carrying a biological child, not Vance. Sure, I might consider adoption down the road, but not yet, not by a long shot. So instead, I was seeing this horrible montage in my mind, picturing myself growing older, my curls graying, my forehead filling with wrinkles, and in every mental image, I was alone. I tried to shut down my spiraling thoughts, to shoo them away like gnats buzzing around my head, but it didn't work. I had to remember that Vance wasn't only with me to have children. Calling on an old tactic, I imagined myself writing a list, scribbling out the things he loved about me, the reasons he would stay: my ambition, my dependability, my devotion to his family. Even my organizational skills. It dawned on me that the list I was creating didn't exactly scream deep, burning love, but I liked that Vance appreciated traits of mine that I appreciated in myself. And of course there was more between us.

I released a long breath, trying to reset. At the opposite end of the room, two women sat together. One of them had a large pregnant belly and was resting a magazine on her baby bump as if it were a tabletop. How nice it must be, I thought, to experience the bodily changes that come with pregnancy.

On the end table beside me, some plastic dispensers held pamphlets for the taking. I pulled out the closest one and opened the front flap. Inside was a list of facts about fertility and medical obstacles that people might face when trying to conceive.

Common factors in infertility include: a woman's age, ovulation disturbances, cervical anomalies, tubal disease, fibroids, and uterine abnormalities.

The list went on and on. My heart sped up as I read further and thought about all the different ways I might be defective. Even without him sitting next to me, I could hear Vance admonishing me for thinking of that word. "Not *defective,* Jess," he would say, dismissing the idea. "Just tense and impatient." Then he would laugh, always so sure that everything would just magically work itself out.

It was no wonder he felt that way. Golden boy Vance, who could somehow sweet-talk his way into a pair of sold-out concert tickets or flash a single dimple and end up with upgraded seats on a fully booked flight. He'd gotten us this coveted appointment with Dr. LaRusso in the same way. If he actually showed up in time for this appointment, I knew he'd waltz right in, totally sure that any fertility issues I had could be easily remedied.

What he hadn't suggested—*wouldn't* suggest—was that maybe he was the problem. Low sperm count could also cause male infertility. Maybe an STI he never knew about or even a genetic condition. As I skipped down to the bottom of the page I was reading, the pamphlet seemed to hear my thoughts and couldn't wait to contradict them.

Infertility is considered a "couples' problem," but the cause can be traced to the female in more than half of all cases.

I snorted a little too loudly at those words, and the women across the room looked up at the noise.

"Sorry," I mumbled sheepishly, returning my attention to the pamphlet.

I wished I could pick apart that statistic in the leaflet and question whoever had compiled the information. Was anyone accounting for the fact that women were probably much more likely to seek treatment for infertility than men? And how could you even call it a "couples' problem" when so many of the people seeking reproductive assistance were single?

Despite the umbrage I felt looking at that page, the idea that my empty womb was somehow my fault felt the most logical, the most obvious. I liked to remind my work associates of Occam's razor, the theory that the simplest explanation is usually the correct one.

The door from outside pushed open just as a car on the street honked. I looked up to see Vance walking in, and my whole body relaxed at the sight of him. Before I even stood to greet him, a nurse appeared at the other end of the room.

"Jessa Gidney?" she called. Her chipper voice was teeming with optimism, an emotion I wished I, too, could feel. Yet as I stood from my seat, nothing but dread pushed me forward.

Dr. LaRusso was an affable man in his late fifties, which Gram always said was the perfect age for a doctor. Old enough to be experienced but still young enough to give a hoot, as she put it. He had a full head of salt-and-pepper hair and a nose that was slightly too large for his face.

After the examination, I changed from the paper gown back into my work clothes. Vance and I were shepherded from the exam room over to a carpeted office, where the doctor was already seated behind a desk.

"Sit, please," he said, not looking up from the folder before him. He was making notes on the paper inside.

We settled quietly into the plush armchairs opposite the desk. Vance reached for my hand and gave it three quick squeezes.

I turned toward Vance, taking in his burgundy V-neck sweater, his black slacks, and the subtle dark circles beneath his eyes. Most days, he wore a suit to work. He felt that being dressed formally allowed him to project the right image when interacting with clients. Today's more casual attire meant something else was going on at work, something keeping him at the office instead of going out entertaining. Normally, I would have known exactly why he was too busy to meet with clients, what deal was heating up, and why he hadn't arrived home before I was sleeping. I realized this with a pang of guilt. I'd gotten so wrapped up in my pro bono case that the only personal issue for which I had any bandwidth remaining was our effort to conceive. Each time he brought up anything else, I found myself tuning out. I squeezed his hand back. He deserved better than what I'd been giving him.

"Right," Dr. LaRusso said, finally looking up at us. He smiled broadly, straight white teeth on display.

"I have several pieces of good news," he started. "First, plenty of healthy couples devote six, nine, ten months to trying to conceive before it actually happens. And longer. A delay of a few months is not a medically significant phenomenon. Many of my peers won't even meet with couples until they've been trying for at least a year. Second"—he held up two fingers—"is the fact that physically, Jessa, you seem to be shipshape. We'll have to wait for the blood work to come back, but on initial examination, you present as perfectly healthy. Though you're in your thirties, you're still young enough to carry multiple children to term without issue. The ultrasound revealed no causes for concern. The fact that your period arrives regularly and without excessive pain is also a promising sign."

"What about the miscarriage?" I asked, referring to my pregnancy the year before.

The doctor nodded like it was a wise question.

"There's always the chance that a miscarriage could result in uterine scarring, which could complicate later conceptions—but initial testing doesn't seem to indicate that's the case here. We can conduct more specific explorations, but I'm not seeing anything to warrant it. At least not yet."

"So what's the bad news?" I asked.

"Not bad news," the doctor said, "just a to-do list." His eyes shifted to Vance. "When the cause for lack of conception is not obvious at the initial stages, sometimes we have to do more digging. I think it'd be worthwhile for you, Vance, to get checked out. A semen analysis is quick and easy. Given the relatively brief time you've been trying, I'm not overly concerned. But if you're feeling impatient, gathering information in the meantime won't hurt. If everything looks okay with the sperm concentration and motility, we can take it from there."

Vance sat up straighter in his chair.

"Shouldn't we wait for the blood work to come back first? Couldn't this be a hormonal imbalance or something?" he asked.

I fought the urge to smack him. Why couldn't he even imagine that he might be playing a part in this—some role other than just the supportive husband? And honestly, was he even doing that?

"Certainly," Dr. LaRusso said. "It'll only be a couple of days for the bloods. By the time you get an appointment for the semen analysis, you'll have heard from me about those results anyway." He opened a drawer from his desk, pulled out a card, and offered it to Vance. "Here is the doctor I recommend for male fertility exams. She's excellent. Unless you have someone else you'd rather see."

Vance looked down at the card and swallowed. A vein in his jaw had begun to pulse, and his visible distress took me by surprise.

Dr. LaRusso seemed to notice Vance's change in demeanor as well.

"I don't want you two to worry," the doctor said. "You are at the very beginning of the process, and science in this area has come an incredibly long way. We will work through this as a team, leaving no stone unturned. You understand?" He gave us another big smile, waiting for each of us to nod in agreement.

After collecting our things, we left the quiet confines of the medical office and emerged into the afternoon commotion of Seventy-Ninth Street. We made our way through the damp wintry air toward Third Avenue, where we would each take different subways back to our respective offices.

"So that was good, I guess?" I asked as we walked, wrapping my arm around Vance's elbow and inching closer to him.

He kept his lips tight and shook his head.

"What's wrong?" I asked. "The news was positive. Shouldn't we be happy that he couldn't find anything the matter with us?"

"With you," Vance shot back. "He couldn't find anything wrong with *you*." He kept his eyes trained straight ahead as we walked. "But now I'm supposed to get put under a microscope too?"

"What's the harm in a quick check, just to make sure nothing's amiss?" I couldn't imagine the fertility exam for men being anywhere near as intrusive as what I'd been putting myself through. As far as I knew, all they needed was a sperm sample, and Vance could take care of that on his own.

"Jessa, there's nothing wrong with either of us except for your glaring lack of patience or, I don't know, your intense and debilitating fear of your own inadequacies."

"Wow, Vance. You're so opposed to a urology visit that you'd prefer attacking me? Why did you even go to the trouble of making this appointment today if you were just going to be a jerk about the whole thing?"

He stopped walking and turned toward me, dislodging my hand from where it'd been wrapped around his arm.

"Jessa, I made the appointment because I'm tired of you freaking out—not because I thought anything physical needed attention. I'm just fed up with your constant fixation, and maybe I was also trying to do something to help you. Like if a doctor told you that you're fine, you'd give it a rest and calm the fuck down. But now this doctor has gone and opened a whole can of worms, and this time the focus is on me. So, what? Now you want me to go down to that office, whack off into a cup? What if I bump into someone I know there? What am I supposed to say?"

"If you bump into someone? *That's* what you care about? What people will think? Really, Vance?" The worst part was that I wasn't even surprised. It always came back to appearances with him. He must have heard the defeat in my voice because he reached out for my hand and lowered his volume again.

"No, all I'm saying is I just don't see why we're going for test after test, putting ourselves through the wringer like this. This is supposed to be a fun and exciting time for us. It's only been six months, Jessa!"

"Right . . . ," I started. "And nothing we're doing on our own is working." I felt my eyes fill with water. Vance saw it too, and his voice softened.

"Look," he said, "I want you to be happy. I know how important this is to you. I thought I could suck it up and jump on the medical intervention bandwagon—even though six months is really no time at all." He looked back toward the door of the doctor's office. "But, Jess, you're sucking all the joy out of this process, making it so clinical. Then each month you get upset that we *failed*. Talking about failure over and over makes me feel like such a loser."

"I never said—"

"You can't even get a diagnosis of infertility until you've been trying for a year," he interrupted. "Why can't we just keep living our lives, and if you get pregnant, great, and if not, maybe one day we find another way to build a family?"

Was he trying to goad me? After all the years I'd waited to have my own family again. To hear an echo of my mother in a baby's laughter or look into a child's face and see the same shade of hazel I remembered from my father's eyes. I longed for the joy of having a shared history with a child, teaching them about my parents and my parents' parents and grandparents. What an amazing experience it must be to forge those common connections with mini versions of ourselves. He knew how important it was to me to try for that.

"You know I want kids," he said. "But . . ." He trailed off as he looked away, his gaze moving toward the traffic light at the corner, where a few pedestrians huddled around a coffee cart.

As I waited for him to find the words, I wondered how we could possibly be so out of sync with each other. I had only a few real goals in my life, but they meant everything to me. Making partner clearly hadn't panned out. Was Vance going to take this away from me now too—the family I'd been pining for ever since my teens?

Finally, he looked back at me. "I feel like it's killing everything else between us. Why am I not enough for you, just on my own? Was I always just a means to an end?"

"A means to an end?" I repeated, my head rearing back in surprise.

Vance's phone chimed from his pocket. He didn't reach for it, but he glanced at his watch with a harried expression.

"Look, I have to get back for a meeting. The Plantico deal is turning into a disaster, and I have to prep for Florida in the morning. Let's table this." He stepped toward the subway entrance.

"No." I grabbed his arm. My voice sounded desperate even to my own ears. I had forgotten that he was leaving for Tampa in the morning.

He was right. The attempted baby-making had damaged other parts of our relationship, all the little things that had been good before. I wondered for a split second if he was right about the other part too—that he was simply the man I'd chosen to be the father of my children, that my love for him wasn't real. Had I just been auditioning men to play a role in the manifestation of some vision I'd concocted as a child? But no, that was ridiculous. I loved so much about Vance, and he should know that.

"Please, you can't just say something like that and then leave."

He glanced in the direction of the subway before answering.

"I just hate that this conception thing is taking over our whole marriage, okay? We don't talk about anything else anymore. I miss *us*."

"But this is all about us. Us, and our next stage as a family." Even as I argued, I knew that at least some of what he was saying was true. I had retreated from him recently.

He looked back at me for a long moment, then just sighed.

"I don't know, Jess. Things are changing between us. You used to come to me for help, but lately it's like you're going rogue on one thing after another. I tell you to dial it back at work, and you ignore me. I tell you to stop with the pregnancy tests, so you go behind my back. This isn't who we are. I don't understand why you're not listening to me anymore, why you . . ." He trailed off for a moment. "I guess I just miss being your partner."

Partners. Was that ever what we'd been? I saw us more as president and vice president—a team, for sure, but not the same. I'd always appreciated Vance's confidence and ability to take the lead on major decisions, shouldering that burden of being in charge. Maybe he just didn't like his VP stepping out of line, and I bristled at the thought. But then I reminded myself how well our dynamic had once worked. I could be doing better too.

He sighed again as he studied my face a moment longer. "I really have to go," he said. He leaned down to give me a perfunctory kiss on the cheek. Then he turned toward the subway, leaving me to stare at his back as he descended into the underworld.

~

The next morning as I drove south on the Jersey Turnpike, I was still thinking about our conversation. After so many years of being in sync and happy, I was allowing my obsession with having a baby to damage everything that had been good between us. I wondered if I was putting even more distance between us by not telling Vance what Gram had shared with me about her childhood. But there was no reason he needed to know. Gram had been visibly distressed when she told me about how her family had to change their last name and move to a new town all because her father had risked his reputation to help somebody. All these decades later, it was still hard for her to confront what her family had been through in the name of standing up for what was right.

I took great pride in coming from people with such strong principles. But I could already hear Vance in my head, arguing that Grandpa Harry should have done things differently, that he could've achieved the same results without losing everything he'd worked for. Even if that wasn't true, Vance was always so sure he knew better than everyone else. I didn't want to give him the opportunity to find fault with Grandpa Harry or his actions. Didn't everyone have secrets they never shared with a spouse anyway, hidden gems they wanted to keep for themselves? I was sure I'd read something like that in one of those Esther Perel books on relationships. This new tidbit about my history felt like something Gram had gifted to me, a fragile but important point of pride that I could savor on my own without having to open myself up to Vance's negativity.

When the blocky concrete facade of Hydeford finally appeared up ahead, I had to force away my personal frustrations so I'd be able to focus. I cleared my throat and coughed intentionally, envisioning the negative energy that was festering inside me floating away like helium balloons released into the wind.

Cutting through the red tape to make this appointment had taken several days, so I wouldn't squander the opportunity. I'd finally found information on the friend Isobel mentioned in our last meeting. After reviewing the files, I now knew the basic facts about Denise Agbar. A twenty-six-year-old woman from Cameroon who'd been in the US since age eleven, Denise had become known to immigration authorities nearly two years earlier when she made a 911 call during a domestic dispute. The situation between Denise and her boyfriend spun out of control, and when the police arrived, both Denise and her partner ended up getting arrested. The charges against Denise were ultimately dropped, but because of her status as undocumented, she was transferred to ICE custody and had been at Hydeford ever since. Currently, she was awaiting the outcome of her appeal to the Board of Immigration Appeals.

The process of admission for visitors to Hydeford was beginning to feel routine, and I was able to get quickly situated in the meeting room. When the male guard arrived with Inmate 541, as he'd called her, I was struck by how young she looked. Maybe it was the woman's wide, alert eyes as she entered the room. She was slender and tall with dark skin and glossy hair twisted into a low bun at the base of her neck.

"You're Denise Agbar?" I asked, wanting to confirm before the guard left. I noted that she was also in the powder-blue uniform, indicating the lowest threat level.

Both she and the guard nodded.

"Ring when you're finished," the guard said as he walked out and closed the door.

"Thank you for meeting with me," I began, taking my seat and motioning for Denise to do the same. As she settled into the chair opposite me, she leaned back and crossed her arms over her chest.

"I hope Isobel explained why I wanted to talk?" I asked.

"Yeah. She filled me in." Denise's words held barely a trace of her ancestral country, no French or Cameroonian undertones. Her voice was filled with oppositional notes, like she was preparing for a fight. "I mean, I think it's great that you want to talk about it, try to help or whatever. But there won't be anything you can do. Nobody's gonna care about what's going on up in here. So I'm not really sure it's worth putting myself at risk."

"At risk? I'm sorry—I'm not sure what you mean."

"Well, everything has a cost, right? I speak up about what happened to me, next thing I know, my commissary account might get zeroed out. Most likely, I get booked on the next flight to Cameroon. I keep quiet about it, keep my head down, maybe things'll go better for me. I got all my family here, both my parents, two sisters. I'm not looking to cause myself any trouble before I get myself back to them."

Denise's words stopped me short. Retaliation? Sudden deportation? Was she for real? I didn't want to make things any more difficult for the women in this center.

Before I could formulate a response, she continued. "And anyway, it's not like it can be undone. The procedure can't be reversed."

"If you don't want to file a grievance, then why'd you agree to meet with me?" I asked.

She shrugged and glanced away, like she wasn't so sure either. Or maybe she just didn't want to say.

"Look," I began, slowly parsing through my own thoughts as I spoke. "What if you just tell me what happened to you? We don't have to do anything with the information unless or until you're comfortable. But I can't know for sure that I *can't* help you unless you share your story with me."

Denise's eyes came back to rest on me, but she didn't answer.

"I'm legally bound to keep everything you tell me in confidence unless you expressly allow me to share it. This would just be talking. Just between us. Nothing more."

She pursed her lips like she was truly considering her options, making me think she actually did want to share her story but was scared of the consequences. That would explain why she had agreed to meet; she wanted to do something, but only if she was safe.

"Maybe we just start with the facts," I offered, positioning my memo pad between us. "Then we can discuss how to handle things."

"And you can't tell anybody what I say?" she asked.

"Attorney-client privilege. I'm not allowed to reveal anything at all."

After a few more moments of silence, she rolled her eyes and began talking.

"So, I was having some bleeding, right?"

I nodded.

"It was just spotting, but it started happening more and more, like at the wrong time of the month. So I told one of the nurses in the infirmary. I guess I was scared something was the matter with me, you know? They took me to that Dr. Choudry over there at Pinelands, the clinic they take us to. We went over in a transport van, in a group. We're all cuffed and whatnot, waiting in the van." She swallowed audibly and shifted in her seat.

"When it was my turn, they brought me to the room, took my cuffs off. The doctor didn't even look at me or make eye contact. Just told me to undress from the waist down and get on the table. No robe or anything. And then without saying anything else, the doctor just went right in and did an internal exam. Nobody told me what was about to happen or nothing. All of a sudden, I just got someone sticking that wand all up in my business without lube on it or anything. So I start saying, 'Stop, stop, stop,' because, well, you know . . ." She trailed off, suddenly a little shy.

I nodded, thinking about how invasive those transvaginal wands could be even in the best of circumstances. Maybe she saw some level of understanding on my face, because she nodded slowly and then continued.

"I was about to start kicking to get myself out of there, but then the doctor showed me the screen and pointed at something. I don't know. It all just looked like black-and-white clouds on that ultrasound monitor. But the doctor said, 'There, that's a cyst. That's what's causing your trouble.' Said my uterus needed to be scraped, a D&C. I forget what it stands for, but I knew it was what they do for abortions sometimes. That freaked me out a little, so I wasn't sure. But the doctor said if I did the procedure while I'm in custody, the government would pay for it. If I waited until I got out, I'd have to pay on my own. The nurse said I'd better make arrangements quick so the cyst didn't get worse and cause me more trouble. I was scared, so I said, okay, fine. They could do what they needed to do."

"And did they explain to you that they might do more than just remove the one cyst?"

Denise shook her head. "Nah. It was much more like, 'Hurry, hurry, sign this.' They got me all worked up about how I couldn't pay for the procedure on my own, so I signed everything they put in front of me. I thought I was doing the right thing."

"Before the procedure, did they warn you of risks or complications?"

"Nah," Denise said again. "Just put a mask over my face and told me to start counting backwards from ten."

I could hardly believe what I was hearing.

"When did you find out they'd done more than the D&C?" I asked.

"Well, when I woke up from the surgery, the nurse was there, and she said . . . She told me . . ." Denise paused and turned her dark eyes toward the wall beside her.

"It's okay. Take your time."

"No." Denise shook her head and wiped at one eye with the heel of her hand. "Now that I started getting on about it, I have to get it all out because they did me so wrong."

I was sorry we were in such a sparse room. Had we been at my office, I would have pushed a box of tissues across the table toward her, offered her a glass of water.

"When I woke up after the anesthesia, the nurse told me the surgery went well. I was real groggy, so they told me to just stay where I was. After a while, the two of them came back to tell me it was time to get ready to go. The nurse said I'd have pain for a few days but not to worry, that it was normal because they had to fix my fallopian tubes. And then Dr. Choudry came in and said, 'Your fallopian tubes were blocked, so I had to remove parts from each. You won't be able to get pregnant naturally anymore, but that's one less thing for you to worry about now, isn't it?'"

"Oh my God!" The words escaped me before I could stop myself.

"I did some looking online. Maybe I could still try to have a baby with IVF, but the chances aren't great with the fallopian tubes damaged." She shook her head as she wiped away the wetness on her cheeks again. "And how would I ever find the money for that anyhow? There's no point even thinking about it."

I was intimately familiar with the difficulty of the IVF process and its middling odds of success. One more topic I hadn't yet discussed with Vance. But I was also well aware of the high cost and the fact that it would be prohibitive for many.

"I always thought I'd have a big family. Now I'm going to have to tell any man I meet up front that I can't ever have kids. How do you think that's going to go?" She didn't wait for an answer. "I never would have said yes to that part of the surgery. How'd they just go in and do that?" She threw her hands in the air in a gesture of defeat.

It was hard to sit across from the willowy woman and just watch her cry, but I could only imagine how much harder the situation was for her. I was irate thinking about what this Dr. Choudry had done.

"If you'd like to pursue a claim," I started, "at least we might be able to change their practices going forward—so they don't do something like this to anyone else."

She snorted as she ran her wet hand against the leg of her cotton uniform, wiping the tears into faint lines on her pants.

"Yeah, it's a little late for that. Saving people," she said, shaking her head. "It's not like me and Isobel were the only ones. There's plenty of others."

"Wait, what?" I hoped I was misunderstanding.

She sighed. "Look. Some of the other girls already tried to speak up, but they're gone now. Back to their countries or whatever. My whole life is here, so I'm just going to keep my mouth shut. You can't guarantee nothing happens to me, right?"

"You mean like sudden deportation?" I asked.

Denise nodded. "One woman, she filed a grievance. She was on an airplane back to Honduras the next day. The very next day."

"That can't be, that can't . . ." I struggled to digest what she was saying. I blinked several times, hoping that would help me see things more clearly. "Denise," I finally began, taking a deep breath. "If you're telling me there's a pattern here, if it's not only you and Isobel but other women in the facility too . . . If you're telling me that those women who've spoken out are being retaliated against, we need to do something. We have to fight for your rights and the rights of every other woman in this detention facility, possibly every woman in federal custody."

"Whoa, whoa, whoa." She held up her hands as if to push my words away. "This isn't *Erin Brockovich*. We're not doing that. These are our private lives, our health. Most of the women here won't even want to tell you about their private business at all. Never mind filing claims or whatever."

"That's exactly it though. Just because you're in here doesn't mean you don't have a right to make your own medical choices. You're telling me that a doctor performed a life-altering procedure on you, without your consent, and that the same thing has happened to other women in this facility. Don't you see?" I was getting frustrated with her unwillingness to cooperate, which I knew wasn't fair of me. I glanced up at the ceiling, thinking of Grandpa Harry and trying to be the very best version of myself.

"If there's a true pattern here," I continued carefully, modulating my tone in hopes that she would see me as the ally I was aiming to be, "the doctor or the facility, whoever is pulling the strings, is forcing involuntary sterilization procedures on women who aren't in a position to resist. It's a blatant violation of your rights, and there's probably some ghastly agenda behind the whole thing that needs to be stopped."

"That's exactly what I don't want. I'm not looking to be part of some political movement." She started pushing her chair back from the table. "The idea sounds great and all, to maybe speak up and help make sure this doesn't happen to anybody else, but I'm not doing that. I'm telling you, a girl speaks out, they get rid of her. Everyone I care about is here in the US. I've got nothing in Cameroon."

"We can take steps to protect you," I said.

She was halfway out of her chair, but at my words, she hesitated.

"If they try to deport you, I can file for an emergency stay," I rushed. "If a whole class of women are alleging the same kind of abuses, they can't deport you all. Doing so would basically be admitting their guilt. And you can be anonymous on the complaint!" I realized. "We'd just list you as 'Jane Doe,' and we wouldn't have to use your name at all. Not anywhere."

She looked back at me for a moment and then settled back into her seat.

"If they try to deport you for speaking up," I said, keeping my voice firm, "I will move heaven and earth to protect you. I promise you that."

She brought her hand to her mouth, rubbing her bottom lip, but her eyes didn't move from my face.

"Look," I tried again, "do you think you could just ask around, see if some of the other women might be willing to come forward? Anonymously, or with the power of a group together?"

She finally began nodding slowly.

"I guess I could talk to some of the others, the ones that are still here. But I'm not promising anything. It's not up to me to decide what they want."

After the guard came back to retrieve Denise, I took a moment to jot down a few more thoughts. As I stood and collected my things, the blond nurse I'd seen on my last visit rounded the corner holding a clipboard. She slowed her pace as she reached me.

"Hey," she said, glancing behind herself and then scribbling something onto a paper on the clipboard. She tore the note from the clipboard, folded it quickly, and thrust it out toward me.

Before my brain could even catch up to what might be happening, I took the crumpled paper from her. I looked down at the note in my hand, where a name was scrawled in blue ink. When I looked back up, the nurse was already scurrying away, continuing down the hallway as if the interaction had never happened.

Carrie

September 1924

I named my daughter Vivian Elaine Buck. She came into the world hollering like she already knew about all the misery that was yet in store for our little family. Mrs. Alice and Mr. John tried to send me to the Colony, where my ma was, but the Colony wouldn't take women who were with child. Instead, I had to stay with a woman they hired from outside of town until the baby came. And then, just three weeks after Vivian was born, they sent me straight to the Colony like they'd wanted from the first.

About six months had passed since the day they came and pulled me away from my tiny baby girl. It took three of those men to get me into the car, what with the way I was carrying on, but they did finally overpower me. Every day since then, I wished for Vivian so hard. I could still remember what my sister, Doris, had been like at six months old, how she'd sat in my lap and smiled at me, pulling on my hair. I wondered if in the six months I'd been at the Colony, Vivian had grown pudgy like Doris had been, if her hair had grown at all, if her chin got slick with drool when she smiled. As I stared hour after hour out the window of the dayroom, the place they brought us out to "socialize" with the others at the facility, my thoughts stayed always with my daughter.

"Carrie." My ma was sitting across from me at the chipped game table.

I turned back to her, waiting to see if maybe she had some new sage words to lift my battered spirits. But we'd already talked the topic to death, so I didn't expect too much. Plus, Ma had never been a sentimental woman, and the years she'd spent at this awful place, the Virginia State Colony for Epileptics and Feebleminded, had hardened her all the more. Sometimes she just shut herself off from the world around her, like she didn't even know anyone else was there. Those times, you could be talking right to her, snap your fingers in front of her face, and she wouldn't even blink.

But she was having one of her good days, playing games with me that afternoon. We were dressed in the same long gray dresses they gave all the patients, the fabric of hers more worn than mine. I'd only been using the clothing for a few months, but she'd been wearing that same dress for years. I couldn't hardly guess how often they might replace a thing like that. Maybe not ever.

I watched as she fiddled with the set of dominoes someone had left at the table. Even when she was acting clearheaded, the look in her eyes was duller than when I was a girl.

Ma was still husky, her shoulders broad above her heaving bosom, but she seemed so much weaker than I remembered her from my youth. Maybe it was how her long hair had gone all gray, the coarse braid down her back making her look like an old lady even though she was only thirty-five by then. But all that time in the facility, surrounded by abandoned women and boredom all the livelong day, I suppose that takes its toll on a person.

She didn't like to watch me mooning over my baby girl, staring out that window with my face drawn and sad all the time.

"It's almost funny, don't you think, Ma?" I asked. "The price of me getting back together with you is being away from my child. Like I can't have you both at once."

"She a pretty girl?" Ma asked.

This was something she asked me most days of the week. Whenever I started talking about my feelings, she would turn the conversation. Always asking if my girl was pretty. I knew Ma thought if she herself had been born with a different face, a slender body, blond hair, maybe she could have had a happier life. Instead, she ended up living with a railroad worker who barely made enough to support us before he up and died, leaving us with nothing but debt after.

"Miss Buck." One of the nurses approached our table, and Ma and me both looked up at her.

"We still got sixty-seven minutes," Ma said, pointing at the clock on the wall behind me.

"Yes, you do," Nurse Williams answered, a prim smile on her face beneath the white nurse's cap pinned to her shiny hair.

I wondered where it was that this rosy-cheeked woman went home to at night, how it felt to come and go from a place like this.

The nurse put a hand to my shoulder, and a wash of alarm took me over. I don't know how I knew, but something inside my bones told me more bad was coming for me soon.

"It's time for you to visit with Dr. White," the nurse said, mentioning the same man I'd met when they first brought me to the Colony. I still got angry each time I remembered how he asked me all manner of ridiculous questions that day. There I was, still crying about being separated from my baby girl, and he wanted to know if I could tie my shoes, did I know the year, and such. He told me that because I could answer his questions, I'd be allowed to room in the outer part of the Colony, where the women with more skills were kept. Male patients, I'd learned, were kept to the other side of the property. There was also a separate ward designated for the "lunatics and idiots," where I didn't have to go. I'd not seen the doctor since that day. I worried that if I was going back to him now, it meant more bad tidings. But then I had the happy thought that maybe it was just the opposite. Maybe my dread was misplaced and I was about to get out.

"You're not getting out," Ma said.

I looked over to her as I stood from my seat.

"They don't hardly let anybody out. And not a girl like you, with no place to go. Ain't like anybody's fighting for you from the outside."

I thought then of Billy and the letter he'd sent me saying how angry he was about everything that had happened. But he never said anything about getting me out.

"Come," Nurse Williams prodded. "It's just your time for a check with the doctor so he can make sure you don't need any new treatments or such. You're not going to give me any problems now, are you, Miss Buck?" She looked over her shoulder toward a large orderly who stood in the corner of the room, the muscles in the man's arms bulging beneath the long sleeves of his uniform.

I followed that nurse through the hallways of the Colony, back toward rooms so far from my dormitory that I'd near forgotten about them since I'd arrived. I noticed a smoking room for the staff and then some empty offices, maybe for secretaries and the like. When we reached a door with a plaque that read "Dr. White," the nurse stopped walking. I made to go into the room, but the nurse took my wrist and pointed at the closed door just beside it.

She knocked lightly and then pushed open the door. Inside was a large room more like a parlor than a doctor's office. There was a plush carpet and a large leather sofa, ceramic lamps, and carved side tables. At the center of the room, across from the sofa, stood a shiny wooden desk that looked large enough for three people to use at once, and different groupings of upholstered chairs. The desk had a few papers piled neatly on top and a brass lamp that had been polished to a gleam. I couldn't think why anyone would want me in such a fancy room. I wasn't sure I'd ever been in a space so turned out before.

"Go on," Nurse Williams said, giving me a little shove into the room. "You can stand yourself over next to the desk. Dr. Preston will be coming in, and you'll want to show him proper respect."

"Preston? But what for?" I asked the nurse. She'd said earlier, I was certain of it, that I was seeing Dr. White. I didn't think I'd ever met any doctor by the name of Preston.

"Oh, I really couldn't say," she said as footsteps could be heard approaching in the hall. "But here he comes now," she added, standing herself a little taller and pushing her shoulders back.

The man who approached us was a stranger to me. He looked to be somewhere over fifty years old, but still, he was comely enough. He had dark brown hair cut to neat square lines around his ears and a crisp linen suit beneath his white coat. He wasn't a particularly tall man, and I stood more than a few hairs higher than he did.

"Dr. Preston," Nurse Williams said, her tone sugary all of a sudden, "this is the daughter, Carrie Buck."

The doctor's eyes slid over to me and he smiled real wide, like one does when trying to make friends with a young child.

"I have *so* been looking forward to meeting you, Miss Buck," he said, his eyes near glowing with delight. "Come." He took me by the arm and led me to the sofa. "Please, sit." Then he motioned with his hand.

It felt a little strange sitting down on that fancy couch while I was in my soiled, shabby uniform, but I did as he said. I thought Nurse Williams would leave us, but she just closed the door and came to stand near where I sat. She held a pencil and a clipboard at the ready.

"We're just checking on some of our patients," Dr. Preston said, his words coming out long and relaxed, like he was adding in extra syllables. "We're trying to make sure we're doing as fine a job in this institution as possible. We want to do the best we can for the good people of Virginia, not cause more trouble. You understand?"

I nodded, though I really didn't understand much at all. Not then.

"We want to help you, Carrie, and I think we may have found a way. Isn't that nice?"

"Yes, sir," I answered. His upbeat attitude had me thinking that my earlier cheery thoughts were on the right track. Maybe I was getting out after all, never mind what Ma had said. I hoped they'd finally realized I didn't belong in a place like the Colony, that I was sent there only because of the pregnancy. Had Mr. John or Mrs. Alice started to feel sorry about how they'd treated me, then come forward on my behalf? Or maybe the nurses had reported on my good behavior. Any which way, I was excited to think about getting to leave that place and get back together with my baby. I knew Billy would help me find a place to live. Maybe I could find a job where I could bring Vivian along with me to work. I was ready to dart out from my seat and run to the exit, except for one important question. "But what about my mama?"

Dr. Preston's eyes jumped back to Nurse Williams then. The two of them shared a look, and Dr. Preston's lips lifted like I'd made a joke. I couldn't say what was funny, unless they might've had good news to share about Ma too.

"No, no, Miss Buck," he told me, talking real slow. "We're just focusing on the younger women so far. Now, if you're ready, I'd like to ask you a few things." He rounded the desk and opened a drawer, pulling out a small notepad before returning to sit on one of the large fabric-covered chairs beside the sofa.

I nodded. I'd have told him my deepest, darkest secrets, whatever he wanted to know, if it meant they'd let me go free.

But then he set to asking me absurd questions that had not one thing or another to do with whether I belonged in the Colony. Most of what he asked, I couldn't properly answer either. Did I know the square root of 121, could I list three battles from the Revolutionary War? I didn't think to remind him that I'd not been to school past the sixth grade. Where else was I supposed to have learned those things? As it was, I knew I'd already forgot so much of what I'd been taught years ago. My figuring with numbers had always been weak, and without practice, I needed my fingers to help me out. Then sometimes I didn't have enough fingers for whatever answer I was seeking, and I would feel mad at Mrs. Alice all over again for pulling me out when she did.

But I pushed my anger away and focused on trying to answer right for the doctor. All the while, he kept on making ticks in his little notebook.

By the time we finished, I felt like I'd been in that office for near half the day. But when I looked at the clock, I saw not even a full hour had passed. Meanwhile, my spirits had dropped so low. I'd likely failed the test I'd been given. I kept my eyes on my dark, scuffed shoes, trying not to let myself cry.

Dr. Preston walked with us toward the door and turned to the nurse.

"This one is perfect," he said. "You've done well."

His words surprised me, and I looked up from my feet. He was smiling bright, as if something excellent had just occurred. And I'm embarrassed to admit that I misunderstood all over again. He was so clearly bursting with delight that I began to hope again that they might be considering my release. Well, shame on me. If I thought anything good could come from meeting with that man, maybe I was just as dim-witted as Dr. Preston wanted to believe.

Jessa

March 2022

Sunday was always my favorite day of the week. Usually, Sundays meant brunches and long walks with Vance or running a couple of frivolous errands before catching up on work that had spilled over from the prior week. But Vance was out of town, and even if he'd been home, I'd still have felt off-kilter, probably even worse. I sat at the Formica table in the narrow kitchen of the apartment where my grandmother raised me, flipping through the pages of a celebrity gossip magazine. Gram was at the sink, sponging pink globs of Goddard's silver polish onto a tarnished serving spoon. A pile of old serving utensils rested on a dish towel beside the sink, waiting to be freed of their black and purple stains.

"Stop reading that garbage," Gram said. "It's obvious you're stewing about something over there, so you might as well spit it out."

I looked down at the magazine and laughed. "I'm not the one who subscribes to these rags." Closing the cover, I took in the glossy photos on the front. In one corner was a picture captioned, "Tom and Gisele: At Each Other's Throats!"

Maybe it should have made me feel better about all the recent arguing with Vance that there were other couples—even rich and famous ones—who couldn't get along either. But for the moment, my focus was elsewhere.

"I can't get Hydeford out of my head," I confessed. "The fact that multiple women had their reproductive organs altered without their permission. I'm just so outraged. We still live in a world filled with monsters—awful, awful humans—and I guess I'm just trying to process it all. It's filling me up with all these warring emotions."

Gram put down the spoon and turned to face me.

"Monsters," she repeated, and I couldn't tell if she was agreeing or reproaching me for the unproductive comment. "Why don't you try to name what you're feeling?" This was something we'd done ever since I was a kid. She said it increased emotional regulation and self-compassion.

I thought for a moment, trying to determine which sentiment was most prominent for me at the moment. "I'm feeling a lot," I said. "Anger, shock, disgust, helplessness, fear. I'm also feeling motivated, thanks to you. If you hadn't pushed me the way you did . . ." I paused, not even wanting to vocalize how I might not have followed up on the situation at the center. I never would have seen the ugly truth for what it was without her prodding. "It's just a lot to digest. Maybe you could distract me with something else?"

She studied me for a moment, her light eyes traveling over my face, like she wanted to say more. "All right," she breathed finally. "Go get my box of photos, if you want. It's on the nightstand on Grandpa's side." Three months earlier at Christmas, Vance's parents had given Gram a picture frame, which she immediately displayed on a credenza in the living room. But she'd never bothered to put a photo in it. "You've spent long enough admiring this beautiful couple," I'd laughed earlier that morning, pulling out the insert that had come from the store.

"We'll find a different picture for the frame," Gram said, "but throw that awful tabloid in the bin on your way."

I tossed the magazine back on the pile of mail where I'd found it and started toward my grandparents' bedroom. "We both know you're going to read it from cover to cover right after I leave," I called over my shoulder.

When I reached the end of the hallway, the floral, citrusy smell of Gram's Jean Naté After Bath Splash was as strong as ever. The shoebox full of photos waited in the same spot as always, on the bedside table next to a stack of my grandfather's business books. Grandpa Walter had died decades earlier, when I was only seven years old. Gram had long since gotten rid of most of his things, but she'd left his nightstand as he'd always kept it, filled with his books and reading glasses and vitamin bottles. I thought maybe Gram liked to open her eyes to that view every morning. Maybe it allowed her to pretend, just for a moment after she woke up each day, that her husband was still alive.

I crouched down for the Cole Haan box that contained many old photographs, but before grabbing it, I paused to admire the framed picture still on Grandpa's beside table. It was a shot of me when I was about six years old, wearing a glittery leotard and posing onstage at a dance competition. I lifted the photo and studied my younger self. The smile on my overly made-up lips was as wide as possible. I could still remember that dance, a sassy number I performed to "My Lovin'" by En Vogue. Back then, I had adored dancing and might've even been talented at it. But after my parents died, I just couldn't do it anymore. Without their smiling faces watching me from the audience, I just didn't see any point.

Looking down at the picture, I suddenly realized why I'd felt so strange when Isobel mentioned the doctor telling her to count backwards from ten. My father used to tell me the exact same thing right before I went onstage as a kid. I hadn't thought about that in forever, but now it all came flooding back to me. His words had been like a shorthand message. Whenever I was afraid to try something, instead of giving me a long, boring speech, my father would tell me, "Count backwards from ten, and then it's showtime."

A knot grew in my throat as I remembered. How could I have forgotten that? It had been something so special between us. I had a pang thinking of how many other special things I must have forgotten—about both of them.

Count backwards from ten. Isobel and Denise had heard the same phrase right before being victimized. The thought horrified me. I wished my dad was still here so I could tell him about the women I'd met. As I pictured his deep hazel eyes and his bushy hair, I was pretty sure I knew what he would say.

I wiped at my eyes and put the ceramic frame back in its place, returning my attention to the box. I'd been through the photos inside countless times over the years, poring over images of my mother from the 1960s, a child with unruly, curly pigtails, then later as a teenager in the '70s, her hair styled into a puffier version of Farrah Fawcett wings. My favorite pictures were from the 1990s, when I started appearing in the images too, a baby in my mother's arms.

With the box in hand, I returned to the kitchen table and lifted off the dusty top. Gram was back at the sink working on the next piece of silver.

"Is there a specific picture you want me to find?"

As I reached into the pile of photos, my phone chimed from inside my tote bag on the floor. I twisted around to reach for it, but she interrupted me.

"Hey now," she said, glancing back to fix me with a halting stare. "I thought we were finished with working eight days a week."

"You know what?" I removed my hand from the bag and held it up, showing my empty palm as proof. "You're right. I'm not at their beck and call anymore." I wondered for a second if it might be Vance calling, but then I remembered his flight schedule. As the phone continued buzzing inside my bag, I willfully ignored it.

"Not at their beck and call?" Gram repeated. "Didn't you work late Friday night and then spend the whole day at the office yesterday?"

"Not for any paying clients," I said.

After meeting with Denise, I hadn't wasted a moment. I'd begun researching case law on medical care in detention facilities, retaliatory actions by correctional officers, prisoners' rights, and the requirements for consent in medical procedures. I still needed more proof, but so far, everything pointed toward the women at Hydeford having a strong case against the facility and potentially even the federal government. I was trying to figure out what relief to seek, how to get justice for the women who'd been harmed, and how to prevent any further damage.

"It was for the women at the detention center. I wanted to do it while Vance was away."

Gram blinked twice. I hated how she always managed to see right through me.

"You haven't told him you're looking into the surgeries?"

"No, I did," I said, but I could see by the tilt of her head that she knew I was holding something back. "I mean, partially, just broad strokes about medical mistreatment," I admitted. "But then he told me I should hand the whole thing off to another attorney. He's not behind me on this, and . . . I don't know, I guess I just didn't feel like listening to him discount any more of my ideas or the reasons why it's important for me to be involved."

She nodded slowly, putting down the cake server she was holding and drying her hands on a dish towel.

"I'm going to tell him," I hedged. "I mean, I'll have to. It's not as if I can move forward on a case like this in secret. But I'm not ready to talk to him yet."

"I want to argue with you," Gram said, pausing as her gaze seemed to shift inward. Then she shook her head. "But who am I to preach brutal honesty when I only just told you about my father and all the ways his crusade affected our family?" She picked up another utensil but then put it back down. "Sometimes we're just not ready to share certain things, and I suppose that has to be all right. You don't have to beat yourself up over needing a moment to come clean."

My nose prickled, the level of understanding in her words threatening to make me weepy.

"Thanks, Gram," I said, clearing my throat.

"Well, that's settled then." She tapped her hand against the counter before coming to sit beside me. "Let's find ourselves a photo." Pulling the box of pictures closer, she began riffling through them.

"Maybe this one," she said, lifting one from the messy pile. "One of my all-time favorites."

It was a picture of me and Mom. We were at some zoo in Florida where we'd been allowed to feed milk to a baby tiger from a dropper. When the cub yawned, my mom had screamed in terror, thinking the animal was going to bite little eight-year-old me. When Gram snapped the photo, we were laughing over Mom's oversized reaction, our faces pink. Our grins stretched wide as ever as we looked at each other with glee.

"I can't believe that place actually let people hold the tigers," I said, staring down at the picture with a smile. "It's hard to imagine anyone allowing something like that now." I often thought about how much the world had changed since my parents died, all the things that would be new to them—iPhones, Uber, streaming services, my trusty Alexa. But then I thought about what was going on at Hydeford and worried that maybe there were still too many things that hadn't changed at all.

Gram pulled out another photo and held it up. It was my mom as a toddler in the 1960s, sitting in a sandbox with two little boys. My eyes drifted to the swing set behind them and the old-fashioned cars in the background before I looked back at the kids.

"I mean, the clothes these poor children are wearing." I laughed lightly as I examined the sweater vests and saddle shoes for another moment and then glanced up at Gram.

"I used to love to dress your mother," she said wistfully. "The sailor dresses and bows." She shook her head. "It was a different time, not like when you were a kid with your neon sweatshirts and ripped jeans. How we made it through." She looked toward the ceiling with a *what can you do?* gesture.

"I still don't understand why you won't just put these in an album."

"Don't start." She looked back at me with a mock frown. "We all have our quirks. Leave me be."

Except maybe I did understand now. After I'd heard more about Gram's childhood, everything was clearer. That day when Gram and I went walking in the freezing cold, she'd opened up about so much I'd never heard before. She told me that Grandpa Harry had been part of a tight-knit community of scientists and medical professionals, many of whom had been investigating methods of eradicating certain human genetic abnormalities. When Carrie Buck's case went to trial, everything came to a head. Gram's voice had faltered as she'd restated the facts of the case and what had led Carrie to court—how frighteningly similar it was to what was happening at Hydeford. Grandpa Harry stood up to the scientists and politicians though, filing his own brief with the court in hopes of defeating their agenda and defending Carrie's rights. Gram said his activism cost him his job and his good name.

No research institutions would hire him after that. The eugenics community had dubbed him a troublemaker and a naysayer, smearing his reputation however they could. When Gram's family's money began to run out, they had to leave their home on Long Island to start over in a new place. They even changed their last name so the negative publicity wouldn't follow them. It was years before they were back on their feet. Eventually, my great-grandpa was able to open the clinic I'd always heard about, but as Gram had made clear, the years in between were incredibly difficult. Their family had been ostracized by so many along the way.

It was no wonder she often avoided talking about parts of her past. Unlike Gram, I had the luxury of looking back at her story and seeing only the heroism and selflessness of it all, but for her, so many upsetting memories remained.

Rather than argue, I did as she bid, continuing to sort through the remaining pictures. We finally settled on a photo for the frame, a shot of Gram and Grandpa Walt as young adults on a tourist trip to London. After positioning the picture inside the glass, I returned the frame to its spot in the living room and then stepped back to study the younger versions of my grandparents. They were huddled under a red umbrella with wide, toothy grins on their faces and Big Ben in the background. Neither of them had any idea then that they'd have only a few more years to enjoy each other. I'd long known that my grandparents had an intense love affair, one that lasted until the day my grandpa died. I wondered if they'd have been that blissful if Gram had kept secrets from her husband too.

My phone let out another little chime, and I remembered that Tate might be looking for me. We had talked earlier in the week about meeting for a walk at the Reservoir that afternoon.

I returned to the kitchen and nudged Gram away from the sink so I could extract the trash bin from the cabinet beneath it.

"What else can I do for you before I head out?" I asked as I hoisted the full bag out of the bin and tied the handles closed.

"I've been taking care of myself just fine for decades. Go enjoy your Sunday." She gave me a gentle shove on the arm. "If I need anything else, I'll ask Manny." The weekend doorman, Manny, had been doting on her forever, becoming indispensable to her as both handyman and friend.

After I hugged Gram goodbye, I carried the trash to the rubbish room in the hallway on my way to the elevators. While I waited, I pulled out my phone and saw that Tate had indeed texted. Instead of an outdoor walk, she suggested we avoid the rainstorm that was now predicted for the afternoon and meet to sample cosmetics at Bloomingdale's instead.

Below Tate's text was another message from a number I didn't recognize, all written in Spanish. As the elevator doors opened and I stepped inside, I lamented that Spanish was a language I'd never learned. I puzzled over the message, deciphering only a few of the words.

"Si, podría hablar con usted, pero no hablo inglés. Espero que no sea problema. Yo trabajo hasta las seis y media, pero usted podría venir a mi casa después de esa hora. Estoy libre el miércoles. Déjeme saber si le parece bien."

Then a follow-up came through from the same number.

"*Soy Jacinta Morales*," the message announced.

"Oh!" I said aloud as I saw her name.

When the nurse had handed me that note at the detention facility, she'd written down the name *Jacinta Morales* with a partial address. After just a little digging, I'd been able to find a phone number for a Jacinta Morales on the very street listed. A landline. I hadn't determined yet how the woman was connected to Hydeford, whether as an inmate or maybe another nurse or staff member. But I felt certain the nurse at the facility had been trying to help by slipping the name into my hand. With any luck, the woman would be able to corroborate some aspect of what was happening at Hydeford and maybe even provide some insight into how to convince Isobel and Denise to take action.

I had called Jacinta's number the day before and left a voicemail, saying I hoped she might be able to shed light on services a client at Hydeford needed. I'd kept the message intentionally vague, worried that if I disclosed the true nature of my call, she'd get frightened and refuse to meet.

I examined the message again. The only information I was able to cull from the text was that Jacinta didn't speak English. Three years studying Mandarin during high school was completely useless in this moment. I wondered if maybe Jacinta could understand spoken English but struggled to write it. I pressed my thumb to the phone number above the text, considering trying my luck with another call—but then I thought better of it. I was too anxious to find out why the nurse had pointed me in Jacinta's direction and didn't want to bungle anything by trying to communicate too hastily.

As the elevator doors opened into the lobby, I could see rain falling outside the building's floor-to-ceiling windows. I emerged reluctantly into the dampness of the afternoon and headed toward the subway. As I walked, I dialed Tate.

"Do you speak Spanish?" I asked. The rain was only a light mist around me, but it was still wet enough to warrant digging through my tote for the umbrella buried deep inside. I passed by a crowded restaurant where a cluster of outdoor tables was jammed full of boisterous weekend customers. The patrons were mostly fresh-faced hipster types who looked to be in their early twenties. Large patio umbrellas with stripes of burgundy and ochre shielded the tables from the mist, leaving the diners to continue their revelry dry and unbothered. How nice it must be for them, I thought, as I wondered about their careers, these young people who could find time to drag Sunday brunches well into the middle of the afternoon.

There had been a time when Vance and I were part of that brunch scene, urban professionals spending our Sundays waiting in line at Barney Greengrass or lounging on hotel rooftops with mimosas in hand. But neither of us had really managed to lean into those experiences. We were both too focused on our careers, antsy to get back to the assignments waiting on our laptops. Our friend Lou had given Vance so much grief for constantly checking his phone that Vance eventually decided we should just stop going to those big group gatherings. I remember thinking back then it was a relief—like we had found time for getting more work done.

Putting in those extra weekend hours was supposed to propel us both toward unparalleled success. At least it had paid off for Vance, who'd managed to remain the permanent darling of his investment bank even while building a labor-intensive podcast on the side.

"Not really," Tate answered, bringing me back to the moment. "I took it in high school and one year of college. I could order you a great drink at a bar in Cancún, but that's about it."

"I'm going to forward you a text. See what you can make out."

"You do know you can just Google Translate it, right?" Tate asked.

"Can you just look at it for me? My hands are full, and it's starting to rain."

"I'll do my best," she offered.

I took the phone from my ear and sent off the text.

"Got it," Tate said. Then she went quiet as she took a moment to read the message. "This is for your immigration case?" she asked.

"Yeah. It's a witness I want to interview."

"It's pretty basic stuff," Tate said. "She says she can meet with you but she doesn't speak English. She works until six thirty, but you can come after. And then she said she could see you on *miércoles*."

"What's *miércoles*?"

"Uh . . ." She sounded sheepish. "It's either Tuesday or Wednesday. Or it might be Thursday. I'm Googling now."

"Do you think I should call her back?" I asked as I neared the stairwell to the subway. "Or maybe text her and hope she has someone who can translate what I've written?" I moved under the awning of L'Étoile, a French patisserie Gram loved, and leaned against the cool bricks beside the window. I didn't want to go underground and lose reception before I was finished with the call.

"Yeah, but what about when you actually meet with her? The firm can pay for an interpreter."

"Maybe." I wasn't ready to tell the powers that be about this other potential aspect of my new pro bono assignment. "This isn't really part of the actual case I was assigned. I'm still just collecting information."

"Oh!" Tate suddenly blurted into the phone, her voice rising with excitement. "You know who speaks Spanish? Dustin Ortiz. You should ask him."

"Ugh, no," I groaned. "I am not asking him for anything."

"I still don't get your aversion to him, Jess. He's a pretty good guy."

"Different strokes for different folks," I said. "I'm at the subway. See you at Bloomie's."

"If you'd rather go find a weekend happy hour, I'd be game for that too," she offered. "Nachos and margaritas make rainy days so much sunnier."

"Nah, I'm trying to cut down on alcohol."

"You are?" She knew how much I loved a glass of good Chardonnay. "Wait, you're not off alcohol because . . ." She let the suggestion hang in the air.

"No, I am most definitely not pregnant." I failed to conceal the dejection in my voice, even though I hadn't told Tate everything

I was doing to get pregnant or how I was doubling down on my attempts to make it happen.

I'd read that alcohol could disrupt ovulation. So in addition to tracking my nutrient intake, avoiding antihistamines, swearing off raw fish, and limiting caffeine to tragically low levels, alcohol was out.

It had been months already since I'd whispered excitedly to Tate that Vance and I were trying for a baby. My continued silence about it ever since probably spoke all the volume it needed to.

"This will work out," Tate said gently. "You'll see. Now hurry up and meet me."

"Yeah. See you soon."

As I started down the stairs toward the train, I wished I could be as much of an optimist as my friend. Instead, I was focused on all the things that could still go wrong.

~

The next day at work, I caught sight of Dustin walking past my office door and almost called out to him. He was carrying a paper coffee cup in one hand and what looked like a box of bakery treats in the other. I could just imagine all the admins swooning over him as he dropped off the croissants and muffins he'd picked up for them. There was something so self-important about him that just got under my skin. I closed my mouth before calling his name.

An hour later, I forced myself out of my chair. I still hadn't come up with a better idea for interviewing Jacinta Morales in a language I didn't speak. I couldn't allow my personal feelings to interfere with the investigation, not when so much was at stake. As I walked toward Dustin's office at the other end of the hallway, I passed his office mate, another first-year associate named Helen, fawning over the box of pastries with a few others in the kitchen alcove.

When I reached his office, I knocked lightly on the open glass door.

"Hey, do you have a sec?"

Dustin looked up from his computer, swiveling in his chair to face me head-on. He wore his typical uniform of khakis and a French-blue button-down shirt with silver cuff links. His sandy hair was perfectly in place as always, curling just a little at the collar. I imagined he'd gone to great effort to achieve the admittedly disarming look.

"Sure. What's up?"

I was quiet for a beat too long as I gathered my thoughts, and his eyes began to narrow.

"You're about to saddle me with more document review, aren't you? It's fine—I can make time if it's too much for you." He started clearing some space on top of his desk.

Right, because the great Dustin Ortiz could handle anything. Despite my urge to scoff at his "anything you can do, I can do better" attitude, I forced myself to stay on task.

"No, not at all," I said, noting that I was suddenly nervous to tell him what I needed. The issues I was researching about the women at Hydeford felt private. It was unnerving to share my thoughts on the topic, especially with a man—and a man I didn't care for at that.

"Do you think Helen would mind if I sat for a minute?" I motioned toward the empty desk chair.

"Please." Dustin held out a hand in invitation.

I tried to steady myself with a deep breath as I turned the chair to face him and sat.

"So you know how I've been working on an immigration case?"

"Yeah, I heard that." He nodded, leaning toward his desk to pick up a small blue stress ball nestled beside his penholder. He started tossing it from one hand to the other as his dark eyes surveyed me.

"It's impressive that you're finding time for pro bono work with all the other cases you're staffed on. You're the lead on, what, four other cases right now?"

I couldn't decide if he was being snarky or genuine, so I just plowed on with what I'd come to say. "I might have stumbled upon some medical abuse at the detention facility, but I'm not sure. There's a woman who may have useful information for the case. Truthfully, I don't know much about her except that she's living in Brooklyn. And I want to interview her, but she doesn't speak English."

"Ah." Dustin's head moved up in the start of a slow nod. "You want me to be your interpreter."

I nodded back, hoping he was on board.

"But the case is non-billable," he said.

"Correct." Of course he'd want to hound the point that I'd sunk to the level of asking the great Dustin Ortiz for a favor.

"So then"—he put out his empty hand, palm up—"what's in it for me?"

"Ugh, forget it." I popped up from my seat so fast that the chair banged against the wall behind me. "I knew I shouldn't have asked you," I snapped as I turned on my heel.

"Wait, Jessa. I'll do it."

I paused and turned back to face him.

"I just meant, like, can I track these hours as if I'm on the case with you?"

"You should be aware," I answered in a defensive tone, "that your pro bono hours won't count one iota toward building a track record for making partner. Sometimes you can just do someone a favor without a quid pro quo."

"Look, I wasn't trying to be a dick," he said, "but you know as well as anyone that it's a rat race out there, and we're not all as good at juggling as you are." He paused, glancing at the little ball he was still holding. "Impressive stress ball demonstrations aside." He smiled sheepishly, and my bravado dimmed.

I was the one who needed help, after all, and I could try, one more time, to give the guy the benefit of the doubt. "Sorry, yes, of course. I'll tell Don Halperin that I needed you, and I'll make sure to let him know afterward that you were invaluable. We'll just try to keep the hours down for you so I'm not depleting firm resources. In the meantime"—I walked back toward him and held out my phone—"can you please text this woman and tell her we'll be there on Wednesday night?"

~

That Wednesday evening, I pulled to a stop in front of house number 176 on a tightly packed block in Brooklyn. For the majority of our car ride from Manhattan, Dustin had been stuck on a conference call about another case, which was just as well. Listening in on a discussion about another securities case seemed preferable to having to make conversation with him. As it turned out though, Dustin stayed silent nearly the entire time he was on the phone. With the exception of a few words of agreement, he appeared to be observing the call simply to learn. I was surprised by his deferential behavior, as I so rarely saw him hold his tongue.

As I pressed the button to turn off the ignition, Dustin removed the buds from his ears.

"Perfect timing," he said. "Call just finished."

We stepped out of the car, and I took in our surroundings. The street was filled with petite two-story houses piled so close to each other that the trash cans could barely fit between any two homes. Most houses had wrought-iron fences surrounding their walkways and square patches of grass in their tiny front yards. For all the years I'd lived in New York, this part of Bensonhurst was somewhere I'd never been. I'd always thought Bensonhurst was primarily an Italian-American neighborhood, but I'd learned since Jacinta's text that it also included a thriving Guatemalan community.

I pushed open the gate and began making my way to the front door.

"No," Dustin said from behind me. "She said they're in the back apartment." He pointed toward a short, concrete stairwell on the side of the house, the front door about four steps up.

"Did she tell you how many people she lives with?" I asked, berating myself for only thinking to ask that question now. I'd already hit Dustin with a barrage of questions about his brief call with Jacinta. He'd managed to ascertain that she had been detained at Hydeford, but only for a matter of weeks.

"She just said she lives with her family. I didn't ask for details," he said as he followed me up the steps and then reached over me to push the buzzer.

A wrinkled woman, stooped and fragile looking, appeared on the other side of the screened door.

"Come, come," she said briskly in accented English, pushing open the door and beckoning us in before we even introduced ourselves.

We stepped inside, and I was hit immediately by the alluring scent of savory food—garlic, onions, something fried—and my stomach rumbled. As we made our way into the tight kitchen, the woman called toward the back of the apartment, shouting Spanish words at a rapid-fire pace.

A moment later, another woman appeared, younger than the first. She was about the same height as my five foot four, with a complexion much fairer than the woman who'd shown us inside. She had dark hair pulled back into a tight bun and wore eyeglasses with bright pink frames. She smiled kindly and motioned to the vinyl-covered chairs at the small table in the room's center.

"*Hola*," she said, looking at Dustin. "*Soy* Jacinta."

Dustin reached out to shake Jacinta's hand, and I felt an instant jolt of annoyance at how he'd somehow commandeered the meeting from the get-go. But I batted the feeling away just as quickly. Of course Jacinta would speak to Dustin first. He was the one who'd talked to her on the phone, and surely he'd told her about my lack of Spanish skills. I reminded myself that he was only attending this meeting as a favor to me, so I had to be more patient with him.

As we took our seats, a commotion arose from the back hallway, the sounds of young children arguing. Then a man's voice sounded, emitting an aggravated string of Spanish words, and the bickering stopped as suddenly as it had begun.

Jacinta looked at us sheepishly and said something to Dustin.

"Her niece and nephew," Dustin interpreted.

I smiled warmly at Jacinta as I pulled my laptop from my tote, placing it on the table.

"Dustin, please tell Jacinta," I started, "that we're grateful she's willing to help us with our client at Hydeford and that we'll try to keep our questioning brief."

Dustin interpreted and Jacinta nodded. She glanced over at me and smiled. I understood the expression as a tacit apology that we couldn't communicate directly, and I offered a matching smile in return.

Then, through Dustin, I launched into a series of questions: Did Jacinta know Isobel Pérez at the facility? How close had the two women become to each other? Did Jacinta ever see Isobel being mistreated by any of the guards? And so on. Jacinta answered everything, responding to Dustin in a tone that sounded cooperative and sympathetic throughout. As she talked, Jacinta periodically glanced back to me as if for approval. She was chatty, giving lengthy responses to each of the questions, seemingly glad to be helpful.

Then I asked if she knew Dr. Choudry. Even before Dustin interpreted the question, Jacinta's smile faded.

"*Sí.*"

I waited for more, but she just lifted her chin and said nothing.

"Ask her if she knows about what the doctor did to Isobel."

This time, Jacinta offered a longer response, and it was impossible to miss the outraged tenor of her clipped words.

"Yes," Dustin said, meeting my eye. "She knows Dr. Choudry and will never forgive that woman for the things she has done."

"Woman?" I asked, confused. "What woman?"

"Dr. Choudry," he said.

"No," I corrected him. "Dr. Choudry is the doctor from the women's health clinic, a man."

Dustin repeated my words in Spanish, and Jacinta looked back at me.

"Dr. Choudry *es una mujer. La misma.*"

I turned wide-eyed to Dustin, assuming Jacinta must be confused.

"She's talking about the same doctor. Dr. Choudry," Dustin said.

"But . . ." I couldn't continue. I was struck dumb trying to process this new piece of information. It had never crossed my mind that the doctor might possibly be a woman. I had just assumed from the beginning that Choudry was a man, but now as I mentally replayed my meetings with Denise and Isobel, I couldn't remember them ever specifying one way or the other. How on earth could a woman be butchering other women in the ways that had been described?

"Dr. Choudry is a woman?" I asked again, feeling stupefied by what sounded like the ultimate betrayal.

"*Sí,*" Jacinta answered.

Stunned, I found myself at a loss for what to ask next. So many questions were suddenly swirling through my mind, making so much noise I couldn't actually hear my thoughts at all.

But then Jacinta began talking to Dustin, saying something new. He glanced at me as she continued to speak at length, but he didn't interpret. After the revelation about Dr. Choudry, I was almost glad for the reprieve, a moment to pause instead of having to process any additional sucker punches. But as Jacinta's comments began to stretch into something of a monologue, I found myself growing frustrated. After two minutes dragged out to four or five, I finally gave Dustin's foot a little kick under the table.

"Hey," I said, trying to remind them both I was still there.

Dustin held up his finger, instructing me to wait, and it was all I could do not to smack his finger back down.

Finally, he turned back to me, his eyes wider than I'd ever seen them.

"They're sterilizing the women," he said, his voice thick, like he had something stuck in his throat.

I sighed. "Yes, that's why we're here. To find out about it."

"No." Dustin shook his head. "I mean, I knew you mentioned medical abuse, but this . . . You never said anything like this. How can that be happening?" He ran a hand through his hair and let out a long breath.

I knew it was hard to believe. Here we were in 2022, and women were being sterilized against their will. I still couldn't parse out what would be motivating the doctor, the guards, the government, to let this happen. Was it because the women were foreigners? People of color? Less educated? Or was it a scam involving money from insurance payments? Maybe all of the above.

"It's barbaric," Dustin said. His eyes darted around the room, as if he'd gone into fight-or-flight mode. "In our own country. My God, Jessa . . . This is really serious." His usually sunny face had drained of color.

"Yes, Dustin, I'm aware." Perhaps I should have been gentler, given him another moment to adjust. At least his first reaction had been one of trust; he'd believed Jacinta and whatever she'd told him. It was probably more than I had expected of him, but I was too focused on what was happening at Hydeford to waste time reconsidering any part of my perception of him.

"What else did she just say?"

"Other women in the facility complained, but then they were deported."

Jacinta watched Dustin closely as he continued relaying her words. "She's willing to tell us more about what Dr. Choudry did, but she doesn't want to be involved beyond that. It's behind her now, she says. She just wants to forget what they did to her."

"To her? To Jacinta?"

Dustin glanced back at Jacinta.

"Is okay," she said in English, giving him permission to continue.

"They removed her uterus," Dustin said quietly.

"She . . ." I looked over at Jacinta, who met my eyes and nodded. "But I thought you were a witness," I said, forgetting that Jacinta wouldn't understand the English words.

"Sounds like she's both," Dustin answered quietly. "Witness and victim. She was only in detention for thirty days," Dustin said. "For filling out a form improperly when her green card expired. She said she didn't even complain of any physical problems before they brought her to the clinic. They told her the visit was a routine checkup, so she assumed it was protocol for all the women when they first arrived. But the doctor did some tests and said she needed to have a procedure to remove two cysts. When she woke up, her uterus and ovaries had been taken."

I felt myself gripping the arms of my chair, attempting to steady myself in the wake of this news. It was too much.

"Did they tell her beforehand," I asked, "that they might remove other organs?"

Dustin repeated the question, and Jacinta shook her head.

"*Ellos solo me ponen a dormir*," she said, then she made a motion to mimic a mask being placed over her nose.

"Nothing. They just put her under." Dustin's voice was so quiet it was nearly a whisper, but I thought I could hear anger simmering underneath.

"Does she have any children?" I asked.

As Dustin interpreted, Jacinta motioned toward the hallway behind the kitchen and said a few words.

"No," Dustin answered, and I fought the urge to vomit.

How many more women could there be? How many had been brutalized? I wanted to get up and call the police. This was an emergency, and wasn't that the thing to do in an emergency? A crime was being committed at that clinic, over and over and over. Someone had to get in there and stop it. But calling the cops wouldn't achieve anything here. We were up against a government facility shrouded in red tape and a glaring lack of transparency. The most effective way to help the women would unfortunately be the most cumbersome one—filing a lawsuit.

"Did she tell anyone? Complain?" I asked.

Dustin translated and relayed Jacinta's answer.

"Other women knew about what happened. Some came to her and gave her their condolences." His eyes continued to dart between Jacinta and me. "That's how she put it: condolences." He grimaced and then continued. "She stayed in the infirmary for a few days, and then they moved her back to her regular cell. Three different women told her they'd had similar procedures, at the same clinic, all with the same results."

Condolences. My heart stuttered at the word because it was exactly right. How many times had I heard that word when I was a child—people always wanting to offer their condolences? On one particularly bleak afternoon about two weeks after my parents' double funeral, I'd actually taken Gram's dog-eared

Merriam-Webster down from the shelf to look for the definition, wondering how this word I didn't entirely understand was supposed to make me feel. Nothing could change the fact that my parents would never pick me up from dance practice again, never teach me to drive, never watch me graduate high school. *Condolences*, as it turned out, was just an empty expression of sympathy, an acknowledgment that all was lost. Thinking about what had been taken from Jacinta, I was reminded of what I'd discovered long ago—that the worst kind of sadness was the kind that came with no hope.

"Why didn't she file a formal complaint?" I asked.

Dustin asked my question.

"Since she only had two weeks until she was getting out, she didn't say anything. Didn't want to jeopardize her position, end up getting deported. She had been warned by friends. Of the other women who filed complaints, one was on a plane back to El Salvador the very same day. Jacinta doesn't know what happened with the other one."

"Can you explain to her that if she doesn't speak up, the doctor is going to keep doing this to more women?"

Dustin rattled off a few sentences, and Jacinta started shaking her head.

"And tell her," I added almost frantically, "that nobody in the facility has control over her anymore since she's on the outside. She won't get in trouble."

He tried to translate, but I interrupted again.

"She has legal status now. Tell her she's safe."

Dustin turned back to Jacinta, but I yanked his arm and interjected once more.

"Tell her that without her, we won't have a case. We need someone who's willing to speak up."

"If you'd let me speak to her, I would." He looked down at my hand on his arm, and I instantly withdrew it.

"Sorry, sorry," I said, forcing myself to stay quiet after that.

When Dustin's Spanish words finally trailed off, Jacinta looked from him over to me, her dark eyes pensive. She tilted her head from one side to the other, like she was beginning to think through the possibilities. Glancing at Dustin, I could see cautious optimism in his eyes.

"Please," I said in English, hoping the woman would understand. "Think of all the other women like you, still hoping to have children. I can't imagine what that would be like for a woman who has waited her whole life to have kids"—my voice broke, betraying my emotions, but I kept on—"only for her to find out some stranger has taken that away from her." Twin tears escaped from my eyes, racing each other toward my chin.

Dustin began repeating for Jacinta what I'd said, but he continued talking for long enough that I could tell he was adding words of his own. Jacinta interrupted him, and he responded at length, all the while leaving me in the dark. Finally, Dustin finished whatever he'd been saying. Jacinta's eyes slid back to me, and we were all silent. I wasn't sure what I'd do if Jacinta refused to work with us. If the women were all too afraid to speak up, how could I even help?

"*Sí,*" Jacinta finally said. "*Lo haré.*"

"She'll do it," Dustin said, his voice still quiet but firm.

Then Jacinta said something else, and from the tone, I could tell she was hedging.

"But she doesn't want to be the only one," Dustin said. "She'll only do it if you convince others to speak up as well. This is not about her, she said. It's about all women."

Carrie

October 1924

It wasn't but a couple of weeks after my meeting with Dr. Preston that I got summoned back to his office. When I arrived, another fellow was already with him, an older man with a shiny bald head and a crisp suit. They were standing close together in the back of the room, each holding a glass filled with amber-colored liquid.

"Ah, Carrie." Dr. Preston greeted me with a broad smile, like he and I was old friends. "Come and have a seat." He motioned me toward the sofa as he and the other man came closer, each taking seats in the armchairs across from me.

"This here," Dr. Preston said, looking toward his friend, "is Mr. Sterling Whitmore. He's going to be your lawyer."

A lawyer! Joy overtook me and I smiled big. Now that they'd got me a lawyer, I figured they were getting me out after all, that there was just procedures we needed to do or some such.

Dr. Preston faced Mr. Whitmore. "As you can see, the girl is quite simple. So many characteristics of a textbook imbecile."

He spoke those unkind words as though I weren't even in the room, and it wiped the grin off my face real fast. I worried I'd misunderstood why they wanted to see me.

"I'm sorry, sir," I said to Dr. Preston, "but what exactly are you planning for me that would render me needing a lawyer for myself?"

The two men shared a small smile before Dr. Preston looked toward me again.

"Well, you're the lucky girl we've chosen to receive a very wonderful procedure."

I wasn't sure what he meant, so I kept silent, waiting for him to explain.

"Yes, yes," the other fellow said. "I certainly do see it. Very limited."

"You see," Dr. Preston went on, "medicine is a wonderful field, and we have discovered a way to make your life easier now, and for your whole future. You'd like that, wouldn't you, Carrie?"

"W-well . . . well, yes, I suppose," I stammered as I tried to figure out what-all was going on.

"Girls like you, Carrie, the hardworking kind, when they have only a little schooling and scant means and, well, tendencies like yours . . ." He again shared a look with his friend. I knew he was thinking about my pregnancy, suspecting that I was a promiscuous girl. I didn't defend myself like maybe I should have. The business with Clarence was my private story that I wasn't wanting to tell. He didn't wait for me to speak anyhow, but just kept talking at me.

"You wouldn't want to be saddled with more responsibilities, obligations a girl like you could hardly satisfy," he said. "Especially if you were to end up with one child after another, after another, after another. Can you imagine the hardship on a person like yourself?"

"I'm not so sure, sir," I answered, thinking that a home full of babies would be a blessing for a girl as lonely as me. It'd be quite the opposite of hardship in my opinion, but I didn't think the man really wanted to hear my thoughts on the matter.

"Well, we can save you from all that, Carrie. With a very simple procedure, we can make it so you never have to worry about conceiving another child, not ever again."

"No more children?" I couldn't keep quiet about that. "That's not something I want at all. No, thank you." I stood from my chair, ready to leave. I wasn't going to let them do any such thing to me.

"We don't mean to do it this instant." Dr. Preston laughed and turned to Mr. Whitmore. "Look at her, champing at the bit." He turned his attention back to me. "No, not right now, Carrie. You see, there are rules about these things. We need special permission from the government of this state, so as we don't get in trouble. Mr. Whitmore here, that's how he's going to help."

"But I don't want the procedure," I said. "I do want more babies one day."

"Come now, Carrie," Dr. Preston said. "A girl like you can't hardly know her own mind. How would you take care of those children you're imagining for yourself? What money do you have to feed and clothe them? To educate them and ensure they don't grow into socially inadequate adults? Criminals, loose women, and such?" He looked at Mr. Whitmore, who nodded back in agreement. "We've come to understand that feeblemindedness like yours is hereditary. That means it passes from a mother to a child, you see. Like it did from your mother to you. And then you'd pass it to your child, and so on. Most likely, any babies you bore would end up back in this very institution, wards of the state just like you. Even more members of the Buck family line would be separating the good, taxpaying citizens of Virginia from their hard-earned money. But with a simple procedure that takes only a few minutes, we can save everybody from all that trouble."

"I know my mind, and I don't want your procedure!" I was hollering now. There weren't nothing wrong with my mama nor with me, and I didn't like all the mean words he was saying. I looked back toward the door, feeling myself in danger in that very moment and hoping again for some way to escape that god-awful facility. Dr. Preston followed my eyes.

"There's nowhere else for you to go, Carrie. You should be grateful to be here. Getting free food, free medical care. And now that we've chosen you as the test case, you'll receive the sterilization procedure for free as well." He said it like I'd won some sort of prize.

"I don't want any procedure, and I won't do it. You'll see. I won't!"

"Well, then, Miss Carrie"—Mr. Preston sounded mad now—"I suppose it's a good thing you have this lawyer here to try to stop me."

"I . . . I don't understand," I said, looking from one man to the other.

"No," Dr. Preston said, "of course you don't, which is just the point I've been making. But I will try to be very clear. You see, we here at the Colony, we'd like to offer these sterilization operations to a certain category of girls and women, those like yourself who simply shouldn't be reproducing. There's a wonderful new law in Virginia that should allow us to do as we please, but until a court of law has the chance to review this new law, certain rules are a bit unclear. If we take your case to court, letting a judge uphold the new law precisely as it's written, then we'll get our answers. After that, we'll be able to proceed with these operations at a breakneck pace, I wager. We just want to do what's best for the inmates, you understand, and society as a whole. Just think of it." He turned to Mr. Whitmore again. "With enough time, we could cleanse society of mental defectives entirely."

He stood then and rang a bell so the nurse would come fetch me and return me to my room. Dr. Preston was right about one thing: I didn't understand what he'd said to me, not at all. How could these men think anyone would benefit from what they described? How had I ended up in a place of such great danger? The only thing that eventually became clear to me was that I had played right into their despicable hands.

Jessa

March 2022

On the way back to the city, I cranked up the volume on the radio to save myself the discomfort of conversation with Dustin. I didn't want to get into any of the reasons I'd nearly cried in front of a potential client. To his credit, Dustin turned his attention to his phone. It had started raining hard during the time we'd been with Jacinta, and now, as we made our way back to the Belt Parkway, I felt anxious to get home. Even with all our recent arguing, I suddenly wanted nothing more than to sit beside Vance, curled up under his arm.

After we'd been driving for twenty minutes, Dustin reached out and silenced the song playing on the radio.

"You ready to talk about it?" he asked.

"Ugh. No, thank you."

"My mom couldn't have children," he said.

Why'd he even ask if he was just going to charge ahead anyway? I didn't bother to hide my exasperation. "And yet, here you sit, your mother's son."

"I'm adopted."

I should've been polite after he revealed something personal, but I was so utterly uninterested in having this kind of conversation with him. No one seemed to understand why the idea of adoption didn't adequately address my desire to have a child. It was a great option for lots of families out there, and maybe we'd end up going that route one day—but I wasn't ready to talk about it. Or think about it. So instead, I lashed out.

"What makes you think you know anything about my life? Yay," I said flatly. "You're adopted. Want a gold star?"

He just raised his eyebrows in response.

I attempted to rein in my emotions. "Look, I'm not trying to disrespect you or your experiences here. I just . . . I just really, really want a child who's biologically mine. A person like you, who's grown up in what I'm assuming was a perfectly lovely and wonderful home with glorious parents who adopted you, probably couldn't understand why I feel that way."

"Then why don't you explain it to me? Might be good to try it on a fresh set of ears."

I was surprised by the sincerity in his tone. It actually *would* be nice, I thought, to talk to someone about everything I was feeling, someone who hadn't heard it all from me before, someone who had zero stake in the outcome. But where would I even begin? When I was twelve years old, watching reruns of *Boy Meets World* in the den off the kitchen, and the phone rang? I could still smell the Mallomars I'd been eating. Greta, the babysitter who came over if my parents went out at night, shrieked in horror from the next room. I remembered the way the cookie melted inside my clenched fist as I ran to the kitchen, where Greta stood with the phone to her ear, suddenly quiet, almost whispering, "Now what happens? Now what? Now what?"

Should I tell Dustin how I hadn't touched foods with marshmallows ever since? Or maybe I should tell him about the time my grandmother forced me to go bra shopping and the salesgirl kept referring to Gram as "your mother," and I cried for so long in the fitting room they had to call security to unlock the door? Or the year after that, when the school sponsored a daddy-and-daughter dance and I helped four of my friends choose their dresses, only to spend the night at home, crying over old photos? No, the thing I probably should tell him was how with each passing day, as Vance and I tried and failed to conceive a child, it seemed less and less likely that I'd ever get back a piece of my parents.

But then I looked back over at him and couldn't bring myself to share anything at all. Not with Dustin. The fact that he was suddenly acting like a good guy didn't erase all the asshole moves he'd made in the past.

"Nah, that's fine," I said, turning the music back up.

~

That night, as I lay in bed beside Vance, I couldn't sleep. My thoughts kept boomeranging between my own fertility struggles and everything that had happened to the women at Hydeford. I felt a crushing sense of sorrow for myself, but even more so for the other women. No matter what relief we sought in court, Isobel, Denise, and Jacinta would never birth more children of their own. There was no restoring what had been taken, no adequate consolation that could be granted after the fact. A lawsuit to stop the facility from harming any more women, a hefty monetary settlement—that was all I could offer these women, and I wasn't sure I could even accomplish that. I needed the firm's permission to file any new case, and the more I thought about moving forward with a class action, the trickier it seemed.

"Stop stressing and go to sleep," Vance mumbled.

"I can't."

He flipped over to face me, our noses only inches apart on our pillows. Just enough ambient light flowed through the closed shades to help me make out the contours of his face, the sleepiness of his heavy lids.

"Honestly, Jess, you're putting me over the edge here. You're the one who wanted me to go for testing. Now it seems like it's causing you *more* stress."

I resisted the urge to sigh dramatically in response to his off-base comment. Again, Vance and I were out of sync.

"It's not the sperm test." I flipped onto my back to stare at the dark ceiling. "I have to speak to Andrew in the morning," I said, mentioning the firm's supervising attorney. "I just . . . if he doesn't go for it, I won't be able to help those women. Not them, and not the women who come after them. I don't know if he'll trust me to do this. And then what? I can't just do nothing."

I'd finally come clean to Vance the day before about the nature of the medical abuse I suspected at Hydeford. If he started up again about how I couldn't possibly be right about the clinic, I was going to lose it on him. I now had actual testimony from three different women, and he *still* thought I might somehow be misinterpreting the situation. All I wanted from him was support, not judgment. Over the years he'd talked me through so many complicated work scenarios, helping me decide what to do. He had an uncanny ability to understand complex situations between partners and associates and how they related to the firm's overall success, but I was beginning to wonder if all that collaborating we'd done had really just been Vance giving me instructions and me doing as I was told. Now that I was disagreeing with his directives, we were painfully out of step.

"It's been four years, Jess," Vance said, focusing on the topic I actually *did* want to discuss. I felt my shoulders relax. "The only one who's not over what happened with the Shantrane case is you.

It's going to be fine." He reached for my hand beneath the covers and held tight.

"Maybe," I answered half-heartedly, turning back onto my side, this time facing away from him.

"Come here." He pulled me closer and nestled me against him, my back against his firm chest.

After another minute, he started running his hand along my rib cage down to the hem of my tank top, which he began pushing up in slow motion.

"Vance." My tone was halting, a shorthand to shut down his advances.

"Oh, come on," he whispered beseechingly. He leaned down and put his warm lips to the part of my side that was now exposed. The only thing I felt at the contact was annoyance.

"You know we're not supposed to tonight. Don't make me be the bad guy here." I reached under the covers to shift my shirt back into place. Undeterred, Vance started untying the drawstring of my sweatpants. "Vance." My voice was harsher now. "Seriously, stop. You're going to mess everything up."

"I promise my sperm supply will replenish itself plenty by morning." He tugged at my waistband, but I pushed away his hand with force.

"I'm not doing this." My voice was loud. "They said to abstain until after your appointment tomorrow, so that's what we're doing." I sat up and turned on the lamp on the bedside table. "I don't even understand. Every time I say it's a good night to try, I feel like I'm forcing you to have sex with me. Yet all I have to do is say no once, and you turn into a horny teenager? Why can't you be on the same page as me? Like, ever?"

Vance sat up too, his expression clouding over with anger.

"Because that's exactly it. We're not on the same page. Not anymore." He swung his legs over the side of the bed and grabbed the quilt we kept folded at the bottom of the bed. "I'm going to sleep in the other room."

"The other room? Because I said no? On the one night you're not supposed to ejaculate? Seriously?"

"No, not because you said no." He made it halfway out the bedroom door, but then he stepped back toward me. "Because you don't give a shit about what I want in this baby quest of yours. It's all about you and your grief and your search for 'connection.'" He made quotes in the air as he said it, mocking me. "I don't even know what else, but you are making me miserable."

"Miserable?" I was shouting now too. "But you *want* babies. All those times you talked about teaching your children all the little things—to love *Where the Wild Things Are*, to make your grandma's matzo balls, to run track in high school . . . Why are you acting like I'm the only one these things matter to?"

"Because you are, Jess!" He moved closer to the side of the bed and bent his head so we were eye to eye. "What I wanted, Jess, was you. Would I also like kids? Yes, you know I do. But that's not all I want from life. What I'd really like to know is what will happen if it turns out we can never have kids, biological *or* adopted. Would we survive, just you and me? Would I ever be enough for you on my own?"

His question was ridiculous. There was no reason to think we wouldn't ever raise children. Certainly we could adopt one day if we chose to go that route. Plus, IVF and surrogacy were still on the table—so many options we hadn't explored at all. The only reason to drum up a scenario like the one he'd described was if he was actively trying to upset me. But I wouldn't take the bait.

"Stop. Just stop. You're going to screw up your test, your body chemistry—"

He interrupted me with a guttural roar, and I understood belatedly that returning to clinical topics was probably the wrong move.

"I just can't be near you right now," he said as he turned and walked out of the room, the navy blue quilt trailing behind him.

~

The next morning, I checked the time on my watch again. Andrew Hendricks, the chair of the litigation department, was at an off-site client meeting and was expected back at noon. That's what his assistant had said an hour ago.

Noon was also the time of Vance's appointment at the doctor. When he'd made the appointment following our visit to Dr. LaRusso, Vance insisted he didn't need me to accompany him. I thought I should be there for moral support, but he seemed to feel self-conscious, so I'd backed off. After our argument the night before, I found myself worrying that he might not even show up for his testing, that he might skip the appointment just to spite me.

When I'd woken up, the apartment had been empty, the blue quilt from our bed folded neatly on the end of the sofa in the living room. Vance had clearly tiptoed around to avoid waking me before he left, and I was choosing to take that as a good sign, that he was being considerate instead of trying to avoid me. Maybe the folded blanket, left so carefully in place, had been meant to tell me he was ready to reconcile. I could only guess.

Had he stuck around until I was up, I huffed to myself, maybe I'd have at least some inkling of what he was currently feeling. Five years earlier, when we got married, I'd thought marriage would change my life and end my time of feeling alone. After all the years of therapy and planning and bucket lists, I had turned myself into a carefully curated person, finally able to live a happier life. That's what marriage had signaled to me. But as I sat at my cluttered desk that morning taking stock, I was unsure of who exactly I'd become since then or whether I was actually any happier now than before I met Vance. Somehow everything had just gotten more complicated.

My office phone rang, and the admin on the other end of the line informed me that Andrew was back and ready to see me.

"Jessa." Andrew smiled warmly as I stepped into his office. He was seated behind his large glass desk, three computer monitors aglow on its gleaming surface, and his cell phone in his hand, dinging with notifications. As usual, he was dressed in a crisp, pastel button-down shirt, obviously expensive, the sleeves rolled to his elbows. A pair of eyeglasses rested on top of his snow-white hair. For someone in his late sixties, Andrew didn't show any signs of slowing down, still always doing a million things at once. "Just one more sec." He looked back to his phone and began typing something.

While he tapped out the communication, I stood there awkwardly, looking around his meticulous office. Andrew's setup always reminded me of my dad's office at his old firm, which was still headquartered only three blocks away. Andrew's office had clearly been attended to by a professional designer, with its intentional placement of desktop accessories, floor statues, and area rugs. A pair of wooden giraffes in one corner stood about four feet high, and an enormous framed black-and-white depiction of a Ferrari covered in graffiti graced the far wall. My father's office hadn't been anywhere near as flashy, but partners at his firm had each decorated their offices in varying themes. Mom always loved how it gave the stuffy corporate attorneys a little bit of charisma. The offices here at Dillney, Forsythe & Lowe were more sterile in their uniformity, except for Andrew's, with its burst of personality. Sadly, I knew already that despite the decor, Andrew was just one more by-the-book lawyer. I felt myself starting to sweat in anticipation of our conversation.

"All righty then," he finally said, placing his phone on the desk and sitting up straighter in his chair. "What can I do for you?" He motioned to one of the two purple leather chairs opposite him, and I dutifully sat down.

"I've been working on this pro bono immigration case," I started.

Andrew nodded, but his eyes slid over to one of his computer screens. He was already losing interest at the mention of a non-billable matter. I decided to get straight to the point.

"I think I've uncovered a pattern of serious medical abuse at the detention facility, and I want to file a class action suit. That's why I'm here, for authorization."

Andrew leaned back in his chair and let out a long, slow breath.

"Jessa." He said the one word like it answered everything.

"Please, just hear me out." A droplet of sweat trickled between my breasts, and I was glad I'd worn a dark high-necked blouse. I should have known he'd try to shut me down from the get-go.

"You're on the Witlock matter, and you're basically running the show on Everson Towels and Matherson's negotiation. It just doesn't make sense," he said, steepling his fingers and leaning even farther back. He regarded me a moment and then continued. "Now that you're thriving again, to put you back into the limelight like that, especially when you're in the middle of another negotiation . . . We can't do it." He shook his head as he finished.

I'd prepared myself for him to bring up Shantrane, expecting him to point to that case during our meeting. I just hadn't expected him to get there so quickly.

"It was four years ago, Andrew," I said, echoing Vance's words from the night before. Shantrane had been one of our most important clients, and four years earlier, I'd been quite proud of myself when, at only twenty-seven years old, I'd been staffed as one of the leads on the matter. I spent months working with them on a complex negotiation, and when I finally got the other side to agree to Shantrane's patently unreasonable demands, I'd been a star of the firm.

But then I'd accidentally sent the opposing side an earlier draft of the agreement to sign, not the final version. Both parties signed before our client or anyone at the firm realized the error. The client was stuck with terms significantly less favorable than the ones they'd have gotten had I just double-checked the attachment to one email. Not surprisingly, the firm swiftly lost Shantrane as a client, and I lost all the respect I'd been working so hard to earn.

I would have been fired at another firm, but Andrew's longtime friendship with my father saved me. Andrew arranged for me to keep my job so long as I kept myself under the radar with clients. Recently, after all this time had passed, and with the solid work I'd produced, I thought I'd finally gotten back to a place of trust and esteem with my colleagues. But not making partner, and the current furrow to Andrew's brow, said otherwise.

"Our firm has a reputation to uphold, one you greatly jeopardized the last time you were the lead on such a high-profile case."

"I understand. I really do. And I'm grateful for the chance you've given me to prove what I can do. But this case is more important than reputation." Speaking slowly, I said, "Women in federal custody are having their uteruses removed without their consent, Andrew."

He flinched at my words, surprise and horror flashing across his features. I was desperate to make him understand the urgency of the situation. "It's forced sterilization. It's . . . it's . . . eugenics."

Instead of jumping to his feet to lead the charge like I would have hoped, he stared back at me stoically.

After a beat he asked, "You're basing this on what? You have proof you can show me?"

Even though I understood many of the senior attorneys at the firm had ceased taking me seriously, I'd been under the impression that Andrew still believed in me, that he thought I was an attorney worth nurturing and supporting. I needed to show him how very serious I was.

I began rattling off all that had been alleged by the women. As I listed one horrid detail after another, he returned to an upright position in his chair again, his gaze intensifying as if I actually had his attention now.

"But only one woman is willing to be named in the complaint?"

"So far," I answered. "Only one woman so far. But the others—I know I can get them on board once they know they're not alone. They're afraid of the retaliation. But with each one who steps up, I think others will follow. Meanwhile, this doctor, this butcher, is getting away with it."

Andrew went silent as he thought over my words. He stared blankly down at his desk, the way I'd seen him do so many times in the past. He would retreat into himself when he was parsing through complex issues until he came up with a solution. The longer he maintained that vacant stare, the more optimistic I began to feel.

"Please, Andrew. What if it were your daughter at risk?" The moment the words escaped my mouth, I wished I could take them back. It was the wrong thing to say. A man like Andrew could never envision his own daughter in a situation like this. He clammed up again and shook his head.

"I'm sorry, Jessa. It sounds like a worthwhile case, but I can't put our firm on the line like that. A case like this would be all over the news, and if it turns out you're wrong . . ." He let me fill in the blanks in my mind. "It's too big of a risk for the firm. You're talking about going after the federal government."

"That's exactly the point," I answered. "I have to bring the case, Andrew."

"I'm sorry, but for the sake of Dillney, Forsythe & Lowe, I can't let you do it." His tone said the matter was settled, but I refused to back down.

"What if I took a leave of absence?" I surprised myself with the suggestion, but suddenly I knew it was the right thing. "I could file the case on my own, as a solo practitioner. If I did that, would you let me come back? After the case was over?"

He let out a long sigh as he regarded me.

"Honestly? Depending on how it goes, this could become a very high-profile case. If you lose . . ." He trailed off, and I once again heard everything he wasn't saying. His lack of support was a surprising betrayal, his willingness to totally shut me down providing a rude awakening about where I actually stood with him. I waited, determined that I wouldn't make this easier on him.

"Jessa," he said, his voice tired, "if the press decided the case was some kind of political move or a wild-goose chase, it'd be too much of a liability. Especially with the bad press after Shantrane, all of it focused on the same one attorney. Clients would wonder why we kept you on, and it'd weaken trust in the firm."

"Well, then I guess it's a good thing I won't lose," I said.

"You're really willing to take that chance?" Andrew asked. "You think this is what your father would want?"

I felt a burst of anger that he'd bring my dad into this, especially when he knew how important my father was to me.

But maybe it was exactly the right question.

"This is definitely what my father would want," I answered, realizing as I said it that it was absolutely the truth. I pictured my dad telling me to count off in my head, and I felt new strength. "I won't lose," I repeated, as much of a promise as it was a wish.

"I really hope you're right, Jessa. At least this time."

Carrie

November 1924

We went over to the Amherst County courthouse on a day so cold that the air came up and bit you. The wind was like pins and needles against the skin, the sting of it so unusual for autumn in Virginia. Even so, I was glad for the opportunity to be outside the walls of the Colony. Laying my eyes on new scenery felt like enough of a gift, even if my knees shook with the chill of the day.

The novelty continued when we stepped inside the courtroom, where I saw one face after another that was unfamiliar to me. There was a buzz of conversation throughout the room, as men dressed in fine suits milled about in the aisle and others shoved themselves into the rows of wooden seats. Mr. Whitmore, that bareheaded lawyer they gave me, he took me by the elbow and steered me toward a table up front, showing me where I was meant to sit. He was dressed in a charcoal wool suit, all gussied up for the occasion, while I was still in my regular uniform from the Colony. They'd given me a scratchy dark coat to wear for the day that was far too small for my frame, but even as my shoulders pinched beneath, I didn't remove it. The ratty dress underneath was worse to look at, for sure. As I lowered myself into the empty chair, I felt eyes on me from all around the room. I tried not to be nervous or to let myself wonder why it was I had to be the one at the center of all this fuss.

After some time, they called the court to order, and everyone got real quiet as the potbellied judge tromped in wearing a black cape over his clothing. He sat himself at a big desk up front, and then up shot Mr. Aubrey Strode, the lawyer for Dr. Preston. Also dressed in a fine-looking dark suit, the man looked fairly similar to Mr. Whitmore, except for the heavy dark hair on his head that was combed neatly to the side. He explained who he was and told the judge all about how wonderful a place the Colony was, and what good care they provided their patients.

"Your Honor," he said after he'd been speaking for some time, pausing to pull his suit jacket in around his middle, buttoning it back into place. "The girl before you today is feebleminded and must be sexually sterilized for both her own good and the good of society. She's part of the lowest grade of the moron class. The evidence is clear that these regrettable traits pass from one generation to the next. We needn't leave the fine, upstanding citizens of Virginian society saddled with the financial and moral responsibility of caring for additional mental defectives. There is a straightforward, affordable, and humane method through which to cleanse society of this burden, and we are today in a position to avail ourselves of its benefits." He looked around the courtroom, meeting eyes with many of the folks who were sitting and listening. "And I'd wager the good people here in this room today would thank us for saving them from such a drain on their resources."

I wanted to stand up and holler at the man that I would take responsibility for my own babies perfectly well, thank you very much. I'd tell everyone in that courtroom about how I'd cared for Doris and Roy when I was barely more than a baby myself. But my lawyer, Mr. Whitmore, he'd already told me I had to sit quiet and not call out, no matter what.

Mr. Strode wasn't finished anyhow. He began pacing to and fro in front of the judge.

"I'll tell you what we can do, Your Honor," he said, a proud smile on his face, like he knew the answer to everything. "It's called a salpingectomy. A simple procedure that Dr. Preston can perform without any risk to life or limb." He gestured toward where I sat. Our eyes met, and it was all I could do not to spit at him. "Afterward, girls like Miss Buck can be rehabilitated. Instead of remaining locked up for all her reproductive years, which could stretch as far as three more decades, she can be trained and made ready to rejoin society on some moderately productive level."

After he finally finished harping on about all the reasons why a person like me shouldn't be allowed a child, he invited up someone named Millie Hart, a primly dressed woman about Ma's age. He said she was a nurse. As the woman climbed into the box up front, I felt sure I didn't recognize her, and I wondered if she worked at the Colony. To my surprise, she told everyone in the courtroom that she'd known me for more than a decade.

"Yes, I knew the mother, Emma, even better than I knew little Carrie all those years ago," Miss Hart told the lawyer. "The mother, she was on the charity list. Well, on and off, but mostly on."

Mr. Strode asked her then, "And could you tell this court how Emma Buck's mind was, if you would consider her feebleminded?"

Miss Hart nodded like she'd been waiting for just that question. "That woman behaved no better than a twelve-year-old girl. Socially irresponsible and morally deficient. So yes, feebleminded sounds just right."

"No more questions, Your Honor," said Mr. Strode.

As he sat back in his chair at the table across from ours, I hoped now was the time my lawyer would stand and defend me—tell everyone all the ways in which I could prove I was not of any feeble sort of mind.

Mr. Whitmore pushed back his chair. As he stood, my heart banged loud against my chest while I waited to hear what he'd say.

"Miss Hart, how well are you acquainted with my client, Carrie Buck?"

That's right, I thought to myself. *He'll show them how that woman doesn't know a darn thing about me.*

"Well, I didn't see as much of her after she went off to live with that other family. I know she was poor and at times unruly. I did hear she made a problem in her school, that she was badly behaved, inferior in her appearance. And there was an incident involving passing a note with a boy."

"And would you call all young girls who pass a note at school feebleminded?" Mr. Whitmore asked.

"Well, that depends on what they put inside the note." Then she pursed her lips tight like she didn't want to say another word about that.

"Anything else you can tell us about the girl?"

"Well, like I said, her mother was of dubious morals. I wouldn't repeat in polite company the sort of things that were suggested about her." The woman's eyes shifted to the side, and she looked at the judge before turning her attention back to Mr. Whitmore.

"No further questions, Your Honor."

As my lawyer made his way back to the chair beside me, I thought maybe I'd misunderstood why Mr. Whitmore was there with me. I turned in my seat to ask why he'd stopped with his questions so soon, but he just held a finger to his lips, reminding me to keep quiet. Shame on me, but I did as he said, afraid as I was of doing anything to make things worse.

Next, Mr. Strode brought up three different teachers to talk about my behavior in school. Not one of those teachers knew me;

they admitted as much themselves. But they told Mr. Strode that I was known to be dull. A "misfit," one of them said. My neck got hot listening to the way they described me. Maybe it was true that I'd kept too much to myself at school, making room only for Billy, but it didn't seem fair to call me dull, especially not all these years later. Weren't lots of children at school shy sometimes?

Finally, they called up someone I did recognize: Caroline Fillmore, the pretty nurse from the Red Cross who'd brought me to the Colony when I left Charlottesville. She climbed into the box and put her hands neatly in her lap.

"Why was it, Miss Fillmore, that Mr. Dobbs wanted you to accompany Carrie to Lynchburg?" Mr. Strode asked her.

"Oh, he wanted her committed," she said matter-of-fact. "He had come to the welfare office to report that the girl ought to be in state custody on account of the fact she'd gotten herself pregnant. He said he wouldn't keep a girl like that in his house for even one day longer."

"And what of Emma Buck, the mother?" he asked Miss Fillmore. "What do you know of her?"

"I know that Emma Buck has borne multiple illegitimate children." She didn't say whether she'd ever met Ma.

"And what do you know of Carrie Buck's illegitimate child?" At the mention of my Vivian, I sat myself up taller. "I understand you've seen her. Can you tell us what you observed?"

"I saw the child just recently, shortly before her eight-month birthday. The Dobbs family has agreed to raise the child, so long as they needn't house the unwed mother."

It was hard for me to imagine what Vivian must look like now, already eight months old. I wondered if she had any hair growing in yet, dark like mine or lighter like Doris. Did she have a pointy chin like her uncle Roy? Round cheeks like her granny Emma? The harder I tried to picture her face, the heavier sat the weight against my heart.

"And how did the baby seem when you examined her?" the lawyer asked.

"Not quite right."

Something was wrong with my baby? Was she sick? Sitting quiet in that seat then, instead of shouting out for more answers, was one of the hardest things I've ever done. I had to let them drone on, talking about where the nurse had earned her credentials and how long she'd had her job, while I waited so anxiously to find out more of what was the matter with my girl. I knew I had no choice, so I waited nervously to hear what she would say next.

"Returning to your impression of the Buck child," Mr. Strode finally said, "how could you tell something was off with it?"

"Well, the adult daughter in the Dobbs house, Loretta, she has a baby of her own about the same age as the Buck child. I was able to view the infants one beside the other, and there is simply a certain look to Miss Buck's baby."

"What kind of a look, exactly?" Mr. Strode asked.

She shrugged. "Just something . . . odd looking, not appealing like a baby should be."

Not appealing! That woman deserved a smack across her cheek. But Mr. Whitmore, he must have known I thought so, that I was maybe fixing to go at her, because he looked at me out of the corner of his eye. He held up a finger, waggling it back and forth to tell me to keep still.

I wasn't sure I could keep myself hushed like he wanted, not with them saying those things about Vivian. Maybe my baby girl was just feeling blue about being separated from her mother. Had they even thought of that? And what kind of attention was she getting in the Dobbs house anyway? I wanted to know. What if all the favor was going to Loretta's baby, leaving my girl little better than just fed and watered? That'd be enough to make any child forlorn.

When Mr. Strode said he was finished asking the nurse questions, Mr. Whitmore again pushed himself out from his chair. I thought surely this time he would do his job, if not to advocate for me, then at least to defend my poor Vivian.

"Have the record show," he said from where he still hovered beside his chair, "that all parties are here. Including Miss Buck's appointed guardian." Then he sat right back down and said no more.

In my shock at his behavior, I finally did shout out, this time at my own lawyer. "That's it?"

"Not now," was all he said, patting my arm to shush me.

"But aren't you going to ask any questions?" I protested.

"Carrie, enough! You'll hurt your case." He looked at me so fiercely that I clamped my mouth shut.

Then Mr. Strode said, "I'd like to call to the stand Mr. Harry Laderdale."

From the back of the room rose a man so handsome that I felt certain he must be good on the inside too. With a head full of dark, bouncy curls and blue eyes that looked to be sparkling with delight, it seemed impossible that he could be there as anything other than a helper, someone who would protect me.

After the man settled into the witness seat and stated his name, Mr. Laderdale said, "I have served as the superintendent of the Eugenics Record Office in Cold Spring Harbor, New York, since it opened in 1910."

"And what is it you do over there at that office?"

"Quite a bit, in fact." He smiled widely like he'd made a joke. "We are at the forefront of the research on eugenics, studying the effects of ancestry on hereditary traits and promoting race betterment." I didn't understand what-all type of work he did, but from the way his chest puffed out as he spoke, I could tell he was right proud of himself for it.

"Can you elaborate on what you mean by the word *eugenics?*" Mr. Strode asked, and I guessed I wasn't the only confused one in the room.

"Of course. Through the study and practice of eugenics, we can improve the composition of the entire population of this country and beyond. If we encourage reproduction of the brightest, healthiest individuals among us, we will propagate strong, capable, attractive humans. It follows naturally that limiting reproduction of the weaker, less intelligent, less fit individuals will eventually lead to the extinction of their undesirable traits. So long as we discourage activities that could potentially dilute a superior gene pool."

As Mr. Laderdale talked on about science and breeding, I set to stewing about that Red Cross woman and what she'd said about Vivian. I could hardly even pay attention to the conversation between those two men. Mr. Strode was asking Mr. Laderdale all manner of questions about science and passing behaviors down from generation to generation. They weren't even talking about me anymore, so I stopped listening, thinking instead about Vivian and what she must be doing every day over there at the Dobbs house. I supposed Mrs. Alice thought looking after Vivian somehow made up for what she and Mr. John had done to me. I wondered if they had my baby sleeping in that same little alcove off the kitchen where they'd once put me, or if maybe they'd created a nursery for both Vivian and Loretta's baby. Even if they didn't want to admit it, Vivian was one of their relations. I imagined a bassinet with yellow butterflies painted on the wood.

When I heard Mr. Laderdale mention breeding cattle, the words caught in my ear and brought me back from my musings. It seemed awfully odd for them to be discussing animal husbandry. With his crisp collar and polished cuff links, Mr. Laderdale hardly looked like the type of man who'd know a lick about farming.

"Farmers do not breed the runts," he was saying. "It even bears out with crops. Agriculturalists always replant with the best seed. The human race is the only one remaining that has not tried to weed out the unfit before allowing the weaklings—the duds, if you will—to create additional inferior beings."

"I see, I see," Mr. Strode responded, nodding along. "And what is the reason you are so invested in this process?"

"It's my life's mission to create a superior human race," Mr. Laderdale answered solemnly. "Think what we could do for American society if we could cleanse it of deviance, defect, and anomaly. Not just physically abnormal like cripples and dwarves and such, but all forms of undesirables could gradually be bred out. From vagrants to epileptics, even loose women and sodomites. The standard of intelligence throughout the country would increase," he continued. "Crime would be reduced, and taxpayer money would be saved in myriad ways. This is why I've written the model sterilization law, on which Virginia has based its new statute."

"Ah!" said the lawyer, as if Mr. Laderdale had said something of great importance. "Can you tell us: What is the purpose of this model sterilization law?"

Mr. Laderdale smiled wide, looking quite pleased to get to explain another thing. "Well, the law provides for the sexual sterilization of the feebleminded, insane, criminalistic, epileptic, inebriate, diseased, blind, deaf, deformed, and dependent, which also includes orphans, tramps, and paupers."

They talked at length then about the words of the law and how it was meant to work. When Mr. Strode finally finished, my lawyer stood again. Mr. Whitmore objected that the man had talked too much about laws, which were outside of his expertise.

After his objection was noted, my lawyer said, "Let's now move back to the plaintiff." Was he finally, *finally* going to fight back for me?

"Let us say, just for the sake of argument, Mr. Laderdale, that everything said here today about Carrie Buck and why she ought to be sexually sterilized is correct—that she is morally degenerate, feebleminded, of limited capabilities, and all the rest. Let's imagine she is sterilized and released from the Colony. Perhaps she will even be taught to be passably productive in some useful occupation before she is let out. Once she is on the outside, will she not resume her promiscuous behavior? Is she not likely to pick up venereal disease and then spread it? Haven't we heard today that such conditions can be so easily caught by women like her? How would letting her go around giving men syphilis be of any benefit to society?"

I stood and shouted before I could stop myself.

"I don't have syphilis!"

The two orderlies who had come with us from the Colony were instantly upon me, pushing me back into my seat.

"Please forgive the interruption, Your Honor." Mr. Whitmore turned his back toward me again, as if I didn't matter at all. "Your answer, Mr. Laderdale?"

"Well, I'd say those men would likely be getting what they deserved," the witness scoffed. "Promiscuous women can spread such diseases whether they're sterilized or not."

"Fine. Then tell me more about the procedure you espouse. Doesn't the law prohibit removing organs from the body unnecessarily?" Mr. Whitmore asked.

"Nothing is taken out. Only a cut is made," the scientist answered.

"And then the organ is destroyed?" Mr. Whitmore asked.

"No." Mr. Laderdale looked up at the judge. "The nip simply removes a pathway for the egg to reach its destination. It only prevents reproduction."

"Can you tell us then," said Mr. Whitmore, "why Dr. Preston has chosen Miss Carrie Buck for sterilization?"

"Well, she's the perfect candidate, you see. She's eighteen years old, which means she could continue reproducing for decades yet. To prevent such a thing, she would need to remain in state custody for all that time, costing the state nearly two hundred dollars a year in the meanwhile. Conversely, with the salpingectomy surgery, we'd remove that possibility. She'd heal up in no time, could reenter society, and have her liberty restored, such as it would be for a person like her. She can be sterilized without any detriment to her general health, and with great benefit to her future and society overall."

Mr. Whitmore began to ask another question but was interrupted because the witness had more to say.

"Miss Buck has borne already one mentally defective child. She has a chronological age of eighteen, but mentally, she displays the age of a child of only nine years. Is this what we want? Nine-year-olds having babies that become wards of the state, only to repeat the cycle generation after generation? Perhaps it's time we all agree that three generations of imbeciles is enough."

"And then what?" Mr. Whitmore asked. "After the operation."

"I've seen this procedure performed on more than eighty women nationwide. Now, near sixty of those same patients are out in the world, working for upstanding folk, engaging in occupations as seamstresses, hotel workers, and such. Without the operation, such inmates must remain locked up, draining resources that could be put to better use. Listen," he said, sounding frustrated that he had to keep explaining something that was so obvious to him. "These people belong to an ignorant, unindustrious, useless class of contaminated whites. There is no reason to allow them to replicate themselves when we have the means to stop it."

I wanted to argue about so much. The way that man had said I had the brain of a nine-year-old, that I belonged to a lesser class of people. But hearing him say I didn't deserve to make more babies, it just made me feel so hopeless. I was beginning to understand that there wouldn't be any point to me arguing, so I just sat there waiting for it all to be over.

When they finally wound down their conversation, the judge said Mr. Whitmore could bring in witnesses of his own to talk against the sterilization. But Mr. Whitmore said he didn't have anyone to bring up, that we were finished. I was tired from the long day of listening to people drone on, so I was relieved to hear it. I stood and stretched my back. As I twisted and turned my gaze over my shoulder, my eye caught sight of Mr. Laderdale over near the exit. He was shaking hands with another fellow, smiling and chatting away. He must have felt someone watching, because his eyes suddenly landed right on me, and our gazes met from across the room. It was the first moment he'd looked me in the eye all that day, I realized, and I recoiled at the connection. He didn't keep focus long, but turned right back to the men crowding round him—as if I could have been any other person in the crowd, someone he didn't know from Adam. I couldn't hear what he was saying over the din of voices, but I could still see him plain as day as he threw back his head and bellowed with laughter. His shoulders shook so hard from mirth, it almost looked like he was having a seizure. For all his complaints about my mental stability, he looked like the true lunatic among us.

Jessa

March 2022

I slammed my laptop shut and fought to catch my breath. Nothing Gram told me had been true.

I'd just finished reading the trial court record from Carrie Buck's case. After telling Andrew Hendricks that I was taking a leave of absence to represent the women of Hydeford, I thought it'd be fortifying to learn more about my own great-grandparent who'd put himself on the line with similar goals. But when I tracked down the witness testimony from the case, I discovered that my long-fabled, heroic grandpa Harry had actually done just the opposite. He'd ruthlessly and intentionally destroyed any chance she'd had.

My phone battery was running low, so I riffled through my desk drawer to find my portable charger. I pushed aside a tube of hand cream, a little troll doll my nephew gave me the year before, and a container of almonds that were probably too old to eat. Had I not been so focused on the sickening revelations of the past hour, I might have gotten nostalgic about all the ways I'd made this little space mine over the years—my framed degree certificates hanging on the wall, photos of Vance and me on my desk. But I was in too much of a fog. I barely managed to shove the charger in my tote, grab my travel coffee mug, and hurry toward the elevator.

When I finally reached Gram's apartment and let myself in, I found her standing at the stove, wearing an old floral apron and stirring a saucepan full of meatballs.

"Jessa!" she said with delight in her voice. "What a nice surprise." But then she took in the look on my face and her smile dropped.

"You told me he was a hero," I said.

She stayed frozen for a moment. Then the meaning of my words settled on her, and she nodded almost imperceptibly. Reaching toward the knob and twisting it to turn off the burner, she said, "I suppose we'd better go sit on the couch."

I followed her numbly to the old striped sofa in the living room, the mint and powder-blue hues that had always been so familiar suddenly seeming foreign and strange to me.

"Why?" I didn't even know how to phrase the rest of the question even though I had so much to ask.

"I wanted to tell you," Gram said as she reached out for my hand, but she seemed to think better of it and took hold of her own hand instead.

"I Googled him," I said. Oh, how I wished I could unlearn what I had read on the internet about Harry Laderdale all afternoon.

"I was going to tell you after your first meeting at Hydeford. But then I realized there was no reason to ruin the beautiful image you've always had of my father, how much you've savored your impression of who he was. That day we went walking, I was planning to come clean, but then I looked at you with your cheeks pinking up in the cold, your dark curls bouncing just like Grandpa Harry's, and I lost my nerve. I wanted you to know how important the Buck case was to your legacy without taking anything away from you."

"Take anything away from *me?*" I snapped. "Have you read the testimony? You told me he saved Carrie Buck. Are you kidding me? He put every last nail in her coffin!"

"Yes, I'm aware," Gram said, managing to keep her composure despite my obvious outrage.

But then an air of resignation settled over her. She got a faraway look in her eye and started talking.

"Some of my earliest childhood memories are from glamorous affairs where my father was the guest of honor. My mother would put me in a party dress to match my sister, Faye. How Faye hated to have me following her around in an identical dress." She smiled fondly at the recollection of her long-deceased sister. "Other times we'd have to stay home, and my parents would come back at the end of their evening smelling of champagne and cigarettes and success."

I'd already heard this bit about Gram's childhood, about her family attending wonderful parties, but it was dawning on me that I'd never been told anything about the hosts or other guests. And I'd never thought to wonder. I'd pictured Gatsbyesque events in my head—pearls and flapper dresses, cigarette smoke and champagne glasses, all being enjoyed against a backdrop of art deco furnishings. But now those images were tainted by my knowledge that Gram's family had gained all that finery at the expense of so many other tragedies.

Her tone shifted as she began to tell a new part of the story.

"Everything was different after the war. Attitudes changed, and my father was no longer viewed as a luminary. Especially after Nuremberg, people understood. My father's findings . . ." She paused and swallowed hard. "Well, his findings were credited with being a major influence behind the Third Reich's notion of a master race."

I sucked in a sharp breath. Even though I'd read as much earlier, hearing the words straight from Gram's mouth was so much worse.

"The Eugenics Record Office got shut down," she continued resolutely. "So he lost his job as director. No more requests to serve as an expert witness like in the Buck trial, no more payments for his testimony. Certainly no more parties. By the time I was a teenager, he was struggling to support us. Faye and I had been cast out by our friends at school and even by some teachers. But the worst was when Faye got sick and we couldn't find a local doctor willing to treat her. That was when we finally moved and changed our name. The Laderdale family became the Larsons."

She met my eyes again as she finished, and I just stared back at her, absorbing the weight of her words.

Finally, I asked, "What about the medical clinic he ran? Was that even real?"

She nodded again. "He was a scientist, not a doctor, but that didn't prevent him from starting the center. He managed it all, but he wasn't a clinician like I may have implied. Just the supervisor."

"May have implied," I said, repeating her words. How thoroughly I'd been misled. Gram opened her mouth to respond, but I interrupted her. "Did my parents know?"

"It wasn't appropriate information to share with a twelve-year-old girl. You shouldn't feel any sense of betrayal that they didn't tell you."

That wasn't what I'd been thinking so much as wondering how my mother had dealt with the information.

"The honest truth," Gram said as she fiddled with an apron string, "is that I whitewashed it a bit for your parents too. I wanted them to know, but I saw no reason to give them all the gory details."

"And now what am I supposed to tell Vance?" I demanded. "I hadn't even worked up the nerve to tell him that Grandpa

Harry had changed his last name, that he'd lost a job over this case. Oh my God, this is so much worse than losing a job!" And then I thought of something even more problematic. "Gram, his podcast."

She opened her mouth to answer, but I interrupted.

"His whole platform is about authenticity, uncovering items lost in the Holocaust, righting the wrongs of the past. But look who he married!"

She tilted her head at me, her lips folding in disappointment, as if I was being childish or foolish.

"What?" I demanded.

"Why would you even consider telling him?" she asked.

"What? How can I not tell him something like this?" Somehow, I was still surprised by her bias for secrecy, even after the decades she'd spent keeping me in the dark.

"There's no benefit, Jessa, to either of you. I know it feels uncomfortable, keeping these things to yourself, but trust me when I tell you it's a kindness to protect him from it. I'm only sorry you have this burden to bear now. I wish I could have taken the information with me to the grave."

"Even if you hadn't told me, it wouldn't change anything. I'd still be the descendant of a monster."

"Jessa," she snapped at me. "He was my father."

"And he did terrible things! And now the consequences of all that—*that's* my legacy."

"No." She reached for my wrist, a fierceness in her voice. "The evil he did does not negate the good. People can be many things. Altruistic clinic directors, loving fathers, and yes, also bigoted, racist, intolerant scientists responsible for great tragedies. Your legacy will be what you make it, and that is why you are defending these women, so the footprint you leave behind in the world is the exact opposite of the one my father left."

Could I really keep something like this from Vance? Just stash it away in a locked compartment in my brain?

But it wasn't just Vance I'd be lying to. His whole family would feel this was important information, something that should have been shared with them. If they found out I was keeping this awful news a secret, they'd hate me for the secrecy, never mind for the information itself. Images of my in-laws, Renee and Howard, flashed through my head. I thought of Vance's brothers and their wives, especially Jiyana and the boys. Over time, they might be able to get over my connection to Harry Laderdale, but Vance was a different story.

"It's so much more complicated with Vance," Gram said, as if she'd heard my thoughts. She knew how deeply Vance had loved his own grandfather, how profoundly he would hate that I was related to someone who'd had any part in causing the man's pain. Or maybe she was thinking of the podcast and how my connections might undermine Vance's success, even if only in his own mind. "I just don't see what you'd gain by telling him."

"It feels too huge. How can I lie to him like this when we're trying to have a baby together, Gram?"

"Sometimes," she said, "we seek to reveal secrets so we can unburden ourselves, when in fact we're only putting the burden on someone else. Sharing that information wouldn't add to the good in the world; it would just undermine your relationship with your husband. If you love Vance as much as you say you do, why would you want to upset him about all this?"

I didn't want to upset him. I'd done plenty enough of that recently as it was. Maybe Gram was right, that keeping this to myself would be a kindness to him, and to the rest of his family too.

"You told Grandpa Walt though, didn't you?"

"Yes," she said. "But it was a different time. Of course he thought the research was awful, the whole idea of eugenics. But he came at it from a different place. Nothing about the Holocaust, or even the war, had touched Grandpa's family. He couldn't trace any of his own family tragedies back to Harry Laderdale. It won't do any good for you to show Vance that he can."

I thought about how things might play out once I told Vance even a portion of what I'd learned, how he'd chart a path back from the present straight through history, just like he did for people seeking stolen artifacts, until he knew every last horrible detail. The bond he and I shared felt increasingly fragile these days, and I wasn't sure we could withstand more stress between us. If keeping the information to myself could protect our relationship, I supposed it was worth it.

~

The next morning, Vance directed the old Subaru down a narrow, pebbly road in Brookville, Long Island. The car was a hand-me-down gifted to us by Vance's dad, Howard, years earlier. We had resisted at first, telling Howard that we'd never need a car in the city. But the car came in handy more often than we'd expected, not just for driving to professional obligations outside Manhattan, but also for excursions like this one, visiting Vance's cousin Dalia and her husband, Yuval, who'd moved to the suburbs.

As we made our way closer to the right house, every bump and jolt caused me to grimace. I was thinking about Vance's sperm, which had been inside my body since we'd had sex earlier that morning. I hoped the jostling wasn't making it more difficult for one or two special swimmers to reach their intended target, that the bouncing wasn't interfering with their goal.

It had been two days since my meeting with Andrew, and I still hadn't worked up the nerve to tell Vance that I was taking a leave of absence from the firm. I thought about how I'd arrived at this place, keeping so much hidden from my husband. Maybe that's just who I was now, a person who kept secrets. I wondered if I should stop beating myself up about it and instead embrace the idea of being a cagey, elusory person. I let out a loud breath, and Vance looked over at me.

"I have to tell you something," I said.

"Uh-oh . . . ," he said lightheartedly, as if nothing I said could possibly upset him.

"I'm taking a leave of absence from work."

He beamed at me. "That's amazing. Why do you look like it's terrible news?"

"It's amazing?" I asked, feeling hopeful that I had misjudged how he'd react.

"Yeah. You can finally take some time for yourself, de-stress like I've been saying. I'm glad we're in agreement now. It's the right thing for you."

"Vance."

Before I said more, I started to wonder if maybe I didn't have to. Maybe I could keep the entire immigration case a secret from him and let him think I was actually taking the leave he wanted for me, a few quiet months to rest. If I was embracing my dishonest side, maybe it was time to go big or go home, as Vance himself liked to say. But it was a ridiculous thought. With any luck, this case would be all over the news, and I would be working so hard that doing the whole project on the sly would be impossible. Besides, I didn't actually want to embrace my duplicitous side. The whole point was to avoid creating any more secrets than those I'd already squirreled away.

"I'm taking the leave," I said, "because the firm won't let me file a class action for the Hydeford women."

"It's probably for the best that the firm's letting it go, given how much evidence you're still lacking. Even if you have enough to support the claim of substandard medical care, that doesn't prove the part about unnecessary sterilizations. Look, do I think the women should have been given more information before their procedures? Yeah, seems like it. Could the doctor have done a better job explaining the risks or making sure interpreters were present? Yes and yes. I admit that something concerning is going on, but the facts you have don't prove any intent to do harm or even that the procedures were not medically necessary, lifesaving interventions."

I couldn't believe he was still refusing to get behind me. I wanted to grab him by the collar and shake him for insisting that I had to be missing something. What I was missing, it seemed, was the supportive husband I thought I had.

"Evidence isn't the problem. We'll get that. It's me. It's because I'd be the one bringing the case. The firm doesn't want my name front and center on another case that may end up in the news." I felt a fresh wave of shame, thinking about the partners' opinion of me, their persistent reluctance to take me seriously, an attitude that had reached more of my colleagues than I'd ever realized.

"I mean, I'm not sure *I* want your name front and center in the news about this either. You're not the only person whose reputation would be affected, and with the podcast—"

"Vance!" I turned toward him in my seat, ready to lay into him, but he held up a hand like a stop sign.

"Hear me out," he said. "Why don't they just put another attorney on the lead? If they believe someone is actually orchestrating the sterilization of all these women?" His tone was fanciful, as if that intentionality was an utter impossibility, as if he were talking about ghosts or time travel. "Shouldn't somebody put a stop to it?"

"Right. Which is why I'm taking the leave. Because the case needs to be filed. And if I'm working on my own, I don't need anyone's permission." I wanted to add, *Not even yours, Vance.*

"On your own? But if they give it to someone else at Dillney, there can still be more investigating, which you could skip. And then if it turns out it's more than just chasing shadows, whoever did the investigating could bring the case, and you wouldn't have to risk your spot at the firm. You can just work on something else."

"No." I shook my head, knowing we were treading closer to matters I didn't want to discuss. "It has to be me."

"Why? Plenty of attorneys at your office could handle it."

The chances of another attorney at the firm following up seriously were slim at best. As Andrew had made clear in our meeting, the expectation at Dillney was to focus on billable hours and career advancement. If I handed off the case, it'd be a matter of weeks before the whole thing fizzled and died. I wasn't going to abandon my clients like that.

"Because . . ." I struggled to answer Vance, wondering how to tell him the universe had sent this case to me specifically, how it had everything to do with what Gram had shared with me about my family's past. "It just does. It has to be me."

"What about your salary? You're not going to get paid? Don't you see how rash you're being?"

I huffed audibly before answering.

"We have plenty saved. Even without your ridiculous Wall Street salary, we could live off savings for six months."

"So it's only for six months then? No matter what?"

I clenched my teeth and turned toward the window. Looking into the seemingly endless thicket of trees along the side of the road, I tried to choose the right words, but Vance spoke first.

"Let me guess. They'll only take you back if it goes well."

"Yup."

"So what you're saying"—his voice began to rise—"is that you'll be working twice as hard, earning nothing, and adding even more stress to your system. All for something that might not even be happening?"

"Precisely," I deadpanned.

When he didn't respond, I turned toward him with a sheepish expression, hoping he could just accept this.

"Jessa, this isn't a joke!"

"Trust me." My words came out clipped. "I'm well aware."

Vance's neck began to turn pink, a telltale sign that he was fuming. He seemed to be running through all the different things he wanted to say, trying to choose where to start, and I braced for the impact of hurtful words. But then I saw a marker for house number 1799 at the end of the road, the lively blue and yellow hues of the painted mailbox so at odds with the weight of the moment we were having.

"It's there." I pointed.

Vance swallowed and turned into the partially hidden gravel driveway. Once we rounded the first bend, we could see Vance's cousin's new home. An oversized colonial with brown shingles, gray shutters, and three symmetrical dormers, it was every bit the quaint pastoral retreat that would inspire a young couple to finally move from Manhattan to the suburbs. It was a place where parents could raise a growing family in the fresh open air, admiring lightning bugs and bunny rabbits on summer nights. I tried not to be jealous of the perfection of it all.

Vance pulled to a stop outside the two-car garage and moved the gearshift into Park without looking at me.

"Come on," he said, his words tight as he opened his door. "We're already twenty minutes late." He was out of his seat in a flash, slamming the car door with significantly more force than necessary before starting toward the front door. I hadn't even taken off my seat belt yet.

After emitting a frustrated huff, I climbed out of the car too, grabbing the cheesecake we'd picked up at the bakery on our way to the Midtown Tunnel. The gravel crunched under my sneakers as I scrambled to catch up to Vance. I'd misjudged the day's weather, and the cool March air made me shudder under my denim jacket. I reached the top step just as the front door swung open, revealing Vance's cousin Dalia and her three-year-old daughter, Sadie.

"You're here!" Dalia held out her arms in apparent joy. Even with her blond hair and fair complexion, Vance's cousin still looked so much like him. She had the same heart-shaped face with its broad forehead and cheekbones, the same full lips and button nose, and the same penetrating stare that could make a person feel like they mattered more than anyone else on earth. I liked to joke that Dalia was simply "hot-girl Vance." Except, looking at Dalia now, I realized how long it had been since Vance had fixed me with that signature gaze, the look that said nothing other than me was on his mind. It brought more clearly into focus how much our relationship had changed since I'd stopped trying to fit so neatly into his idea of perfection.

I pasted a broad smile on my face and gushed, "This house is enormous!"

Dalia's movie star–handsome husband, Yuval, appeared in the foyer behind them, an unopened can of artisanal seltzer in his hand.

"It took you two long enough," he said in his thick Israeli accent. "Six months since we moved, and only just now you come?" He smiled to show he was teasing, pushing the door wider and ushering us inside.

After Dalia took the bakery box from my hands, I bent down toward Sadie.

"Hey, sweet girl." I tugged lightly on one of her brown braids. "Will you show me all the best parts of your new house?"

"I'm getting a new baby," the girl answered.

"Oh?" I looked up at Dalia.

Dalia smiled and nodded, putting a hand to her still-flat abdomen. "It's early days still, but . . . yeah. I guess we're having another one." She shrugged like she didn't even know how it had happened.

"That's the best news!" I tried so hard to sound genuine despite the wave of jealousy in my gut. As I wrapped Dalia in a tight hug, I was horrified by my selfish, immature reaction to her happy news. I marveled at how everywhere I looked, every last thing suddenly seemed to be about babies. God seemed to be taunting me, making me think about reproduction all day every day, all while withholding the grand prize. Maybe it really was karma, a curse on my family. I'd never been into supernatural ideas, but current circumstances had me reconsidering.

"Mazels." Vance reached out to fist-bump Yuval. "That's awesome for you guys." His smile looked sincere, even as he seemed to be avoiding my eyes.

After a grand tour of the home, including the multiple empty bedrooms that I imagined would soon be filled with a whole gaggle of button-nosed babies, we all settled into the kitchen to enjoy the spread Dalia had prepared for lunch.

Yuval sat beside Sadie, carving her grilled cheese sandwich into bite-sized pieces and trying to convince the cherub-faced girl to eat. Meanwhile, I listened to Vance and Dalia at the other side of the table, catching up on the various members of their extended family. In between bites of avocado salad and poached salmon, Dalia told Vance all about how Uncle Mort was dating a woman half his age and their cousin Lydia was finally moving back from Sweden. Dalia's younger sister, Naomi, had just accepted a position as an exhibition manager at the US Holocaust Memorial Museum in Washington DC.

At the reference to the Holocaust, I tensed. I shouldn't have been surprised that someone would mention it. The Holocaust had a way of coming up at nearly every single visit with Vance's family, whether as a passing mention or as material for yet another philosophical debate. Typically, I might chime in to make a comment or offer my own opinions, but now I felt like an interloper, a traitor. Long ago, I assured Vance that I'd be comfortable raising our children in the Jewish faith—but suddenly I wondered if I even had that right, given who I came from and everything he'd set in motion.

"The Holocaust Museum," Vance said, and I assumed he was going to mention the ways he'd collaborated with that institution for a few episodes of his podcast. The museum's international tracking system was a valuable tool for hunting down documentation pertaining to art and other heirlooms that had been stolen from families. But instead, Vance sighed. "That'll be pretty rough stuff, being confronted by the images in their exhibits day in and day out. It's different than just talking about it. Some of those photos . . ." He let out a loud exhale, shaking his head at the notion. "I'd never be able to face all that horror on a regular basis."

His words reconfirmed my decision to keep my secret to myself. I had no other choice. "Sounds like the perfect job for Naomi though," he continued. "She was always the most committed to our heritage out of all the cousins."

"Says the man who refuses to drink from anything other than his grandfather's sixty-year-old kiddush cup at Jewish holidays," Dalia said. Then she lowered her voice to imitate what Vance always said: "Because it's what Saba would have done."

"Touché." Vance laughed. "Well, still, this position makes so much more sense than the taxidermy she was doing at Natural History."

"Right?" Dalia popped a grape into her mouth. "Her senior thesis was on all the ways the world would have been different if the Holocaust had never happened. My dear sis has always been a crusader."

"I'm well aware," Vance said between bites of fish. Then he finally looked at me across the table. "Remember when you first met her?"

Naomi had been the only member of the extended family who'd taken issue with Vance dating a non-Jew, grilling me about my background and my plans for our future children. Vance had felt bad about his cousin's uncouth behavior, explaining over and over that their grandparents' experience in the Holocaust had traumatized the entire family. I didn't want him to start talking about all of that again, the specifics of what his grandparents had endured, the stories he'd grown up hearing.

"But what about you?" I asked Dalia, trying to change the subject. "What's the latest in your life? I mean, besides . . ." I motioned toward Dalia's stomach.

"Actually," Dalia said, her shoulders slumping, "I'm having an existential crisis, I think." She laughed lightly as she reached over to snag a piece of Sadie's grilled cheese for herself. "I finally found a job out here, but now with the new baby coming, I'm thinking of taking off a few years." She looked at Yuval, who nodded encouragingly.

"I keep telling her to do whatever she wants," he said. "It is her life, so it must be her decision. You agree?"

My eyes shot over to Vance, but he was happily spreading cream cheese on a bagel and nodding along.

"I just don't know," Dalia said, grimacing. "If I'm gone for too long, I'm afraid I won't be able to find a position when I'm ready."

"You just have to leave the right way," Vance said assuredly. "Shore up your contacts now, while you're still there, and then you could take some time away without too much detriment to your résumé. Just remember that you have a very marketable skill. I mean, people always need nurses, right?"

"You would think," Dalia answered. She reached for a platter of roasted vegetables in the center of the table and began serving herself some eggplant. "It certainly feels like the nurses run everything, like we're the only ones who actually know what's going on with any given patient."

With Dalia's words, I thought of the nurse at Hydeford. I had been meaning to track down the woman, but I'd gotten so caught up in the meeting with Jacinta and everything it revealed. Dalia was right though: The nurses always had the inside scoop. That woman at Hydeford clearly wanted to help. Otherwise, she never would have given me the note. I needed to find her again to see what else she was willing to share.

"Right, Jess?" Vance said.

"Sorry, what?" I hadn't heard anything over the din of my thoughts.

"That a nurse with Dalia's character traits will always be in demand." They all looked at me expectantly.

"Oh, yeah. Of course." That was a no-brainer. Dalia had an indescribable quality that made people want to share all their burdens with her because they somehow knew instinctively that she would do her very best to take care of them. "If all healthcare workers were as kind and selfless as Dalia, this world would be a much better place."

As we drove back toward Manhattan, this time with me at the wheel and Vance in the passenger seat, my thoughts felt like a collection of Ping-Pong balls bouncing in every direction. I had so many ideas and new questions as I considered how the nurse from the detention facility might be able to assist with the case. I tried to corral my herky-jerky thoughts and started to create an interview outline in my head. I wanted to know how long Hydeford had been using Dr. Choudry, whether Choudry was the only doctor performing gynecological surgeries for residents of the facility, if the sterilizations were openly discussed among supervisors or staff, and whether other medical abuses were being perpetrated on the incarcerated women. The list went on and on.

"I can smell those fumes," Vance said, interrupting my internal deliberations. "Just say it and get it over with." The edge had returned to his voice.

"Get what over with?" I glanced over at him and saw that his expression was strained, the corners of his mouth tilting down so pointedly that they were almost cartoonish. Turning my eyes back to the road, I told him, "I honestly have no idea what you're even talking about right now."

"You're just going to get more upset if you keep it inside, and I have too much work waiting at home to deal with this later. So go ahead, spill."

I started to worry he was talking about what Gram told me, that he could tell I was keeping something important from him. When I stalled, he said, "So you're not upset about Dalia and Yuval? It didn't bother you that they have another kid on the way?"

"Well, apparently it bothered *you*."

I leaned forward to punch the dial on the radio, and "Uptown Girl" came bursting through the speakers. I turned the knob to the right, raising the volume to drown out further conversation. I raised my eyebrows at Vance, who leaned his head back against the headrest and shut his eyes in frustration.

For the first time in a long time, I was focused on something other than getting pregnant—and I wanted to keep it that way. The questions I'd been asking myself about Hydeford were important, and I was trying to concentrate. Having to manage Vance's emotions on top of everything else required bandwidth I just didn't have. Let him stew in his own anger and resentment, so long as he kept quiet and let me think. I was finally feeling the smallest flicker of hope for the Hydeford case, and that was where my focus needed to be. Vance, and his ever-present need to be in charge, could wait.

A few days later, I was back at the detention facility. As I waited for Isobel in one of the private meeting rooms, I arranged my memo pad and pen on one side of the long white table. Then I walked back toward the closed door, peering out from the little glass window in its center. I was hoping for a glimpse of the blond nurse, an opportunity to get her full name at least, but the hallway was empty.

I stuck to my post by the door, shifting from one foot to the other as I waited. I reached up to the small silver hoop in my right ear, a modest, discreet piece of jewelry that I thought was appropriate for today's meeting, and pushed the backing more firmly into place. My eagerness to find the nurse was coming out in my every nervous fidget.

A moment later, Isobel rounded the corner with an unfamiliar male guard escorting her. My shoulders dipped as I moved back from the window, and I settled into my seat at the metal table. Any interaction with the elusive nurse would have to wait.

"Ma'am." The burly guard nodded as he brought Isobel into the room. "Buzz us when you're through." He motioned with his head toward the box on the wall before stepping out and closing the door.

Isobel was dressed in the same jumpsuit as usual, but she had her hair up in two buns at either side of her head, Princess Leia–style. The way she kept her shoulders pulled back and her chin tilted slightly toward the sky had me wondering whether that aura of strength she projected was as effortless as she made it seem. Or maybe it was a crucial component of surviving in a place like Hydeford. As she sat down in the opposite chair, she looked at me expectantly.

"Everything is prepped and ready for your hearing," I told her. "But that's not why I'm here this time."

Isobel's top lip twisted, and she shook her head slowly, like she was disappointed in me.

"I knew you were going to come back here asking about my personal business. I don't have anything else to say about it. Nope." She folded her arms across her chest and glanced toward the door. "I'm done talking about that. Everything that happened is none of my concern anymore, so it most certainly shouldn't be any of yours."

"We have a woman who wants to sue," I answered, "to bring a lawsuit against Dr. Choudry and the clinic, against Hydeford, maybe others. She's on the outside now, but she was detained here."

Isobel showed no reaction, so I continued.

"The woman has legal status to stay in the country, but after what they did to her in here, she can't ever have kids. And she's ready to do something about it. She wants someone to be held accountable."

Isobel shrugged, her eyebrows slightly raised, like my comments were utterly irrelevant to her.

"Isobel, please."

"Why do you even need me if you've already got somebody else to do this fight? I told you already, I cannot get deported over this, and that's what's going to happen if I start running my mouth." She looked down at her hands.

"We can do certain things to protect you from retaliation. They didn't do this to just one person, Isobel. From what I'm hearing, there's a pattern. A group of powerless, under-resourced, dark-skinned women have been targeted and abused. Somebody has to put a stop to it before more people are hurt. I'm not looking to be the hero here. That has to be you. What if you can stop this from happening to more people?"

Isobel did more machinations with her lips, biting on the lower one, twisting the top, as if words were trying to escape her mouth but she was using a great deal of energy to hold them in.

I wanted to say more, to continue rattling off all the reasons why Isobel's participation was so crucial, but I reminded myself of what my father always used to tell me: that sometimes sitting quietly is the most effective way to argue.

Finally, Isobel spoke.

"What exactly do you need?" she asked.

"Tell me about Fern, the nurse who works here."

~

At eight thirty that evening, I was still at my office. Andrew and I had settled the terms of my leave, deciding that I'd finish out the week before making it official. Over the last two days, I'd handed off most of my work to various colleagues, which left me free to focus all my attention on the immigration case.

A few younger associates were in the hallway outside my office, arguing over who would go to the lobby to retrieve their food delivery. I wondered if I'd miss the camaraderie of the firm while I was working on my own, but I'd never really bonded with anyone at the office besides Tate, so probably not. As the associates discussed their dinner, I glanced at the clock on my computer screen, unable to remember if I'd even eaten lunch.

I'd been glued to my desk since returning from Hydeford earlier that afternoon, following up on the meager information I'd collected from Isobel. After finally relenting earlier, Isobel told me the nurse's last name, Kraska. She said the nurse had been working at the facility since well before Isobel's arrival there. But that was the sum total of either what Isobel knew or what she was willing to share. Either way, I was beginning to worry that I'd hit a dead end.

I dialed a number from the list I'd made and listened to the ringing on the other end. After a long afternoon of combing the internet, I had located the telephone numbers for all but one of the

F. Kraskas who lived within a hundred miles of Hydeford. This was the second-to-last F. Kraska remaining. If whoever answered this call was not the correct Fern Kraska, only one more shot remained before I might have to admit I was entirely out of ideas.

On the third ring, a woman picked up. "Hello?"

"Hi, is this Fern Kraska who works at the detention facility in Hydeford?" I asked.

"Who's this?" The woman's words were clipped and impatient sounding, similar to all the others who'd answered my earlier calls. They probably thought I was trying to sell them something or steal their credit card numbers.

"This is Jessa Gidney. I believe we met when I was at the facility interviewing a client."

"You're Isobel's lawyer."

My heart bounced and I pumped a fist into the air.

"Why are you calling me at home?"

"I was hoping you might be willing to speak with me about some of the medical treatments the women are receiving," I said.

"Not on the phone, no. I have nothing to say." The panic in the woman's voice was so palpable that I imagined her looking around the room in her own house, making sure she was alone.

"Perhaps you'd be willing to meet me for coffee?"

"I work all week. I can't get away for coffee with someone I barely know."

"Saturday then," I said. "I'll come to you."

To my surprise, the nurse rattled off an address.

~

When Saturday rolled around, I was so nervous I almost called Dustin to ask him to join me. But my leave had officially begun, and going forward, I would need to refrain from using the firm's resources. I was tackling this case on my own.

I knew in my gut there were more victims of Pinelands at Hydeford, but if I couldn't get Nurse Kraska to open up to me, I wasn't sure how I could help them. Under my arrangement with Andrew, if I ever wanted my job back, I had six months to file this case and show a likelihood of success on the merits. Whether it was negligence by the facility or the medical clinic, or intentional targeting by the government, a guard, or Dr. Choudry—I couldn't yet say. But even if I failed to meet Andrew's deadline, I would not give up, whatever the cost to my career.

When I pulled my car up in front of the small clapboard house in northern New Jersey, I glanced in the rearview mirror to check my appearance. I decided to quickly pull my unruly curls into a ponytail so I'd look more professional. But then I pulled my hair free of the rubber band just as hastily, deciding that a more casual, approachable look was probably best for this meeting.

When Fern opened the door, she was just as I remembered. Somewhere in her midfifties with long blond hair, which she now wore in a low braid, and thick, sturdy limbs. She was dressed in loose jeans and a faded lavender sweatshirt, and she held a steaming cup of coffee in her hand.

Her eyes swept over me, and then she shepherded me inside. "Come, we can sit on the deck. You'll want to keep your coat on," she said, as she pulled her own parka off a coat-tree near the door.

As we passed through the living room, I saw the home was modest but tidy. Colorful area rugs and decorative table lamps filled the space. The shelves in the living room were lined with picture frames, many of them holding multigenerational group photos full of smiling faces. The unmistakable aroma of pancakes wafted toward us from the kitchen, and I wondered if anyone else was in the house. As we continued through the cluttered kitchen toward the glass sliders leading to the back, two tabby cats appeared at Fern's feet. She shooed them away before opening the glass door.

Outside, two coffee mugs and a carafe waited for us at a patio table.

"I started early," Fern said as she held up the coffee cup in her hand and pushed one of the mugs on the wrought-iron table to the side. "We might as well get straight to business." She motioned for me to sit down, took her own seat, then poured hot coffee into the cup in front of me. "What is it you wanted to know?"

"I went to see Jacinta. Thank you," I added, taking the cup. "We met at her home in Brooklyn. I brought an interpreter and heard about the procedure she underwent. We're going to file a complaint in federal court."

Fern offered little more than a nod in response, but I thought I saw a flicker of satisfaction cross the woman's face.

"So what else do you need from me?" she asked. "Sounds like you're all set." She glanced back toward the door to the house.

"Jacinta doesn't want to do it alone. She'll probably back out if we can't get others to join the complaint, and then we'll be nowhere. I don't think I can help the women at Hydeford, or the ones who come after them, unless I have a fuller picture of what's going on. I also need a better understanding of what's happened to women who were there in the past."

"And what makes you think I'd be able to help you? Or that I'd be willing?" Fern asked. "I did my part." She pulled at her gray parka, tightening it around herself as if physically holding in whatever information she might have.

"Nurses always know more about what's going on with patients than anyone else," I said, repeating what Dalia had pointed out the week before. "And the fact that you've chosen to work as a nurse tells me you care about helping people. You're not going to sit by and do nothing while women are at risk." I hoped those words were true.

Fern sipped her coffee but didn't answer.

I stayed quiet too, my heart beginning to race as I worried I'd hit another dead end. But then I had a thought. "How long have you been working for ICE?" I asked.

"I don't work for ICE," Fern said. "Hydeford is a privately run facility. I work for DeMarke Corrections, an outside company. The government hired them to run the place. I'm pretty sure that's how it works at most detention centers these days. DeMarke runs more of these centers than anyone else, and they could have put me anywhere. I requested Hydeford because it's closest to where I live."

I hadn't even known the facility was privately run. Realizing that I'd been ignorant of such a basic and important detail was another blow to my confidence, jolting me awake to the fact that I still needed to learn so much—not only about this particular case, but also about the nuts and bolts of detention in the US. I'd recently become aware that the government often hired private contractors to help with various aspects of immigration detention, but I hadn't realized the entire operation at Hydeford could be for-profit. Knowing now that I was dealing with a business enterprise, I wondered more seriously about the kind of insurance reimbursements they must be getting for all the medical procedures happening there.

"Can you tell me how medical treatment generally works at the facility?" I asked, hoping the open-ended question would get Fern talking.

"I can't lose my job," she said. "My husband's been out of work near two years. He's helping out on some construction jobs, but we've got three kids. You know how teenaged boys eat? I can't lose my job," she said again.

"I understand," I told her. "I'm not asking you to get involved. Just maybe point me in the right direction. Tell me who else to talk to?"

"I don't know if anybody else would be willing. Some women in the past have filed grievances. But then you see those women get deported back to their countries, sometimes the next day, sometimes only hours later. The other women see it too. Makes it so people want to keep quiet, you know?"

"How is that even possible?" I wondered aloud. "To make the deportations happen so quickly? Aren't there protocols? Last I heard, it could take weeks to even get an asthma inhaler in one of these places, yet somehow they can ship a woman off like it's nothing?"

"I imagine if they get those women to file a request saying they want to be sent back to their origin country, arrangements can be made very quickly." She looked off toward the yard next door. "The guards just have to persuade them to say they don't actually want to stay in the US after all."

So now there was coercion to add to the complaint too. I felt a pounding in my head.

"Can you tell me about Dr. Choudry?" I asked, switching gears.

Fern swallowed audibly. "She works at Pinelands Women's Health. It's an outside facility the women go to. They have a contract with DeMarke, and all the women go there when they need medical visits. Choudry's been there a few years. From what I hear, she's not even board-certified."

"Have you ever been there, to Pinelands?"

Fern shuddered. "You couldn't pay me to step foot in that place."

"Why?" I sipped my coffee and tried not to grimace at the bitterness of it. Something about it tasted off.

"You should see the women when they come back from the place. Shell-shocked, bandaged, confused. Lots of the women don't speak English, don't even know what happened to them. I wonder near every day how many women still don't know exactly what was done to them over there."

"Why does it continue? Who allows it?" I couldn't keep the incredulity from my voice.

"The people who run DeMarke, I guess." Fern said it like she wasn't very sure. "Sometimes I think they're just punishing the women for trying to find their place in the good ole US of A. God forbid they should have the right to live how they want." Fern was getting worked up, confirming my suspicion that she cared more than she'd initially let on.

At the sound of the slider opening, I twisted around to see a brown-haired boy, about thirteen years old, poking his head out the door.

"Mom, where'd you put my cleats?"

"They're at the front door, Pete, right where you left them last night." Fern sighed and glanced at me.

As the boy closed the door, I hoped Fern would continue what she'd been saying, but she was quiet a moment and then just pushed back her chair.

"Look," Fern said, "I can talk to the women. Try to get a few of them to reach out to you on their own. Can't make any promises though. They'll need real assurance that you can protect them from sudden transfers or deportation. None of them will like the idea of putting themselves in further jeopardy. And like I said, some of them don't even speak English."

"That's fine. I have someone who can join me to interpret. At least for Spanish. I can find other interpreters as needed." I prayed that Dustin's conscience would keep him amenable to helping me, at least for a little bit longer.

"Give me your number again," Fern said, taking her cell phone from her pocket. "I'll see what I can do."

~

When I walked into the lobby of our apartment building, I caught sight of Vance already waiting at the elevator bank. His back was to me, and he wore a sleeveless t-shirt and a pair of baggy gray sweatpants. His arms and neck were slick with sweat. Earbuds peeked out of his ears, and he didn't notice me approaching. I paused, taking a moment to study him. He was apparently still energized from his Saturday morning run as he bopped his head along to the music playing in his ears. A few months ago, I would have wrapped my arms around him from behind and kissed his cheek, not minding the dampness of his skin. Now, I felt awkward and unsure. There had been so much fighting and stress lately. Everything between us felt changed.

He turned slightly and noticed me. His lips began to spread in a smile as he reached up to remove one of his earbuds.

"Hey. How'd it go with the nurse?" he asked as I reached him.

The elevator doors opened, and we stepped in together. The routine of it, the sameness, shook something loose inside my heart, sending a wave of melancholy through my whole body. In a different version of reality, in the world before our "fertility journey," I'd have already called Vance to fill him in on my meeting, eager to talk through every nuance with this beautiful man who'd given me so much emotional support over the years. For a long time I couldn't have imagined making a major decision without his input. But things had changed between us. Somewhere between all the foiled, unpleasant attempts at baby-making, or maybe because of his constant doubts about my judgment, the magic between us had been steadily evaporating, like shallow puddles after a summertime storm. *Soon there might be nothing left at all,* I thought, and the realization made me profoundly sad. I wasn't prepared to let him slip away from me, not yet. I had to protect our closeness, all past mistakes and omissions aside.

I knew keeping secrets from him was only making things worse. But with the growing chasm between us, I saw no other choice.

Even if I couldn't reveal the horrible story of my family's past, I could still make sure to be immensely, excessively forthright going forward. *No new secrets*, I promised myself, and maybe with enough honesty, I could push the old secrets further and further away.

"The meeting was kind of great." I smiled tentatively as Vance nodded. Maybe he was warming to the idea of me pursuing this case. "She's going to try to get me a few more names, women who might be willing to talk. I also found another party we have to name as defendant. Turns out, the facility isn't even run by the government. They hire private companies to run these places. She said this one was called DeMarke."

"DeMarke? You mean DeMarke Corrections?" Vance asked.

"Yeah, how—?"

"They're a client. Not of mine. Arjun manages the account. I think they've been with our bank for a long time, like more than a decade. They run Hydeford?"

I nodded, stunned by the coincidence. The elevator doors re-opened, and we stepped out in tandem.

"You can't bring a suit against DeMarke," Vance said as he continued toward the apartment door. "So I guess that's that."

The flippancy with which he said it stopped me in my tracks. "What the fuck are you talking about? You just said it's not your account."

"Still," he started, turning back to where I stood, but I interrupted.

"You and Arjun aren't even in the same group. How could this matter at a company as enormous as yours?"

"Jessa, are you kidding? They're an important client of the bank. I can't have my wife dragging them into court on some witch hunt. Do you know how that would look for me?"

"Witch hunt?" I snapped back, and the accord I'd been hoping for was gone in an instant. I was once again brimming with rage. "If you can't respect what I'm doing, then maybe we have a bigger problem than who's getting named in the complaint."

"Yeah," Vance nearly spat back. "Maybe we do." He reached into his pocket for his keys, turning his back and marching down the hallway. I stayed rooted to my spot. I couldn't bring myself to follow him after what he'd just said, and I wasn't fool enough to miss the metaphor in that. There was a small bench opposite the elevator, and I lowered myself onto the faux leather to collect my thoughts. I felt like I was seeing Vance in a whole new light. I'd always thought he trusted my choices, but now I was wondering if those choices had actually been his, not mine, all along. Maybe every single time. I had let him direct me in so many ways, professionally, socially, romantically, because it felt safe. How easy it had been to fall in line because I generally agreed with his suggestions, but now it seemed we no longer saw eye to eye on anything at all.

Witch hunt. Fuck him. Suddenly it was all just too much—having to fight Vance, knowing what had happened to Denise and Jacinta and Isobel, discovering what had been taken from them. Their whole futures, worlds of possibilities, had been ripped away, literally yanked from their bodies. A sudden sob escaped me as I thought of them now, young women who would never get pregnant, never birth more children of their own, no matter how desperately they wished.

I wiped at my eyes. A neighbor could step off the elevator at any moment and find me weeping in the hallway, but I didn't care. I needed this moment to simply let myself feel. I replayed everything in my mind again, how the women had been cuffed in the exam room, how they'd been forced to sign unclear paperwork, pressured to submit.

I wondered then if I'd told any of those details to Vance. I'd pulled so far back from him that I couldn't even remember what I'd shared.

Reminding myself that I was partially at fault for our current discord, I tamped down the fierce anger in which I'd been stewing. I could do better too.

When I stepped into the apartment, I heard Vance already in the bathroom with the shower running. I went straight to the kitchen, reaching for the bag of sliced sourdough bread on the counter. I had skipped breakfast in my rush to meet Fern earlier. As I pulled two slices of bread from the bag, I tried to think dispassionately about the conflict of interest with DeMarke. It was unfortunate that Vance might have a difficult situation at work because of the case, but if anyone was to blame for it, that would be the people at DeMarke, the people at Hydeford, or Dr. Choudry. And yet, Vance probably wouldn't see it that way.

But this was just too big. I wasn't going to drop this case simply because it might cause a problem for my husband at work. Besides, everyone loved Vance at his bank. Whatever happened, they'd figure things out. And not for nothing, maybe Vance should encourage the bank to drop DeMarke as a client. Unless he liked working with people who supported discrimination and abuse. He couldn't possibly be okay with that, given his lifelong feeling about what his grandparents had experienced.

We'd had so many conversations over the years about what his grandparents had been through, how they'd never really recovered, how he and his brothers had tried so hard to heal their grandparents' pain. Yet now, amid a situation where people were suffering in real time, their pain didn't matter to him?

I pushed the bread into the toaster, trying to keep my mind blank. I needed a few minutes of rest from my turbulent emotions. Taking a container of hummus from the fridge, I crossed the small kitchen for a butter knife, relieved by the mundanity of these tasks. As I removed the cover from the spread, the tangy, garlicky smell of the chickpea paste instantly turned my stomach and I raced to the sink, ready to vomit. The feeling passed almost as suddenly as it had arrived, but it left me reeling nonetheless.

Could it be? I remembered my distaste for Fern's coffee earlier. So many women said that nausea was their first sign, the symptom that tipped them off about their pregnancies. I tried not to get excited. It was probably just the beginning of a stomach bug. I pulled my phone from my back pocket anyway, then opened the period tracking app.

To my great surprise, I saw that my cycle was already two days late. I couldn't believe that despite my hyperfocus on getting pregnant, I hadn't noticed. I'd been so wrapped up in the case and all the stuff with Gram that I'd actually managed to lose track of when my period was due.

My hand shot up to my breast, and I poked at it to see if it was tender. It was not. Even so, between the two-day delay of menstruation and the unexplained nausea, I dared to hope. Come to think of it, I'd been a little queasy at my last meeting with Isobel too. I wouldn't say anything to Vance until I knew one way or the other. And at that moment, I didn't feel like saying anything to Vance at all.

My brunch forgotten, I grabbed my purse from the hook near the door and headed back to the elevator. I'd used up my supply of pregnancy tests and needed to buy more at the pharmacy. Vance would wonder where I was when he got out of the shower and found an empty apartment. After the way he'd spoken to me, I didn't care. Let him sweat a little.

Twenty minutes later, when I returned to the apartment with a bag from Duane Reade in hand, Vance was gone. We hadn't made any concrete plans to spend the afternoon together, but we had tickets to see *The Music Man* on Broadway in the evening with Vance's parents and Gram. Maybe he needed more alone time before all the family togetherness later, but still, it wasn't like him to leave without telling me where he was going.

Except I had done it too. *So at least we are still on the same page about one thing,* I thought glibly.

Rather than dwell on Vance, I hurried to the bathroom to take the test. I'd used so many of these home tests over the past few months that I didn't even glance at the instructions. When I set the wet test stick down on the counter, I flushed the toilet and pulled out my phone, planning to sit on the edge of the tub and scroll through social media while I waited the required five minutes for the results. I checked my reflection in the mirror first. My curls were pulled back in a low ponytail, and I had a slight flush to my cheeks. There were little blue half-moons under my eyes, probably because of the late nights doing research. I'd heard that a woman's face sometimes changed during pregnancy, but so far I just looked like a tired version of my regular self.

My eyes drifted back to the test stick, and I saw something already beginning to appear. I leaned in closer, not believing my eyes. Two lines! The control line was significantly darker than the test line, but there were definitely two lines.

"There's a second line!" I said into the empty bathroom.

Could it be that I was actually pregnant? In the very worst month of my entire relationship with Vance, I'd managed to conceive? I closed the toilet seat and sat down to stare at the test stick for the duration of the testing time so I could make sure the line didn't disappear. *Does that ever happen?* I wondered. *Do lines disappear after they've shown up?* This was uncharted territory, and suddenly it seemed I was not an old pro at pregnancy tests at all.

When my phone alarm went off and the test still showed a positive result, I laughed out loud. I had given up hope of getting pregnant without some sort of medical intervention. I'd been so sure we would need serious fertility treatments and that even then, we might not see any action inside my uterus. It seemed utterly unfathomable that simply having sex with Vance could have resulted in me finally becoming pregnant again.

I thought then of my last time, how I'd been pregnant one minute, and the next, not. Was I going to fall in love with the fetus this time, only to lose it again? I wrapped an arm around my belly, willing the little cells, the beginnings of a baby, to stay put and keep doing their thing.

A few months earlier I would have called Vance immediately, shrieking in excitement. But right then, I was so frustrated with him that I didn't even want to share the news. I wanted to hold on to it as a private nugget, for me alone, to simply bask in a moment of joy without any strife or disagreement. Maybe I could keep it to myself for a few days, like my own special treasure, before I had to tell him. I realized then that if I did that, my pregnancy would become just one more secret I was keeping from my husband. But for a few blissful moments, I simply didn't care.

16

Carrie

October 1927

I'd been trapped deep inside the walls of the Colony for three whole entire years. Just a few months earlier, I'd had my twenty-first birthday, but all I got to show for it was an extra pinwheel cookie after supper that night. During my time inside, I'd gotten more familiar with the place, working different jobs and even getting friendly with some of the other patients. The first year, I'd been in the laundry, scrubbing soiled linens. Then at the start of my second year, they moved me to the cafeteria on account of my good behavior. I'd been working breakfast and lunch ever since. Folks around the Colony didn't mind that I liked to keep quiet a lot of the time. It wasn't as if they had so many choices when it came to keeping company anyhow. Some of the patients were in a truly bad way, never uttering a word, staring out the windows at nothing for all eternity. Those of us who were more alert, we kind of stuck together. When work shifts were over, we idled with each other in the little recreation room. There we could pass the minutes squabbling over who'd get the next turn with the marbles and such.

One Tuesday afternoon, I was sitting with Ma and a pretty lady named Lindy, the three of us arranging dominoes on a square game table. Lindy'd only been at the Colony a month, but with the way time moved inside, it felt like I'd known her forever. Meanwhile, Ma was having one of her clearheaded days, which had been getting fewer and fewer.

"Put one here," Ma said, pointing to a spot I'd missed.

I was doing just as she said, taking care not to jostle the others, when that young nurse, Miss Bradshaw, brought in the day's mail. Only a handful of us ever received correspondence. Gerty Sims, who had nine children on the outside, received a note from her oldest daughter from time to time, and Rosalie Barlow, who'd been brought into the Colony because of her addiction to alcohol, got mail near every week, but she would never tell us who-all was sending it to her.

"A letter from your fella," Nurse Bradshaw said, dropping an envelope on the table and nearly toppling our dominoes.

"Ooo-eee! From your fella!" Lindy hollered, teasing me.

"He's not my fella," I said, just like I did every time a letter from Billy arrived. When I'd first come to the Colony, Billy sent me a letter every month. As the months dragged on though, the letters started coming slower, maybe every eight weeks when I was lucky. The other women heckled me every time, saying Billy and I were sweet on each other. I never paid it mind, but for some reason that day, I found myself wondering if Billy hadn't met another girl yet. I didn't like the way it made me feel inside to think of that. There was a tightening in my belly as I held on to that envelope and wondered again if I'd made a mistake not marrying him when he'd asked. Doing so would have saved me from being trapped where I was. That much I knew for sure.

"Well, go on," Ma said. I guess she wanted the entertainment of news from the outside too.

Opening the envelope with my short fingernail, I expected to find much the same as usual in his letter, updates on his brothers and some news about his construction job. I wanted to hear tidings about my baby, Vivian, but he never offered any tidbits having to do with her. Before I got the letter out of its jacket, a newspaper clipping fell into my lap. Unfolding it, I saw the words up top said, "Supreme Court Votes to Uphold Virginia Sterilization Law."

It had been near three years since they'd taken me to that courthouse, and I'd not heard anything about it since. I thought, after a time, that the matter had been put to the side or forgotten, and I'd been relieved, allowing myself to forget it too. But now that I saw the news Billy sent, my heart started to hammer once again.

I read through the article quickly, and I was comforted to see that it didn't say anything about me. It talked instead about that man Laderdale, who, at the trial, had more to say than anyone else. I remembered how he'd compared wanton women to inferior cattle that could be bred out from the herd. I'd been shocked by it at the time, but my outrage had long since faded, the way things do when you get further and further away from them. But as I held the article all those years later, I worried that someone like the horrid Mr. Laderdale might be coming back for me.

Reading on, I learned that the Supreme Court of the United States, which I knew to be the most important court in all the country, had said Virginia's sterilization law was just fine. The article reported that a great humanitarian by the name of Oliver Wendell Holmes had written the decision for the court. It spoke of his legal arguments, much of which was too confusing to make heads or tails of. I skipped forward to see if there was any mention of the Colony. As my eyes moved down the paper, one sentence about what Mr. Holmes had written did jump out at me.

"It is better for all the world," the court's opinion said, "if, instead of waiting to execute degenerate offspring for crime or to let them starve for their imbecility, society can prevent those who are manifestly unfit from continuing their kind."

A weight settled in my stomach as I remembered afresh the things said about me when they brought me to the Amherst County courthouse. Though I'd hoped that nonsense had been forgotten, the article in my hand said different.

The newspaper praised the court's decision as being broad-minded and called anyone opposing it a sentimentalist. Then it talked more about that man Laderdale and how his model sterilization law was fit to be adopted in states all throughout the country. Laderdale, they said, was a hero who would be responsible for reforming the entire human race. They called him progressive and said he worked tirelessly to educate other scientists. He had support from our country's richest families, like the Carnegies and Rockefellers, and others I'd never heard of, and he was getting money from all of them to do more research. His work was keeping immigrants out of the country and preserving the high quality of the American population.

The author of the article seemed to like the idea of sterilization, explaining that Mr. Laderdale found a way to measure the size of heads and arms to know who should be considered "unfit." He also figured out how to arrange qualities of the feebleminded into "pedigree charts," which the author said was one of the best pieces of support for the new law. The reporter said medical experts could use the charts to stop people with bad traits from making babies and passing on whatever it was the scientists didn't like.

I started to read the article over again from the top so I could make better sense of it, but Ma interrupted me.

"Well," she said, "we're waiting. What's your friend got to say for himself?"

Only then did I remember to check for a note from Billy. It was there inside the envelope, in his neat, tight cursive. My hand shook as I unfolded the paper.

Dear Carrie,

I've been holding on to this article for many weeks, unsure whether to send it to you. But knowing as I do what happened at the county courthouse soon after you went away, I thought this was something you should see. I hope it doesn't frighten you unnecessarily, since by now, everyone in that awful place must know that you are not of feeble mind. Even so, I decided you should read it so you can continue to take great care.

Always your friend,

Billy

When I finished reading the letter aloud, Ma asked me to read out the article too.

"He's right," Ma said. "They know you here now. You got nothing to worry yourself about."

It took only three days for me to learn how very wrong she was. Thirty minutes before I was meant to start the breakfast shift, Nurse Bradshaw arrived at the door of our dormitory with two large orderlies behind her.

When she called out, "Carrie Buck!" from the entry, the other ladies in our shared room started hooting the way they always did when a girl was about to get punished for breaking one rule or another.

I knew why they'd come for me though, and it was for a lot worse than a scolding.

I looked all around me for another way out, as if I didn't already know that the windows were barred.

The nurse called for me again, now sounding angry. "Miss Buck!"

I sat down on the scratchy blanket atop my cot, searching my brain and calling on God to help me think of what to do.

"You better go, Carrie," Gerty called from her bed. "You're just making it worse."

But nothing was worse than what they wanted to do to me.

Jessa

April 2022

Two days had passed since I discovered I was pregnant, and I still hadn't told Vance. It should have brought us closer, this happy news, but if anything, I was retreating from him even more.

Now I was at Dr. LaRusso's office, lying on the exam table, staring up at the ceiling, a paper sheet draped over my legs. I hoped with all my heart that the doctor would say the pregnancy was real. I had taken two more tests to confirm the positive result. But still. I'd read all about chemical pregnancies, faulty test batches, early miscarriages. I was afraid to get too excited.

"Go ahead and sit up," the doctor said, rearranging the sheet so I was more fully covered. He removed his latex gloves and rolled a few feet back from me on his little round chair. "So I *am* seeing early signs of a pregnancy." He smiled and I felt myself grinning back. "We'll confirm everything with the bloods and also make sure your hormone levels are where they should be."

At the words *hormone levels,* I felt another burst of panic.

"What if they're not right? My hormones?" I asked.

"Then we supplement what your body is already doing with synthetic hormones to support the pregnancy. I know you're concerned, Jessa, but I see no signs indicating you're at any particular risk for miscarriage."

"Okay." I nodded, trying to absorb the doctor's words, trying to believe them. "Then what should I do now?"

"Other than taking the prenatal vitamins and cutting out certain foods, there's not much else I would recommend yet. Mostly, just try to avoid undue stress, alcohol, lifting anything particularly heavy. No scuba diving," he added with a chuckle. "That's about it."

I let out a heavy breath, unsure whether it was a sigh of relief or concern.

"We'll make an appointment for about eight weeks from now for the first ultrasound." Dr. LaRusso stood and closed the folder that held my information. "You'll want to bring Vance so he can hear the heartbeat."

It all seemed like magic, sorcery, the idea that there could soon be a second heart beating inside my body. I was already wondering whether the baby would be a girl or a boy. I thought of my parents. Would it be a baby boy with a cleft in his chin, just like my dad's? Or would it be a girl, maybe with my mother's singing voice? My mom would have made the best grandma, the kind with a signature cookie recipe and a never-ending supply of exuberant hugs. I wished all over again that they were still alive so I could share the joy of this moment with them. If only I wanted to share it with Vance too.

As Dr. LaRusso prepared to leave the room, I realized I still had so many questions.

"When you say avoid stress," I asked, "could you elaborate on that?"

He waved a hand in the air dismissively.

"There's no conclusive data really linking stress to miscarriage, but many of us in the medical community believe stress can impact pregnancy, or a mother's health overall. That said, a fetus is generally hardier than a lot of people give it credit for. I wouldn't worry too much. It's the nature of being pregnant, I think. Worrying about worrying," he joked, patting my elbow.

After the doctor excused himself, I used the paper sheet that had been covering me to wipe the gel from myself. I got back into my yoga pants and shoved both the sheet and paper gown into the aluminum trash bin beside the exam table. Eight weeks seemed like an awfully long time to wait to confirm a baby was still growing inside me. And the doctor wanted me to avoid stress? Laughable. The only time I could imagine being calm about the pregnancy would be in about nine months, when—if!—I had an actual living, breathing baby in my arms.

As I slipped my feet back into my sneakers, I tried to push away my panic and focus on other things. I had meetings lined up over the next few days with four different women whom Fern had sent my way, two still at Hydeford and two who'd been released. I had to finish prepping for those appointments, and I also wanted to start drafting a complaint, even though there was still much information to collect. If I wanted to help save the current and future women at Hydeford, as well as my position at Dillney, I really had no time to waste.

I made my way out of the doctor's office with an unfamiliar feeling in my chest, as if an electrical current were pulsating inside me. It was part excitement, part dread, and so much more that I couldn't put a name to. I knew I had to share the news with Vance. I was also entirely confident that he would be thrilled—which was why I had to keep asking myself why I was so reluctant to tell him.

~

Hours later, I sat cross-legged on our living room carpet with my back against the sofa and my computer open in my lap. I was surrounded by the different file folders I'd created for each distinct legal issue in the immigration case, as well as folders of information pertaining to each different witness. Even though my method was old-school, I always preferred having hard copies of important documents on hand as I did my work. This was proving especially useful as I typed out page after page of the draft complaint.

At the sound of keys in the door, I stiffened. I was in the zone with my work and had a million tasks I still wanted to finish, so it really wasn't the best time for a pregnancy announcement. Vance and I had spent the last two days passing like ships in the night, barely interacting since our last argument. In all likelihood, he was about to storm into the apartment and march right past me again, just to make some sort of point about my unreasonable behavior. *Allegedly* unreasonable.

Even so, as he pushed the door open, I pasted a smile onto my face.

"Still at it, huh?" he asked, without any of the obvious rancor I'd expected. He dropped his messenger bag near the door and came to sit beside me on the floor, mimicking my cross-legged position as he sat against the sofa next to me. I figured he'd finally come to terms with the fact that I was moving forward with the class action, whether he was on board or not.

"Yup." I leaned over on one hip and kissed him lightly on the cheek, just as I normally would to reconnect after a long day apart. "Just working on the complaint."

"Wow," he said, glancing at the computer screen. "I didn't realize you had enough information to be at the drafting stage already."

"I don't, really," I confessed. I made a few clicks to save the document and then shut my laptop. "But I wanted to start on it anyway to help clarify my thoughts. I thought writing it down would highlight which areas need more attention and which information I should still be trying to collect. It's helping me to see the case from more of a legal perspective and not just through the lens of my moral outrage. Does that make sense?"

I looked at him for confirmation that he was following along.

He nodded. "Yeah, sure." Then he rocked to the side so his knee bumped mine in a gesture of solidarity. "What else are you thinking about it?"

"I mean, it's crazy, the case law and history that I'm finding about similar situations. Ever heard of the 'Mississippi appendectomy'?"

Vance shook his head.

"Yeah, I hadn't either. Apparently it was the name given to unnecessary hysterectomies at teaching hospitals in the South in the 1970s. Women were misled to believe they were having procedures like appendectomies and then were sterilized instead. The victims were mostly poor women of color, many of whom were never told what had really been done to them. It was training for the med students. A practice so prevalent it got a name, Vance."

He shook his head slightly, as if stunned by the thought.

"And then there's California," I continued. "They banned coerced sterilization as a form of birth control in prisons in 2014 after detained women came forward about what was happening to them. In 2014!" I still couldn't believe it myself. "It's so recent, like . . . I can still smell the flagrancy of it. And that doesn't even take into account the twenty thousand people in the state who were sterilized between 1920 and 1979 because they were deemed unfit to reproduce. It's everywhere. Virginia sterilized at least eight thousand people during that time period for the same reasons. North Carolina sterilized over seven thousand. The list goes on and on. Oh, and guess what percentage of *those* victims were women of color?"

"It's hard to believe it could happen in our country," Vance said, rubbing a hand over his eyes. "But isn't it illegal?"

"If only it were that simple," I scoffed. "In the 1970s, a judge in one case acknowledged that the US was sterilizing somewhere between 100,000 and 150,000 people a year, all of them with lower incomes." I started flipping through my folders to find the printout of the case. "Relf," I mumbled as I rummaged through the folders. "Relf, Relf. Aha!" I held it high in the air like a blood-stained weapon at a crime scene. "They threatened to take away their welfare benefits if they didn't comply. It says so right here." I waved the paper again. "The judge in that case prohibited federally funded sterilization without 'informed consent.' But it doesn't say anything about state funding. It doesn't stop the states from doing the exact same thing."

"Yeesh." Vance shook his head. "And nothing has changed in the fifty years since that case? How can that be?"

"In Tennessee in 2017," I told him, "a judge offered reduced sentences to any inmates willing to use Nexplanon, a birth control implant that prevents pregnancy for four years. At least that dude was an equal opportunist because he offered men the option of reduced sentences too, but only in exchange for vasectomies. But 2017! And that California prison? That was also less than a decade ago. It's not over, not even remotely, Vance."

"Yeah, it doesn't sound like it," he said. "I just . . ." He hesitated, but I nodded to encourage him to speak freely.

"Look," he said, "I agree one thousand percent that if this shit is happening at Hydeford, it has to be stopped. But I really wish you'd bring this case back to the firm, let them handle it."

"But you know they won't."

"Jess," Vance continued, "all you know is that they won't move forward if you're the lead attorney on the case. You never asked if they'd take the case if you removed yourself."

"But I can't remove myself. I have to do this. It has to be me."

"Why?" Vance asked.

I clamped my lips closed to prevent myself from mentioning my great-grandfather. I knew Vance's first response would be about how my sordid family history reflected on him. He'd worry how it would impact his image with his own family to have chosen someone who came from a man like Grandpa Harry. Never mind the embarrassment he'd feel with his podcast community if it came out that he'd married the descendant of someone responsible for so many of the losses the podcast was meant to rectify.

But if the truth ever came to light, as the truth so often does—and if I won this case and better protected the women at Hydeford—Vance would have that to hold on to. Despite my deplorable family history, I would have tried to help the Hydeford women. What kind of person wouldn't? And yet, the case seemed to be turning into a compulsion for me, maybe because it had the power to redeem me—the power to redeem us both. But I couldn't tell Vance any of that.

"Because I feel this in my bones," I said instead. "Maybe because I'm a woman? I don't know. I just worry the firm won't do what needs to be done, and I don't understand why you're so dead set against me working this case."

I could see the disappointment settling over his face as he let out a breath and uncrossed his legs, rising from where he'd been sitting.

Moments ago, we might have been making progress, and now I'd ruined it again.

"There's leftover Chinese in the fridge," I told him, realizing suddenly that in my current "teeny bit pregnant" state, maybe I shouldn't be eating food with MSG. Or was MSG even a thing anymore? I clearly still had a lot to learn about being pregnant. Starting with how to best share the news with my husband while also being utterly at odds with him. Even so, it was well past time to tell him. I took a deep breath, preparing to just blurt it out.

Before I formed the words, Vance said, "You know, I just don't understand what's with you lately. You've gone from this organized, deliberate, up-and-coming attorney to a woman who seems intent on destroying everything in her path. You're literally lighting your whole life on fire. Why? For the women at Hydeford? I understand how awful it is, whatever's happening to them. What you're describing sounds like an Orwellian horror movie, and of course something like that has to be stopped—but by you alone? You're on some ego trip, insisting you can do everything on your own when these women would clearly fare better with someone else taking the lead. You certainly don't care one iota how this could impact my own reputation at work. I mean . . ." He let out a cynical laugh. "Who's to say you won't fuck this up just like you fucked up Shantrane?"

I blinked at his words.

"Wow, Vance," I said, trying to digest what had just come out of his mouth. "Just . . . wow. You don't understand one-millionth of what you're talking about, and you're being a complete and utter asshole."

Vance stared back at me long and hard, his Adam's apple bobbing in his throat. "I don't know what is happening here, but I can't do this. I thought . . . I don't know what I thought, but I just can't do it anymore."

"Can't do what?"

"This. Us." He motioned between us with his hand. "I have to go."

He walked into the bedroom and called over his shoulder, "I'm packing a bag."

"Wait, what? Vance, no." I hurried after him, but he was already pulling a duffel out of the closet and filling it with clothing. "You can't just leave because we had a fight."

"A fight? This isn't just one fight, Jessa," he said. "I'm talking about weeks and weeks of arguing, of us never agreeing about anything, of you going full steam ahead, never pausing to let me into your thought processes, and on and on you go, ignoring what I tell you to do and just bulldozing everything in your way."

As he stuffed clothing into his duffel, I floundered.

"But . . . no! You can't just run away from this. Where are you even going?" I demanded.

"I just need out. Out of all of this." He waved his hands in the air, like he was indicating everything that constituted our life together.

"You're leaving me?" I nearly shrieked. My hand shot to my abdomen, as if to protect the secret fetus from the sight and sound of what was happening around it.

"Yes, Jessa." Vance spat out the words. "I. Am. Leaving. You."

Within minutes he was out the door. It happened so quickly, it felt like I might have imagined the whole thing. He couldn't really mean it, right? He'd cool down and come back in the morning, wouldn't he?

I needed to talk to Gram, the only other person who would understand what I was going through and help me think through my next steps. But as I picked up my cell phone, I noticed it was already close to eleven o'clock. She would be sleeping, and I didn't want to wake her. Even if I were to try, she slept like a hibernating bear and wouldn't pick up anyway.

Moving back to the living room, I flopped down into the corner of the sectional sofa. It was always my favorite place to curl up next to Vance when we were reading or watching a movie. But now Vance was gone. And I was alone. The apartment was silent except for the quiet hum of the refrigerator coming from the kitchen. I realized that, at thirty-one years old, I had landed exactly where I'd always been most afraid of finding myself: with nobody. But then

I thought of the baby growing inside me. I was *not* alone. I had the baby. As I held my hand against my belly, thinking of the little life working itself into existence, I knew the only way I could mother any child was to stand up for what I believed was right. No matter what else it cost me.

Carrie

December 1927

One month after they completed the sterilization procedure, I was released from the Colony. They said that since I wasn't at risk of getting pregnant with any more children, the time had come when I could be rehabilitated to reenter society.

Mrs. Libby, the woman who'd agreed to take me in as a housemaid after my release, was younger than Mrs. Alice, and kinder. She lived in Timberlake, which wasn't too far from the Colony back in Lynchburg. But the house was more than an hour's drive from Charlottesville, where my baby, Vivian, was still living with the Dobbs family.

Mrs. Libby had a yellow bun atop her head and a brown apron she wore day in and day out. She gave me a room at the back of the house with its own door to the outside. There was a real bed on a wooden frame and even a small bureau that was just for me. When she saw how little I'd brought with me from the Colony, she went through a pile of her own castoffs and handed me sweaters and coats like I was from the charity bus coming to pick them up.

Mrs. Libby trusted me with a lot of tasks I'd never done at the Dobbses' home. Not just the marketing, but also looking after her two small children, Flora and James. That was my favorite part of the job, but most days Mrs. Libby was with the children. Even so, it was better at Mrs. Libby's than at the Colony, so I tried always to be on my best behavior with her. I saw no use in sassing her when nothing that'd happened to me was any of her fault anyway.

In the beginning, she did the cleaning and laundering alongside me so I could see just exactly the way she wanted me to keep house.

"Carrie, dear," she said one morning while we stood side by side in the sewing room, "after you finish starching the linens, take the list beside the cupboard and go on to the market. Money's there on the counter." It was a cold day, and she reminded me to wrap myself up in the worn red coat she'd given me.

As I made my way toward Main Street, huddling in on myself to keep the wind from getting at me, I tried not to think too hard about my Vivian. Sometimes there weren't room for anything else in my brain except for Vivi, Vivi, Vivi. And then I'd remember how I wouldn't have any other children either, and sometimes it was all I could do to keep putting one foot in front of the other without falling right down to the ground. I stuck my chin higher in the air, telling myself I had to be strong, otherwise I'd surely never get my daughter back. Then I'd be alone for the rest of my days.

I'd barely gotten past the turnoff from Mrs. Libby's street when I heard a familiar voice behind me.

"Well, as I stand and breathe, if I ain't coming right up on Miss Carrie Buck."

I turned around and saw my one true friend standing across the street. It was Billy, and for all the world it felt to me like he'd just appeared out of nowhere, brought up out of the dust on the street. He was smiling wide as he started toward me. I could tell he was happy as a squirrel to have stumbled upon me, like I was just what he'd been searching for. And my Billy, he was a sight for sore eyes. He looked just the same as he did when I'd left him, but so much more grown.

Turned out, he'd come over to Timberlake to visit a cousin. It was good luck that he was walking back toward town to catch the train when I passed by. He said he would come along with me to the market so we could catch up, that there was a later train he could take.

We dallied there in the grain aisle of Barton's Grocery, still exchanging all sorts of pleasantries, mostly just soaking up each other's presence. I should have been searching for tupelo honey, like Mrs. Libby asked, but I could hardly remember why I'd come to that store in the first place, as delighted as I was to see my old friend. Shoppers were coming and going, walking around where we stood crowding the path.

Finally, after he inquired after Ma and then told me all about his brothers, I asked what I wanted to know most of all.

"Now tell me the truth of it," I said, leaning closer and catching a whiff of Ivory Soap coming off him. "Have you seen Vivian over at the Dobbses' at all? She must be so grown."

His face fell, and I felt a panic bubble in my gut.

"You haven't heard?" He sounded kind of stunned, maybe even angry.

"Heard what?" I asked, and that balloon of worry inside me grew bigger.

"Carrie," he said, putting his big hand on my arm, "she got measles." He looked to the side, and then his eyes dropped down to the ground.

"Okay." I nodded, urging him on. I'd had the measles back when I was seven years old. At the same time I had it, so many other children from our one elementary class had it too. Our little school had been forced to close up until enough of us were able to come back to make it worthwhile to hold class again.

"Well, she got better." He shifted from one foot to the other. "But then she got some sort of infection, a secondary thing." He breathed in real long. "Carrie." His voice broke, and I prayed I was wrong about what was coming next.

"Don't say it, Billy."

"Carrie." His voice was real gentle.

"No! No, no, no. Billy, don't say it!" I was shouting now, and I guess I was making a scene, but I didn't care.

"She passed on back in June."

He might have said more after that, but I didn't hear any of it. I had sunk to the floor of that grocery store, where I lay keening like a wild animal. My Vivi was lost, and I'd never even known her at all. I'd never seen her smile nor felt her little hands wrap around me. And now she was gone from the earth. Lost. Like she'd never even existed at all. I howled in pain, nearly unable to breathe. She was my only one, and now she was gone. And there would never be another to remind me of her.

At some point, Billy carried me out of the store. He brought me back to Mrs. Libby and explained why I was in such a state. She helped me into bed and put a damp cloth to my forehead like Ma used to do when I was a toddler with a fever.

For the next four days, Mrs. Libby didn't ask one thing from me, letting me lie there staring at the wall. She brought my meals to me and everything. But then on the fifth morning, she was back in the doorway at 6:00 a.m. I reckon she thought she was doing right by me to finish up her coddling.

"Rise and shine, Carrie!" she said. "You've got chores a-waiting." She marched right into my little room, already wearing that brown apron of hers, coming to stare down at my bitter, sorrowful body. "No time to waste," she told me, but I wanted more time to grieve for my child—and all the children I might have had, who would never come to be.

"You can put me out," I told her. "Send me away and have done with me. I'll not be doing work today." I grabbed at the comforter and pulled it higher over me.

"Now, you listen here, Carrie," she said, moving over to the window. She pushed aside the curtain to let in the first slivers of morning light. Then her voice turned gentler. "You've suffered a terrible loss," she said, coming back toward my cot and sitting herself down on the edge. "I remember just what it's like from when Alfred passed last year. You think you can't get through it, that you'll never be all right again, that you won't ever have good reason to greet the morning. But you will, and you must. And the best way to push through what you're feeling is to put yourself back to work, to remind yourself that you are still alive. No matter what or how much has been taken from you, you are still here. Now what are you going to do with that?"

I stared back at her with what I imagine were vacant eyes. Even so, I somehow ended up rising to my feet and doing as she said. I dragged myself from the bed, pulled my work dress over my head, and got back to work. I didn't feel much alive then, I can tell you that, but somehow I started the day like she wanted.

~

Four weeks later, when I was fixing supper for Flora and James, I was still ruminating over all I'd lost. As I spooned creamed collards onto the children's plates, there came a knock at the front door.

"I'll get it!" James shouted, jumping out of his seat. He was always hoping the Bible man would be coming back around to tell the children more stories. Following behind him, I wiped my hands on my smock. Mine wasn't brown like the one Mrs. Libby wore all the livelong day, but a light pink that had pleased me back when I'd first arrived at her house. I hurried to help James reach the latch before Mrs. Libby heard the knocking carrying on too long.

When the door swung open, there standing on the stoop was my old friend Billy again, and I'll confess, my heart took a deep breath at the sight of him. He was holding a small arrangement of daisies, and he wore an expression on his face that I recognized from years past. To my surprise, this time I welcomed the question in his eyes. With all that had been took from me, I realized then, I must do like Mrs. Libby said and move forward in any way I could. I was not whole, nor would I ever be. I had been robbed in all the ways that mattered to me. I had but one thing left, and that was my own heart. I took Billy's hand and invited him in.

Jessa

April 2022

When I awoke, my arm moved reflexively toward Vance's side of the bed. My fingers found the covers still perfectly in place on his side, as if even the bedding wanted to hound the point that Vance was gone. Really gone. I was still stunned he'd left. I didn't know where he would have gone. Maybe a friend's apartment or a hotel. Could he have taken the car and driven out to his parents' home in Locust Valley? At the thought of my in-laws, my heart sank. I didn't want Vance to tell his parents anything about what had happened between us. I didn't want to think about Renee and Howard listening to Vance's version of events and shaking their heads, as baffled by my behavior as Vance seemed to be.

As I swung my legs over the side of the bed, my phone pinged from the bedside table. It was a text from my grandmother, ever the early riser.

"Hate to think of you alone with your work all day. Get yourself out of the apartment and come over for lunch."

Gram must have had a sixth sense about when I needed her. I tapped out a quick response agreeing to meet. At least I still had

Gram. I closed my eyes to quiet the words that inevitably followed. *For now.*

After I brushed my teeth, I fixed myself a sad breakfast of dry whole wheat toast. It was one of the few meals that didn't make me gag. When I finished, I rinsed the dish and put it in the drying rack next to the sink just as the apartment's buzzer phone warbled for attention. My first thought was Vance. But that was ridiculous because he wouldn't have needed the doorman to ring up. Then my stomach clenched as I remembered: Before the argument with Vance, I had emailed Dustin, asking him to stop by and translate some of his notes from the interview.

But now, the idea of spending time with him was even less appealing than usual. And that wasn't even accounting for the constant low-level nausea I was suffering. But I needed his help, and we both knew it.

I asked the doorman to send him up and quickly cleared a space at the dining table for us to work.

"Hey." I tried to sound nonchalant, even pleasant, as I opened the door. As usual, Dustin was dressed meticulously, though he looked a little like he was on his way to a nightclub, all turned out in his black slacks and sleek black button-down. He had a fresh shave, and his thick hair, curling just slightly at the collar, caught my eye in a way I wasn't prepared to acknowledge. Taking in his appearance, I felt that much dowdier, still clad in the sweats I'd slept in.

"Sorry for the mess," I said as I ushered him inside. "I've been printing hard copies of everything that seemed relevant. It's just easier for me, so please don't tell me I'm acting like I'm a billion years old. I'm aware that digital files exist." I scooped a stack of papers off the table and deposited them on the credenza behind us.

"I got staffed on a new matter last night," he said, taking a seat catty-corner to mine. "Everyone's going into the office today, so I'm more rushed than I expected. But I'll stay as long as I can."

Dustin's mention of the office, and the thought of energized attorneys getting together on the weekend to discuss a brand-new case, the intensity and excitement of it, made everything about my choices feel suddenly more conspicuous—taking the abrupt leave of absence, jeopardizing my career, risking my entire livelihood. He must have noticed the dismay on my face as he opened his laptop and said, "I thought you just wanted to review the notes from the meeting with Jacinta. That shouldn't take too long."

"No, no." I tried to shake off my bigger concerns. "You're right. I didn't realize you were on the clock. But hey," I said, pulling my laptop closer, "I'm meeting with four other women soon. Well, if I'm lucky. At least two of them will require a Spanish interpreter." I looked at him hopefully.

He looked up from his computer screen and sucked in air through his teeth.

"What?" I asked, even though I knew what he was about to say.

"Come on, Jessa. You know I can't do it. This case isn't on the firm's roster anymore. It's one thing for me to come over and talk about it on a weekend, but it's a whole different level to keep going with you to client meetings."

"Right, right, no, I know." I nodded my head, trying not to sound as disappointed as I felt. I'd have to find another interpreter, but I could do that. There were probably lots of human rights organizations out there that would be more than happy to provide the name of someone who could help.

"Jessa," Dustin said, reaching for my hand.

I looked up at him, startled by the physical contact, and even more surprised that I wasn't entirely opposed to the feel of his warm hand on top of my own. "I'll do whatever I can to help. You're just putting me in a tough spot. I can't risk my job. I'm still new, so I don't have the kind of savings that would allow me to be cavalier. As it is, I'll be paying off my student loans for a thousand years."

"No, I get it," I said. "I didn't mean to make you feel guilty or obligated. This is my fight. I know that."

He nodded and let go of my hand, and I felt the retreat like a loss. I turned my eyes away from him quickly, back toward my computer screen, wondering how I had arrived at a place in my marriage where my husband had walked out and I was actually relishing touches from Dustin, of all people.

"Let's just get to it," I said.

As we dove into the notes from the interview, examining each detail Jacinta had given us and considering the various points of law that might be supported by her testimony, I tried not to get discouraged. Even though I had so adamantly declared my intent to represent the women on my own, I hadn't really expected to be *alone* alone. I thought I'd at least have Dustin's brain to pick and Vance to bounce ideas off. But nope. It was Jessa against the world. Which, frankly, was a feeling I'd experienced so many times in my life that sinking back into it now was like putting on an old, reliable sweater. There was an odd sense of comfort to the familiarity of it.

It didn't take long to get through the notes, and before an hour had passed, we were already finished. Dustin rose from his seat and twisted from left to right, like he was stretching his back. It was a move I'd seen him do in the office countless times.

"You have back trouble?" I asked as I, too, scooted my chair backward and rose to my feet.

"Just an old surfing injury," he answered. "No big deal." Something about the way his eyes darted away from mine told me the very opposite was true.

"When did it happen?" I asked, suddenly filled with an unexplainable urge to know about Dustin's past. Was I so desperate for company that I'd listen to Dustin's life story just to keep another warm body in the apartment? Yes. Yes, I was.

"About five years ago," he answered. He'd made his way to the door and was looking back at me expectantly, as if waiting to be dismissed.

I quickly parsed the timing in my head. "That would have been right before you went back to law school."

"Yup." He nodded, rubbing the back of his neck with a hand while his eyes moved to his feet.

At his obvious discomfort, I connected the dots. "That's why you went to law school," I said. "Because you couldn't surf anymore." The realization irked me, all my judgmental feelings about Dustin's prior life choices resurfacing. The path I had chased since my childhood, the education and career I had hustled to achieve for so many years, was simply his pivot, his plan B when his laid-back surfer lifestyle stopped working out. "Seems like a drastic change for you." I scoffed. "One minute you're chilling on the beach without a care in the world, and the next you're knee-deep in torts outlines?"

"I was hardly *chilling*," he said, his tone suddenly hard as he stepped closer to me. "It was my job."

"You were a professional surfer?" I asked.

"Yeah. And I worked my ass off to get to the top."

My head tipped to the side in surprise. This new piece of information didn't comport with the impression I'd been carrying around about him since our very first meeting. He seemed to sense I was doubting something about him or his story. Then he pushed his shoulders back, dipped his chin, and began to refute everything I'd previously thought of him.

"I was training all the damn time," he said, "in and out of the water, regimenting my nutrition, constantly educating myself about the science of the body, the ocean currents, the boards.

Early mornings and late nights trying to be the best I could be." He shook his head slightly and added, "I did love it though, even when I was just a kid. For years, surfing was the only thing that mattered to me, so maybe it's not fair to call all of it work."

I blinked back at him, my eyes shifting in surprise. I'd never imagined him as anything other than a slacker, when in fact a great deal of substance might be hiding behind his bro facade.

I wondered what else I didn't know about him.

As I considered him, I looked back up at his face, and our gazes connected with a sudden zing. Alarmed by the electricity I felt buzzing between us, I stepped back. I wasn't going to be that woman. I wasn't going to start thinking about someone else just because I was having trouble with my husband. And Dustin was still a prick, even if he was a complex, substantive prick.

"Hey, can I ask you something?" I said, working to keep my voice neutral.

"Shoot." He pushed his hands into his pockets and waited.

"How come you've always been such a jerk to me at the office, but now you're acting like a total nice guy? What changed?"

"I haven't changed, Jessa," he said. "You have." He glanced down at his watch. "I'm late," he said. "Sorry." He let himself out, closing the door behind him and leaving me to wonder what he'd meant.

~

By lunchtime, I was in my usual chair at my grandmother's kitchen table, picking at the crusts of a turkey sandwich. I'd just finished giving Gram the *Reader's Digest* version of what happened with Vance, how he'd left in a huff with no indication of where he was going or how long he intended to stay gone. Gram sat opposite me, her lips pursed in the way that meant she had a number of her own thoughts on the issue.

"There's one other thing," I said, waffling between excitement and nerves.

Gram raised her eyebrows as she lifted her teacup from its saucer and sipped delicately. English breakfast had always been her favorite, and the familiar wet-grass smell of it was comforting, making me feel bolder.

"I'm pregnant."

"Jessa!" Gram's face lit up and she straightened in her seat, a bit of tea sloshing out of her cup as she put it back on the table. But then, almost as quickly, her expression soured. "And Vance left anyway? What a thing to do to your wife. That . . . that . . ." She seemed to be struggling for a strong enough insult.

"No, stop." I shook my head to intercept Gram's outrage. "I didn't tell him. He doesn't even know yet." I regretted that I'd brought even more duplicity into my marriage. "This is apparently what I do now. I keep all sorts of secrets from Vance. It's becoming a hobby or something. I just conceal one thing after another. Actually, not so many things, just the big things that really matter. I'm just a big fat liar, a rotten, worthless fraud of a wife."

"No, don't do that," Gram said. "You cannot compare not telling him you're pregnant with the other secret you're keeping."

I ran my finger over the painted flowers on the saucer in front of me. "If I just dropped the case, begged for my old job back, and forgot about Hydeford, I know Vance would come back. But I can't just put my life back the way he wants me to. I need to do this. He doesn't understand why it's so important to me to represent these women. But, Gram . . ." My eyes filled with tears, and the room blurred.

"Oh, honey," she said, reaching across the table and taking my hand. I held tightly to her bony fingers, trying to still myself, but a sob escaped anyway. And then another and another, until I was weeping in my grandmother's arms. She let me cry, waiting silently as she ran her hand over my long curls.

When I finally began to quiet, she sat back regarding me.

"That's better," she said, handing me a napkin to wipe my face. "Now, let's talk a little bit about blame, shall we?" She looked at me pointedly, as if I should already know what she was trying to convey. But I didn't have an inkling, so I just stared back. She sighed in the way of a teacher repeating a lesson to the child who hasn't paid attention in class.

"You are not the only one to blame here, Jessa. Maybe I gave you bad advice. I was the one who encouraged you to keep our family secret to yourself. I thought it was the right thing to do. But perhaps . . ." She paused, her eyes searching my face. "Perhaps that was just my own childhood trauma influencing me."

"Are you saying I should tell him?" I asked.

She was quiet another moment, and I watched as her expression changed. She was going back in time, and I could almost see the file drawers opening inside her head as she pulled out old memories.

"Mother told us we were never to talk about our past, that we were to forget where we came from. I did love my father. I can't say that I didn't. But I can never forgive him for what he did, the evil he brought into the world. I did everything I could to remove myself from it, including keeping it secret." She looked down at her lap for a moment before meeting my eyes again. "I didn't want you to ever feel the kind of shame I did, not when it wasn't your shame to bear. But I see now the toll it's taking on you, keeping this secret from Vance. I'm beginning to think that keeping it tucked away is doing you more harm than good. And now with a baby on the way . . . Maybe it's time to sit down with Vance and just tell him everything."

After she'd been so adamant about keeping our history to ourselves, doing otherwise felt nearly impossible to consider.

"But you said—"

"Forget what I said." Gram swatted an invisible obstacle in the air. "I'm just an old fool. You have to do what's right for you. And for your marriage."

I took a deep breath as I digested her words, trying to decide how I felt about them. I leaned closer to her, resting my head on her shoulder and closing my eyes. Of course I would tell Vance about the baby. If I told him about the baby but nothing about my great-grandfather, I was certain he would come back. But I didn't want to bring our child into the world knowing I was keeping other secrets from his or her father. That was not the type of parent I wanted to be, nor the type of person. Once Vance knew the whole truth, would that be the end of our marriage?

~

Vance wasn't answering my calls. I'd been trying for two days. Not until I texted him saying I needed to share important news did he finally call me back. Now we were sitting across from each other at a crowded Starbucks near our apartment building. Several people were lingering at the counter, waiting to retrieve their orders. We had managed to find the last empty table, wedged into a corner close to the restroom. My throat felt tight as I held the wrapper of my straw between my fingers, twisting it into a tight coil.

"Well, I'm here." Vance sounded frustrated. I noticed that the circles under his eyes were darker than usual.

I stared back at him, still unsure what to say first.

"Jessa," he groaned, "is there anything you actually need to share? Or was this just some kind of ploy to get me to return your call?"

His unkind words shocked me into admission.

"I'm pregnant."

He shook his head like he had water in his ear, like he hadn't heard me properly.

"What?" he asked, his voice still laced with irritation.

"I'm pregnant," I repeated, and I watched his face slowly begin to change. As the words sank in, the accusatory glare melted away, and in its place appeared an unfettered expression, as if he was opening himself up to the news, to possibilities, to me. A cautious smile grew, slowly overtaking his face.

"Jess!" he nearly shouted, his voice full of joy. His eyes darted around the room as if he was looking for other people to include in his celebration. The older man at the next table was focused on his laptop and didn't look up.

I was so relieved by Vance's excitement and his complete 180. Moments before, he had looked at me like I was gum on the bottom of his shoe. I nodded back at him with a goofy grin on my own face.

He reached across the table and took hold of my hand, gently pulling the straw paper out of my grasp before closing his fingers around my palm.

"I'm so sorry," he said, "for the way I left. For storming out on you and not giving you the benefit of the doubt, for not waiting longer to figure things out. I should know better. We're going to make this work. Whatever you need. How long have you known? Did you call the doctor? What do we do next?"

I found myself getting caught up in his excitement, nodding and laughing at how frenzied he sounded. I'd been so worried about his reaction that I hadn't imagined the great pleasure I might take in finally sharing the joy of the pregnancy with him. But then I remembered the rest, that there was more I needed to tell him.

"Wait, Vance, slow down." I smiled sadly. "There's more."

"Is everything okay with the baby?" he asked, fear creeping into his voice.

I shook my head. "Yeah, no, the doctor said everything's fine, although it's super early. It's something else."

"You don't want to drop the case? Or Hendricks already fired you for good?"

"Vance, just let me talk!"

"Sorry, sorry. Go ahead." He released my fingers and took hold of his coffee cup with both hands, as if to show he was behaving. I would have reveled in the adorableness of the gesture had I not been so distracted by worry.

"There's something important I learned recently that I haven't told you. I didn't want to upset you. I guess I thought I was protecting you . . . or protecting our relationship. But I can't bring this child into our life with any secrets between us."

"Secrets? What kind of secrets?" He looked at me quizzically.

I took a deep breath and dove in. "My great-grandfather, Gram's dad, was named Harry Laderdale." I paused for a second, waiting for a reaction, even though he'd likely never heard of the man.

"Laderdale?" Vance asked.

"Yes. They changed their last name to Larson after World War II, to hide who they really were."

"After World War II?" Vance tilted his head slightly, one corner of his mouth lifting. "Are you about to tell me you're part Jewish? My mom would be thrilled."

"No." I shook my head and reached for my iced coffee. I noticed my hand was shaking. "It's actually almost the opposite."

"What?" He laughed lightly, still not appreciating the enormity of the moment. "What's the opposite? That you're part Nazi?"

"Vance," I said pleadingly, "this is serious—and probably worse than anything you can imagine." I took a deep breath for strength and launched in. "My great-grandfather was a scientist, a eugenicist. He compiled data, studies, that argued certain types of people should be bred out of the population. He started here in the States in the 1920s, sterilizing women at psychiatric facilities so they could no longer have children. Which is part of why I've been so obsessed with my case." I realized I had started to cry. "He said he did it for the nation, for some warped notion that his work could improve American society. But it's even worse, Vance. His findings eventually made their way to Europe. His work gave the Nazis the idea of racial cleansing. It was his publications they relied on when they started killing non-Aryans."

As I talked, the color drained from Vance's face and his features went slack. He looked stunned, as if he'd just been injected with a tranquilizer but hadn't yet collapsed to the floor.

I seized on his silence, continuing my confession, spouting out every last horrid detail before I lost my courage.

"He helped create the Immigration Act of 1924 that kept so many Jews from coming to America in the '30s." I knew I was just making this worse for Vance, but if I didn't tell him everything now, I might never be brave enough to finish—and I couldn't have this hanging between us anymore. I needed to reveal every horrifying, disgusting truth. "He sent films to American high school students," I said, the words rushing from my mouth, "to teach them about the importance of eugenics in Germany. The Germans based their sterilization law on a model he wrote. He defended Hitler's Nuremberg decrees as scientifically sound. He was awarded an honorary doctorate from the University of Heidelberg in 1936. He—"

"Stop! Stop!" Vance held up a hand as if to protect himself from my words. "That can't be right. What are you even talking about? None of this makes sense." He shook his head vigorously.

"I didn't want you to know," I answered on a sob.

"Are you serious? Gram's father did all of those things?"

"He did," I said, choking up again. Instead of finding a napkin to wipe my tears, I studied Vance's face. I couldn't gauge his reaction.

But then something in him shifted.

"Wait." He pushed back his chair as if to stand. "You knew? You knew about all this and didn't tell me?"

"No! I only just found out a few weeks ago." I reached out for his wrist.

"Weeks?" he snapped, pulling his arm away. "You've known this for weeks and only thought to tell me now?"

"I should have told you sooner," I said. "You have no idea how horrible this has been for me. I don't know why I waited." I searched his eyes, hoping he could forgive me.

"I know why you waited. Because you knew I would never want to be with someone who came from a person like that," he said, venom in his voice. "Fuck, Jessa." He looked around, as if remembering his surroundings. He was silent a moment and then began to speak. The effort he was making to control himself was clear. "You knew how much I would hate this. And you didn't think to tell me, not once, while we were trying for the baby or when I was prepping episodes for the pod? Not even when we were spitballing all your eugenics theories about Hydeford? Wow." He shook his head, a smirk on his face as his gaze traveled toward the ceiling. "It all makes sense now."

I thought he was going to keep talking about the legal case, but he shifted back to himself. "You know how strongly I feel about everything that happened to my family. You didn't think, maybe once, before trying to get pregnant, that you should have shared this information?"

I couldn't say for sure if I'd conceived before or after learning about my family history—but I didn't think it was the right moment to say as much. I had a different point I needed to get across.

"Don't you see now?" I asked. "This is why *I* have to take the Hydeford case, why I can't give it up no matter how many times you ask. It's my chance to separate myself from what my great-grandfather did, to separate myself from the sins of my family. This case coming to me felt like fate."

"You are so obsessed with this fucking case!" Vance slammed his palm against our table, and this time the guy beside us did look up.

Noticing the man's glare, Vance mumbled a quick, "Sorry," then turned back to me.

He inhaled a slow, deep breath. When he spoke again, his voice was quieter. "The fucking case is the least of your problems. Nothing you do can undo what your great-grandfather did. And nothing can undo what *you've* done either."

He stood, pushing the heel of his hand against his forehead and closing his eyes for a moment. As he blinked, I could see a new thought occurring to him.

"And now my baby is going to be related to this man? What are my parents going to say about their grandchild sharing the same blood as a fucking Nazi?"

"He wasn't a Nazi," I said weakly, as if it made any difference.

"No," Vance said. "I guess not. From everything you've said, he might've been even worse. If such a thing is even possible." His eyes were stony as he glared down at me. "I can't look at you. I have to go." He pushed his chair back toward the table with too much force, leading it to tip and fall to the floor with a thud. He didn't turn around as he marched toward the door and back out to the street.

I stayed in my seat, ignoring the stares from the people who'd witnessed the scene. A young woman walking by lifted the chair and offered me a weak smile. I was too upset to even thank her.

In the span of one trip to Starbucks, I had somehow saved my marriage—only to destroy it all over again.

Jessa

April 2022

Once again in the Hydeford parking lot, I was sitting in my car waiting for Dustin and hoping he hadn't changed his mind about coming.

I was scheduled to interview two of Fern's four contacts, and I had basically begged Dustin for one more interpreting session. He was reluctant, but I pulled on his heartstrings until he caved. Except now, as the meeting time was approaching and he still hadn't arrived, I worried his fears about undercutting his position at the firm had gotten the better of him.

I hoped not, because these interviews were crucial. With four new women who'd agreed to testify, albeit anonymously, plus Jacinta, others might finally come forward too. I felt more compelled than ever to convince Isobel and Denise to be part of this. They deserved to be heard and at least get some modicum of justice.

I looked down at my stomach, still flat, and rubbed a palm across it wistfully. It had been three days since I'd heard from Vance. The day after our argument, he'd sent a text saying to reach out in case of a medical emergency, but otherwise he wanted no contact. I kept checking my phone for a follow-up text saying he just needed some time, or that his departure wasn't permanent, but there was nothing. My dream of the perfect family had almost come true, but now it appeared that was all it'd ever be—a fantasy.

I felt a single tear leak from my eye, but I hastily wiped it away just as Dustin pulled up beside me in a bright orange rental car.

"They don't make it easy to find this place," he said as we stepped out of our separate cars. Even though it was April, it didn't feel like spring yet, and I shoved my hands deep into the pockets of my wool coat.

"It was good of you to come all this way," I said, taking in his freshly shaven face and the crisp white collar of the shirt beneath his open parka.

He twisted from side to side, stretching his back in that way of his, and laughed lightly. His eyes darted to the ground and then back up to me. "I guess I find it pretty hard to say no to you."

I felt a flash of surprise at his words, both in their kindness and in their implied intimacy. I raised my eyebrows and tried to think of the right response, but then he seemed to backtrack.

"And you can be one pushy-ass attorney when you need something."

I twisted my lips in disbelief. "That's it? You're here because I'm pushy? I don't think so. Talk all you want, but I know you don't regret trying to protect these women. I saw the way you reacted at Jacinta's house." As I said it, I realized it was true. Dustin had clearly been deeply affected listening to Jacinta. "Like it or not, I see you, Dustin Ortiz."

"Whatever." He rolled his eyes and turned toward the entrance, but I could hear the smile in his voice. He motioned that we should make our way inside. "You don't have to rehash everything you said on the phone. I cleared the afternoon, but I really won't be able to do this again. I mean it. As important as this case is, crucially important, I don't have seven years of goodwill at the firm under my belt like you do. I also don't have the same freedom to devote time to a pro bono case, as much as I wish I did. I have some financial hurdles to clear first."

"Yeah, yeah." I waved a hand in the air and swatted away his words. "You'll be back." I stopped at the entryway and reached out to pull open the heavy door, but Dustin grabbed my wrist, stopping me.

"Jessa," he pleaded, his eyes holding mine. "I'm serious. My dad has been having some serious health issues, and I've been sending money to my parents every month. I can't slack off at the office when this job is the only thing paying the bills." He took a deep breath. "I really can't keep doing this, no matter how much I enjoy being in your company."

"I'm really sorry to hear about your dad, I am," I said, "but let's be real. My company has never been something you've enjoyed. I'm not completely obtuse."

"Yes, Jessa, you are." He pulled me back from the door, making it clear he had more to say. He looked down at me for a moment before he began again, his hand still clasping my wrist. "If I've been a dick to you, it's only because I can't figure out how to act around you. I haven't been trying to make you hate me so much as trying to protect myself from getting close to you. I mean, look at you." He gestured in my direction like he'd finished making his point.

"I don't know what you mean," I said cautiously, my mind coming up with too many possible scenarios of what he was trying to say.

"Even the first time I met you . . ." He shook his head as if he were saying something obvious. "I walked into the conference room on my second day, and there you were, holding court and dissecting every last facet of Odeon's legal strategy like you were in the Matrix, remember? I was mesmerized. You're whip-smart, but you don't lord it over anyone. You've clearly got an incredible friendship with Tate, but you're also kind of closed off, like people have to earn it with you before you let them in. You have this quiet confidence about you, and you're so freaking competent that every case you touch becomes a slam dunk. Add in those big eyes of yours, your hair . . . I was crushing on you hard. When I found out you were married, I guess I put up some walls. I don't think it was even a conscious decision. Acting like a bit of a bastard just put a little more space between us and made it easier for me to share the air with you. I didn't want to be pining away over a married woman, and I can admit now that I was pushing you away intentionally. But then you went and turned into this bleeding heart, and I guess I couldn't do it anymore." Then he shrugged, while I stared at him in shock. "I'm not trying to put you in an awkward situation. Just being honest."

We regarded each other for a long moment as I tried to decide how to respond. A look of panic flashed briefly across his face, like he wished he could take it all back. In another life, I would have been thrilled about attracting someone like Dustin—a successful, good-looking, and apparently very caring guy who worked his butt off to help support his parents. But I did, in fact, have a husband. At least, I hoped I did.

"I don't believe you," I finally said.

"You think I'm making this up?" He sounded incredulous.

I put my hands on my hips and continued to study him.

"If you've been rude in order to mask some alleged feelings for me, or to snuff them out or whatever, why have you all of a sudden started acting nicer?" It was entirely possible that he was just manipulating me for some reason I hadn't yet figured out.

Dustin nodded. "Fair. Leave it to Jessa Gidney to find the holes in any argument." I thought I heard a fondness to his tone.

"You didn't answer my question."

"It was that day in the car," he said. "When we drove out to Brooklyn to talk to Jacinta. I saw that you were struggling with something, and . . . I don't know, I just didn't want to cause you any more distress, no matter how insignificant. Even though you didn't want to discuss your personal business with me, you were clearly feeling something very deeply. As usual, I admired your passion, and I decided during that car ride that I didn't want to add anything else to your clearly full plate."

I was floored. All this time I thought he was a callous frat boy. I had the urge to knock against his chest to see if the other Dustin Ortiz was hiding somewhere inside. I'd been so wrong about him in so many ways. Something tugged at my heart while he spoke, almost pulling me toward him. But like he said, I was married. *Married.* And I couldn't give in to the pull. Not when my marriage was hanging by a thread. My loyalty had to be to Vance, even if he was AWOL.

Before I could think of what to say, Dustin shrugged again like he'd just finished telling a funny little story—not laying bare his secrets. "Let's get in there."

He turned back to the entrance, and I followed behind, wondering why my life seemed to be getting more complicated with each passing day.

The meetings with Romina Ignacio and Yamileth Navar went just as Fern had predicted. Yamileth arrived at the visitation room dressed in the same blue jumpsuit I'd grown used to seeing at the facility. She had wavy brown hair she wore loosely around her pale face. I knew already that Yamileth was thirty-four years old and had been subjected to a procedure at the hands of Dr. Choudry that left her sterile.

With Dustin interpreting, Yamileth explained that, like Isobel, she'd not been told anything about a hysterectomy until after she'd woken up. She had been under the impression they were removing a cyst from an ovary, and she swore she'd never given consent for anything else.

With each word of Yamileth's that Dustin relayed, I felt my skin growing itchier. I tried to imagine being trapped in a doctor's office without the ability to leave of my own free will. The table full of surgical tools. The locked doors.

"She asked the nurse for an interpreter, but they didn't bring anyone," Dustin said, repeating Yamileth's statements.

"How did you know they wanted to do anything at all without an interpreter?"

As Dustin repeated the question in Spanish, Yamileth nodded like she'd been waiting for me to ask.

"I have a few words in English," she answered through Dustin. "'You're sick,' the nurse told me. The only other words I understood were, 'Doctor fix,' and when I asked for the interpreter, they said there was 'no time.' They finally got the interpreter *after* the procedure to explain how I should care for the incision. That's how I found out what happened to me.

"There was one woman," Yamileth told us as Dustin interpreted, "Stella. Her bed was next to mine, and we sat together at every meal. They told her if she made a complaint about the clinic, she would have to spend another seven years in prison."

"Where is she now, your friend Stella?" I asked, thinking maybe she would also be willing to join the class action if she understood she could do so anonymously.

Even though I didn't understand the Spanish words that Yamileth said next, the anger came through loud and clear before Dustin translated.

"She disappeared. Nobody told us what happened to her."

The meeting with Romina, Fern's other contact, was different. Unlike the other women, Romina had not been operated on. She explained in a mix of English and Spanish that she had been given a shot of Depo-Provera, a contraceptive injection meant to make a woman sterile for several months. The doctor injected her without explaining what was in the shot. She only found out when she climbed back into the transfer van with a Band-Aid on her bicep and one of the other women asked if she'd gotten "the birth control shot." When Romina got back to Hydeford, she asked the attending nurse what she'd been given. The nurse checked the file and confirmed it.

Romina was awaiting a hearing on the appeal of her deportation order. She begged us to keep her name private, lest her participation influence the outcome of her case. I wished I could do more to reassure her, but why would a woman in Romina's position trust anyone at all?

After we finished the meeting, I walked with Dustin toward the exit to say goodbye. I had to go back in for my appointment with Isobel, but Dustin's work was done.

"So that went as well as we could have hoped, I think." I still felt awkward from our earlier conversation.

Dustin nodded as he opened a locker near the facility's entrance and removed his messenger bag.

"Yup." He didn't meet my eyes as he slung the bag over his shoulder.

"Listen," I said, but he held up a hand to stop me.

"No." He shook his head. "Let's not make this weird. I said what I said. I'm just a guy who's more comfortable laying it all out there. I know there won't be anything between us." He swallowed hard before a playful glint crept into his eyes. "Especially because you promised to leave me alone now so I don't lose my job. Not everyone has years of savings and your stellar résumé, never mind an investment banker spouse to get them through times of unemployment."

I didn't want to tell him I actually might *not* have my banker spouse anymore, that I might have successfully destroyed my marriage. I let my eyes rove over Dustin for a long moment. It was appealing, the idea of seeking comfort from him. Maybe any man who wasn't always angry with me would have been appealing at this point. And Tate had been right. Dustin was a good guy, not just a handsome one. But I couldn't give up hope that Vance might come back to me, not yet. The last thing I needed was to complicate matters further by thinking about another guy.

"Thank you," I said, offering him a regretful smile.

He nodded once more, and I watched as he walked away.

A few minutes later, I was back in the meeting room greeting Isobel. I noticed a small grease stain on the sleeve of her jumpsuit and wondered how often the uniforms were washed. When the door clicked closed behind the departing guard, Isobel took the seat opposite me and offered me a tight smile, the kind that said she wasn't pleased at all.

"You've got to stop this," Isobel said, "coming in here over and over just to ask me about my hysterectomy. It's my business, and I told you already, I'm not comfortable making a public fuss about it. I got my family to think about."

"I'm not here to pressure you," I rushed out. "I just thought you'd like to know that five women have now agreed to join a class action."

"A class action?" Isobel let out a little laugh. "Denise told me she called you Erin Brockovich a while back. She meant it as a joke, but look at you now." Isobel leaned back in her chair and gave me an approving once-over. "You're really trying to stick it to them, huh?"

"I have to do *something* and do it without exposing any of you. Some of the women will be listed on the complaint as Jane Does, so we'll have Jane Doe #1, Jane Doe #2, and so on. If you wanted, you could add your name to the action as another Jane Doe." I ran a hand over my own abdomen as I spoke. "Or not. It's up to you, but I wanted to keep you informed."

Even though I hoped so deeply that Isobel would decide to join the fight, I couldn't force her. If she wanted to sit this out, I would respect her wishes. I was well aware that I had absolutely no idea what it was like to walk five steps in any of these women's shoes. But I did know what it felt like to dream of a family. I hoped that if ever someone robbed me of that, I would still have the will to fight. But who could say? I prayed Isobel would find that will within herself.

"Who exactly are we suing?" Isobel asked. "The government?"

At hearing her say "we," I tried not to smile.

"A lot of people. The defendants, at least so far, will be Hydeford Detention Center, DeMarke Corrections, Dr. Choudry, Pinelands, the director of the local ICE field office that oversees this facility, the secretary of Homeland Security, and the director of US Immigration and Customs Enforcement. I'd like to add more employees at the clinic and several individual guards too, but we're not quite there yet."

"People here are going to go crazy if you really file a complaint." I sensed a warning in her tone.

"Somebody has to do something about what's happening in here."

"And why is that somebody going to be you?" Isobel challenged me.

"You sound just like my husband," I said without thinking.

"He doesn't want you doing this?"

Despite my usual efforts not to discuss my personal life with clients, I was so raw I couldn't suppress the urge to say a little something about what was happening with Vance.

"He thinks I should have more proof before I start blowing up everything in my own life to start something he calls a crazy crusade. But I know what it is to want a baby. I miscarried last year, and I don't know if this one . . ."

I trailed off, realizing I had just accidentally revealed my pregnancy to Isobel too. The last thing I wanted was to make her feel worse about her own infertility.

"You're pregnant?" she asked. "I shouldn't be surprised with the way you've been rubbing your belly since we sat down."

I yanked my hand down to my side.

"My husband," I said, "thinks if I get too stressed, I'll lose this baby too. The arguing has been endless. He left, and I honestly don't know if he's ever coming back."

"Yikes," Isobel said, taking in a sharp breath and regarding me.

I gave a little shrug, suddenly self-conscious, and Isobel shook her head.

"No, don't do that," she said. "Don't act like it's no big deal. I've been real with you. Now you be real with me." She continued studying me. "Tell me something," she said. "Why does it matter to you so much that we bring this case?"

I thought for a moment, trying to put my emotions into words. I wouldn't tell Isobel about my family history. That was simply too much. I was still struggling to face it myself, and it was hardly the most important part of this picture anyway.

"If you don't stand up for yourself," I finally said, "people will keep getting away with it, taking control of women's bodies and making choices for them they have no business making. We all come at these decisions with our own personal histories. When

I was a little girl, my mom used to button up my raincoat for me on wet spring mornings, singing a song about 'one button, two buttons, three buttons, four.'" My voice cracked as I chanted the words, picturing my mother in those moments. "I often imagined myself doing the same thing for my own child one day, bouncing my shoulders to the rhythm in the same goofy way. And now I think about all the women in here who had their own dreams when they were little girls, and how those dreams are being ripped away from them. Nobody else has the right to decide which ones of us are fit to bear children, which ones of us are 'good enough.' What does that even mean? This isn't about individual worth or merit. It's about our rights."

Isobel sighed heavily, but she didn't respond.

"We have to stand up for ourselves and for each other," I repeated, my voice rising. "Think about your daughter. She's going to make her own judgments about who her mother is. Who do you want to be for your child? I know who I want to be for mine."

Isobel stared back at me, her face blank, and I worried I had gone too far.

"Listen," I said, my bravado dimming, "I know you only wanted a lawyer to help with your deportation. I won't bother you about this again, and I'm really, truly sorry if I've been too pushy."

I closed my notepad and put the cap on my pen.

"I'll set up an appointment to prep for your next court appearance," I told her. "We're good until then."

I rose from my seat and moved toward the intercom box.

"For fuck's sake," Isobel said.

"I'm sorry, what?" I asked.

"I'll do it. But you have to keep me anonymous. Someone in here's going to figure out who's involved. You got to keep an eye on me the whole time, from start to finish. I am *not* getting deported over this."

I hurried back into my seat and opened my notebook again.

"We will not let that happen," I said as I took Isobel's hand and squeezed. We stared at each other for a moment, and a million little messages seemed to pass between us—grief for all that had been lost, acceptance of the challenges ahead. A lump formed in my throat as I thought how bittersweet it was that Isobel and I had really come to understand each other. She squeezed my hand back, like she knew just what I was thinking.

With a quick nod, I pushed past the lump and told her, "Now, let's get to work."

~

Driving back to the city, I was exhausted by the back-to-back interviews and the thought of all the work that lay ahead. Merging onto the highway, I found myself ensconced in thick, slow-moving traffic. As I inched along, I thought of all the wrongdoers I'd listed to Isobel earlier. This case was drastically different from anything I'd worked on in the past. Representing corporate defendants—big companies that sold insurance or frozen vegetables or Bitcoin—was something I could do with one hand tied behind my back. At the bottom of every case, those clients were mostly just fighting over money. But filing a class action, in an urgent effort to stop violent and irreparable damages to vulnerable plaintiffs, was completely new to me. I found myself questioning all over again whether I was equipped to handle it. As I worried I might fail them all, I tried to ignore Vance's voice in my head, gaslighting me. But pushing away all the doubts he'd been stoking since I first told him about the case was proving difficult.

Thinking through the steps of the case, I decided I'd try to get attention from the press quickly. Should the complaint play well in the court of public opinion, my clients might have a fighting chance of winning this thing. But what would happen until then?

I considered all the discovery we'd need and found myself nearly gasping for breath. We'd have medical records, correspondence, financial information, daily logs from the facility, all of DeMarke's records, and whatever else I could require the medical facility to produce.

Amid cases like these—the ones with enough defendants to field a football team and an enormous number of documents to scour—Tate had been a real godsend. She could lead a team of paralegals in the initial stages of document review like nobody's business. I again thought of Vance saying that I was doing these women a disservice by taking the case without more help. On this point, he probably was right.

Now that I'd let the fear seep in, it began to run wild in my mind. What if my actions somehow made everything worse for the women inside? Was I just being selfish and using their case to make myself feel better about who I was and where I came from? Thoughts began swirling like a violent storm, and I felt my breath growing shallow. I couldn't have a panic attack in the middle of the highway, even if the cars were moving at a snail's pace. I was approaching an exit—if I could just hold it together until I made my way up the exit ramp. My car moved up one inch at a time. I just tried to breathe deeper and deeper. Finally, I pulled to the side of the road and cut the engine.

I leaned my head against the wheel and shut my eyes, breathing slowly and allowing my tempestuous thoughts to run free. My throat burned, and I felt nearly paralyzed with fear.

I couldn't say how much time passed before a knock at the window made me jump. There, beside my window, was a police officer. Because of course there was.

I rolled down the window and looked up at him. He was a Black man deep into middle age, with a salt-and-pepper beard and a slight paunch at his middle.

"Everything all right here, miss?"

"Yes, sorry, Officer," I said, wiping under my eyes with my knuckle. "I was upset about something. I just needed a minute."

"This isn't a safe place to stop your vehicle," he said. "Cars coming off the highway here are still passing by fast. They mightn't see you in time." He motioned toward the traffic light up ahead. "At that light up there, you make a left, and it'll take you to Dina's. You'll see it on your left. She'll fix you right up."

"To Dina's?" I asked, confused.

He nodded without offering an explanation, tapped the side of the car twice, and walked away.

I couldn't imagine what he meant, but I had to go in that direction to wrap back onto the highway anyway.

As I turned off the access road onto a busy thoroughfare, I passed only a couple of storefronts before I saw a big magenta awning with "Dina's" written in flowery cursive. The name was positioned diagonally across a drawing of a frosted cupcake. It was a fun-loving design, with confetti sprinkles and a maraschino cherry making the awning aggressively perky.

I scoffed. I should have been used to other people belittling my feelings, especially men, but I bristled all the same. He was sending me to a freaking bakery? My problems were hardly the kind that could be fixed by a pretty cupcake.

That wasn't going to cut it.

Then I had a jarring thought: Maybe I was just like that cop. There I was, thinking I was really going to help these women, even though I didn't have the right experience and had never represented an entire class of plaintiffs. Suddenly my plan seemed like a metaphorical cupcake—a cute idea but woefully inadequate.

If I really wanted to make a difference for the detained women, I should probably hand over my findings to an actual immigration lawyer. But if I abandoned them like that, Isobel and the others might see it as another reason not to move forward. I'd promised to stand by them, and I couldn't renege on that. As I merged back onto the slow-moving highway, I considered another option: a way to give my clients the best of both worlds. I laughed out loud as I realized the cop might have been pretty insightful after all. He'd offered me the best he could, given the circumstances. And maybe sometimes offering your best was enough.

When I finally drove over the bridge into Manhattan and merged onto the FDR Drive, my dashboard lit up with an incoming call. Vance's name flashed on the screen, and I hesitated to answer. He might be calling to say he was never coming back, to tell me we were officially over, soon to be fighting over the custody of a child. Of course, custody would only be an issue if he wanted anything to do with our baby—something I wasn't sure of now that he knew the whole story.

"Hello?" I said tentatively.

"We need to talk." Vance sounded breathless, his voice echoing. He was probably in the stairwell at his office, seeking privacy for whatever vitriol he intended to spew.

"Yeah," I answered, girding myself.

"I can't now," he said, "but in a couple hours. Please tell me you can meet tonight."

I sighed loudly, allowing Vance to hear it, but then agreed. "Just tell me when and where."

"I'll come to the apartment. Around eight thirty. I have to run."

As the call disconnected, Vance sounded like he couldn't stand another second of hearing my voice. It was a new wound at a difficult moment in our relationship, perhaps our complete unraveling.

When 9:00 p.m. rolled around and Vance still hadn't appeared, I began to wonder if he'd changed his mind and no longer wanted to talk. A call letting me know as much might have been nice, but maybe such courtesy was simply too much to hope for with the way things were between us.

I was sitting on the couch with my computer in my lap, scrolling through websites about fetal development. I landed on a page that detailed an average baby's growth from week to week, comparing the size of the fetus to various common items, mostly foods. Since I was just a few weeks along, our baby would only be the size of a grain of rice or a pomegranate seed. I smiled as I read that at this early stage, the baby would resemble a tadpole. Thinking of my offspring as a nascent amphibian was equal parts wonderful and gross. Reading further down the page, I learned that in order to hear the fetal heartbeat before twelve weeks, doctors would often perform a transvaginal rather than an abdominal ultrasound. I hadn't realized that's what I was in for when I scheduled my follow-up with Dr. LaRusso. Would Vance come to that appointment? The thought of him standing beside me reeking with disdain while a doctor maneuvered a wand inside my body brought new meaning to the word *awkward*.

The sound of a key at the door startled me. When the door opened and I saw Vance's face, I was hit with a wave of longing that nearly knocked the wind out of me.

He was dressed in black slacks and a blue shirt, the one patterned with tiny diamonds that I'd helped pick out at Bloomingdale's the year before. The shadow along his jaw was dark, as was usual for this hour of the evening, but his eyes were bright. If I didn't know better, I'd have thought he looked happy to see me.

"Hi," I said stiffly, moving my laptop to the end table and standing. I didn't approach him. I wasn't sure what to do with myself or why I had risen from my seat in the first place.

"Hi," he said, closing the door. "I'm so sorry I couldn't get here sooner." His tone was harried but kind. "I have to tell you what happened at work today. Sit." He motioned to the spot on the couch I'd just vacated.

"Okay . . . ," I said tentatively, lowering myself down again. He was acting like we were normal, like we weren't in the middle of falling apart, like I shouldn't feel as utterly wrecked as I did.

Instead of joining me on the couch, he sat on the large wooden coffee table across from me. There wasn't much space between the table and the sofa, and his legs ended up flush against mine.

"So you know how I've been underwater on the Wagner deal?" We were at eye level with each other.

I nodded, even though I had only the vaguest sense of that deal.

"Well, I finally came up for air for thirty seconds today, and of course Arjun immediately asked me to be another set of eyes on some reports for him."

Vance often joked about how Arjun, arguably the smartest person on their floor at work, was constantly asking for "a quickie second opinion." Even though no one was more likely to understand the complex business or accounting issues at play than Arjun himself.

"Yeah," I said, looking down at where our knees touched and wondering where this was going.

"They're doing due diligence on some matters related to DeMarke."

My eyes shot back up to his.

"He had financial statements," Vance continued, "showing earnings at the different facilities they manage." He took a breath. "DeMarke manages twenty-one facilities, but one number was out of sync with the others. The profit margin at Hydeford is 40 percent higher than all the other facilities DeMarke manages."

"Wait." I sat up straighter. "Hydeford is their most profitable facility?"

Vance nodded, almost frantically.

"I knew it!" I was suddenly on my feet again. "It's the insurance payments! Why else would one detention center be getting so much more money than all the rest? The other facilities DeMarke runs have just as many inmates or more. So why would this one place have such a different economic outcome? They're not just butchering people over there—they're making a massive profit off it."

"Jessa, I'm so sorry. I can't believe I doubted you," he said, reaching for my arm and pulling me back into my seat. "I don't know why I was so stubborn, why I kept insisting you had to be wrong. Maybe I'm just not used to seeing you charge ahead without needing my input." He swallowed audibly, and I watched his Adam's apple bob in his neck. "But I should have listened, Jess. You always knew."

His hand landed on my leg, and the warmth of it seemed to spread all over my body. I allowed myself one brief moment to sink into a wave of relief at his about-face. Maybe things could still work out for us and I could be finished sleeping alone. But then my mind returned to the case. I had no time to linger on my feelings.

"I have to get on this, like, yesterday!" I turned back toward my laptop.

"Wait, Jess, just wait." He reached for my arm to slow me down. "This could get me fired. You can't know what I just told you. You have to find the information some other way, not from me."

Right. I had put him in a difficult position at work after all.

"I get it. It's fine. There must be other ways to find this information. A lot of it is probably publicly available, and whatever's not, I should be able to access through discovery."

"And you won't tell anyone you heard it from me?" He could have made a dig then about how practiced I was at keeping secrets. I was relieved he didn't.

"No, of course not," I assured him. "But wait." My mind was running on overdrive, new thoughts bombarding me. "Do you think this means everything is coming from the top at DeMarke? That it's not just some underground scheme at Hydeford? It's starting to look like company policy, unofficially sanctioned." I felt faint at the very notion.

"Well, DeMarke is headquartered in Atlanta," Vance said. "If it were company-sanctioned, it wouldn't make sense that among so many detention centers, only one would be engaging in fraud."

"It's not just coming from the doctor though," I said. "Now we know that at least."

"Right," he said, glancing down at my laptop as if he wanted to start doing more research, together.

"I've looked into how these facilities are structured," I said, thinking back to all the information I'd been able to find online. "They have a local company for on-site management. There's a facility manager, and his compensation is tied to the profitability of the center. The better the center does, the more the manager gets paid. The sterilizations may not be company-sanctioned, but they definitely appear to be facility-sanctioned. Encouraged even. So this isn't just about controlling these women's bodies," I said, still mentally parsing through the information. "It's also insurance fraud."

"It backs up everything you've been saying," Vance said, squeezing my hand. He was suddenly so very present for me. "They're preying on people, doing some sort of eugenics or whatever you want to call it. And then they're profiting from it to boot. The math proves it," he said again, his voice thick with admiration. He looked at me with a light in his eyes I hadn't seen in weeks, and I wanted to bask in it.

I grinned back at him, so relieved to have finally convinced him of what I'd known all along. I allowed myself another moment to absorb that Vance finally believed me, believed *in* me. He had seen hard evidence, which had restored his confidence in me. But then

I felt the familiar clench of annoyance creeping back into my chest as I wished he hadn't needed outside evidence—that he'd simply believed in me from the start.

I couldn't think about that now though, because I finally understood the true enormity of what I'd uncovered at Hydeford. Vance had been right about one thing all along—I'd bitten off way more than I could chew on my own.

"Vance." I let myself collapse back against the couch. "With all these new possible defendants, this is too big a job for one person. It's too big a job for two people or five people."

"Let me help you," he said. "I've stood in your way long enough. Let me help clear the path."

Suddenly he was the Vance I'd been hoping for ever since my first trip to Hydeford. Of course I wanted his help. Needed his help. But it wouldn't be enough.

"But what about us? You left me."

Vance released a long breath.

"I didn't really *leave* you," he said. "Let's not call it that. I just needed some time. I was angry. I mean, you did keep a huge secret about your identity from me. Even if you'd only known the truth for a few weeks, you still hid it."

I didn't interrupt to tell him that by saying the secret was tied up with my identity, he'd just validated my deepest worries: that he wouldn't be able to separate me from my ancestral lineage.

"I mean, it's not surprising that I would need a minute to process, right?" he continued, at least having the decency to offer an abashed smile. "Here I thought I'd married a straight arrow. Always coloring inside the lines, not breaking the rules, never straying from a certain narrow path. And then it turns out you have this nefarious family history that's inspired you to go rogue, running into the craziest legal scenario you've ever dealt with, headfirst and all alone."

It was true. I *had* always been a rule follower, white-knuckling my way through life, single-mindedly pursuing my limited list of life goals. But the way I'd been living of late, trying to stand up for what was right instead of focusing on some grand master plan, felt so much better.

"You're my wife," Vance said, knocking his leg into mine in an affectionate gesture. "You're carrying my child. And I love you. We're going to be our own little family soon."

I felt the tears that had been pooling in my eyes spill over at his words.

"Hey," he said, moving next to me on the sofa. "Come here." He wrapped his arms around me, and I relaxed into his hold. We stayed like that, clinging to each other. As I took comfort in our closeness, an image of Dustin flashed into my mind, unbidden. I pushed it away, unwilling to consider what it might mean.

After a while, I pulled back, wiping the sleeve of my hoodie against my cheek.

"Thank you for bringing this information to me, for trusting me with it and finally believing me," I said, my voice wet. "But, Vance, I can't take myself off the case."

"Well, yeah, no. You can't." Now he was all matter-of-fact, like he'd never suggested otherwise. "I've been trying to think of a way for you to handle it. There has to be something in between working too hard and not at all. Right?"

It seemed he had more to say, but I held up my hand. I didn't need him making a plan of action for me yet again. Whatever he was about to say would only fuel the resentment I was still feeling for the way he'd abandoned me, physically and emotionally. Besides, I had already hatched an idea on my own. Something I'd begun contemplating after my run-in with the cop. And now I knew what I would do.

"Vance," I said, the word an instruction for him to stop talking. "I've got this. I know what I'm going to do."

"You do?"

I tried not to be offended by the surprise on my husband's face, and instead of laying into him for being condescending, I said, "I know this case should have a huge team of people working on it. I mean, we should be pushing for a congressional investigation and bringing down every last person and agency who is complicit in this situation."

Vance nodded in agreement.

"We need people to help. And I know who to ask. I'm starting with Will Carbone."

"Who?"

Will Carbone was my former law professor. He ran a clinic at NYU, but I'd only taken his course on evidence. The clinics allowed students to help with pro bono cases to gain experience while litigants benefited from free legal services. Many law schools had similar programs, and now I was sorry I hadn't participated in the one at my school. Professor Carbone ran the Immigrants' Rights Clinic along with a partner professor whose name I couldn't recall. They focused on social justice issues in protecting newly arrived or detained immigrants. It could be a perfect fit. What's more, if I remembered correctly, the clinic often partnered with outside community-based organizations that provided all kinds of pro bono legal services. Now that I had settled on this idea, I couldn't believe I hadn't reached out to them sooner. And NYU was hardly the only school with that kind of clinic. I could check in with Columbia, Cardozo, Fordham, and so many others. An entire team of legal partners was materializing in my mind's eye, growing by the second.

After I explained all of this to Vance, he reached forward and hugged me.

"I knew you'd find the right support in the end." He said it with relief, like it was what he'd been waiting for all along.

What I didn't say in response was that I wasn't doing this to lighten my own workload. I'd still be working my ass off because of the enormity, and the importance, of the case.

As he pulled back from the embrace, his expression told me he wanted everything to go back to normal between us. I wanted that too. I took in the soft light of his Coca-Cola eyes and the warmth on his face, and I tried to imagine picking up where we'd left off. A movie reel played in my mind as I pictured us moving forward together again—eating takeout on the sofa while we binged new shows, spending weekends with family, or doing our work side by side like before. And of course, now, becoming parents together. Yet the images in my mind left me feeling anxious and empty somehow, and I worried that the life I was imagining was simply no longer possible.

Jessa

May 2022

I turned down the narrow side street in Greenwich Village, weaving a path around other pedestrians on the bustling sidewalk. It was one of the first warm days of spring, and the streets were crowded with people enjoying the weather. I hurried along past quirky lunch spots, smoke shops, tattoo parlors, and hipster clothing stores. Most passersby probably wouldn't even notice the narrow three-story structure where I was headed. But to me, the building was a beacon, a safe haven that seemed to call out to me as I approached.

For the past four weeks, I'd been stepping into the inconspicuous brick building that housed the Manhattan Immigrant Defense Center on a near-daily basis. I pushed open the heavy glass door, checking my watch again. I was relieved to see that despite the subway delay on my ride downtown, I wasn't as late as I'd expected.

As I made my way toward the building's interior stairwell, I rounded a corner and nearly collided with Will Carbone.

"Jessa!" he exclaimed as we each stepped back to avoid toppling the other. Will was dressed in one of his signature three-piece suits. His white hair was combed neatly to the side and his eyes, beneath round tortoiseshell glasses, were especially bright. "We're really getting there, kiddo," he said, and I felt myself puff up at the pride in his voice. With each day that passed since I'd first told him about Hydeford, he'd proven how right I'd been to reach out.

"I'm running late for my granddaughter's birthday," he said with an air of apology. Then he made his way around me. "Lydia and I got so caught up."

When I had contacted Professor Carbone the month before to ask about working with NYU's Immigrants' Rights Clinic, I didn't think he'd even remember me. Eight years had passed since I finished law school, nine since I'd been a student in his evidence class. I needn't have worried. When I reintroduced myself on the phone, he immediately referenced a law review article I'd written as a student and joked that he always lamented when promising young legal scholars landed at corporate firms instead of academic institutions. Buoyed by his apparent confidence in my abilities, I launched into the reason for my call, but as soon as I uttered the words *class action*, he stopped me short.

It wasn't going to work, he said. Although the students in the NYU clinic were very talented, he explained, a large class action lawsuit would be too complicated for them to manage without additional oversight. He suggested looping in Lydia Brass at the Manhattan Immigrant Defense Center to partner with us.

Since that time, we'd created a larger and more formidable team than I ever could have dreamed. Lydia and her colleagues contacted several other human rights organizations in New York and New Jersey, and even the National Immigration Project of the National Lawyers Guild in DC. I felt as if I'd barely blinked, and suddenly I was co-counsel alongside some of the biggest names in immigrant defense law.

And then there were the NYU clinic participants. Those students were devoting countless hours and providing invaluable support. At any given moment, I found myself surrounded by four or five dedicated 2Ls and 3Ls who were worth their weight in gold.

I made my way to the project room on the third floor, a windowless conference space large enough for ten or twelve people to work together. Under the room's fluorescent lighting, I found a group of students focused on their individual laptops. I walked to an empty seat at the large oval table and pulled out my own computer. The others acknowledged me quietly, glancing up with silent nods and small smiles.

While I waited for my computer to power up, my eyes roved over the four students seated near me, each of them working intensely. Wanda and Reese, two young women sitting beside each other, had been walking the six blocks to and from NYU's Vanderbilt Hall multiple times a day to comb through case research, check case citations, and organize the growing piles of supporting documents. Sean, who'd joined the team only the week before, was working on a preliminary press release. Then there was Mia, in her wire-frame eyeglasses and hot pink combat boots, who was so well-versed in the requirements of various immigration orders that I had trouble remembering the young woman was still only a student.

In the four short weeks we'd been working together, there'd been laughter and hugs each time any of us found a new piece of law that worked in favor of our clients. With our shared passion and all the hours of quiet work together, I'd found myself feeling more connected to these colleagues than I had to any of my peers at Dillney. Although Will Carbone had offered to let me remain lead attorney, I'd declined. For the first time in as long as I could remember, it didn't matter to me who oversaw a particular case. I was just glad we were all doing our best to help our clients. It felt pretty incredible to work alongside other people who were putting forth so much effort for reasons that had absolutely nothing to do with their holiday bonuses.

As I returned my attention to my computer, opening Westlaw to continue my online research, Lydia appeared at the door with three large binders in her arms.

She spotted me and smiled warmly. With gray hair cut close to her head and a face that was only just beginning to wrinkle, she was dressed with her usual bohemian flair in tan bell-bottom pants, a flowing floral blouse, and long earrings made of pink feathers that reached below her shoulders. Despite her fun-loving style, she could tear apart a weak legal argument in a matter of seconds. She hurried around the table, making her way toward my seat.

"You're just in time," she said in a half whisper, then dumped the binders on the table. "I think it's ready to go," she continued in a hushed tone.

She was talking about the complaint. We'd been going over it with a fine-tooth comb for the past several days, making sure we hadn't left out any important claims or any possible defendants. Once it was finalized, we'd send it over to our co-counsel, the New Jersey Alliance for Immigrant Justice, who would file it on our behalf in the morning.

"The kids finished the cite checks last night. All that's left is the final proofing now. You want to take a turn?"

Back in my life at Big Law, being tasked with proofreading could have been considered an insult, or at least a waste of a senior attorney's valuable time. Proofing was a dreaded assignment endured only by junior associates and paralegals. But I was glad to be involved in all stages of the case. Instead of simply drafting theoretical documents, I was getting deep in the weeds, doing the tasks that kept a person feeling connected to a case. And anyway, Lydia had turned her focus toward discovery and the different sources from which the team would be seeking information. There were bucketloads of work involved in that too.

I nodded enthusiastically. "Give it here," I said, reaching for a binder.

I picked up a pen and began reading from page one. It felt like I'd been over the familiar document a thousand times already, but judges could be sticklers for perfection, and I didn't want to risk even the smallest error. As I read, I rubbed a hand against my belly. I still wasn't showing, but my stomach wasn't nearly as flat as it had been eleven weeks earlier. Only one more week remained until the coveted twelve-week mark, when the risk of miscarriage would drop dramatically. I was still trying to maintain some emotional distance from the baby growing inside me. Just in case. But I was doing a woefully poor job of staying aloof.

As I continued turning pages of the complaint, I became engrossed in the facts of the case all over again. Each time I was confronted with the details from Hydeford was just as jarring as when I first discovered what had been happening to the women. I could see the events unfolding all over again, like a horror movie playing in my mind.

Nearly an hour later, as I reached the end of the document, the section enumerating the relief the plaintiffs sought, the quiet was interrupted by Lydia's legal assistant, Asahi.

"I brought food!" he called gleefully. He held up two take-out bags from Loukoumi Taverna, our favorite Greek restaurant, famous for their cumin-spiced falafel wraps.

Sean whooped in response, like he'd just won a prize. "You are a legend, Asahi!"

The scent of garlic made its way toward me, and instead of making me queasy, it caused my mouth to water. In recent days the nausea had subsided and I'd been ravenous. For breakfast alone, I could go through two English muffins, fully loaded with eggs, cheese, bacon, and avocado. No matter how much I ate, it never seemed to be enough.

Asahi placed both bags on the lacquered table. People rose from their seats, gathering around the bags to extract foil-covered pita wraps and plastic containers of salads and dips.

I waited while the others rooted around, not wanting to seem as piggish as I was feeling. Wanda noticed me still in my seat and tossed me a wrapped sandwich.

As I smiled gratefully and began opening the foil, Sean came up behind me, glancing at the complaint on the table.

"You're almost finished. Good." He pulled out the chair beside me, unwrapping his own sandwich before continuing. "Then you can help me with the request for the Senate investigation. If we can get the Permanent Subcommittee on Investigations to look into this . . ." He took an aggressive bite of his gyro, then grinned sheepishly as he worked through the large hunk in his mouth. "They'll find everything. Hopefully they'll even shut down the facility while the investigation is pending."

"We should definitely be aiming for that," Reese said from across the room as she settled back into her seat. She had the kind of long, straight blond hair I'd always envied as a kid. She was a beautiful young woman with a bright future ahead of her. She was also a white all-American girl, probably just the sort of person my great-grandfather would have wanted to clone.

"Getting Hydeford closed, it's a more immediate solution," Reese said. "At least then the women would be moved somewhere else where the threat of retaliation would be reduced."

"I was thinking the same thing," I said. "Although I don't know why I keep allowing myself to get distracted with this part of the case. I know the DC attorneys are handling the filing with the Office of Inspector General. I should really be working on this list for discovery with you guys."

"I know why you're focusing on it," Asahi said from across the table. "You want to see those fuckers pay as quickly and dramatically as possible."

I laughed. "Well, I guess that too." As I bit into my sandwich, I couldn't tell whether the warm sensation coursing through my limbs was from the falafel or the camaraderie filling me up. Probably both.

After everyone finished eating and the room quieted down again, I returned to the complaint. Even with only a few pages left to read, I couldn't regain my focus. The talk of discovery had brought Dustin to mind, probably because we worked together on multiple discovery teams at the firm. Or, more likely, because he simply kept invading my thoughts unbidden, and I was having an increasingly difficult time banishing him. There had been so many times over the past several weeks when I'd wanted to call him, just to tell him what was happening on the case. I thought he'd want to know. But I also didn't want to confuse myself or Dustin about any feelings we might have for each other, especially not while everything was still so fragile with Vance.

And things *were* getting better with Vance. Well, sort of. Ever since the night of our reconciliation, we'd both been on our best behavior, and we hadn't had a single argument.

I sighed thinking about him now. Despite the recent détente, something still felt off. I knew he was trying—like when he started making me flavored decaf coffees every morning, poor but thoughtful substitutes for the espresso shots I'd used as fuel before pregnancy. He bought me a new pair of fuzzy slippers and a full-sized body pillow that was supposed to help prevent back pain as my pregnancy progressed. But such things did not make a relationship satisfying. I was getting what I'd thought I wanted, but it turned out the little gestures didn't matter to me at all, not when there was still so much we weren't saying to each other. At times I would catch Vance staring at me from the other side of the room, thinking unknowable things. I wondered in those moments if he was looking for traces of evil in my face, second-guessing his decision to make peace.

A noise caught my attention, and I glanced up from the document. As if conjured by my thoughts, Vance stood in the doorway of the project room. He was wearing a dark long-sleeved t-shirt and the gray cargo pants he favored for weekend outings. He raised his eyebrows at me expectantly, beckoning me over. I held a finger to my lips and hurried around the table toward the door.

"What are you doing here?" I whispered as I took his arm and pulled him farther into the hallway.

"Can I kidnap you for a while?" he asked, moving me toward a window. "Take you out for some fresh air and a walk to Washington Square?"

"Vance, I can't," I said, trying to sound disappointed. In truth, I was outraged he would ask me to step away when he knew we were nearing such an important deadline. "We're filing tomorrow, remember? I need to be here to finish this with everyone."

He smirked. "Trust me, I'm well aware." Annoyance seeped out of each clipped word. It was the first time in recent weeks he'd used that irritated tone with me. I almost felt relief at hearing the rancor and knowing he was at least being genuine with me. I figured all that hostility had been lurking there, simmering underneath his gentlemanly behavior all this time.

Before I could give it more thought, he backpedaled. "I just wanted to see you. Can we sit, just for a few minutes?" He motioned toward a bench at the end of the hallway.

I nodded and followed. As he sat, his expression turned so serious that I began to worry. His lips were pinched, and he seemed to be holding his breath, gearing up for something.

"What?" I demanded.

"I talked to Gram today," he started.

"Gram?" I said with sudden panic. "Is something wrong?"

"No, no, nothing like that." He waved away the concern. "I just had some things I wanted to talk through with her."

"Why? Like what?" I felt immediately defensive.

"You've been so slammed. I knew you had to cancel brunch plans with her, so I called and offered to take her."

"Why?" I repeated. "Were you trying to find out more about her father?" Had he co-opted the date simply to interrogate her? A protectiveness welled inside me as I worried about what he might have said or done.

"What? No." He seemed affronted by the thought. "I had no ulterior motive. You can relax your shoulders." He laughed lightly. "I just wanted to do something helpful for you while you're so busy. Can't I try to take care of you, of your family?" He reached toward my face, where a stray curl had fallen from my messy bun, and he tucked it behind my ear. "Gram's *my* family too, you know."

As I berated myself for wrongly assuming the worst, I couldn't stand the constant flux of my feelings toward him.

"Did you know that Gram met Carrie Buck?" Vance asked.

"Wait, she what?"

"She met the woman from that court case, Carrie Buck. The one you told me about. They met in the 1980s. Carrie was elderly, and you weren't even born yet. Gram said your mom and dad were trying to get pregnant with you, and I guess they'd been having a hard time."

Gram had never told me about this. Nor had she ever mentioned my mom having fertility issues. Were my own struggles with fertility genetic? It would have been nice, during those recent months of worry, to be able to connect my own struggle with my mother's. Doing so might have somehow softened the blow of it all.

"I have no idea what you're talking about," I said.

"Gram told me today when we were at brunch. Your mom had a second miscarriage, and she thought it was a consequence of everything her grandfather had done, that God was punishing the family. Apparently, your mom insisted they do something to change up the bad juju or whatever. I didn't understand the trajectory exactly, but somehow they came up with the idea of going to see Carrie Buck. I don't know. You'd have to ask Gram about the rest of it. She said she'll tell you. I thought you might want to go see her to find out more."

"Go see her? Like, today?"

He nodded.

"You thought that while I was finalizing a huge complaint that's getting filed in literal hours, I'd want to take off for the day to chat with my grandmother?" I couldn't help myself from snapping at him. The combination of this new information and Vance's stupid suggestion was almost too much to bear.

I hadn't known my mom had miscarried even once, let alone two times. It was strange, learning something new about my own mother all these years after her death, and from Vance of all people. He'd never even known her.

"Actually, yeah," Vance answered defensively. "I guess I kind of did think that."

In spite of my annoyance, I was still stunned by this news and completely intrigued. "So they went to meet Carrie in person? How could Gram not have told me? Especially after coming clean about everything else." I wondered what else my grandmother still hadn't shared.

"I really don't know, Jess, but here's the thing: Carrie forgave them. That's what Gram wanted me to know. I think she wanted me to understand that if Carrie Buck could forgive your family, then I can forgive you too."

"Wow." So much was going on inside my head, I didn't know where to start. "I can't believe they actually met her." After all the time I'd spent ruminating over the woman's history, always picturing Carrie as a young woman, it was hard to imagine her as a wrinkled elderly person, sitting in a room with my own mother and grandmother. I tried to keep my thoughts focused on that amorphous visual because I didn't want to acknowledge Vance's other comment—that he *might* be able to forgive me, that this was something he was still working on. Was I supposed to thank him after his epiphany? Was that supposed to be my takeaway from this conversation? I was so much more interested in the other information he'd revealed.

"You should call her later," he said. "In the meantime, I can take a hint. I'll leave you to it." He rose from the bench and motioned with his head toward the conference room. "Crushing it on this case is the best way to show those guys at Dillney that they'd be fools to lose you."

Standing back up too, I wrapped my arms around his waist and lowered my head to his shoulder, desperate to feel the closeness we once shared. We stood there for a long moment, silent, our arms snaked around each other. I soaked in the familiar lines and curves of his lean muscles, the safe smells of cedar and pine that wafted toward me from his skin. As I clung to him, I realized that he'd never understand what this was about. Whatever happened with Dillney, I knew I'd always be able to find another job. I was doing this for the women at Hydeford. I couldn't say that to him though. Not now, while we were still so raw.

When I finally pulled back, I asked, "What do you think's going to happen after we file tomorrow?" As if anyone could know the answer to that question.

Vance shrugged but answered anyway. "I bet it will make the news. You'll be famous," he added with pride in his voice, pulling me back toward him to give me an extra little squeeze.

"Oops," he said, letting go quickly. "Don't want to smoosh the baby."

"About that," I said, leaning back again so I could see his face. "I'd like to tell your parents about the pregnancy tomorrow night. After the filing is done."

"But it's only eleven weeks," he said. "I thought we were supposed to wait until after the first trimester, just in case."

"If anything goes wrong," I said, "I want your family to be part of our grieving process. But right now, I think we should include them in our joy too."

"So that's the deal now?" he asked lightly. "We just tell everyone all our secrets? All this honesty is getting to be a bit much. Are you sure you can handle it?"

I smiled back without answering. I was beginning to see that I could handle so much more than either of us had yet given me credit for.

Jessa

May 2022

I stepped off the Amtrak train in Penn Station and waved goodbye to Lydia, Sean, and Asahi. The four of us had traveled to Trenton that morning to file the complaint for declarative and injunctive relief and damages in the US District Court of New Jersey. We also attached a petition for a writ of habeas corpus, seeking release of any plaintiffs who were still being held at Hydeford as a way to protect them from retaliation. Each time I thought about the fact that we'd just submitted a book-length complaint against the federal government, I found myself shaking my head in disbelief again.

As I started up the stairs from the underground terminal, people rushed past me, scurrying in every direction in typical New York style. Now that the first step in commencing this litigation was complete, I wasn't sure what to do with myself. The defendants would have thirty days to answer the complaint, and in the meantime, much of the case would simply be a waiting game. Vance and I weren't due at his parents' house on Long Island for a few more hours, and I thought maybe I should take the opportunity to do something frivolous and fun in the meantime—a quick break before sitting down again to strategize about next steps.

I pulled out my phone and sent a quick text to Dustin.

"Filed the complaint this AM. Wish us luck!"

I didn't let myself overthink why I felt the need to reach out to him. Instead, I just smiled and tossed my phone back into my tote. But then I thought of Gram. Before anything else, I wanted to speak to her about her meeting with Carrie Buck.

As I reached the top of the escalator and stepped onto Seventh Avenue, I squinted my eyes against the bright sunshine and dug back into my bag. Walking uptown with my cell to my ear, I waited for Gram to pick up. As I listened to the phone ring for a third time, I felt a rush of wetness between my legs.

"No!" I yelped into the air. "No, no, no!" I hadn't realized that I'd stopped walking until an older woman approached me from behind.

"Are you all right?" the woman asked. "You need help?"

I looked down to see if any fluid or blood was visible on my pants, but I saw nothing.

"No, no, thank you," I said. I began scrolling frantically through my phone for Dr. LaRusso's office number.

I hailed the first taxi I saw and told the driver the obstetrician's address. The doctor's office hadn't answered yet. As it rang, I put the phone on speaker and texted Vance.

"I think I'm bleeding. Meet me at Dr. LaRusso's? Oh God, Vance."

Then I realized I was crying.

"You okay, miss?" The driver turned to glance at me from the front seat.

"Please, just hurry," I answered. "I think I'm losing my baby."

~

Two days later, I lay in bed staring at the wall. The light in the room had begun to dissipate, letting me know the sun was setting. I heard the apartment door slam shut, Vance returning from his office.

"You're still here," he said as he walked into the room. His top button was undone, and his tie hung open around his neck.

"Oh good, a joke," I deadpanned.

The doctor had put me on immediate bed rest. Forty-eight hours earlier, an ultrasound had revealed that I had a condition called placenta previa, meaning the placenta was in the wrong place and was causing my bleeding. To protect the pregnancy, I would need to stay off my feet, preferably in bed, for most of every day.

"Chin up," Vance said as he sat beside me on the bed. He pushed the hair out of my face and rested his hand against my forehead. Physically, I felt fine, though I probably looked awful, still clad in the t-shirt and sweats I'd thrown on the day before. My teeth and hair had gone unbrushed for more than twenty-four hours.

"The doctor said most of these cases resolve as the uterus grows," Vance reminded me. "You'll be out and about in no time."

The doctor hadn't seemed overly concerned, and Vance certainly wasn't, but I couldn't relax.

"And look, you've already gotten pregnant two times. If anything were to happen—"

I interrupted before he could utter the words.

"Don't."

"Well, we wouldn't try right away, of course," he began.

"No, never."

He looked down at me with a confused expression, and I pushed myself higher on the bed, bunching the pillows behind me.

"All I've been doing is lying here, worrying about who I'm going to lose next. Gram, this baby, or you." The way I'd felt during the cab ride to the doctor's office, when I thought I was really losing the baby . . . I couldn't go through anything like that again. I'd had plenty enough grief for an entire lifetime.

"Look," he said. "I know I was on your ass to slow down, and you were right to tell the team you needed some time off. But I also don't think the placement of the placenta inside your body has anything to do with how you've spent the last few months. You've been crushing it out there, Jess, and nothing about this situation"—he waved his hand over the bed—"has anything to do with your work."

Oh, *now* he was enlightened? Now, after I'd spent the last day negotiating with God, promising I'd give up everything else that mattered to me if the baby could just make it safely to term?

The day before, I had attempted to run a conference call to discuss reducing my responsibilities just partially, and only temporarily. But I'd felt myself getting ramped up about every topic raised. Even as I struggled to pull back, I knew this case wasn't something I could do at half tilt. Either I was all in or I was hiding under my covers. There didn't seem to be a workable in-between. Unfortunately, Vance seemed unable to grasp the nuance.

"Jess, look. If you want your position back at Dillney, I think at this point, you kind of have to get back to work. There's nothing to stop you from getting on your laptop or making phone calls from bed."

"Yes, there is." I squeezed my eyes shut in irritation. "I'm not in the right headspace to make decisions that will affect other people's lives. How am I supposed to solve anyone else's problems when I'm such a mess?"

Vance looked away from me, turning his gaze toward the room's wall of windows and running a hand across the back of his neck. He massaged his own shoulder for a moment, like he needed to rub away the tension I was causing him. Then he looked back at me.

"I don't mean to be callous here. I know this is an incredibly hard time. But the reality is, any decisions you make now can have long-term impacts."

I felt myself sag even more deeply into the pillows behind me. Maybe he was right, but in that moment, I simply didn't care.

He stood and started to change out of his work clothes. As he walked toward his bureau, he spoke over his shoulder.

"By the way, did you ever talk to Gram about Carrie Buck?"

I had spoken to Gram about the bed rest, but I'd hurried off the phone. I was panicked about the baby and didn't want to talk about anything else yet. Since then, I'd been intentionally avoiding my phone, trying to pass the hours watching old movies instead. I could handle Michael J. Fox traveling through time, but I couldn't face anything out in the world, not yet.

"I'm so tired," I said instead, which was ridiculous since I had done precisely nothing all day. "I have to go to sleep." I rolled over and closed my eyes.

The next morning, Vance was back in the same spot at the side of the bed, staring down at me. I'd been watching him get dressed as he prepared to head back out like it was any normal day.

"It's fine," I told him, after he'd announced he needed to stay at the office a little late that night.

Having him home while I languished in bed didn't do me any good anyway. It just left me feeling guilty that I was disappointing him in yet another way. My faulty anatomy, the bad luck that followed everything I touched. I could breathe better when he wasn't there.

He stood beside the bed awkwardly for a few more moments, as if he wanted to say more. Finally, he leaned down to kiss the side of my head and left.

Before I knew it, I felt a hand gently shaking my shoulder. I opened my eyes to see Tate standing above me.

"What are you doing here?" I asked, flipping onto my back.

She was wearing a chic white blazer and a full face of makeup. But of course she was. She was still out in the world, living her life and doing exciting things like everyone else. Looking at Tate all dolled up, I felt like she and I were inhabiting different planets.

"I got the key from the doorman."

Vance had given the doorman a list of approved visitors so I wouldn't have to get out of bed when they showed up.

"I need to show you something," she said.

She reached into the tufted orange tote bag that was hanging from her shoulder and pulled out her iPad. As she typed in a search on the screen, she plunked down on the edge of the bed with a graceless thud, as if there wasn't a physically and emotionally fragile woman hiding inside it. She pushed at my leg under the covers, wordlessly demanding more space for herself. If I'd had more energy, I would have told her to get out, that she was misreading the room and I didn't want to see whatever it was she wanted to show.

"Here." She shoved the screen toward my face.

It was an article from the *New York Times*. I almost pushed the device back toward her, but then my eye caught the headline: "Advocacy Groups Allege Immigrants Subjected to Unwanted Gynecologic Procedures in Federal Facility."

"What is this?" I asked, even though I already knew. Clearly the *Times* had picked up the news about the complaint, just as we'd all hoped. I didn't look up at Tate but kept reading.

> A coalition of immigrants' rights groups has filed a complaint in the US District Court of New Jersey alleging that female immigrants held at the Hydeford Detention Facility have been subject to significant, invasive, and unnecessary gynecological procedures without their consent. In particular, the complaint alleges a high rate of unwarranted hysterectomies performed on detained women. Several of the women joining the complaint have chosen to remain anonymous, citing a fear

> of retaliation by immigration authorities. The procedures at issue have been completed at one particular medical facility. That clinic has not responded to request for comment.
>
> The director of ICE disputes the allegations that detained women are being "used for experimental medical purposes" or that there has been any infringement on the right to reproductive autonomy of minority groups. The agency did not respond to requests for information on the number of hysterectomies, tubal ligations, or other sterilizing procedures that were performed.

The article then went on to list the other allegations included in the complaint about poor medical oversight, rough treatment of the detained women, and inadequate precautions regarding COVID-19.

That the article had been published was fantastic news. Really fantastic. If the team wanted to win the case, and to make institutional reforms going forward, we needed people to know what was happening and to feel outraged about it.

"Okay, thanks for showing me." I averted my eyes from the screen and handed the iPad back to Tate. A week ago, I would have jumped for joy, seeing how the article had focused on all the right bullet points. But now I just wanted Tate to leave.

"There's more," she said as she put the iPad back in her tote and then, to my dismay, kicked off her heels. She readjusted herself on the bed, settling into a comfy sitting position at the foot and crossing her legs under herself. "That nurse you went to see? She's been trying to reach you."

I didn't remember ever telling Tate about Fern.

"She somehow managed to get in touch with Dustin," Tate said.

Dustin.

After I texted him from outside Penn Station, he'd written back almost immediately. I hadn't even read the message until long after

I'd gotten home from the obstetrician's office. Just a simple note: "*You've got this.*"

Had I not been so distraught over the pregnancy, it probably would have been exactly what I needed to hear.

"You told him? About . . . this?" I gestured toward my belly.

"Of course not." Tate flinched. "Since when do you think I tell people your private business?" She looked offended, and I felt a little bad for being so churlish when she was just trying to help.

"No, I know you're a vault. Sorry I'm a grouch." I forced a repentant half smile. "Dustin can tell the nurse to just call any of the co-counsel on the case for whatever she needs. I'll give you a list." I twisted to the side to look for the phone I'd been so aggressively avoiding.

"No, no list," Tate said. "She wants to talk to *you*. She told Dustin more women want to come forward. People who saw the article in the news. They want to join the complaint."

"Oh." As I processed Tate's words, something tugged at me—a pull to get up and call Fern, to track down the new defendants and create the amended filing—but I pushed all of it away. I couldn't trust myself to be a helpful advocate while I was so worried about my own situation. I wouldn't be able to focus, which wouldn't be fair to our clients. "That's great news," I finally answered. "It'll make a difference for them all. Still, tell her to call Will Carbone at NYU. Or Lydia Brass, or anyone else at the Manhattan Immigrant Defense Center. I'm out."

"I can't believe you're saying this." Tate squinted down at me like she was struggling to recognize me. "After everything you've put yourself through for this case, now that it's really moving forward, you're *out*?"

This wasn't about what I wanted. But all I could think about was the baby and whether my every movement was putting it in further jeopardy. The women deserved more than the small sliver of mental space I'd be able to devote to legal work at the moment. I already knew from Shantrane that I was capable of making careless errors with disastrous consequences. I couldn't risk something like that again.

"Look, I told Will Carbone and the rest of the team that I was having a medical emergency. They've got everything under control. They don't need me."

"Yes, they do, Jessa. You're the one these women have connected with. You're the one who inspired them to come forward. The case wouldn't exist without you. You're their best advocate. Don't you see that?"

Tate's words hit me hard. The team had just filed a second complaint with the Department of Homeland Security, and they'd begun reaching out to members of Congress. Since the beginning, I had promised the women I would be there. Right there with them. I let out a long breath as I thought it over again. But then I shook my head.

"I appreciate what you're saying, but I just can't. Thank you for coming, Tate." Then I turned onto my side, away from her.

"Jessa, come on," she persisted.

In response, I just closed my eyes, shutting out my friend, trying to shut out the world.

She stayed on the bed a moment longer, obviously reluctant to go. But eventually the bed shifted and I heard her stepping back into her shoes. Seconds later, I heard the apartment door close and the room was silent once again. I lay in the bed, exhausted, sad, afraid.

Before long I heard the front door opening again, and I figured Tate must have come back to argue another point. I kept my eyes closed, hoping to discourage her from saying whatever else she wanted to say. But then I heard my grandmother's voice.

"Enough," she said.

I turned over to find Gram marching into the room holding a paper grocery bag. She was wrapped in a cheery floral pashmina, but she wore a stern expression on her face.

"Enough," she said again, waves of moral indignation wafting off the word. She dropped the grocery bag on the nightstand and moved toward my work bag in the corner of the room. Bending low, she dug into the bag and retrieved my laptop.

I pushed up on my elbow. "What are you doing?"

"Fire this thing up." She held it out to me. "Check your emails."

"What? Why?"

"Do as you're told," she said, her tone steely.

I felt wounded by her harsh pitch. She had to know how much I was struggling, how scared I was of something happening to the baby. I reached out for the computer.

"I'm making you a sandwich," Gram said, picking up the bag again and turning on her heel. I didn't bother to protest that I wasn't hungry.

Within seconds, I could hear her rooting around in the kitchen, the clamor of drawers opening and closing. It all sounded so ordinary, as if this were just a regular day and not another moment in my life when I was petrified of losing what I cared about most. I didn't want to read whatever was waiting on my computer. I'd already seen the one article from Tate. I couldn't face any more real life today. Caught in my own panic, I simply didn't have it in me.

I stared at the computer's lock screen with its artful picture of Arizona's red rocks until Gram finally walked back in, a plate of finger sandwiches and a glass of water in her hands.

"I'm not ready to do this," I said. "I just need to be alone." I pushed the computer closed and twisted toward the nightstand to get rid of it.

"No, you don't," Gram ordered, putting the food down on the dresser and hurrying to the nightstand. She snatched the computer back up, holding it to her chest. "I heard you," she said, looking down at me. "And two days ago, I respected your position. I know you need to process this on your own, to worry, to be vigilant. And you've done that. But no more. Now you need to get back to work."

"But the baby—"

"No," Gram interrupted. "No 'but the baby'!" She held the computer out again, and I reached for it even though I had no intention of using it. As if Gram could hear my thoughts, she persisted. "The baby is fine. There is no medical reason why you cannot work from the comfort of your bed. You can take calls, you can write emails, and you can continue what you started. You will not abandon these women. I raised you better than that!"

I flinched at her words.

"I just can't. Please, can you understand that?" I looked up at her pleadingly. "I'd only be worrying about the baby the whole time because . . ." I didn't even know how to explain what I was feeling, the terror of despair.

"Jessa." Gram fixed me with a stern look. "Losing your parents as a child was hard, yes. Nearly impossibly so. Believe me, I know. I lost my only daughter that day. But you are so much more than a girl who was orphaned at twelve. You have to stop living your whole life based on the worst thing that's happened to you."

"Really?" I asked, the anger rising in me like a flame. "Isn't that just what you've done? Have you not defined yourself by your parents? Or are you more than the daughter of a villain? Living your whole life in shame, telling your family half-truths and hiding where they came from . . . If that's not basing your life on a singular part of your identity, I don't know what is." I hadn't yelled at Gram like this since I was a teenager.

Gram stepped closer to the bed. "As a matter of fact," she said, her voice rising, "I've done the exact opposite. I've *lived*!" Her face filled with color as she continued revving up. "I married, had a child, got a wonderful job, made friends, and then pushed through terrible tragedy to raise my grandchild. I did everything I could to be a better person than my father. Yet you . . ." She looked around my bedroom, which had been growing messier as I lingered in bed. The curve of her lips deepened in disapproval. "You're languishing here, letting everything else that matters to you wither away instead of making the most of the best parts of who you are."

"Yeah, well, maybe you didn't raise me as well as you think. You're the person I trusted most in the world, yet somehow you kept an enormous secret from me my whole life rather than face something that scared you. Maybe I learned it from watching you, Gram. Pathological avoidance seems to be exactly what you've taught me."

I could see such sadness in her expression as she regarded me, her eyelids sliding to half-mast and the corners of her mouth seeming to pull her whole face down. I began to regret my harsh words.

"Gram," I started again, "I didn't mean—"

She interrupted before I could finish.

"Nope." She shook her head. "Don't do that. You said your piece, and you meant it. It's good for you to tell me what you're really feeling. Especially when there's so much truth to your words."

"There is?" I asked, reaching for a tissue from the box on the bedside table.

"I need to work on sharing the truth, even when it's hard for me. And you, my dear, need to work on remembering that loss is a part of life, and we can't live our entire existences focused so intently on everything that has been stolen from us. Sometimes you need to concentrate less on what's been taken and more on what you have to give instead."

I could hear the logic in Gram's words, but somehow the idea didn't seem to pertain to my own circumstances. The losses hurt too much.

"Now," Gram said, as if we'd settled the matter, "I brought you something I think you should read." She moved toward the bedroom door, where she'd left her oversized purse. With a satisfied grunt, she pulled out a marble composition notebook, the kind I used to practice my penmanship in when I was in the first grade. The notebook Gram held was badly faded and warped with age. "I know Vance told you that I met Carrie Buck," she said, coming to sit beside me on the bed. "So it's time you and I have a little chat about that."

"Yeah. I wanted to ask you about it, but then everything with the baby . . ." I looked toward my midsection before pulling the duvet higher to cover myself. "How come you never told me you met her? Like, not even after telling me all about your father?"

Gram let out a long sigh. "I don't know, Jessa." She looked up at the ceiling, as if searching for her response somewhere in the ecru paint above us. Then she brought her eyes back to mine.

"It was a long time ago when we went to see her, in the early '80s, and nearly ten years before you were born. She was living in Waynesboro, Virginia. A widow by the time we met. She gave me this." Gram lifted the notebook. "I've kept it all these years, but I never actually opened it, not until last week. I tried when she first gave it to me, but I was too full of guilt, too afraid of what I'd find inside. Eventually I just hid it away. But watching you these past weeks, I knew it was time for me to confront whatever I'd find in the pages. The woman filled the whole thing, and her handwriting does leave something to be desired. But I think you should read it."

"Why would she give it to *you*? What about other people in her family?" Right away, I realized the answers and regretted asking.

"She never had more children, obviously," Gram said pointedly. "Her husband had already died by the time we met. She didn't have any family to give it to." She placed the notebook on the bed beside me. "She seemed to feel we had a bond—because of my deep regret over what had happened to her, I suppose. Maybe she hoped I would do something with it. Try to set things right." Gram cleared her throat, and I thought maybe she felt shame about not doing more with Carrie's writing. "She told me she'd learned that the only way to move on from the pain of the past was to try every single day to make the world a little better somehow."

"But who did she think you were? Didn't she think it was random the way you and Mom reached out?"

"I told her straightaway who my father was, and she remembered exactly the role he'd played in her life. We talked for a while, the three of us. Toward the end of the visit, she told me it was time to release myself from the burden of my own guilt. She forgave me and insisted that I follow her example."

"I don't understand," I said, shaking my head. "What reason did she have to be so gracious?"

"Your mother and I couldn't fathom it either. But I think I understand now. And my point in bringing this to you, Jessa, is that if she could do it, after everything she went through, you can forgive too. Forgive *yourself*. Stop blaming yourself. It's time. Well past time, in fact." The look she gave me then was so knowing, she seemed to be aware of every last secret I'd ever kept.

I had never spoken to a soul about my guilt over my parents' death, about how they were on that icy road because of me. If not for me and my school's parent-teacher conferences, my mom and dad would have been at home that night, watching sitcoms instead of skidding off the road, flipping not once but twice, before slamming into a hundred-year-old oak tree. I hadn't talked about this with anyone, not even my childhood therapist. I knew what people would say—that it was ridiculous to blame myself, that some things are just fate. But I'd always felt responsible just the same. The role I played in the greatest loss of my life was perhaps what made it so difficult to bear, even all these years later.

Gram stood and collected her things, retrieving the plate of sandwiches from the dresser and moving it to the nightstand beside me. She left the notebook for me as well, telling me to call if I wanted to talk over what Carrie had written.

Once I was alone again, I ran a hand over my eyes as if to clear them. I stared down at the journal in my lap. I wasn't sure I could bring myself to read it. I related to my grandmother in that moment.

I traced my fingers along the edges of the closed journal, the aged cardboard delicate and pulpy against my skin. Slowly, I opened the front cover and looked down at the page, where I found tight, slanted letters waiting.

It was one of them blindingly bright Virginia summer days. That's what I remember most about the morning the ladies came to take me away. I was home watching after the babies like usual because Mama was downtown again, looking to find herself a day's work. Doris was crawling across the dusty floor, stopping now and again to stare at her toes, and I felt a little sorry at the way the milk-white skin of her knees had gone gray from the dirt of the planks. Baby Roy was asleep in the old bassinet we'd got from Miss Jenny, who lived with her brother's family on the second floor of the house. Our family had two rooms on the first floor, right below them. I was just six years old at the time, you understand, but I loved to look after my own brother and sister, to be the one taking charge. Even if they was only half-related to me, that one-half was enough.

My cell phone rang, interrupting me. I fished through the rumpled bedcovers until my hand connected with the phone. It was my doctor's office.

"Hello?" I asked, bracing for whatever bad news they might deliver.

"Hi, Jessa? It's Kendra from Dr. LaRusso's office. The doctor just wanted me to check in to see how you're feeling."

"Oh, um . . ." I wanted to say, "*I'm scared to death*," but I knew that wasn't what the woman was really asking.

"I'm good, I think," I said instead. "I haven't had any more bleeding, and I've just been lying here in bed the whole day, like the doctor said."

"You're still in bed?" Kendra asked.

"Yup. I've been very well behaved."

"Oh no, honey. The bed rest was just for the first twenty-four hours as a precaution. You can get yourself up and move about now. Just so long as you avoid strenuous exercise and such."

"But the doctor said full bed rest."

"He did, for twenty-four hours. I know, sweetie, sometimes when we're stressed we don't get all the facts. That's why the doc always likes us to call patients to check in after a scare."

"You're sure? I'm allowed up?" I asked, nervous to follow the wrong advice.

"I'm sure."

"But . . . ," I began, not sure how to politely explain that I wasn't prepared to accept medical advice from the receptionist.

"I'll tell you what," Kendra said. "I'll have Dr. LaRusso call you himself after he finishes with his patients today. Until then, there's no harm in a hardworking pregnant mama keeping her feet up for a few extra hours, right?"

I hoped Kendra was right. Even just the two days of bed rest had me feeling like I was spiraling toward an abyss of fear and depression. But if full bed rest wasn't necessary, then perhaps the baby wasn't in the kind of jeopardy I had been imagining.

"That would be great. Yes, please have him call, and I'll stay in bed until then. Thank you."

Besides being upset with myself for confusing the doctor's instructions, what I couldn't stop thinking about after I hung up was the difference in care between what I was receiving from my fancy Upper East Side doctor and what the women in Hydeford had gotten from Pinelands. I had been spoken to in my own language, by a doctor of my own choosing, in a clean and comfortable medical office, and *still* I had misunderstood what was happening and how to take care of myself. The contrast with what the detained women had experienced was glaring. I thought of the personal and emotional nature of gynecological care, the importance of the doctor-patient relationship, the fragility of so many moments that occurred only in exam rooms. Those women still needed my help. There was plenty I could contribute from home—even from bed, like Gram said. I needed to get back to work.

~

By 8:00 p.m. I was sitting comfortably at the dining table. Dr. LaRusso had called a couple of hours earlier, just as Kendra promised, and he'd clarified that the bed rest was, indeed, intended as only a brief precaution. As my uterus continued to grow and stretch with the pregnancy, the doctor explained, the placement of the placenta would, in all likelihood, correct itself. In the meantime, now that the bleeding had stopped, I could resume my usual routines without concern. He told me to take it easy physically—no strenuous exercise and no sex—until the placenta moved to a new position. But returning to other regular activity was no problem.

The thought of avoiding sex with Vance was a surprising relief. Ever since he abandoned me for those few days the month before, I hadn't wanted to be intimate with him, to have him touch me in that way. If I was completely honest with myself, I still felt uneasy being around him at all. Had my feelings toward him changed altogether? Or did I just need more time to move past what he'd done? I used to rely on him no matter what. But what had felt safe and comforting before was now making me feel small and stifled. I worried our relationship might have always rested on the building blocks of my emotional baggage. But then I reminded myself that I was chock-full of hormones, so maybe I shouldn't entirely trust my current feelings.

For the time being, I needed to turn my attention back to the old case I'd been searching for online. When I'd finally returned Fern's calls earlier that afternoon, I learned that one of the new Jane Does joining the complaint had experienced severe abdominal pain and a diagnosis of endometriosis. She had been told, prior to her incarceration at Hydeford, that she needed to have one of her ovaries removed. After the woman was settled in the facility, she agreed to have the surgery. Unfortunately, when she awoke, she learned that Dr. Choudry had removed the wrong ovary, taking out the healthy organ. The woman needed a second surgery to remove the faulty one, leaving her in an infertile state. Jane Doe #6 had relocated to South Carolina after her release, but she was willing to travel to New Jersey to testify if it meant someone would have to answer for what happened to her.

The case I had been looking for was one I'd read in my torts class in law school. A man had gone into surgery to have his left hand removed, and when he awoke, he found his right hand had been amputated instead. The doctor in the case had been found liable of negligence, and the hospital was held to account. As I copied down the citations from the case, I heard a key in the front door.

Vance walked in with his messenger bag draped across his body and an empty bottle of iced tea in his hand. He startled at the sight of me. "You're out of bed," he said, stating the obvious.

"Apparently we misunderstood Dr. LaRusso. It was only a twenty-four-hour bed rest."

"No, you should get back in bed." He put down his bag in a hurry and started moving toward me.

"Vance, I spoke to him. He said it's okay, that he never meant for me to stay in bed longer."

Vance shook his head and reached into his pocket for his phone, but then, presumably noting the time, tossed it onto the table. "I'll call him in the morning to figure this out."

"Vance," I protested as he came closer to my chair, as if he might lift me out of my seat and carry me back to the bedroom. "I literally spoke to the man a matter of hours ago. I don't need my husband to act as an interpreter."

"Still, I should follow up with him."

"What the fuck is wrong with you? Don't you think I can have one single conversation with a doctor and understand what he's saying all by myself? Why are you always second-guessing me?"

Vance scowled. "Jeez, Jess. I'm not trying to second-guess you. I'm trying to take care of you. The way I always have."

Vance *had* always taken care of me. But somewhere along the line, his tendency to swoop in and take control had gotten completely out of hand. His care had begun to feel oppressive, like an insult. I could take care of myself just fine. I could stand on my own, figuratively and literally. But I couldn't bear another argument. Not now, when I was finally coming out of my funk.

"Fine. Call him in the morning if you want. In the meantime, I'm sure I can sit in a chair for a couple more hours without any problems. I just want to get through a few more cases."

"You're working here?" He looked horror-struck.

"If you're worried about my stress levels, then let's not do this." I didn't want to devote the next hour to rehashing the same old arguments when I had so much work to do.

"You know what?" He threw his hands in the air and marched toward the kitchen. "Fine. Don't listen to me," he said, grabbing the take-out menus. "I'll order dinner."

"Well, won't that be wonderful." I tried to keep the sarcasm out of my response, but I didn't quite manage it.

~

The following morning, after a tense night of picking at chicken tikka masala and snapping at each other, Vance was once again chipper. He had just hung up with Dr. LaRusso and was pleased to report that my required period of bed rest had, indeed, concluded. I waited for him to apologize for his despicable behavior, but he just leaned over for a quick peck on the lips and headed out the door.

Instead of dwelling on his over-the-top mansplaining from the night before, or his failure to apologize for belittling me, I hurried to my closet. I was excited to put on my first pair of maternity trousers. I'd ordered them online after growing tired of using a rubber band to hold the button of my regular pants in place. As I pulled the gray slacks up to my middle, I marveled at the loveliness of an elastic waistband. Tugging at the flexible fabric, I tested how far I could stretch it out. Would my belly grow as far as the fabric extended, or even beyond it? Putting on those new pants made the pregnancy feel very real, and I had to remind myself to temper my excitement, for all the obvious reasons.

As I finished getting dressed, my thoughts returned to the case. Adding women to the complaint would require additional filings with the court. The night before, I'd arranged a meeting with Lydia and our co-counsel from New Jersey to take care of completing the necessary motion. I was just heading out the door when my cell phone rang. Pulling it from the front pocket of my tote, I checked the screen.

"Hello?" I said, feeling a little uneasy.

"Finally, she picks up!" Dustin joked on the other end.

"Yeah, sorry about that. There's been a lot going on."

"No, no worries," he said, his voice bouncy with excitement. "I heard from Tate that more plaintiffs are joining the action."

I rolled my eyes as I walked out the apartment door, cradling the phone between my ear and shoulder. It had been less than sixteen hours since I'd texted Tate. I should have guessed from the preponderance of smiley face and fist bump emojis in her response that she'd share the happy news of my return to the case with someone else.

"It's like I said," Dustin continued. "The smart bet is always on Jessa Gidney getting it done."

"I appreciate the vote of confidence," I laughed into the phone. "But you might want to wait a little longer before calling your bookie."

"I just wanted to tell you that I filled in some of the partners," he said. "I hope you don't mind, but I was so amped up about your progress that I couldn't keep it to myself. Hendricks and the others are pretty excited. They're all patting themselves on the back now, saying how your involvement is going to reflect well on the firm. I think they might be asking you to come back sooner rather than later."

"But nothing's really happened yet. We only filed three days ago."

"Things are happening, Jessa. Trust me. You haven't checked the news?"

"Tate showed me the article," I said.

"Article?" He laughed. "It's not just one article. The story is everywhere. And the fact that more women are coming forward is huge. The partners know you assembled an entire team and that you're on your way to winning a high-profile case. I thought you'd want to know I'm not the only one who believes you've got what it takes to win this. Just don't be surprised when Hendricks calls, begging you to come back."

I laughed at his words. And then I shocked myself by wondering if I even wanted to go back to Dillney. I hadn't missed being in the office for a single day since taking the leave. I didn't miss my other cases or any of my colleagues beyond Tate. And apparently Dustin.

I'd reached the elevator bank and was hovering beside the down button. I didn't want to risk losing the connection.

"I'm sure you'll get the temporary restraining order too," Dustin said. "You'll see." He was talking about the request our team had made for an order preventing any of the Jane Does from being deported until the merits of the case were litigated.

I allowed myself one moment to bask in his unbridled support, closing my eyes in gratitude.

"Thank you for saying that," I said as I pushed the elevator button. "Speaking of the TRO though, I'm on my way to a prep meeting, so I'd better run. Thanks for checking in."

After my meetings, I rode the 6 Train uptown. Winding my way through the tightly packed train, I maneuvered to a spot where I could clutch one of the stanchion poles while the train rocked from side to side. Looking around at the crowded car, I wondered if soon my belly would grow large enough that others would begin offering me their seats on rides like this. It was hard to imagine reaching such a different point in the pregnancy, where simply standing up would feel like hard work. I prayed again that I'd get there.

As the train sped north, my mind wandered back to Carrie Buck's journal. After the call from Dr. LaRusso's office, I'd been in such a hurry to start working again that I'd put the notebook aside, hiding it deep within the drawer of my nightstand. Tucking it away like that had probably been a gesture of protectiveness, a safeguarding of Carrie's secrets. Or maybe I was just protecting myself from more of Vance's gaslighting. Either way, now that I was caught up on the new developments with Hydeford, I was eager to see what else Carrie's pages revealed.

I wondered what Carrie possibly could have written about at such length. If it turned out to be page after page condemning Harry Laderdale, I decided I wouldn't hate that. I imagined there would have been some catharsis for her in filling a journal with all the things she never got to say to the men who trampled her rights, Harry Laderdale being at the front of the pack. But I doubted Gram would have shared the notebook in that case.

When I finally reached the apartment, it was only six o'clock. Vance wouldn't be home for another couple of hours.

I made a beeline for the nightstand, removing my blazer and tossing it across the foot of the bed. I kicked off my shoes and climbed onto the bed, settling myself against the plush pillows. Then I reached into the drawer for the notebook and began to read.

~

After more than two hours, I was nearing the end of the journal when my phone rang. I ignored the call, instead reaching for a tissue on the nightstand and wiping at the wetness under my eyes.

I'd read all about Carrie's life, starting with how she ended up in foster care, then the sexual violence she suffered, followed by her subsequent transfer to an institution for "mental defectives." I struggled to keep turning the pages. When I read about the loss of her baby, Vivian, and how it shattered Carrie so completely, all my prior thoughts about curses and karma started coming at me again. Breathing in and breathing out, I reminded myself that panic wasn't good for me or the baby. Then I returned my focus to the scrawl of Carrie's writing.

In the last few pages, Billy had shown up in her life again, taking a second chance at asking for Carrie's heart. Carrie finally had relented, figuring maybe it was time to let him in, to embrace the one good thing she had.

And then I was on the last page. As I stared down at her final words, I realized that the entire time I'd been reading, I'd been hoping Carrie had written something about mercy and forgiving the unforgivable. All along, I'd wanted to believe that if she could find a way to forgive those people, then maybe I, too, could find a way toward compassion and forgiveness like Gram had said. I was so very tired of holding my anger and disappointment like a force field around me, clasping the despair like a talisman. I felt almost desperate for guidance from Carrie—a way out. Pulling the notebook closer in, I turned my eyes back to the page, equal parts nervous and eager to see what those last few paragraphs would reveal.

Carrie

April 1970

I feel near certain God won't forgive those men for what they took from me. I still can't figure how it was they thought they were in charge of deciding who should and shouldn't be allowed to make babies, who was or wasn't good enough. Lord knows it was never up to them.

All these years later, I suppose I've come to understand much that was unclear to me as a girl. Folks might say I've lived a small life, just being a wife, cleaning house, keeping to myself, and not much else. I never had an important job, going off to business like the young girls do now. I didn't travel hardly anywhere either, born and likely to die in this here state of Virginia.

Yet I'd say I've been through more than most. I never would have got past those days after Vivian died, nor the long years of missing the other children I never had, if not for the way I learned to rely on myself. Billy, he tried, but he was just the icing on top, not the answer itself. In the quiet days of my little life, I learned to believe in my own self and my own strength.

I did choose to love my old friend Billy the way a woman loves a man. But I set him straight right from the start that I was going to be making any decisions for myself all on my own. I knew by then for sure that I always needed to be true to myself.

I gave Billy a good life, I think, except for the children he never had. He would have loved getting to watch his own babies grow like weeds in the garden. They'd have been beanpoles surely, just like him, those same freckles dotting their cheeks. Even now, on lonely days, I like to imagine boys like that, doting all the time on their father.

A little stream trickles along behind the house here. When we first settled in, right away Billy set to building me my own special bench out beside it, a place where I could rest myself when I wanted a quiet moment to remember Vivian. It's been years now since Billy passed, and here I still sit, remembering Vivian and Billy both. I try not to let my mind wander away with all the what-ifs. Even so, one thought keeps creeping back up on me: If only I'd been born some years later. Surely what happened to me would never happen to a young woman today. But then I remind myself there's no use carrying on that I didn't land up in better times.

All the while, I'm still scribbling in this here book. Sometimes when everything else falls away, we finally see the clearest. I didn't ever give myself enough credit for pushing through the hard times. I focused so hard on what I'd lost and how it'd been taken from me. I wish I'd come to understand sooner that I should be grateful for my own two feet, the very same footing that held me up all along.

Jessa

May 2022

I closed the journal, glancing at the clock and discovering I'd been reading for three hours. I'd expected Vance back earlier, but whatever delayed him had given me a chance to read to the end of the diary.

It was hard to wrap my mind around everything Carrie Buck had been through. One thing painfully obvious from the journal entries was that the woman had never been feebleminded. No, she'd just been a poor girl from the wrong side of the tracks who had neither the education nor the support necessary to beat a system that was rigged against young women like her.

I rose from my spot on the bed, stiff from all that time sitting. As I stretched my arms toward the ceiling and then twisted back and forth to loosen myself up, the movement made me think of Dustin, and I felt my lips tick up. I couldn't say for sure what emotion welled inside me at the thought of him. Was it just a surprising fondness? Actual longing? I almost began to berate myself. But then I thought of Carrie and her insistence on being true to herself, so I allowed myself to simply feel what I was feeling. I shrugged to myself in the empty room. If the feeling persisted, sooner or later I'd be able to name the emotion.

I took my phone from the counter to check my missed calls and saw only one notification, but not from Vance. The voicemail was from Lydia, letting me know that ICE had responded to the plaintiffs' request for a temporary restraining order to prevent any retaliatory deportations.

"Call me back!" Lydia had shouted in the recording, sounding frantic. "Doesn't matter what time!"

I instantly panicked, wondering if ICE had responded with some defense we hadn't anticipated. As I hit the callback button and waited for an answer, I hoped the urgency I'd heard in Lydia's voice wasn't because of something even worse, like one of the women already being put on a plane to be shipped out of the US.

"Finally!" Lydia declared as she picked up on the other end. "I've been waiting and waiting."

"What happened?" I asked. "Is it Isobel? Denise?"

"It's all of them," Lydia said.

"They deported them *all?*" I balked. "But half of them weren't even in custody!"

"No, no, no. Nobody's been deported. That's the whole point. ICE stipulated to the terms of the injunction request."

"They stipulated?" I repeated. "Wait, so they're safe? Everyone's still here?"

"Yes, yes. This is good." Lydia chuckled. "They're all still here." But then her tone turned serious again. "Sadly, they're exactly where we left them. But the little bit of happy news is that ICE has at least agreed not to deport any of the plaintiffs while the case is still being adjudicated."

I couldn't believe it. "Without even a hearing?"

"Without even a hearing."

"But why?" I asked. "Why would they do that?"

"The media! You did a great job, Jessa. Mailing out those press releases the day we filed the complaint was genius. The story is everywhere. ICE must be shaking in their boots. They've got to know they can't get away with retaliatory deportations with all eyes on them. Maybe they figure stipulating to this one request will help them play better in the court of public opinion."

"Wow." I lowered myself onto the edge of the bed, stunned. It was a win. Not *the* win, but it was something.

"I know," Lydia said on the other end of the phone, as if she could hear everything I was thinking. "You did good, my friend. We've just got to keep it up. Now, go get your rest, and we'll talk in the morning."

~

Three days later, I got the call Dustin had predicted. It was Andrew Hendricks. He knew all about the filing, the additional plaintiffs joining the case, the government's agreement to comply with the terms of requested injunctive relief. He was impressed. He was proud, he said. I scoffed at that. Proud. As if Andrew had anything to do with what I'd accomplished with the case.

And he wanted me to come back.

That was what I was telling Vance and his cousin Yuval as the three of us ate dinner that night. Both Yuval and Vance had come uptown straight from their offices to meet me at the little Middle Eastern café we loved. They were dressed in almost identical outfits. Each had on tan slacks and a light blue button-down shirt with French cuffs. A few weeks earlier, I might have been uncomfortable being the only one at the table in casual clothes, but I'd recently begun thinking that jeans and boots were more my style than dress pants and sweater sets after all.

"Turning him down felt beyond amazing," I said, and I could feel my cheeks straining from how widely I was smiling.

"Good for you." Yuval reached out, giving me a light punch to the arm.

"You did what?" Vance squinted at me like he couldn't comprehend what I'd said.

"Dillney's not the right place for me." I shrugged like it was no big deal, then stabbed a ball of falafel with my fork. "It's so clear to me now. I guess sometimes you have to move away from something to make sense of it."

"But we're having a baby," Vance said. "You need that job."

"A baby?" Yuval exclaimed. "Mazel tov!" He leaned over the small bowls of hummus and eggplant salad between us, punching me in the arm again, this time a little harder than the first. "We have much to discuss, no?" He nodded encouragingly. "Only a few months behind our own. Now you will have to come and live near us. The babies will be friends from the very beginning."

I smiled back at him. It was nice to think of our child having a cousin and playmate. I hadn't let my mind wander to things like playdates or "mommy and me" classes yet. But I'd finally hit the end of the first trimester, so maybe it was time to let myself dream a little. "Moving to the suburbs is definitely not part of the fantasy for me," I joked, "but the rest sounds pretty good."

"So yes to the playdates, no to the burbs. Got it." Yuval smiled back and then held out his fist to bump with Vance.

Vance returned the gesture half-heartedly before turning back to me.

"But, Jessa, the money," he said, prodding as if I hadn't understood what he'd said.

"No, I get it. But I was thinking of doing something else."

"But why? That was a great job. Of course not making partner was disappointing. I get that. But losing out was a blessing in disguise. Without jockeying for a promotion, it's just a good, steady job at a well-regarded firm." He looked at Yuval for agreement, but Yuval just shrugged and bit into his pita. "You can take whatever work they assign you," Vance continued, looking back at me. "And not worry about fighting for the high-profile cases all the time. You get to avoid all the crazy, intense situations but keep the cachet of being a Dillney attorney. You just take your paycheck and go home."

Ah. Now I saw things more clearly. Vance didn't want me working too much when the job was stressful or challenging, but if I could be a cog in a wheel, accepting a paycheck to work on cases that didn't matter to me at all—that, he thought, made good sense.

I opened my mouth to argue, but he cut me off.

"That's what we decided. That's what you said you wanted."

I didn't know what I wanted exactly, but I certainly wanted enough agency to find out.

The waiter was back at the table asking if we planned to order dessert.

Yuval declined, then Vance rattled off the items he and I would share. Honey cake, vanilla ice cream, and berries.

After the server walked away, Vance turned back to me expectantly, like he was waiting for me to agree with what he'd said.

As I met his gaze, a window shade seemed to lift, and I could finally see through the glass behind it. Vance had once represented everything I thought I wanted, but looking at his face over the glowing candle, I finally understood, with stark clarity, that we no longer fit. I simply wasn't the person he wanted me to be. Not anymore.

"I'll talk to Andrew tomorrow," I told Vance, then turned toward Yuval. "For now, I want to hear about the trip you guys are planning. Dalia told me there's a babymoon in the works?"

Vance turned to listen to Yuval with an easy smile. Probably because he thought he'd won. As always. Why wouldn't he assume I'd agree to maintain the status quo when, for so long, keeping safe and steady had been my primary goal? Except somewhere over the past several months, I had changed, even though I might not have noticed it right away. It was time for my choices to change along with me.

When we got home from dinner, we settled onto the sectional sofa and Vance picked up the remote for the TV.

"Wait," I interrupted him. "I want to talk."

"What's up?" he asked, pulling his phone from his pocket and glancing at it before placing it on his lap.

"I'm not even sure where to start," I said, struggling to believe I was about to take such a leap. "I think . . ." I paused, taking a deep breath, then started again. "I think this isn't working for me."

"What isn't?" he asked, glancing at his phone again.

"Us. Us being married to each other."

"What are you talking about?" He looked back at me, his eyes narrowing.

"I don't think we're working as a couple." I hated having to spell it out. "We need to make a change. Maybe not be together."

"What do you mean 'not be together'?" He made quotes with his fingers in the air. "What, like, get divorced?" He laughed, like the idea was ridiculous.

"I don't know," I said, forcing myself to be completely honest. "Maybe? I mean, that's where my mind is going. So yeah, that *is* what I mean. A divorce."

"No, you don't." His tone was still light, like we were simply misunderstanding each other. "What are you even talking about? Is this because of what I said about you going back to Dillney? Fine, don't go back."

"No," I said, frustrated that he wasn't taking me seriously, even during what was possibly the most serious conversation of our entire relationship. "You and I, we don't want the same things, Vance. And we haven't for a while."

"What are you even talking about?" he said again, except now he was beginning to sound angry. "What? Don't we both want the baby? Jessa, we're making a family. Why would you say this now? It's all you've ever wanted. I'm getting over your family history. I'm getting over all of it and just trying to forget it already."

"But I'm not, Vance. I'm not getting over it because it's a part of who I am. I need to acknowledge that and live a life that makes me proud. This dynamic between us . . ." I paused, trying to come up with the right description of how I felt. I finally settled on the simplest explanation. "I just need different things now."

"Yeah, but . . ." He motioned toward my stomach. His mouth kept moving, but no words came out, like he was still trying to decide if I was being serious. "What are you trying to get out of this conversation? You want me to be more supportive about Hydeford? To listen better? What?"

"Vance." I sighed, determined to make my point. "It's none of that. Or maybe it's all of it." I reached for his hand, but he pulled away from me. "I'm always going to care about you, and you're right. We are having a baby together. We will still raise the baby together. We just won't live with each other anymore."

His eyes hardened, as if he was finally hearing me, and my breath hitched. I thought of my entire in-law family, especially Jiyana and the boys, and my palms began to sweat. But I knew I was doing the right thing, so I pushed myself forward.

"Or if you don't want to be in this child's life, I will raise it on my own. Either way, Vance, I can't stay married to you. I need to stand on my own two feet."

Epilogue

Eighteen months later

I hurried across Lexington Avenue, half jogging in my patent leather pumps as I pushed the stroller toward Gram's apartment building. Nearing the door, I saw my grandmother was already outside waiting for us, along with her college-aged neighbor, Vanessa.

"I couldn't pass one more second without my beautiful great-granddaughter," Gram said, walking toward us and smiling down at the baby. "Come to Grammy," she cooed, reaching down to unfasten Vivian's seat belt straps.

As Gram lifted my little girl out of the stroller and held her high for a loud smooch, I marveled again that one-year-old Vivi looked so much like Gram and, unfortunately, not at all like either of my parents.

"Isn't she a sight?" Gram said to Vanessa, making a silly face at the baby.

As much as I wanted to linger, I had to get going to make my train.

"Don't forget, the daycare opens at noon," I said, lifting the diaper bag from my shoulder and attaching it to the back of the stroller.

"I know, I know." Gram pulled the stroller closer. "And Vanessa has graciously agreed to hang out with us because she doesn't have class until the afternoon." It was fortunate that Vanessa was still living with her parents next door to Gram and could help out with any heavy lifting. "Don't miss your hearing," Gram told me. "Not after all this."

It had been a year and a half since we filed the complaint in the Hydeford case. During that time, more than fifty women had joined the class action, but little else had been achieved in federal court. Small motions had been decided, like whether certain pieces of evidence would be discoverable. Luckily, the court had decided most of those motions favorably to the plaintiffs. But the case was still ongoing, and nothing of any substance had yet been declared.

At least the complaint we'd filed with the government had yielded more results. In the time since we'd first requested the congressional investigation, the Department of Homeland Security had closed the Hydeford Detention Center, transferring all its inmates to another facility, and a lucky few had even been released. DeMarke and ICE were no longer engaging the services of Pinelands, and Dr. Choudry had been let go. I couldn't say what else had become of Dr. Choudry, except that she had denied all claims of wrongdoing and consistently refused to comment on inquiries from the press.

But now, at last, the Department of Homeland Security's Permanent Subcommittee on Investigations was holding a hearing on the medical treatment of women who had been detained at Hydeford. I knew the committee had questioned dozens of witnesses, scoured records, and consulted with experts, and that maybe, maybe, some positive ruling would be made.

I hailed a cab and asked the driver to hurry to Penn Station, where I would be meeting Lydia, Sean, and Will Carbone to board an Amtrak train to Washington DC.

As I clicked my seat belt into place, my phone chimed with a text. I glanced at the screen and smiled.

"Good luck today. Don't worry about Vivi. I'll take her back to my place after daycare, and I reminded my mom already about watching her tomorrow, so you don't have to."

It had taken some time, but Vance and I were finally on good terms again, coparenting like champs, if I did say so myself. He'd offered to find a new place to stay so I could keep our apartment, but I was much happier finding a new apartment where Vivi and I could live. I'd set us up in a place on Ninth Street in the West Village, the area of the city I'd always loved best.

As far as I knew, Vance hadn't started dating anyone seriously yet, and neither had I. But we both probably would. And that would be okay. For now, I was happy to spend my time focused on my daughter, my grandmother, and my work. I'd taken a position as a professor at NYU Law School, where I was teaching 1Ls about administrative law. I loved being surrounded by the students and was hoping to add additional courses to my load when Vivi got a little older.

As the cab sped down Fifth Avenue, I scrolled through my other text messages. Dustin had written, wishing us luck just like Vance had. Except looking at his message, I got a tingly sensation in my chest. Maybe soon I would allow myself to explore that. But not yet. For now, I had other things on my mind. I was nervous about how things would go in DC and whether progress would be made for our clients.

I reached into my tote and pulled out the letter again. Four months earlier we'd finally won Isobel's immigration case. The removal order had been canceled, and she'd since received her green card. She and I had hugged so hard that day at the courthouse as we alternated between tears and laughter. Then Isobel had climbed in the car with her grandmother, ready to reunite with her daughter, Sia.

A few weeks later, I found a letter in my mail.

Dear Jessa,

I got my old job back at the nail salon (and I'm still the best manicurist in the neighborhood!). Some days, after work, I'll watch Sia hanging out with her friends, almost teenagers now, and I think about what I'd want someone to do for her if she ever ended up in a situation like mine. I think a lot about how to protect her. I pray the world will change and we'll come to a place where the people in charge can no longer use women's bodies to get what they want—not for money, power, anything.

The only hope we have is knowing there are people out there like you. You showed up at that detention facility to do just one small thing (though not small to me!), but you left there dead set on doing another. You took one look at us and you saw us. So many of us in there were feeling helpless, lonely, hopeless, destroyed. But you marched yourself into our lives and didn't let us give up. You, with your pushy attitude and your fancy pens, you challenged us to see the other parts of ourselves, the best parts. We know you're still out there doing everything you can for us, trying to finally get some justice, make someone acknowledge what they took from us.

We see you too, Jessa, and we will always be grateful for you. Whatever happens with our case, you've already done more for us than you can know. You helped us find strength in ourselves again, and no words could sufficiently thank you for that. You better make sure you remember our gratitude every single day. Now, go win that case!

The letter was signed by each of the women who had joined the class action. Somehow, between Fern and Isobel, they'd managed to get signatures from all the women who were now part of the suit, all fifty-three of them. I hoped that after today, I would have news they'd be relieved to hear.

I folded the letter and placed it gingerly back in its envelope. Closing my eyes for a moment in the back seat of the cab, I counted backwards in my head, centering myself and getting ready. It was showtime.

Washington DC

Special Subcommittee of Investigations Hearing
Senator Marshall Lowell Presiding

It is the bipartisan finding of the subcommittee that female detainees at the Hydeford Detention Center in New Jersey were subjected by a DHS-contracted doctor to excessive, invasive, and often unnecessary gynecological procedures with repeated failures to obtain informed medical consent. This is an extraordinarily disturbing finding. It is, in our view, a catastrophic failure by the federal government to respect basic human rights. Among the serious abuses this committee has investigated since its inception, subjecting female detainees to nonconsensual and unnecessary gynecological surgeries is one of the most nightmarish and disgraceful. Those involved must be held accountable . . .

Author's Note

Back in 1995, when I was a high school senior, my history teacher assigned a final project asking students to choose any US Supreme Court case from 1900 to 1945 and write a research paper about it. As I trudged to the library and searched through different cases, nothing grabbed particular hold of me. But then I stumbled onto the 1927 case of *Buck v. Bell,* where the Court considered whether eighteen-year-old Carrie Buck should be subjected to a sterilization procedure against her wishes.

The legal question in the case was whether Carrie had been denied due process when the Supreme Court of Appeals for the State of Virginia affirmed a judgment ordering the State Colony for Epileptics and Feebleminded to perform a salpingectomy (surgical removal of the fallopian tubes) for the purpose of preventing her from reproducing. Carrie, as well as her mother and her infant daughter, had been deemed "intellectually disabled," and the argument, from a eugenics perspective, was that any additional offspring Carrie produced would most likely be intellectually disabled as well. Medical providers in Virginia were hoping that a court of law would uphold Virginia's new sterilization law as constitutional, and doctors would then be able to perform these salpingectomies without fear of reprisal. All they needed was a "test" case. Doctors at the Lynchburg Colony saw Carrie as the perfect subject because her mother was also institutionalized, and her infant daughter, like any infant, could easily be cast as "feebleminded." The facility hired a lawyer to represent Carrie, but he was allegedly in cahoots with the doctors at the Colony all along. Worth noting is that subsequent writings about the case show clearly that the three females involved were not disabled and, in fact, possessed adequate cognitive ability to be considered intellectually average.

The uncharacteristically brief opinion of the Supreme Court allowing for the sterilization was written by the esteemed Justice Oliver Wendell Holmes Jr., wherein he made one statement after another that shocked me back in the 1990s and continue to shock me today. Among other things, he stated: "It is better for all the world, if instead of waiting to execute degenerate offspring for crime, or to let them starve for their imbecility, society can prevent those who are manifestly unfit from continuing their kind."

The Court went on to equate sterilizing the "mentally unfit" with requiring compulsory vaccination, both of which were deemed small sacrifices made for the benefit of society at large.

Finally, Holmes concluded the opinion, sealing Carrie's fate as he wrote, "Three generations of imbeciles are enough." (A slightly altered version of this statement is voiced by a different character in the novel for the sake of narrative flow, but the appalling nature of the sentiment remains.)

Even as a high school senior with an extreme case of senioritis, I was horrified by the injustice of the case. As part of my project, I studied the principles of eugenics, a field that had become popular in the 1920s as a way to "better" the human race. I learned that in the years following Carrie's case, over seventy thousand people were sterilized throughout the US.

So many aspects of the case stayed with me after I finished the project. Seven years later, when I graduated law school, I had the passing thought that even though I'd taken twenty-four different courses during my time as a law student, the case of Carrie Buck never came up. I figured it must have been overturned somewhere along the way and was no longer relevant in modern America, where women's rights to bodily autonomy were safe and secure.

It wasn't until eighteen years later that I was thumbing through a women's fashion magazine and stumbled on a headline about a "uterus collector" who was allegedly performing hysterectomies on immigrant women. The article explained that women at the Irwin County Detention Center in Georgia were claiming that a doctor there was performing unneeded gynecological procedures and removing the reproductive organs of detained women without their prior knowledge or consent. In 2020! I immediately thought of Carrie Buck. The more I read about the situation in Georgia and the allegations of these women, the more outraged I became. I couldn't get over the parallels I was finding between Carrie's case in 1924 and the immigrants' statements nearly an entire century later. The stories the women were telling haunted me, and I knew I had to do something—which, for me, meant writing a book.

I jumped into the research and was shocked to discover that *Buck v. Bell* was never overturned after all. The case is *still* good law (although the specific Virginia law allowing for Carrie's sterilization has been repealed).

I also dove deeper into the related history and sociology and discovered that the eugenics research performed by American scientists was funded by many of our country's greatest philanthropists (think Rockefeller, Carnegie, Kellogg). The very same research was then used as a touchstone and inspiration, relied upon by Nazis and the Third Reich in their quest to "cleanse" the human race of the unfit, to create a "master race" instead.

To properly show the ripple effects these research theories foisted on so many innocents throughout society, I have included some mature content in the story, showing the myriad ways a woman like Carrie could be deprived of power. She was denied the right to get an education, to say no to the advances of a more powerful man, and even to keep her own daughter—and for all of this, the courts deemed her deviant.

In a time when women's reproductive rights have once again taken center stage in the news, I thought it important to show that blocking abortion access is not the only avenue for female reproductive rights to be exploited. Whether because of private facilities seeking inflated insurance payments or because of individuals chasing power or other personal interests, women's rights to bodily autonomy are still very much at risk. This revelation propelled me to dream up the scenarios imagined in this book and write *Counting Backwards*.

Additional Reading

For those interested in more reading on these topics, I recommend the following sources:

Black, Edwin. *War Against the Weak: Eugenics and America's Campaign to Create a Master Race*. Washington, DC: Dialog Press, 2012.

Bruinius, Harry. *Better for All the World: The Secret History of Forced Sterilization and America's Quest for Racial Purity*. New York: Vintage Books, 2007.

Cohen, Adam. *Imbeciles: The Supreme Court, American Eugenics, and the Sterilization of Carrie Buck*. New York: Penguin Books, 2017.

Das, Alina. *No Justice in the Shadows: How America Criminalizes Immigrants*. New York: Bold Type Books, 2020.

Largent, Mark A. *Breeding Contempt: The History of Coerced Sterilization in the United States*. New Brunswick, NJ: Rutgers University Press, 2008.

Lombardo, Paul. *Three Generations, No Imbeciles: Eugenics, the Supreme Court, and Buck v. Bell*. Baltimore: Johns Hopkins University Press, 2022.

Acknowledgments

Writing this book has been both a humbling and harrowing experience. While I am honored to be able to tell the stories of Carrie Buck and the fictional women of Hydeford, I am devastated that we still have so much work to do to protect human rights in our society. I crafted this novel in hopes of spreading information and compassion far and wide. During the process, I had the support of so many. Please bear with me as I thank them all here.

First and foremost, Samuel Abrams, my twelfth-grade history teacher. He has probably long since forgotten me, but I certainly remember the way he sparked my interest in important pieces of our nation's history. Without him, I might never have learned of Carrie Buck and the difficulties she endured.

Speaking of teachers, I am indebted as well to my former professor Barry Friedman, Jacob D. Fuchsberg Professor of Law at NYU Law School. He has remained a staunch supporter of my career-related endeavors, both legal and creative. Thank you for introducing me to Nancy Morawetz, co-director of the Immigrant Rights Clinic at NYU, who was incredibly generous with her time in walking me through the legal clinic process and experience. She also pointed me toward Alina Das's work, which has provided me with invaluable education on recent situations in immigration courts.

I'd like to thank Ann Garcia at the National Immigration Project for explaining finer points of certain case law and the Catholic Charities Volunteer Team for connecting me with individuals willing to speak regarding immigrant experiences. Thank you to my friend Ian Dumain for his patience as I put my own lawyer hat back on and badgered him with questions. Thank you to José Olivares for uncovering and reporting on the allegations made by women in detention and then generously speaking with me about his experience. To the other sources with whom I spoke but who requested anonymity, thank you.

I am so grateful to my wonderful, kind, brilliant agent, Kathy Schneider, and the whole team at the Jane Rotrosen Agency, for invaluable advice, input, and tireless championing of my work. Thank you for helping me find the perfect home for this book.

This is my fifth novel, but my first with Harper Muse. Thank you to my extraordinary editor, Lizzie Poteet, for everything, but especially for asking all the right questions, for lending your keen eye and remarkable wisdom, and for providing your unwavering support throughout this journey. Thank you to Jocelyn Bailey for sharing your masterful language skills, your enthusiasm, and your thoughtful care and attention. This book is so much better for all of it. Thank you also to Patrick Aprea, Caitlin Halstead, Margaret Kercher, Nekasha Pratt, Taylor Ward, Jere Warren, and the entire team. You've all made this book so much more than it could have been without your help. I feel incredibly lucky to be a Harper Muse author.

Thank you to Nicola Wheir for your thoughtful comments on an early draft of this book. They helped more than you know.

Thank you to Brooke Warner and Crystal Patriarche for your unwavering support. I have learned so much about being an author from working with you, and I will be ever thankful for your guidance and unequivocal enthusiasm for my work.

Since beginning my career as a writer, I have built meaningful relationships with many other authors that transcend anything I expected from "work friends." Corie Adjmi, Lisa Barr, Jenna

Blum, Amy Blumenfeld, Fiona Davis, Karen Dukess, Daisy Florin, Avery Carpenter Forrey, Elyssa Friedland, Heather Frimmer, Reyna Marder Gentin, Alison Greenberg, Alison Hammer, Sally Koslow, Rachel Levy Lesser, Lynda Loigman, Annabel Monaghan, Zibby Owens, Camille Pagan, Amy Poepell, Ines Rodriguez, Marilyn Simon Rothstein, Jessica Saunders, Susie Schnall, Dan Schorr, Courtney Sheinmel, Rochelle Weinstein, and Kitty Zeldis, I don't know how I'd navigate this experience without you. An extra-special shout-out goes to my writing group buddies / soul sisters, Samantha Greene Woodruff and Brooke Lea Foster, who step up to support, guide, cheer, and hug me at every opportunity.

To the book bloggers, bookstagrammers, and bookfluencers—where would all the authors be without you? We owe you so much for the endless ways you help keep books alive and relevant: Melissa Amster, Holly Berfield, Barbara Bos, Alissa Butterfass, Suzy Weinstein Leopold, Andrea Peskind Katz, Brad King, Robin Hall Kominoff, Lauren Blank Margolin, Sue Peterson, Jamie Rosenblitt, and Renee Weiss Weingarten.

To my friends from outside the writing world, the ones who continue singing my praises and flooding their friends' feeds with information about my books, thank you. I believe that showing up is the most important thing a true friend can do, and you all have that mastered. From attending my events once, twice, three times, or more; inviting friends; posting, reposting, and then posting again—each and every action means so much to me. Thank you to Julie Breakstone, Jenny Brown, Jocelyn Burton, Lissy Carr, Bonnie Davis, Bree Schonbrun Dumain, Amy Federman, Jackie Stone Friedland, Reena Glick, Ali Isaacs, Michelle Kantor, Jessica Levinson, Andrea Lieberman, Ari Mayerfield, Nancy Mayerfield, Daria Mikhailov, Michele Mirvis, Jenna Myers, Robyn Pecarsky,

Gisela Perl, Michal Plancey, Aliya Sahai, Julie Schanzer, Abby Schiffman, Aviva Seiden, Renana Shvil, Dina Spiegel, Amy Tunick, Stacey Wechsler, and Mimi Sager Yoskowitz.

To my nieces and nephews, thank you for all the fun you bring to our many family gatherings and the joy you bring to my life. To Sheila, Bob, Allison, Ben, Samantha, and Mike, thank you for your enthusiasm and support for my work. I hit the in-law jackpot with you all. To my father, teller of the best "dad jokes"—I'm sure of it—I will always love finding the humor in words with you. To Seymour, I love you and appreciate you every day. To Kelly and Harry, who are the most loyal people I know and who support me whenever I need it. To my mother, thank you for teaching me to persevere and never take the easy way out. I am happiest when I know I'm making you proud. To my children, the joy you bring me knows no bounds. I couldn't possibly be prouder of the people you are and continue to become, and I love you endlessly. And to Jason, who tells it like it is and still has so many wonderful things to say. None of this would be any fun without you.

Discussion Questions

1. Before reading this novel, what did you know about America's pre-war eugenics practices? After reading it, has your perception of our history changed?

2. How does the book portray the issues of immigration, fertility, and motherhood? Did it make you reconsider your views on these topics? How does this resonate with current events?

3. How does the author handle the theme of reproductive injustice? In what ways does this theme connect to the experiences of both Jessa and Carrie?

4. Jessa's story involves a fight against medical malpractice within a detention facility. How does this storyline make you reflect on the current state of healthcare and justice for immigrants?

5. Carrie's story is based on a real-life person and a landmark Supreme Court case. Does knowing this fact influence your perception of her character and her struggles?

6. How does the novel challenge societal expectations of women, particularly in relation to motherhood and career?

7. In what ways does the revelation about Jessa's family history impact your understanding of her character and her motivations?

8. How does the novel explore the concept of self-determination, especially in the context of the two women's stories?

9. The novel is described as a compelling exploration of empowerment. What are some ways the characters in the book embody this theme?

10. Does the author's use of dual-timeline storytelling impact your understanding of the issues presented in the book? How does this connection affect your perception of their individual stories?

11. The book explores the theme of women charting their own paths professionally and personally. Discuss the importance of women helping women in the book. Can you provide specific examples of this theme in action?

12. How does the book challenge societal expectations of women, particularly in the context of motherhood and fertility?

13. Discuss the relevance of the Supreme Court case allowing forced sterilization in 1927 to the events in the book. How does this historical event impact the present-day narrative?

14. How does the author explore the theme of self-discovery and change in the characters' lives? How do these transformations affect their decisions and actions?

15. How does the topic of reproductive injustice intersect with the issues of immigration and eugenics?

16. How does the author use the character of Jessa to explore the idea of family in different forms?

17. After finishing the book, what key themes, takeaways, or emotions stayed with you? Why?

18. How does the author use the cover design to elicit a sense of intrigue? Did this contribute to your reading experience?

About the Author

Photo by Rebecca Weiss

Jacqueline Friedland is a *USA TODAY* and Amazon bestselling author of historical and contemporary women's fiction. After graduating from the University of Pennsylvania, she earned a law degree from NYU and a Master of Fine Arts from Sarah Lawrence College. Jackie regularly reviews fiction for trade publications and appears at schools and other locations as a guest lecturer. She lives just outside New York City with her husband, four children, and two dogs.

Connect with her online at jacquelinefriedland.com
Facebook: @JacquelineFriedlandAuthor
Instagram: @jackiefriedland
X: @jbfriedland